THE FALL OF BRADLEY REED

A GRUMPY SUNSHINE REVENGE ROMANCE

SEASON OF REVENGE

MORGAN ELIZABETH

PLAYLIST

brutal - Olivia Rodrigo
You're Losing Me - Taylor Swift
Kill Bill - SZA
Hello Cruel World - Paramore
I Bet You Think About Me - Taylor Swift
Everything to Everyone - Renee Rapp
Tell That Mick That He Just Made My List of Things To Do Today -
Fall Out Boy
The Lucky One (Taylor's Version) - Taylor Swift
She's a Lady - Forever the Sickest Kids
Cold Coffee - Ed Sheeran
Fool's Gold - 1D
Growing Sideways - Noah Kahan
Paparazzi.- Lady Gaga
Untouchable (Taylor's Version) - Taylor Swift
Lose You to Love Me - Selena Gomez
closure - Taylor Swift
Mine (Taylor's Version) - Taylor Swift

A NOTE FROM MORGAN

Dear Reader,

Thank you for choosing to pick up my story. If you're anything like me, your TBR list is thirteen million miles long so choosing to bump this up means everything to me.

The Fall of Bradley Reed follows Olivia Anderson and Andre Valenti and is a standalone romance in an interconnected series. You do not have to read the previous book(s) in the Season of Revenge series, though you will meet some of the characters in those books.

Writing this story (like most of them, if we're honest) started with the unhinged idea of, what if I had an FBI agent watching my chaotic searches and what if he somehow fell in love with me through them? It's been a blast to write.

. . .

This book does feature content some may find triggering. These include: mentions of infidelity, (not with the MCs) anxiety, bullying, drinking/alcohol, use of edible marijuana, mention of verbal abuse, narcissistic partners/parents, and fatphobia. As you can always expect in my stories, it has a liberal use of profanity and lots of spice. It is intended for readers 18 and older.

As always, please put yourself and your mental health first when reading. It's meant to be our happy place.

I love you to the moon and to Saturn,
    -Morgan Elizabeth

To my pathological people pleasers:
How's that praise kink coming along?

ONE

Can you manifest a breakup?

SATURDAY, AUGUST 19

Something isn't right.

I don't know what it is, but I feel it in my bones.

In my *gut*.

Some people don't have that sense, the ability to know when something is just wrong, even when you have no substantial evidence to back it up. I'm convinced those people must not be people pleasers.

People pleasers have some kind of genetic makeup deep in the marrow of their bones that just *knows* when something is off.

It's like when your fiancé is in a shitty mood and even though you've barely *seen* him all day, you just *know* he's mad at you. Some self-saving instinct tells you tonight is the night to make his favorite steak, put on the pretty undies, and say *yes* to watching the incredibly boring documentary about Abraham Lincoln on the History Channel.

But now is the absolute *worst time* to have a gut feeling like this.

I'm standing in front of a mirror in a bright white dress (I don't *love* it, but my mother told me would look good in pictures), holding a bouquet of deep-red roses (I wanted sunflowers, but my mother said they weren't classic enough), my hair in a sophisticated updo (again, better for pictures than the beach waves I hoped for), and I know in my heart of hearts, something is so very wrong.

"Did someone die?" I ask, looking over my shoulder in the mirror to where my mother is fixing her lipstick at the vanity.

"What?" Cici, my best friend since elementary school, asks from the floor where she's smoothing out my cathedral-length train.

I didn't want that either. I worried I'd trip and break something on it, which would make for a bummer of a honeymoon.

But think of the impact, *Olivia!* my mother had said months and months ago in the bridal shop, so full of excitement and joy, I had no choice but to say *yes* to a dress I wasn't in love with.

And now, she's groaning at me, the exhausted, annoyed sounding one I'm much more used to hearing.

"God, Olivia. Can we please have just a *single day* where you don't go on your strange little . . . tangents?"

"I just . . ." I take a deep breath, moving my eyes back to the mirror. "Something is off," I insist again, this time quieter.

"Off?" Cici asks.

"Off. Like . . . that feeling when you can't remember if you turned your curling iron or the oven off and you're going away for a week." It's twisting in the pit of my stomach, unable to be ignored. I wish it were as easy as turning the car around and running up to double-check or calling your neighbor who has a key.

"It's just cold feet, Olivia. It happens to all brides. I felt it before I married Huxley. You remember, don't you? I snapped at poor Staceigh about her dress?"

I do remember, but mostly because Cami and I had orchestrated the entire dress debacle.

Finally, the ice in my belly lessens just a hair when I remember the moment and just how *hilarious* it was. But my mother didn't snap at her because of cold feet.

She snapped at her because my mother wanted every single eye on her and her alone during her big day and was afraid her soon-to-be stepdaughter would overshadow her. But that's neither here nor there.

"I don't think—"

"God, she's always been like this," she says with a huff, cutting me off. She's complaining to no one in particular but speaking as if everyone's attention is completely glued to her. "So dramatic, always looking for attention. We're all nervous, Olivia. There are many eyes out there. Get over it."

My lips go tight in a smile and I nod in the mirror, wiping my sweaty palms over the heavy skirt, knowing by now, I'll never win this fight. "You're right," I say, my voice low, eyes moving back over the big dress. It's not worth the argument, not worth the guilt she'll inevitably send my way if I push her.

Plus, she *is* under a lot of stress. The planning of this wedding has taken over her every thought for the past nine months.

Even if she used it as her main storyline on her reality show against your wishes, the voice I always ignore whispers vehemently.

And, of course, my mother is right—there are a lot of people waiting for our grand entrance.

Four hundred and thirty-seven, to be exact, not including the paparazzi sequestered outside the church. (I wanted something nondenominational since no one in our family is particularly religious, but my mother convinced me otherwise. *The photos in a cathedral will be so gorgeous, Olivia!*) They're all waiting to catch a glimpse of the new Mr. and Mrs. Bradley Reed.

Maybe she's right.

Maybe the churn in my gut is just because there are going to be *so many eyes*. It's a big day, after all.

"I drove," Cici says quietly as she stands, brushing her hands down her lavender bridesmaid dress.

"What?" She looks over her shoulder at my mother, who is bossing some poor employee to grab her a new glass of Champagne before looking at me in the mirror once more.

"I drove. If you want to bounce." I smile at her.

"You're a good friend."

"I'm also serious as a heart attack, Liv. You want to be a runaway bride, I'm driving the getaway car."

I laugh before answering, "I'm good. I appreciate it though. Just . . . nerves, you know?" She gives me a tight smile and I know a part of her wants me to agree, to beg her to help me dip out of this wedding.

She doesn't *like* Bradley.

But then again, she doesn't know him like I do.

He's . . . sweet when it's just us, when he doesn't have his fraternity brothers and finance bros to impress.

"Where's Cami?" I ask, and I don't miss the scoff my mother lets out at the name of my father's partner and my business partner.

Once my enemy and now one of my closest friends.

It's a long story, really.

"Helping your dad with his tie," Cici says. "And then they're both headed here."

"I still don't know why she's a *bridesmaid*, Olivia," my mother says, taking the glass from the server who turns away almost instantly, running off like she's afraid if she spends too long in my mother's stratosphere, she'll feel the full burn of her wrath.

"Because she's one of my closest friends and she's *family*."

"She's a wedding planner, Olivia. It's . . . uncouth to be *friends* with the help."

I sigh but luckily, my phone beeps loudly so I don't have to answer. "Can you grab that for me, Cici?" I tip my chin toward my cell. "It might be Cam or my dad." Ever the perfect maid of honor, she nods, moves to the small table where I left my phone, and hands it over.

The name on my screen has my brows furrowing.

"What is it?"

"It's Bradley," I say, my voice low.

An eternity passes as I tap in the password, the world swirling around me, that feeling in the pit of my stomach reaching its tentacles outward, stretching until it touches my fingers and toes. I numbly tap the last digit and it's like some sixth sense knows already.

"He's probably texting you one last time before you're officially husband and wife," Cici says, positivity in her voice.

I appreciate it, but somehow, I already know.

It's confirmed when I see the screen finally, Bradley's smiling face and his name at the very top, the last text I sent reading: *Good morning! I can't wait to marry you today!*

His most recent text reads:

I'm sorry. I can't do this.

And the world comes crashing down around me.

TWO

What do you do with an unused wedding dress?

SATURDAY, AUGUST 19

The pile of tissues is as big as a small child.

A toddler, maybe.

A preschooler?

I don't know.

It's really big.

And as I stare at it, my eyes and nose and head and soul throbbing, I can't help but think I should clean up. It's a hotel room, after all, not my own place. There are more used tissues on the bed and in the little kitchenette. Someone zipped up the gown my mother loved, perfectly tailored to fit every edge and curve of my body in a way that would sell well in tabloids.

We were going to donate the proceeds, of course. It would look too garish to sell your daughter's wedding photos without having a good cause. I had agreed but only under the promise the money would go to Cami's mother's charity, Moving Forward.

Guilt wraps around me, and I make a mental note to ask my grandfather to donate to the charity in my name. I can pay him back in four more years when my trust is open.

The charity shouldn't suffer just because I couldn't get my fiancé to actually tie the knot. It's not her fault the wedding won't happen, that there won't be some glamorous tabloid stories to sell and profits to donate.

Instead, they'll get an even juicer story and they'll get it for free.

My fiancé—*ex*-fiancé, I remind myself—ended our engagement just minutes before the ceremony, and now it's all ruined.

All of it.

And now, I'm surrounded by *waste*.

So much fucking waste.

Who knew a simple wedding could have so much *stuff*?

The tissues.

The gown.

The flowers.

The cake, the food.

Three years of my life.

All of it a fucking *waste*.

The words weigh on my soul, the idea filling me with a heavy panic I don't know how to escape from.

Clean.

That's the obvious answer, of course.

I need to *be* clean, to scrub this day off my skin until there's a fresh layer Bradley has never touched, a new version of me who will be able to stand strong and tall beneath this disappointment, but until then, I need to clean this *room*.

It's suffocating me, and I need it gone.

Standing, I wobble on my feet as if I've been drinking all day, but despite the twenty bottles of Dom Perignon Cami had sent up to the bridal suite (*we weren't going to be having a Champagne toast, after all*), I haven't had a drink since mimosas this morning.

"What are you doing?" Cami asks, her voice like a mother of a toddler who is walking toward a flight of stairs.

"I need to clean up," I say, and my voice is raspy, like it hasn't been used in days.

"Liv, no."

"Cami, there's—"

"Liv, *no.*"

"Cami, I need to do this," I say, panic filling my chest. Cici walks to me and grabs my hand.

"Come on. Let's sit down. We can—"

"I don't want to. I want to clean. I need to do something, I can't just sit there. I need—" The panic is crashing over me like waves and I'm being pulled into the undertow.

"You need to sit down because you're scaring me." I paste on my well-practiced fake smile.

"I'm fine. I swear. I just need to be productive."

"The only mess in this room is those tissues, Liv. It's only going to take a moment," Cami says, her eyes wide. I'm sure mine are frantic, unable to hide my true feelings based on how she's looking at me like I'm a wild animal who has been put into a small enclosure.

Have you ever seen those videos of those zoo animals in terrible enclosures, how they pace and twitch and act completely out of sorts?

That's how I feel.

And the pain in my chest when I watch them, the all-consuming desire to jump in there and let them out is probably how Cami feels.

Shit.

I shouldn't make her feel that way. It's not right. It's not her fault I was left at the altar. It isn't fair to put that on other people, people I love.

I'm making a scene, and I need to stop.

Closing my eyes, I take a deep breath in and slowly release it, trying to come up with a solution.

Something to do.

I can't just sit here.

"What about the venue? It needs cleaning. We'll never get the deposit back if we don't clean up before midnight. We have to—" Again, Cami cuts me off, grabbing both of my hands in one of hers and leading me back to the bed until I'm sitting on the edge.

"Your dad has it handled, honey. He's making sure it gets done.

Damien's with him and a few others. We've got this under control."
More guilt lashes through me, making me angry and in pain at the
thought of my dad having to do *even more*.

He already had to go out front and let everyone who was sitting,
waiting for a bride to walk down the aisle to Pachelbel's *Cannon in D*
(I wanted *Lover* by Taylor Swift, but my mother insisted we go *classic),* know the wedding was canceled. He already had to answer questions and deal with angry guests. After that, he helped clean up the
cathedral, making sure I didn't have to look at or deal with any of it
while in my state of misery.

And now he's doing *more.*

"I should help. That's not fair," I say, my voice cracking, the throb
in my throat near impossible to ignore. Cami's hand tightens in mine,
a silent attempt to hold me in place, to stop me from standing and
running down to him.

"Babe, let him do this."

"Cami—" But she knows me too well, knows how to hit me where
it will hurt, or at least what to say so I'll do as she would like.

"He doesn't know what to do with himself. You know your dad—
he's a fixer. His girl is sad, he wants to fix it, and he has *no way* of
fixing this, Liv. Let him do this. If not for you then for him. If he
doesn't, I genuinely think there's a good chance he'll try to hunt down
the douchebag and give him a taste of his own medicine."

The throbbing turns into a painful ache and finally, the sob I was
holding back breaks free. Cami wraps me in her arms, and I cry into
her shoulder.

"My god, Olivia. I can't believe how *selfish* you're being." Cami's
entire body goes stiff at my mother's words. I hold on tighter to her,
not for my benefit, though.

Because Cami has an unhinged sense of justice and I don't need
to end this day in a prison.

Again.

"Excuse me?" Cami says, not even turning to look at my mother.

"*Cami*," I say low, under my breath.

It's not worth it.

It's not worth it.

I've been my mother's daughter for 26 long years, and this is just *part* of it. She means well, but she was raised to think the world revolves around her. It's not *her* fault.

"You're babying her. She's throwing a hissy fit, but what about the rest of us? What about the guests—"

Cami tries. She really does try to defend me with grace and honor, to reason with the unreasonable. "One of the first things out of her mouth when I entered this room was how she felt bad for the guests, Melanie. It's—"

My mother cuts her off, as if she didn't hear her at all.

"What about *me*?"

And there it is.

I watch it in real-time, I think, the atom bomb inside of Cami imploding.

It's funny since she was the only person who was able to endure my mother long enough to plan Melanie St. George's extensive wedding. Multiple planners ditched after a short time with her unrealistic demands and self-centered thought process, but Cami was able to rise to the top and give her everything she wanted.

"What *about* you, Melanie?" she asks. I try and hold on to her tighter but she isn't having it, stepping back and away from me, detaching with a gentleness I know she is forcing from the set of her jaw.

"Cam—"

"Exactly that. Do you know how *embarrassing* this is? My daughter got left at the altar by a *Reed*. We were so close and she couldn't seal the deal." Her eyes start to water, though I know from experience a tear will never fall; that's the extent of the emotion she'll show.

Emotion creates lines, and tears ruin makeup. But a gentle watering of the eyes . . . it's just enough to look vulnerable and earn compassion.

"And now I'm going to be the *laughingstock* of everything. I can't even believe it. I won't be able to walk into Saks without people *staring at* me like I'm some, some *loser*. Some *freak* they should pity. I'll be a *pariah!*"

"I don't . . . I can't . . ."

It's not often Cami is at a loss for words, but it seems my mother was able to accomplish this feat.

"I told you, Olivia. I *told you* to stop nagging him, to let him be. Men like him, they don't like that."

"I know, Mom. I'm so sorry," I say, keeping my eyes down.

She did. Multiple times.

Like when I called him from the bakery where we were getting the seven-tier wedding cake and he told me he had *better things to do* and to just *pick a fucking cake.*

According to my mother, it was wildly inappropriate I had even *asked* him to attend.

There was the time we had engagement photos, he was three hours late, and for some reason, my mom told me it had to have been *my* fault. I should have put it into his calendar myself, reminded him, told his assistant, and picked out his outfit for him.

There was also the time—

"You're kidding, right?"

My business partner's tone is cold, cruel, and measured.

This is Cami ready to fucking *blow.*

"What?" my mother asks, dabbing at the corner of her eyes with a custom embroidered handkerchief.

"I said, *you're kidding me, right?*" Cami enunciates each word, like she's speaking to a child.

"I don't understand."

"It's just, it must be a joke if you're telling your daughter just an hour after her fiancé left her at the altar it's *her fault* or *you* are the one who deserves pity."

Silence rings in the room and it's heavy. I can't breathe in it, like one of those days where it's so humid, you can't bear to be outside because it feels like you're inhaling water.

"Camile, I know you don't understand how all of"—she waves her hand at the luxury of the hotel room—"this works, considering your upbringing and all, but when you're trying to keep a man like Bradley Reed on your line, you need to cater to him. And obviously, Olivia did not do this."

Cami waits for a beat before she answers. I open my mouth to attempt to stop her, but it's no use.

This fuse has been at risk for months. Years, even.

It was bound to happen. Might as well get all of the shitty experiences over at the same time.

"Olivia is your *daughter*, Melanie."

"I know that, Camile." Now my mother is speaking as if *Cami* is the child.

"She is your daughter who has done *nothing* her entire life but cater to others—to you, to those fucking evil twins, to your family, to Bradley fucking Reed—whether or not any of them deserve her kindness."

"What are you trying to say? I don't deserve Olivia's kindness?"

"Jesus, you know what? Yes. I am saying that. You don't deserve the kindness and attention and generosity Olivia is constantly *giving you*. You don't deserve it because you don't even *recognize it*, much less appreciate it. You just *expect it*."

"I know you don't have children of your own, but if you did, you'd understand that's how it is as a parent."

"No. It's not. That's not how a parent is supposed to act, expecting her child to further their own social career, to cater to them indefinitely. That's fucked up, Melanie. It's manipulative. And Olivia is good—so good, she has sacrificed her own wants and needs her *entire* life to keep you happy because it keeps her life easier to do that rather than to have you give her shit about not doing what you want her to do. She would probably let this shit go, let you dab at your

THE FALL OF BRADLEY REED   17

eyes and whine about what an affront her being *dumped on her wedding day* is to *you*, but I won't."

"I'm not sure what this even has to do with—" Cami steamrolls right over her.

"Because personally, I'm tired of watching her bend over backward for everyone, for *anyone*, but especially for you. You're selfish and rude and, honestly, probably *jealous* of your daughter, but that's a conversation for you to have with your therapist. I'm *done* with you being rude to her in front of me. You can apologize to her and we can all commiserate *for her*, but if you want to sit there and make this a personal pity party, you can leave." My mother's mouth is open, and for once in her life, she seems to be in genuine shock.

"Well, I neve—"

"Yeah, no shit. Maybe if you *had* been talked to like this, you wouldn't be such a cunt, but unfortunately for everyone who has to cross your path, you've never been told no. And you know what, the next time I see you, I'll play the game. I'll smile because it's what Liv wants, but know this: I see right through you, and I'll spend the *rest of my days* trying to undo the *harm* you've done to your daughter, harm her father tried his best to counteract, but there's only so much he can do when every time you waltzed back into her life, you did nothing but tear her down."

My heart beats fast, similar to how it felt right as I opened that text from Bradley.

And just like then, my stomach aches with a gentle sense of relief rushing through me, quickly followed by a healthy dose of guilt.

Relief because I don't have to marry Bradley.

Relief because I would never say any of this to my mother, regardless of its truth, but Cami did. And she did it for me.

It beats and my stomach churns as I stare between my mother and Cami, trying to calculate five steps ahead to see how she'll react.

Maybe she'll have a moment of understanding.

Maybe this is what she needed, this moment to knock some sense into her, and we will always look back on this failed marriage as a bittersweet time in our lives where our relationship took a turn for the better.

Lose one relationship but earn another.

But I should know by now not to expect too much from Melanie Kincaid, now St. George.

She turns to me, her jaw set, those eyes watering in the same superficial way as before.

She's not upset about what Cami said.

She's upset Cami *had the nerve* to say it.

"Call me when you're not with *her*."

What she doesn't say is what I hear.

I'll expect an apology.

She reaches where her small clutch sits on the bed, grabs it, and walks out.

And then it's just Cami, Cici, and me in the room, all staring at the door.

What the fuck is in the air today?

THREE

SATURDAY, AUGUST 19

After my mother leaves, we sit in stunned silence.

Well, Cami does.

I move once more to clean up the mess, to keep my hands—and my mind—occupied.

"You didn't have to do that, Cam," I say, grabbing at the pile of tissues and moving them into a garbage can. "I know it came from a good place, but it so wasn't necessary."

If you didn't grow up with her, I understand how one might be offended or frustrated with my mother. She's brash and not in the fun, Cami way, but she means well.

Truly, I have to believe that.

"I love that you did, really. But she's just overwhelmed. And she's right—she hyped this event up so much to her circle of friends, and you know how those women can be. She's going to be the target of bitchy whispers until the next scandal, and that's my fault."

We've worked with enough of them for Cami to know, for her to understand.

"She wasn't raised to think about other people, only about how it impacts her. I guess we could blame my grandfather—"

"Liv," Cami says finally, breaking into my rambling as she walks to where I'm cleaning, holding my hands in hers to stop me from distracting myself further. "No." Her warm eyes meet mine, holding me in a trance, and suddenly, it's clear just how serious she is.

How much she needs me to understand what she's about to say to me, even if she knows I'm not going to like it.

"I need you to know nothing, none of this, was your fault. *None of it*. Do not listen to her. You did not *deserve this*. And you are not at fault for your mother's emotions nor the way her so-called friends will treat her." I sigh and bite my lip but don't dare break eye contact with her.

"I did nag. A lot." Cami rolls her eyes, and Cici's quiet scoff can be heard from where she's sitting.

"You nagged about what? About things he was supposed to be helping you with *as your partner?*"

"He has a very high-stress job." He was sure to remind me of that often.

"*And so do you, Olivia.*" I shrug.

Public relations and party planning for the wealthy aren't the same as managing the finances of millionaire clients who have unreasonable expectations.

"He makes more money."

"Jesus Christ, who *cares?* If we want to go down that route, *you're worth more money than him.*" She lifts her hands in defense, knowing my argument. "Not that it matters. But if we're looking at things like that, shouldn't he have been worried about you? About what you needed or wanted? If this all boils down to your value—which, Olivia, look at me." I had started to inspect the perfect French manicure I'd gotten the day before. "It *does not*. But if you're going to use that as your excuse, you deserve to look at the full picture."

Digging into that would cause too much turmoil in my already delicate mental state so instead, I break eye contact again, looking at my hands, at my perfectly filed nails, and at the small cut on my pointer finger.

I got that handmaking his gifts for his groomsmen.

"*We can order them,*" *I had said of the intricate flasks engraved with initials.* "*Look, this site makes them and we can get them shipped in just a few days.*" *I'd brought my phone to him to show him the gift site I had found them on at his request.*

"*But it won't mean as much if they aren't handmade.*" *I sighed, taking my phone back, switching tabs, and showing him a new one.*

"*This other site, it costs a bit more but they're handmade.*"

"*Olivia, I really want them made by us. Can you please do this for me?*" *I bit my lip, thinking of the work I had to get done before our honeymoon, of the little touches I still needed to finish for* our *wedding before sighing and opening my calendar.*

"*I can order the materials and get them here . . . Thursday. Friday, we can make a night of it. I'll come to your place and we'll order pizza and do it together.*"

As exhausted as I was, I wanted that: a night with my fiancé, hanging out and spending quality time together, working on something together. It was just two weeks before the big day and a nice way to reconnect.

I wanted some kind of proof, I think, that I wasn't making a huge mistake. I needed the reassurance this relationship was going to last, that we were meant to be like I had convinced myself we were.

But were we really?

"*I'm going out with Casey. I really don't have time for it, Olivia. Can't you just do it?*" *He wasn't even looking at me, scrolling on his phone and leaning on his kitchen counter, and I remember for the first time actually questioning what I was doing here.*

I think I had questioned it a few times quietly, but this was the first time I asked myself straight out.

Why were we doing this?

"*Bradley, I—*" *Finally, he looked up and put on that boyish smile I used to think was so fucking cute, so sweet. I thought it showed a part of him he shared with me and only me.*

That was bullshit, I'm seeing now. A well-practiced look he used to get his way.

He took a step forward, grabbed my chin, and pressed a soft kiss to my lips.

"Come on, Liv. You know I'm no good at that stuff, and you're so great at it."

"I just—"

"This is why I love you," he said, his voice low, and I melted.

I smiled.

And he stepped away, eyes moving back to his phone as he reached for his keys absentmindedly.

"Alright, I gotta go out. You've got that handled, right?" He looked to me but I didn't answer. "Remember to lock up before you leave."

Before I leave because I didn't live there.

We were together for nearly three years and we didn't live together.

That's weird, right?

Neither of us were religious; there was no "living in sin" concern.

I remember watching him walk to the front door and not answering, still holding my phone with the tutorial I was going to show him.

"Later, Olivia," he said, and then the door closed behind him.

That was barely two weeks ago.

Saturday, after I spent the entire Friday making them while he was out with his friends, slicing my finger open on the packaging, I handed him the groomsmen's gifts with a smile. He barely thanked me.

I convinced myself he was anxious. Overworked.

But that little cut . . . it means more to me at this moment.

He wasn't any of that. He wasn't sweet or boyish. He wasn't anxious or overworked. He surely wasn't stressed about the wedding he had no hand in planning.

He was just an asshole.

An asshole who, despite what I hoped, I don't think ever loved me.

Ever.

"I made his groomsmen gifts," I say, my voice low.

"I know," Cami says, and I wonder if she sees it, the switch being flipped in me.

"I listened to *John Mayer. After he was the world's biggest douche.*" Cami cringes but nods.

"I know, honey."

"I didn't have that bachelorette in Vegas because he said it made him uncomfortable, then he went to a strip club with his buddies while *I stayed home and made his gifts.*"

"I'd like it on record I told you I didn't like you choosing a Sunday brunch as your bachelorette because of him but that I would love you despite your terrible decisions," Cici says from where she's sitting.

She did.

She so did, and I laughed it off because she just didn't *get it.*

I thought that was just *what you did* when you were in love.

Why didn't my brain ever think that if you're in love, you shouldn't have to give up things or sacrifice yourself for it?

It should be *simple.*

"I gave up *peanut butter* for him!" I say, panic creeping into my words.

"Why do I feel like of the things you just named, that's what you're most upset about?"

"Because it's *upsetting!* Years without the peanut butter Christmas trees? Or eggs? Or pumpkins? Do you know how *depressing* that is?" I stare at the wall, the one across from the hotel room bed with the ugly, abstract art I was sure would be the first thing I saw the morning after I finally became Mrs. Bradley Reed. After I looked at my new husband's smiling face, of course.

"I did *everything* for him." I say the words low and filled with pain, but I don't finish the sentence out loud.

I did everything for him and it wasn't enough.

I gave up huge chunks of myself—my time, my ambition, my . . .

personality, even—and it wasn't enough to make him love me, not really.

What does that say about me?

Me, a person who so very profoundly wants to be accepted, wants others to like her and view her as *valuable,* wasn't enough when I gave someone my all.

What does that *mean?*

My best friend breaks into my mild mental breakdown.

"You do everything for everyone, Liv. That's your problem—you put everyone else first at the expense of yourself," Cici says, a hand on my shoulder. "Maybe this is a sign to take care of Olivia."

"Or maybe he was just always a piece of shit and you dodged a bullet," Cami says under her breath.

"Cami!"

"Tell me I'm wrong," she says with a bored expression.

Cici can't defend him.

And I'm starting to realize right now that neither can I.

"But in all serious, Liv . . . maybe Cici's right," Cami says, moving closer as well. "Maybe you should take this as a sign. I've known you for three years and never, I mean *never*, Olivia, have you done something selfish. Never have you looked at the world and said fuck it, never have you put *yourself* first."

"Cam, love you, but we met because I was terrorizing you."

"And you sure as fuck weren't doing it for yourself," she says. "You were doing it to keep the twins content in order to keep your mom happy."

I roll my lips between my teeth before opening my mouth to argue because that's not totally true.

"And before you say you were doing *that* so you would get your trust, please remember you gave up any chance of getting your trust early in order to save your father's business." I shrug it off.

"I started a business with you—a lot of that is for me. My mother would have rather I became a socialite looking for a husband. I didn't do *that* for her."

"So not a single part of starting a business with me was to make your grandfather proud?"

She stares at me, knowing the truth, and *goddammit*.

"I'm not saying Event Press isn't your passion, Liv. I'm just saying, when was the last time you did something for you and no one else?"

I stare back.

Then I look away because Cami's gaze can burn a hole straight through your subconscious if you're not careful.

But the damage has already been done.

Her words have hit their mark and I'm thinking about it, really taking it in.

When was the last time I was selfish? When was the last time the people pleaser went back into hiding, the last time I banished her to get what I wanted *solely* for myself?

My body breaks out in a cold sweat because . . .

I don't know.

I don't know.

Oh god.

Oh god.

The panic creeps in, starting in my chest and slowly seeping out, like blood in the ocean, before I shake my head.

Nope. I don't have time for this. No way.

Slowly, I force it back into the bottle, imagining the strands as some kind of corporeal thing I can grab and stuff back in meticulously before putting the stopper back on. Because even now, even as I realize just how detrimental my people pleasing is and how I might need to make some kind of real and concrete change in my life, I know having another meltdown would hurt Cami and Cici.

It would hurt my dad.

And they don't deserve that. The same way I don't deserve being left by Bradley, they don't deserve to have to worry about me.

Still, in this moment, I make a promise to myself.

I'd, at the very least, try.

Try to do things for me.

To put myself first, to be selfish.

A small smile pulls at the corner of my lips with this new resolution, and though the weight is still heavy—so fucking heavy—it's like there's some kind of hope, a light at the end of the tunnel.

If I'm brave enough to walk toward it, that is.

My smile must clue Cami into a break in the hurricane of my sadness. It might just be the eye of the storm, a bit of peace before the tail end hits even harder, but for this small moment in time, I'm . . . okay.

"Let's have your dad order food and we'll drink all the Champagne and you can get your tears out," Cami says with a smile, standing up to get her phone.

I shake my head, reaching to grab her wrist to stop her.

"Oh, no, I'm done crying," I say then stand, grabbing a few of the straggler tissues I missed to toss in the garbage. My movements aren't dazed and slow anymore, but sure and assured.

I'm on a mission.

No more moping, no more sadness.

I'm on a mission for myself.

To find myself, maybe.

Because I think I just now realized I don't know who I am when I'm being what everyone needs me to be.

"What?" Cami asks, confused.

"It's totally okay to cry, Liv," Cici says, clearly thinking I'm putting on a brave face for their benefit.

And I am, but also . . . I'm not.

"I know that. Crying is good, but I'm done." I shrug my shoulders like it's no big deal. "He's not worth it."

It's true but also a lie.

The first plan of action in my *prioritize Livi* plan is, I need them *out* of here.

I need alone time.

I need time to think about what happened, about who I am now and how to move forward with this new version of me I'm determined to craft from the wreckage.

I don't miss the way Cami and Cici look at each other, silently talking, probably wondering if they should schedule me a grippy sock vacation.

The jury's still out there, but for now, I'll use my experience with keeping everyone else happy to my benefit.

Possibly my very first selfish act.

"I'm fine. I promise. This day has been shit. I'm sure I'll need a shoulder to cry on another day, but for tonight, I'm all cried out. I just want to take a hot bath in this fancy ass hotel, order in some junk food, and go to bed. I can face . . . everything else tomorrow." A beat of silence passes while I pray they let me have this. Maybe they'll be so worried about me, they'll give me anything I ask for to keep me from jumping.

A little morbid, Liv.

"Please, guys. I promise, if I have another mental breakdown, I'll call you right up. I'm pretty sure Bradley's card is connected to all these rooms still," I say.

It's a lie.

One I won't admit to them, of course. Unfortunately, I was the one who had to book the rooms after weeks and weeks of hounding Bradley. "So please, go to yours, rack up some room service charges. That will make me feel better." I lie through my teeth, but it turns out, another perk of coming out of the daze of making everyone but myself happy is I'm a really, really good liar and I'm absolutely excellent at hiding all of my emotions.

I wait with bated breath to see if they buy it, if I bought myself some alone time to wallow and be miserable without them hovering over me.

"Livi . . . ," Cici says, unsure, but Cami looks me over and nods.

Whether she sees through my lie the way she always can or she buys it, I don't know, but it doesn't matter.

"Okay, Liv. You call us if you need something. I also need hourly sign-of-life texts in order to keep your dad from busting down the door. At least until you fall asleep."

I relax, knowing I'll be alone for the night, that I'll get the opportunity to just . . . be without them watching. To come to terms with my new reality without them hovering, no matter how much I love them.

"Deal," I say with a weak smile. All the fight fled with my braveness.

Cami sees that, too, shakes her head, and sighs.

I would guess she sees right through me, but my need for this must be just as clear because she claps her hands together and nods at Cici.

"Okay, let's clean up a bit and drag anything exclusively wedding out of here and then we'll leave you be, Liv."

And not for the first time, I'm so incredibly thankful the universe decided to give me Camile Thompson all those years ago when I needed her most.

FOUR

How do you get over being left at the altar?

SATURDAY, AUGUST 19

It's hours later, long after I lied and texted Cami I was going to sleep in order to end my hourly check-ins, long after I actually did attempt to fall asleep, and long after yet another cry session.

I don't even remember what that one was about, to be honest.

I've cried for everything since Cami and Cici left to give me space. Small sniffles and soul-crushing sobs and everything in between, but each and every tear was cathartic.

I've cried for my failed wedding, but not the lost relationship.

I've cried over how fucking stupid I was but gave myself some grace, realizing I wasn't fully at fault.

I've cried over letting all of our guests down but recognize they don't matter in the grand scheme.

I've cried about disappointing my mother but understand it's not fair for her to put that kind of pressure on me.

I've cried over how I feel *guilt* for this failed marriage when I was the only one putting effort into it.

I've cried for the realization that nothing in my life is *mine*.

And at some point, I just cried to cry.

Sometimes, that's the best kind of all.

It's also long after I finished an entire bottle of Champagne that could be saved for a happy occasion but is now forever tainted with poisoned memories.

The buzz is what has me moving to my phone, opening the web search app, and typing in a number of searches, each getting more and more unhinged.

FAILED WEDDING.

WHAT TO DO IF YOU GET LEFT AT THE ALTAR.

HOW TO GET OVER AN EX.

HOW TO GET OVER AN EX YOU MAY HAVE NEVER ACTUALLY LIKED.

CURE FOR PEOPLE PLEASING.

HOW TO PUT YOURSELF FIRST.

JILTED BRIDES.

WHAT TO DO IF YOU'RE A JILTED BRIDE.

HOW TO RETURN REGISTRY GIFTS.

DO YOU HAVE TO RETURN REGISTRY GIFTS?

HOW TO DISAPPEAR AND START A NEW LIFE.

JILTED BRIDE SUPPORT.

That's the one that led me here, staring at a private Facebook group.

Jilted Brides of North Jersey.

A group for women to talk about their experience of failed marriage without pressure or judgment. All welcome!

It could have been the alcohol.

It could have been the fact I flicked that little angel on my shoulder who said, *What would your mother think if she found out? She'd be humiliated,* off and into another dimension.

It might have been I've never once in my life met someone who was left at the altar and here was an entire group of women who had gone through this.

Or because suddenly, in the darkness of a five-star hotel room, I felt unbearably lonely.

Regardless, it's sometime between midnight and two am and I'm still awake and click *request to join*.

Then, I answer the questions required for consideration:

When did your relationship end?

Where do you live?

Would you be interested in an in-person support group?

If yes, leave your cell number.

Not long after, I pass out, my eyes puffy and swollen, my nose raw and red, but my mind content in the fact that, somehow, I'm not alone in this.

And sometimes, that's all you need to get through the day.

●●●

I'm smiling when I walk down to breakfast the next morning.

Not because I'm happy, but being able to leave this hotel at checkout and go back to my apartment without a chaperone depends on looking like I'm so *totally fine*.

I'm not, by the way.

I'm hungover and sad and stressed because I'm not *that* sad, and I'm wearing a pound of makeup, and I'm *mad*. Slowly, I'm creeping into the anger stage of grief, and I think I want to stew there for a good, long time.

Self-care and all.

I think my new version of putting myself first requires giving myself the grace to be fucking furious.

Cici gives me a happy smile when she sees me, the smile widening when she sees mine. Relief takes over her whole face, and I worry for a moment I'm a bad friend for lying to her about how I'm feeling in order to get alone time.

But the new version of me puts me first, and I can't do that if my friends are hovering over me.

"Good morning!" I say, and I wonder if I laid it on a little too thick, my voice sounding fake even to my ears. I refuse to let myself admit a small part of telling them I'm *absolutely fine* is because I don't want my friends and family worrying about me. They've been through a lot the past few days as well, and I refuse to be a bigger bother than I've already been, to let them suffer at my expense.

Nope.

Not admitting that.

Because New Livi does everything for her and herself alone.

Right?

Right.

Guilt still wraps around my belly.

"You're . . . here," Cami says when I sit down at the table next to her and Cici, my dad's worried eyes burning into me from across the table.

"I'm here. This breakfast is the best in the area. I'm not missing it."

The entire table looks at me, faces cloaked in confusion and worry.

Except for Cami.

Cami's face is firm, puzzled, and she's staring at me, trying to decode me.

Cici's hand grabs mine.

"Liv, honey. Yesterday . . . Bradley—" She pauses like the name is poison, like she's worried I might break at the mere mention, and I smile so as to assuage her guilt. It's fake, but they don't have to know that. I lay my free hand on top of hers.

"Cees, it's fine. I'm fine. Bradley called off the wedding and that totally sucks, but I'm fine. It was for the best." The knot in my chest tightens a bit with my words, but I shake it off. "Better to find out now rather than later when it would take much more work to undo."

"It's okay to be sad, Liv," she says, her voice low, and there's my sweet best friend, the woman I've known since kindergarten. The one who walked alongside me through all of my awkward phases and cried with me when boys broke our hearts and listened to me bitch about my mom without judgment. The woman who forgave me when I treated her like shit, when I chose to please my mother and keep my evil stepsisters happy over her.

It's then I let myself put the new Livi on the shelf for a moment, let the old version who wouldn't want my friends and family to suffer because of what happened to me out once more.

I've put these people through enough. I don't need them to worry about me. If I show them this version, this happy, well-adjusted version, they won't panic and can go about their lives.

But of course, I can't be *too* happy, or else they'll think something is up.

It's a very fine balance, trying to convince people you love you are *totally fine.* That becomes even more difficult when I make the mistake of looking around the dining room.

All eyes are on me.

Not all are as obvious as others, some staring at their phones and giving me little sideways glances, some pretending to talk to a table-mate but occasionally giving me stealthy looks, while others are straight-up eyes locked on me.

Waiting to see if I'll break.

Wedding guests.

Friends, family, acquaintances, people I've never even seen before in my life but still know as a far-off family member or a friend of my mother's. I wonder how many of them are texting a friend back home with minute-by-minute updates.

I can't hate on it—I would probably do the same.

But before I can move forward with my mission to convince everyone I'm just fine or attempt to save face further, my phone bleeps with a new text message followed by another and another, and then even more eyes are on me. Most notably, there are three sets of wide eyes I know incredibly well, staring intently.

"Don't look at your phone, Liv," Cami says, her eyes locked to where I'm grabbing my cell from the bag I brought downstairs with me.

"It could be media looking for insight," Cici agrees.

"It could be Bradley," I say, digging in the bag to find it. A part of my dad's duties yesterday, as assigned by Cami, was to go to my apartment and grab some clothes and a bag since everything I hand-picked with me was perfectly bridal white.

I don't want you to be reminded nonstop, Liv, she had said when I objected, not wanting to put my dad out even more than I already had. *And neither does he. Let him do this.*

I caved and this morning, when I was able to put on a light-pink top and a pair of black leggings, I have to admit, I was relieved. Unfortunately, he grabbed the biggest tote bag I own, and I can't find a damn thing in here.

"Even more reason not to grab it," Cami says under her breath.

I ignore her.

Cami is an incredible judge of character, and I should have *known* this would happen when she looked at my now-ex the first time they met at the Beach Club and her top lip went up in the teeni-est, tiniest sneer.

I didn't, of course, so enamored by his smile and the way he paid me attention and the way he held my hand under the table at the Fourth of July party and made me feel . . . special.

If you were to ask me right now what made me fall for Bradley Reed, I'd tell you it was because he made me feel *special.*

Well, actually, I'd probably battle with the lump in my throat and tell you I have no idea before losing said battle and breaking down in tears again despite my brave face, but in a week or so? I'll probably say I was because he made me feel like I might be special.

He made me feel *seen.*

And in a life where I've spent most of it making myself small so my mother can shine, making myself small to avoid any kind of back-lash, that meant something to me.

And it was something I can now recognize faded quickly, some-thing I stopped feeling as soon as we were both comfortable in the relationship, but I held onto that initial feeling and it carried me through the end of our engagement.

Cami calls me a people pleaser—she says it's why I'm so amazing with the public relations and marketing of our events. I know what people want to see, the message they need to hear in order to buy what I'm selling, and I give them exactly that.

I guess she's right.

But that's what also made me blind to all the damn red flags that are Bradley Reed, so it has to go.

In a personal capacity, at the very least.

Everyone is holding their breath when I glance at the lock screen and furrow my brows. "I don't know the number."

"Ignore it, Liv. Seriously," Cici says.

I ignore *her* instead.

I mean, if I ignored everyone's warnings in the first place, I might as well keep that ball rolling, you know?

Tapping my screen, I open the messages and read them.

Then I reread them.

And a third time.

"Who is it?" Cami asks.

"Is it the jackass?" That's Cici, a bit of a shock since she never once said anything bad about him, not even when I was in the peak of my meltdown yesterday.

"Your mother?"

"Your dad?"

"I'm right here," my dad says, but Cici and Cami ignore him.

"Tabloids?" Cici asks.

I continue staring, reading the strange and unexpected message a fourth time.

"No," I say, finally breaking my silence.

"Who is it?" Cami sounds even more concerned than normal, and I think that must be a terrible, horrible indication of the state I was in yesterday.

"It's a . . ." I squint at my phone, trying to decide if what I see is even real. "It's a support group?"

"A support group?"

"What asshole is sending you links to fucking *support* groups?!" Cami says, and the rage in her voice makes me worry she might go run to this person's house with a pitchfork and a torch, *Beauty and the Beast* style. "And even more, a support group for *what?*" She looks at me with a slightly calmer face. "You know you don't need that, right? You've got—"

"Take it down a notch, Cam, it's not in a mean way."

"Of course it is. People are the fucking worst—"

"Let her finish her thought, Camile," Cici says, her voice much calmer than Cami's. I'm pretty sure she glares at my childhood friend, but I don't pay either woman any notice as I read the text for the fifth time.

> Hi, Olivia. This probably feels strange, and we know you're going through a lot right now, but I wanted to reach out. You applied for our Facebook group yesterday and noted you'd be interested in in-person support group meetings. I know it's very soon, but we have our next meeting in three days, so I wanted to let you know.

> There's a group of five of us who meet once or twice a month just to talk about things.

> We've all been left at the altar and are in different stages of our grief. It helps, talking to someone who has been there. We understand if this is too soon, but I wanted to extend the invite anyway.

> Sincerely, Julie Chen.

It all comes back to me.

My drunken searches, the Facebook group.

Jilted brides.

There's a support group for women who have been through this.

A local one.

"What is it?" Cami asks, probably noticing my lack of hysterics. "A client?"

"A tabloid?" Cici asks again. "They've reached out to me already, asking for my thoughts as the maid of honor, but I told them no comment."

That makes me groan.

I didn't even *think* about how everyone will be hounded just as much as I will be.

Everyone I *know* is going to be bombarded. The marriage of a Reed and a Kincaid was already news, but the drama of it falling apart right before I walked down the aisle is too good of a story to pass up.

"How bad are those?" I ask, temporarily distracted from the message on my phone. I'm sure at least *one* of the major trash papers has already started to dish on my misery.

Cami and Cici look at each other and I know instantly.

It's bad.

It means at least one of the big ones has started to post about my big day, whether they have concrete quotes or not. Though, if I'm being honest with myself, they probably do—the people my mother insisted on inviting in order to show off are not the types to keep juicy gossip to themselves, especially when having said juicy gossip could elevate their own social worth.

Fuck.

As the granddaughter of Jefferson Kincaid, the real estate mogul, and daughter of Melanie St. George, the wife of Huxley St. George and one of the newest members of the *Housewives of Los Angeles*, the spotlight was on me before I even *met* Bradley Reed.

But when word got out I would be marrying a man who comes from a wealthy, influential family of his own, the press went rabid. Every moment of my unbearably extravagant wedding was outlined, leaked details splashed across pages of trashy magazines, and in the last few weeks, I couldn't even go to the *gym* without at least one camera following me.

I hated it, but my mother loved it and begged me to lean into it to help her own standing as she climbed the social ladder as an affluent reality star.

I was assured—promised, even—that once the excitement of the wedding died down, once I went back to my normal life, I would mostly have peace.

Unfortunately, I don't see that happening anytime soon now.

"We can worry about it tomorrow. Or the next day," Cami says, attempting to get me to focus. "Who texted you?"

My mind goes back to my phone. I look at it then back at her. "It's, a, uhm . . . another jilted bride?"

"What?" The single word is drenched in justified confusion.

"I mean. It seems like possibly *quite a few jilted brides.*"

"I don't . . . I don't understand," Cici says.

"I . . . I kind of did some searching last night. I found a group of North Jersey women who were left at the altar. I was a little . . . drunk off fancy Champagne." Cami can't fight the smile on her lips even though her face is transforming with shock and anxiety. "And I requested to join the group. There was an option to leave your cell number if you were interested in an in-person meeting and I did."

"You gave strangers your *personal cell number?*" my dad asks, his face aghast. "Liv, that's incredibly unsafe."

"I was drunk, Dad."

"Cut her some slack, dimples. She's been through a lot." He rolls his eyes, but even from here, his smile from the nickname he pretends to hate is clear. Cam reaches over and grabs my cell from my hands. She uses a perfectly manicured finger to swipe to the top of the text chain, and she reads it slowly before handing the cell to Cici, who repeats the process.

"Are you going to reply?" my best friend asks as she hands the cell back to me, my eyes roaming the letters once more.

"Well, yeah? What else would I do?"

"Uh, ignore it?"

"That would be rude."

"I think you're pretty well excused from being rude right now," Cami says. "You don't owe these people anything." Her eyes narrow. "You don't owe *anyone* anything, Olivia."

I know she's saying more with her words, but I ignore that as well.

"I think . . . I think maybe it could be good for me. Worst-case scenario, I get a funny story from it."

"Worst-case scenario, it's a setup and you're being sold out." I roll my eyes at Cici.

"You're such a pessimist."

"I'm a realist," she says. "There's a difference."

"Is there?" I ask with my first genuine smile of the morning.

Instantly, it's clear everyone knows it, too, because they back off. It's like one small move has them all slightly less worried and I fucking hate that. It turns a knife in my chest.

The absolute last thing I want is all of them worrying about me.

"Why do I know there's no way to talk you out of this?" Cami asks.

Again, I smile.

Smiling feels good.

It feels *normal*. I could really use *normal*.

I once read that if you fake smile enough, it tricks your brain into being happy.

I wonder if that's how this is working. The more I smile, the more normal I feel.

But I know it's probably more about having good fucking people in my corner and that is making me feel all light and bubbly.

"Because I'm undoubtedly going to this."

Cami sighs in defeat but suddenly, I feel so less defeated.

Because I think this might be the first solid step into doing things *for me*.

FIVE

What do you bring to a support group for jilted brides?

WEDNESDAY, AUGUST 23

If you had told me six months ago, I'd be walking into some random woman's apartment building to take part in a support group, honestly, I wouldn't have been *that* surprised.

But I couldn't have foreseen *this particular* support group.

A group for daughters of women who will never, ever be happy no matter what happens?

Yes.

Pathological people pleasers?

Absolutely.

Shit, people who start their own businesses and no longer have any sense of work-life balance?

For sure.

But a support group for jilted brides?

Well, I didn't see *that one* coming.

"Olivia!" a pretty brunette with fair skin and a huge smile says as she opens the door. "My goodness, I'm so happy you came! Come in, come in!" She steps aside, and I almost turn around and run down the hallway because I'm fully second-guessing the decision to say *yes* to this.

"Uh, yeah. Thanks for inviting me. This is for you," I say, handing over a bottle of Champagne to who I'm fairly certain is our host.

My mom isn't perfect, but she did teach me to never show up empty-handed.

"Oh, look at you! You are so kind. Come, come, let's meet everyone."

Everyone turns out to be four women sitting around a small coffee table, a large charcuterie board in the center and glasses of wine at the ready.

I don't know what I expected, but it *wasn't* this . . . this book club-looking vibe.

"Everyone, this is Olivia. Olivia, this is, well, everyone," she says with a giggle. A chorus of excited *hellos* comes my way and I force out a smile.

Jilted brides.

This group of women looks more like a group of bored Stepford wives.

That's not nice, Olivia. You don't know these women at all. Judging them is just as bad as what the Bitch Pack did. You're better than that.

"It's so great to be here. Thank you so much."

"Of course! We're so glad you found us."

I sit at the end of the couch, crossing my feet at the ankles and putting my bag in my lap, trying to shake off how uncomfortable I am.

"So, we'll let you settle in a bit and go around and introduce ourselves, just so you know who we are. We've learned it's easier to open up once you hear everyone else's story, you know?"

I nod, unsure of what else I should say.

And then they begin, starting with who I've confirmed is our host, Julie. She was dumped a week before her wedding by her boyfriend of ten years. They had a conversation and despite her wanting to work on the relationship, it wasn't something he was interested in.

Chrissie is a blonde with bright blue eyes who tells me with little to no pain in her voice that her fiancé ghosted her the day before they were to wed and she has never heard from him again. From what a friend of a friend has told her, he's living two states over and is engaged to someone new.

Naomi confesses her ex is already married with a baby on the way despite the fact their one-year anniversary would have been last week.

Simone, a redhead with big curls tells me her ex broke up with her the night before their wedding and get this: they *still live together three months later.*

Strangely, I suddenly feel a bit better about my circumstances.

Which, I suppose, is the point after all, isn't it?

"If you're comfortable, Olivia, we'd love to hear your story. If not, you don't have to talk at all, though. The goal here is to heal and find people who understand what you're going through; part of that is, we know it can take time."

Glancing around at the friendly faces, though, I want to. I want to open up to them, to tell them everything.

"I met my . . . ex at my family's country club three summers ago. I fell hard and he did too . . . or so I thought. Last year, he proposed, and everything seemed perfect. My mother went into overdrive, planning a giant wedding, and he seemed . . . content. There wasn't any sign he . . ." I pause.

I pause because for the first time, I'm ready to admit out loud that there *were* signs.

He gave me so many, and I ignored them all.

"That's a lie," I say, my voice low, my head down as I start picking at my cuticles. My wedding day manicure is almost completely chipped off, the long-lasting gel polish having fallen victim to my anxious picking. "There were signs." I sigh and suddenly, my hand is being held by a light-brown one—Naomi.

"We get it. This is a safe place. We've all . . . We've all been there." A round of murmured agreement circles the coffee table and suddenly, I believe them.

This is a safe place.

Not to say my friends, who would have spent a full year in a hotel room with me while I cried and yelled and broke down, aren't a safe place because of course they are.

But there's an untouched embarrassment I feel when I look back on the past three years and see all of the red flags.

He gave me so many signs he wasn't in this for the long run, that he wasn't *invested in this.*

We never moved in together and never discussed our post-wedding living arrangements.

We never spent more than a night together.

We never went on a vacation in the nearly three years we were together.

He never talked to me about his work, about his frustrations, and anytime I talked about mine, the subject was quickly changed.

I brought it up one time, early in our relationship. I remember it so perfectly.

"I built a business with one of my best friends. A good one. A big one. We have an entire staff, have won awards, and we've only been around for a little over three years." I shake my head, picking at my nails. "I tried talking to him about it once, about an issue we were having. I remember it so well. I was frustrated and I was talking and he came over and tucked my hair behind my ear and smiled at me and gave me this look . . . god."

I shake my head again, remembering his face, a mix of pity and annoyance and boredom, the kind of look you give a kid who has been talking about some video game you don't understand for the past six hours.

Not your adult girlfriend talking about her business.

"He said, 'Babe, you know that all goes over my head. It all sounds so silly to me, parties and whatnot.'" My eyes slip closed and it hits me in a way that hasn't registered just yet.

"He never cared, did he? It was always . . . I don't know. It was always artificial for him or something." I've tried to figure it out a few times now, to decode why he let it get so far, let us get so far, and why he stopped when he did.

Was it for the image boost?

Was it for his ego?

The press?

I guess I'll never know since he hasn't responded to any text or call since that day.

"I think that's the hardest part," I say. I've kept my head down, not looking at them, too embarrassed and unsure of myself. "The not knowing. Not knowing why he ended it but also not knowing why he . . . why he started it. Why he *continued* it. That's almost worse, you know?" I lift my head and finally meet their eyes, expecting to see what I saw in the hotel room when my world burned around me, while the pretty curtain I had hung around my relationship for the past three years fell, leaving me with . . . reality.

The pity.

The sadness.

The concern.

Of course, I could have told Cici all of this. I could have told Cami or my dad or my mom—*okay, maybe not my mom*—and they wouldn't have held it against me.

But I don't want to see it in their eyes. The looks of pity, of dismay.

Of disappointment.

I interrupted their lives with my wedding—both the planning and the actual day itself—and it all could have been avoided if I had just *opened my eyes.*

But when I meet the eyes of each woman in this room, each listening with rapt attention, it's not there.

There's no pity or disappointment or exhaustion.

There's *empathy.*

Understanding.

These women . . . they get it.

They've lived it.

They don't have that look on their faces because they've been there. They've ignored the signs, and they've gotten left at the altar, and from what I can see, they're still standing.

It gives me hope.

Because I'm playing like I have it all together, but the foundation of the life and world I thought I understood has shaken.

And because I need to tell *someone* this, I give it all to these relative strangers.

And fuck, it feels good.

SIX

What is the best revenge on an ex who did you wrong?

WEDNESDAY, AUGUST 23

An hour later, I'm way more comfortable, sitting crisscross applesauce on the couch, munching on a plate of snacks from the nearly decimated charcuterie platter, and feeling a bit fuzzy from Champagne and wine.

These women, though all so very different, are somehow all the same. The same traumatic experience has linked us together, charms on a bracelet, connecting different pasts and presents, different likes and dislikes and aesthetics to make something that just makes sense to this very specific group of people.

I'm popping a chip in my mouth when I ask it, the question I've been wondering silently for days now.

"So, how did you get over it?"

Five pairs of eyes stare back at me.

"What?"

"You all seem so . . . chill. How did you get over your exes? How did you get over the wedding? The . . . disappointment everyone feels?"

It hangs on me like a heavy winter coat, following me everywhere I go. Sometimes, I think I've managed to take it off, to hang it up and pack it away, but then the weight slowly returns and suddenly, I'm suffocating again.

They all look confused.

"The disappointment who feels?" Julie asks.

"Well. The guests. They came a long way. And your families? That kind of thing?" Brows furrow and it's clear I've lost them.

"Well . . . ," Chrissie starts, rolling her lips between her teeth before reaching out to hold my hand. "To be honest, Olivia, I can't speak for the other women, but I mostly have been focused on my own . . . heartbreak. On the loss of that ideal, of that happily ever after."

Oh.

Oh.

Well, duh.

"Oh, yeah, I mean, I feel that too." They blink and look at me like they don't quite believe me.

But I do; there's a bit of that heartache, I suppose, of that loss of a partner.

It's just . . .

The guilt outweighs my pain.

Now that I'm thinking about it, I should definitely bring that up in my next therapy appointment.

"You all seem so put together."

"I mean, to be fair, for the majority of us, there's been some time between the event and now. But we're all on our own journey, Olivia." Heads nod.

"Definitely. And talking about the new issues that pop up, like the anniversary for me, is helpful with processing those emotions."

They all seem so well-adjusted, but it still doesn't fully make sense to me.

"I'm not going to lie, you guys totally lost me." They look at me with furrowed brows.

"How so?" I glance at each of them, seeing that now *I* have lost *them,* before I try to figure out how to put it into words.

"So you guys . . . you like, you get together once every . . ."

"Two weeks, a month. It's not set in stone."

"Got it. So you meet once in a while and . . ." They look at me like I'm insane.

"We talk," Naomi says slowly, like she suddenly is second-guessing if I'm all there. I shake my head and close my eyes, trying to phrase it so they understand.

"What are you doing to *feel* better?"

"What do you mean?"

Somewhere in the back of my mind, something stirs. An excitement or a pull to do more to . . . I don't know.

"We should . . . do something."

"Like what?"

A pull to get even.

"Like *get back at them*." The eyes around the coffee table go wide. "You know. Get closure." I sit up straighter, genuine excitement building with each moment.

"You mean we should . . . talk to them?"

"Fuck no," I say.

"You lost me," Julie says, and all heads nod in agreement. In this moment, it's so painfully clear they're questioning why the fuck they invited me.

But also, an idea is brewing.

Because *fuck* Bradley Reed.

Fuck him and his shitty attitude and his douchey ass and the way he left without a care and doesn't have to deal with the backlash and the way he gaslit me every fucking time I brought up a concern until I was convinced I was the crazy one.

But I *wasn't*.

If I had listened to my gut instead of worrying about how he felt, how my mother would feel, and how it would *look* in the eyes of others, I might not be here.

"I have this friend. She dated this dickhead for a bunch of years and then he dumped her in a really shitty way." Nods tell me they're following me once more, if a bit skeptically, so I continue. "So, she gets really drunk and she and her friends make this list—a revenge list. Shit to give him a taste of his own medicine, to make her feel better. To get her own version of closure."

I lost them again.

That's fine.

Because for the first time in a week, there's a fire in my veins.

Excitement.

A will to do something other than put my head down and work, even if Cami has banned me from the office.

"And then my business partner had these bitchy girls who were trying to destroy her and we got them back, made sure they couldn't fuck with anyone anymore."

Blinks. They have no idea what I'm saying.

Probably because they're normal people.

That's fine. I can show them the light.

"We should show these assholes how we really feel. How they can't treat us like we're . . . space fillers and then leave whenever they want without consequences. They can't just leave us in shambles and get out scot-free."

Chrissie smiles, her eyes lighting up, and I think she gets me. Perfect.

"We should write them letters! It would be so cathartic. Then we can read them in group and send them all together." The other girls all smile and nod.

It is so painfully clear we're on different pages.

"I was thinking more . . . tangible. Men don't respond well to . . . love letters or whatever. We need to do things that they'll remember. Make them regret ever hurting us." Any hint of understanding is gone. "So, my friend Abbie put glitter in the vents of her ex's car so when he turned the heat on, it blew everywhere."

Naomi's eyes go wide and she smiles. "That's absolutely diabolical! The glitter must have been there *indefinitely*." I nod in agreement, sitting on the edge of the couch now and smiling wide.

"And it was because he loved that car so much, it sometimes seemed like he liked it more than her. She also placed all of his coffee orders every morning, so she changed the order just a bit to fuck with him."

They nod, seeming to finally get the point.

I *don't* tell them that she also fucked and then married this boss.

It's not the vibe, after all—ending up with true love after heartbreak.

We're going for cold-hearted baddie vibes. Black Widow-type shit.

But, you know.

Without the murder.

Bodily harm . . . I mean, maybe.

My phone beeps, reminding me I have my weekly call with my mother in half an hour. It was supposed to be the first post-wedding and taken while on my honeymoon, but we all know how that went.

It's a call that's been in place since I was little, when I lived with my dad full time and my mom only came to LBI for the summers and stayed at the Beach Club, spending the rest of the year across the country trying to score some rich husband or get snapped by a paparazzi. Now, it's often recorded for the show, the producers catching her reaction to my every word.

"Shit, okay, I have to head out—this has been so amazing though. Really, thank you so much for inviting me." I look around at the girls, all smiling. "And I'm serious. We should . . . We should all get ours. A little revenge, you know?"

"But how?" Tina asks. She looks interested in my idea but unsure.

"We'll do it together," I say with a smile, the idea forming. "Next meeting is"—I scroll on my phone and find a date two weeks out—"September 10. Everyone comes with a list. The more unhinged, the better." I lift my glass of wine and drink the last sip. "We can whittle them down to find the best options."

"Unhinged how?"

"Whatever you think your ex would hate most, write it down. No matter how crazy. Then we'll brainstorm how to make it happen."

Julie looks nervous, unsure.

"This is . . . We're supposed to be getting *over* our exes."

"Julie, I promise you this: nothing helps more to get over a shitty man than fucking him over the same way he fucked you over. It's . . . a scientific fact." Her brow furrows like she doesn't quite believe me, but that's fine.

She doesn't have to.

I'll *show* her,

"Next meeting!" I say, then I stand, smiling.

"I can't wait," Chrissie says, and I hug each of my new friends before walking out the door, a new, little pep in my step.

Who would have thought joining a support group would be the best decision I'd made in a long, long fucking time? Even listening to my mom gossip and nitpick on our call can't bring me down.

And the entire rest of the night, I get lost in planning my revenge.

SEVEN

How do you cut the brake lines of a Chevy Nova?

THURSDAY, AUGUST 24

It's barely five days past my failed wedding and one day after my meeting with my new group of friends, and I'm starting to feel twitchy with my need to *do something*.

Cami demanded I take off the entirety of the time I had planned for my honeymoon and while I *get it*—she means well and doesn't want me to overdo it in my *fragile state*—I need to be busy.

Being busy stops me from having time to swim in my messy thoughts. I need *work* to distract myself.

It's not an option, unfortunately, since I've been locked out of everything, including my freaking email.

I have had a love-hate relationship with Cami from the very start and I don't foresee that ever changing.

But after last night, after my meeting with the group, at least I have a new motivation, something to occupy my mind. Something exciting and fun—revenge.

I'm in the middle of researching just *how* a vintage car works, including the brake lines, when my phone rings, showing Cami's name on the screen. I try not to roll my eyes (a failed effort) because the woman calls me twice a day to make sure I'm not tipping over the edge,

"How'd it go?" Cami asks as soon as I pick up. I sigh and shake my head.

"What, no hello?" I ask.

"Is that Liv?" my dad asks in the background, and I once again roll my eyes into my skull.

Sometimes, when I'm feeling really introspective, I'm *sure* the universe got it wrong and Cami was supposed to be my mother. That they should have met and Melanie Kincaid never should have been involved in my conception at all.

Granted, Cami was only five when I was born, which would make that not only impossible but ridiculously inappropriate.

Still, I think you know what I mean.

"Zach, stop, let me talk to her," she says, and there's a scuffle like they're fighting over the phone. That's confirmed when my dad's voice is closer this time.

"It's my daughter, angel." I can hear his smile and it tugs at something in my belly. Not because I miss him, but because they have that relationship, that joy and happiness and teasing. The feeling is a strange mix of happiness they have that and jealousy I don't.

That I *never have*.

"Get off me. No. Shoo. Shoo! Go make me dinner or something. Make yourself useful. I'll fill you in later." A door closes loudly before she sighs and a mix of knocking and my dad's muffled laughter fills the line.

God, he's so happy.

That should have been the first sign things would never have worked with Bradley.

He never laughed like that, never looked at me the way my dad looks at Cami. I shake my head, trying to dislodge my unhelpful thoughts as Cami speaks. Focusing on the signs I should have seen, on the things lacking in my life will get me nowhere.

"God, your dad really is a pain in my ass."

"Yeah, yeah, yeah. I don't need to hear about your ass pain in conjunction with my dad." Her catty smile and love to poke fun at me can almost be heard through the line.

"I mean he—"

"Dear lord, Cami, I swear to fuck, I'll hang up."

"No, no, no! I'm sorry. I'll stop. Please!" I sigh, and when she realizes I'm staying on, she speaks. "So, how did it go?" I roll my eyes but answer anyway.

"It was . . . good. They're all very sweet."

"Sweet like a librarian or sweet like Abbie?" Sometimes, she has the most random, unhinged comparisons.

"What's the difference?"

"Abbie's psychotic."

"Oh. I think librarian?" Definitely librarians, especially Chrissie. While I was suggesting we plan some kind of Carrie Underwood-style revenge, she wanted to write a *strongly worded letter*. The idea alone makes me smile.

"Probably for the best. So, what do they *do*?" I sit on her question for a moment because I'm not entirely sure how to explain the Jilted Brides Club.

"I mean, I still don't really get it, but I think they just . . . meet up and talk."

"Talk." Cami sounds skeptical. I shrug despite her not being able to see me.

"Yeah, I guess."

"Are they like . . . really hung up on their exes?" I shake my head even though she can't see it.

"I heard some of their stories. It seems like it's really just a group of friends who happen to have a common experience. They talk about it because . . . it's unique. Others can't really relate."

"Oh. That's . . ."

"Anticlimactic?"

"Well, yeah. Kind of."

I don't know why I feel I should avoid telling Cami about my revelation on getting even with our exes, how I convinced an entire room of women with enough emotional baggage to drown the *Titanic* to write a list of revenge ideas in an effort to make ourselves feel better about our situation, but I do.

That's a lie.

But I also know why I don't tell Cami.

It's because if I did, I know for a fact she would *not* approve. She'd tsk and tell me it's not a healthy way to cope.

A total fucking hypocrite if you ask me, but whatever.

She's in her *healed girlie era* and we love that for her. I just personally am *not* there and more in my *Reputation* era.

And considering the idea of revenge on Bradley Reed is the only thing holding my fragile pieces together, I don't want her raining on my parade.

Cami breaks into my thoughts, finally asking what I know she's been dying to since I answered the phone.

This wasn't a call to ask about my support group—not really. Sure, she wanted to know, but . . .

"Okay, but how are you really?" she asks, and even though the question twists something in my stomach, I smile.

"I'm fine," I insist.

"Olivia. You don't have to play that with me. It hasn't even been a week. You're allowed to feel . . . sad. To mourn. Whatever. If you want to rage and throw shit, that would be so totally acceptable. I know it's not your style but . . ."

I don't tell her that just yesterday morning, I felt that cloud of sadness and mourning, like I ruined everything, that I fucked up somehow. That Bradley might have been *justified* and I simply couldn't see why just yet.

But it's dissipated.

Now I'm burying any pain and sadness beneath a thick layer of anger.

Of vengeance.

Don't get mad, get even is my new motto.

She'd probably understand, given her history, but also, she's reformed now.

And she's protective of me.

And, of course, she's with my dad.

So I won't tell her about my plans, of where my about-face is stemming from.

"I'm totally fine."

"Olivia—"

"Cami, I know it sounds crazy but I'm serious. I promise. I had my little cry session and a few days of moping, but now I'm good. I'd be even better if you let me come back to work."

"Babe, that's not normal. You dated him for over two years."

"Well, I'm not a normal person. We both already knew that." She sighs.

"Olivia—"

"I'm serious, Cami."

And I am.

As of last night, I feel . . . better.

I feel healed.

Like a cloth was lifted from my eyes and now I have a new purpose for my life. A new reason to roll out of my bed other than pleasing Bradley Reed and convincing both of us I'm good enough to be with him.

I wasn't, of course.

I was *too good* for him. That's a fact I'm starting to actually believe. Something I think if I tell myself enough, I'll start to believe it to my bones.

Fake it till you make it and all that.

"I'm good. I'll probably have bad days, but today is not one of them."

I know if she were here in front of me, her eyes would carefully dissect me the way she does with everyone, reading between the lines and decoding every facial expression in order to decide if I'm telling the truth.

And she would see what I want her to see.

I make sure of it always, no matter who I'm speaking to.

But we're over the phone so she just sighs. "I don't want to see you in the office until Monday, Liv." I roll my eyes. "I know you're rolling your eyes. I don't care. You haven't taken a day off since we started Event Press. You can endure one more weekend."

"Yes, I—"

"Emergency gallbladder surgery doesn't count," she declares, cutting me off. I stay silent. "Plus, you worked from the hospital."

"I had client emails to answer! I couldn't leave them hanging!"

"You could have, Liv. But your people-pleasing nature literally self-destructs at the mere thought of letting someone down so you couldn't bear it. I've never met anyone who can write such a concise email under the cloud of painkillers,"

"Until you met me," I say with a smile.

A proud smile, and I know she can hear it through the phone it.

"God, I can't stand you. Call me. If you need anything at all, I can be to you in an hour."

"It's a two-hour drive to Hudson City from LBI."

"And I can be there in an hour."

I smile, knowing she means it, but warmth also blooms in my belly that I have that: someone who would run red lights and possibly start a state-wide police chase just to check in on me.

"Not necessary, but I appreciate it, Cam." There's a long pause before she speaks once more, and I know I've survived another interrogation.

"Love you, Liv. See you soon."

"Love you too, Cami," I say, my throat still closing a bit every time she says those words to me, words that are so difficult for her to say. Then we hang up and I'm in my quiet, lonely apartment once more.

But unlike the previous days since the failed wedding, I don't feel that loneliness coming in to consume me, to swallow me whole. Instead, I use it as fuel.

I open my computer and start searching with a vengeance.

EIGHT

THURSDAY, AUGUST 24

I need this promotion.

I need it more than I've ever needed or wanted anything in my life.

At least, I need it if I'm expected to continue to work here without losing my fucking mind. This becomes clear once more when Peterson, my boss, leans his arm on the top of my cubicle and looks at me, his face serious.

He looks like what everyone thinks of when they picture that higher-up who hasn't done anything since he became a manager and pawns off all of this work to the people below him. His perfectly pressed suit and $500 shoes would do him no good if he had to be in the field, his hair is thinning at the top, and he has a jelly stain on his white button-down from the donuts Sally brought in for everyone.

The sign said, *Please take one,* and I guarantee if you look in the bottom left drawer of his desk, you'll find four wrapped in napkins.

And every fucking day, despite never doing any work himself, he leans on the wall of my cubicle, making the thin particle board bow, and asks me the same thing.

"Anything new?"

This is why I want a fucking promotion.

This.

Well, to be frank, there are many reasons, but this takes the cake.

Because I'm tired of everyone and their fucking mother coming to my desk and thinking it's open game to just chitchat, to interrogate me about whatever assignment I'm working on.

I don't want to see their faces.

I want to sit here and dig and monitor this trust fund baby's movements until I find something concrete to use so I can move on to a better assignment.

I was told in no uncertain words when I was assigned this case almost a year ago and moved into the house across the street from Bradley Reed to keep tabs on the wiretaps we have in his home that if I did well, I would get a corner office.

A corner office.

God. It sounds like a dream.

I got into the FBI because I love information. I love digging, solving problems. I love to sit on my computer and code and hack and figure shit out.

I do *not* love the politics of an office.

I do *not* enjoy small talk.

And I definitely do *not* enjoy reporting to fucking morons who can barely figure out how to open a PDF in their email, much less how to access or process the dozens of recordings captured for just one case every day.

And *no.*

I *don't* have anything new just yet on the Reed case, which makes it even more frustrating.

My current primary assignment is to keep tabs on Bradley Reed, the man who we have substantial evidence is siphoning funds from his investment firm, and his fiancée, whose name he put everything into. Reed is exactly what you might expect—a rich Finance Bro (capital F, capital B) who got a little too confident and a lot too greedy. But he was smart enough to pin everything on his fiancée, so if, say, the

SEC or the FBI got wind, he could claim at least partial innocence and, with his daddy's connections, get *maybe* a slap on the wrist.

His fiancée, Olivia Anderson, who, from what I can see, is not only wholly innocent but utterly unaware of his plan, would take the brunt of the fall.

And because of that, I watch them both day in and day out, trying to make sure neither makes a run for it and attempting to find the smoking gun to pin it all on Reed once and for all.

I can't fucking wait for this case to be done because watching this spoiled rich brat every single day might be more boring than watching paint dry. These days, her social interactions and text messages are mostly friends checking in on her to make sure she's not having a mental breakdown and work.

And her work is fucking *party planning*.

Things got interesting a few days after Reed left her just minutes before she walked down the aisle. It ended in her searching for different forms of revenge on a shitty ex, but that was it before she dove head-first into work.

She's barely even left her townhouse in Hudson City.

I have a theory as to why Reed left her, something I haven't shared with anyone else but also something I haven't been able to substantiate one way or another.

"Not yet," I say, keeping my eyes on my computer screen.

There's nothing there, but if I look busy, maybe . . .

"Remember, Valenti. This case is going to determine if you or Andrews gets that promotion in January."

As if I didn't already fucking know that.

As if it's not the only thing I've been able to focus on for the past six months.

"Got it."

"I want my mug on news channels all over the tristate by Thanksgiving. I don't care who the fuck we pin this shit on, Reed or one of his cronies or the girl. The American people deserve to have someone they can bring to justice."

God, he's such a miserable fuck.

I got into this work because I love computers and love the idea of using that knowledge to help others. I love starting at the surface level and finding out every single thing about a person, from what time they were born to what they had for breakfast, to what app they scroll while taking a shit.

But this—the bureaucracy, the politics, the *egos*—I fucking hate.

And Peterson.

I hate him most of all.

Because he pretends that he does shit *for the American people.*

And *for justice.*

But he does it for the thrill, the power of it.

Olivia Anderson might be a vapid, spoiled brat, but she's not guilty of stealing millions from innocent people. She's just guilty of being too fucking stupid to realize what her now ex was doing. And that's not a crime.

"It's not Anderson."

"You got proof?"

"Not yet, but—"

"Her name is on all paperwork. Her signature is on the bank statements. Unless you've got concrete proof it's not her or Reed admits she was a pawn, it's looking like her."

"Isn't our job to protect the innocent?" I ask the jelly splotch on his shirt.

"Our job is to find people responsible for crimes," he says. It's bullshit and we both know it.

"Except—"

"And *your* job is to either clear her name or make sure Anderson doesn't make the situation worse. Have you done that?"

"Well, she hasn't fled the country yet, so—"

"Perfect."

"But that's not—"

"We moved you in across the street almost a year ago because you were so fucking sure he was having meetings there, and all we've gotten is a fuck ton of pictures of her going in and out of his house and a few heavily coded conversations. Those are the only meetings we have on paper and, again, her fuckin' name is on everything. You've got until the end of November and then I'm wrapping this up and pinning her in the center."

If that happens, I can kiss my promotion goodbye.

I know the only way Peterson will sign off on agreeing I deserve it, despite the fact that Andrews is only here because he's some higher-up's nephew and gets *nothing done*, is if I clear the Anderson girl's name and frame Reed.

But I need more *time*.

"Peterson—"

"November. Talk to you later, Valenti," he says, tapping his hand on the makeshift wall he was leaning on before turning on his heel and walking off to go torment someone else.

I hate him so fucking much.

But he's gone, so there's that.

Just then, a ping comes in, a text to Anderson's phone.

> CAMI
>
> Do you need me to go with you today?

Today. What is today? Looking at my calendar, I move my eyes to the lines written in blue—Olivia Anderson's calendar.

August 24 . . . nothing.

Not even a meeting.

She hasn't met the one-week mark Thompson insisted on as a "break" before she's allowed to formally begin working again.

> No, I'm good.
>
> I'll be in and out, should be simple.

> I can be there in an hour, Liv. You should have someone with you.

> You've got a meeting at the club today.

The "club" is the Beach Club, the fancy country club-esque resort Olivia Anderson's grandfather owns and also where Camille Thompson's personal office is.

> And I can cancel it. What if he shows up?
> You haven't seen him since the rehearsal.

I don't know any of these people personally, but after such a long time on Olivia Anderson's case, I feel like I know them pretty well. Of this entire crew, I like Camile the best.

She doesn't watch her words and *never* takes shit from anyone. Even her rich, prestigious clients who have more money than God— she does what she needs to keep them content but she also sets incredibly clear boundaries and expects everyone to respect them.

Of all of the people who have reached out since Olivia was left at the altar by her fiancé, Camile is the one who doesn't put kid gloves on, instead talking to her outright.

For the record, of the people who have reached out since the failed wedding, the person I can't stand the most is her mother, Melanie St. George.

While Camile is asking Olivia if she needs help picking up the last of her things from her ex's home, Melanie St. George is begging her daughter to try and *make amends* and fix this.

The text she sent last week still makes me curl a fist when I think of it, and I don't even *like* Olivia Anderson.

> This is an embarrassment, Olivia. It looks
> terrible for me, my daughter being dumped
> by a Reed. You need to fix this.

But more interesting was the way Olivia didn't lash out or, at the very least, ignore the message.

Instead, she replied cordially and *apologetically*.

> I know, Mother. I'm so sorry for any inconvenience this has created for you. I know your plate is already so full.

It wasn't said in a snarky way either. I instinctively know.

That's because she's a pushover of the worst kind, a quality I can't stand in people.

But regardless of how I feel about her, Olivia Anderson is a lot of things I detest, but she isn't guilty of embezzlement. She isn't responsible for draining hundreds of elderly people who entrusted Bradley Reed with their investments.

She doesn't have the backbone for it.

She *is* a spoiled princess who was born with a silver spoon in her mouth, despite spending most of her childhood years with her working-class father.

She *does* have a few million dollars waiting in trust for the day she turns thirty, collecting ungodly interest each and every day, so even if her surprisingly successful event firm tanks, she'll never need to worry about money.

She *was* dumb or vain or delusional enough to fall for Bradley Reed's bullshit, to date him and agree to marry him and do everything for him, from taking his clothes to the cleaners to calling up his dentist and rescheduling his appointments, even though he so obviously didn't care about her at all.

And she was dumb enough to become the most obvious scapegoat on the face of this planet.

She was stupid enough that now my job is to keep tabs on her at all times and make sure she *stays out of prison*.

And finally, Olivia Anderson might not be guilty, but she is my only shot at getting out of this fucking job I can't stand.

My eyes move to the monitor on my far right, the one that's a mirror of Olivia's laptop she works from almost exclusively. Usually, she just answers emails, hosts video conferences with clients, or works on documents. Occasionally, she'll be feeling a little more masochistic than normal and start searching her own name and pulling up the tabloids to see what people are saying about her.

But this time, she opens an old window she's had minimized for a week, a tab where she searched for revenge on an ex. There's an accompanying document where she pasted in her favorite options with notes to herself.

Glitter in the vents: overdone, Abbie did that already.

Abbie being Abbie Martinez, married to Damien Martinez, the well-known family law attorney in New York City.

Steal all of his left shoes.

I thought that was a pretty good one—can't get very far with only a right shoe, and it's small enough not to get her in too much trouble.

Rip all the seams on his pockets.

Genius, really. Imagine putting your phone in your pocket and it just falls out every time.

But as fun as this list is, it puts a pit in my stomach because it's not a good sign, her opening it once more. I thought there was a chance she was creating it as a form of catharsis, a silly girl thing I couldn't quite wrap my head around, like a diary used to get the thoughts out so they don't go rancid in your mind.

Something you hide in a drawer and never look at again.

Except she's reopening it.

Looking at this file wouldn't be concerning.

Not really.

Not concerning, at least, if it wasn't for the category at the bottom she labeled as, *Completely unhinged shit that dickwad really deserves.*

Because on the list are things that could land her in prison with an attempted manslaughter charge.

And it's most concerning when she scrolls to the bottom, clicking on the header and letting the writing cursor blink for a few moments, like she's reading the options and going over them once more.

Then, that pit in my gut churns as she moves to another tab and starts searching.

HOW TO CUT BRAKE LINES.

And then she clicks the first result and watches a video.

And then another.

And then searches, *WHAT TO CUT BRAKE LINES WITH?*

And, *CAN YOU CUT BRAKE LINES WITH A KNIFE?*

And then, *HOW TO DISABLE A VIDEO SECURITY SYSTEM?*

Less than ten minutes later, she closes out of the windows and sends a text to Camile Thompson.

> Off to go grab my stuff from he who must not be named.

Fuck.

Fuck fuck fuck.

This is *not* good. Not at all.

My eyes drift to the corner office door, watching the opportunity of it becoming my office come January wither and die because Olivia Anderson is no use to my investigation if she's arrested and booked for murdering her embezzling ex.

Not exactly a *reliable witness.*

Fuck.

I need that promotion.

I don't think I'll be able to handle this cubicle for another year or more while I wait for a new opportunity, won't be able to endure working beneath Peterson.

There's only one option, really.

Olivia Anderson needs to be stopped. She's putting this entire investigation at risk.

I would have begged for nearly any other case a year ago when I was assigned to Reed and Anderson and this is why: petty, rich assholes pretending there are no rules and laws in place, only concerned with themselves.

And now a year of work, a year of kissing Peterson's ass, of moving across the state and working more overtime than I ever have in my life is about to go to waste because some rich bitch is mad her ex dumped her.

Not on my fucking watch.

When I stand, grab my keys, and head to my car without a second thought, I'm not totally sure what I'm going to do, but I can figure that out on the drive over.

NINE

What to do with old photos of an ex?   🔍

THURSDAY, AUGUST 24

My phone buzzes on the center console of my car as I arrive at the small neighborhood I once thought I'd live in. It's cute, if a bit boring, with catalog homes lined up in predictable colors with perfectly green lawns and impeccably maintained landscaping. The homeowner's association is a bitch, tossing any hint of uniqueness out, but it's in a good school district, not too far from the Hudson City office, and the neighbors are all kind and charming for the most part.

I don't even have to check my phone to know who it is, but I do anyway.

CAMI

Do you want me to come with you?

I sigh before answering because I've told her no less than five times I would be doing this on my own.

Nope, I'm good. Just grabbing my things.

Give me an hour, I'll be there with your dad's truck.

THE FALL OF BRADLEY REED   69

> I don't need a truck, Cami. You're grossly overestimating how much of my stuff is at his place.

I hate him, you know.

I've always hated him.

I want to text her she's a liar, that she's saying that because she's a *good* friend, but I also know . . .

She's not.

Lying, that is.

While she never looked me in the eye and said, *I hate that creep. Marrying him is a huge fucking mistake,* she didn't *not* say it. She's Cami, and even if she's *reformed,* she never sugarcoats her words, not about the Bitch Pack, not about my dad, and surely not about Bradley Reed.

I always envied that about her, how she would never beat around the bush in order to save people's feelings, for better or worse. When I go home, I should make a vision board for *New Livi* and put a picture of Cami dead center.

Her intuition is so on point, in fact, I think anyone I date needs to go through some of her rigorous testing in order even to make it to the boning part of the relationship.

Bradley never would have made it through.

> Yeah, I know. Next time, I'll make sure to get your approval.

I guess that it's a good sign if you're already thinking of next time.

Not that you should jump into a relationship. It's just good you're not swearing off men for good.

> Don't worry, I won't be like you and refuse to date anyone for ten years after my traumatic relationship.

Oof, burn.

> I'm allowed to be mean. I was left at the altar a week ago.

How long are you going to use that one?

> However long everyone lets me get away with it.

Queen move, really.

> That's me, a queen. I'll text you when my embarrassingly small box of shit and I are out.

I send the text, and she sends a thumbs-up emoji, and god, she really is spending too much time with my dad.

She's turning into him.

Next thing I know, she'll be sending me the world's worst dad jokes.

I smile at the thought because even though I gripe about the two of them, I love how they found each other and how fucking perfect they are together. The perfect balance.

My eyes move to the door of the house I once thought I would live in. The garage door is open, the display lights on so everyone can see his white Chevy Nova, his pride and joy.

It's not even a good car, not anything impressive.

Maybe for a 80-year-old man, but not a 30-year-old.

Another red flag.

He was in more of a serious relationship with a fucking old man car than me.

I don't know who that's more embarrassing for, if I'm being honest.

Sighing, I reach for the handle, proud my hands aren't shaking even a bit as I head to my ex-fiancé's home to gather the last of my things.

Why isn't it all just in a box for me, ready to go, you ask?

Because he's too much of a twat to be bothered.

I texted him yesterday, asking if he could box up my things and send them to me or if we could meet halfway and exchange them, maybe talk about what went wrong. It was the first time I talked to him since our wedding day. Some idiotic part of me thought he'd be a decent guy, help me get closure or something.

I clearly was losing my mind.

> **BRADLEY**
>
> I can't, Olivia. I have a job.

> So do I.

> They're your things. If you want them, go get them. Leave the key on the island while you're there, too.

Leave the key on the island.

That's what two years of my life boil down to. I don't even get the decency of a sit-down conversation with him, for him to explain why.

I don't know why I would expect that, though. Why I would expect him to give me something he never gave me? I convinced myself for years his lack of compassion was because he was raised that way, closed off and focused on himself. I told myself once we were married, once we were a *family,* it would all change.

I was stupid, of course. That was never going to happen. And now I'll never get that respect, much less closure.

But you know what? Fuck that.

I don't need it. It's a brand of closure that would come with conditions, one that would be given only to make himself feel better, so he could brag to whatever poor girl comes next he *did me right,* probably right before complaining about what a shitty girlfriend and fiancée I was in his eyes.

Just like me, she'll probably be so gaslit into believing it, never questioning it any further.

So no.

I don't need Bradley's shitty closure.

No, I'll get my own.

Actually, I'll *take* my own.

Whether he's willing to give it or not.

My eyes move to the garage as I walk up to the house and all I can think is how much I hate this stupid fucking car, the classic Chevy I'm ninety-nine percent sure he loved more than he ever loved me. Actually, I'm *sure* he loved it more than me, all things considered.

He would only take the car out when the weather was absolutely *perfect*. I remember suggesting we use it as our getaway car after the wedding and you'd think I had told him I wanted to have a wedding ceremony drowning puppies and a dinner of live bugs.

It's what convinced me this would be the perfect revenge: cutting the brakes of his *precious* car so when he takes it out, he'll crash into some light pole or garbage can, ruining it forever. Technically, the body could be fixed, but I know Bradley Reed.

It would be destroyed for him.

Tainted.

It's a trophy for him—he keeps the garage lights on even at midnight so everyone in the vicinity can see the car in *all its glory*. Last year, he got a letter from the HOA because some residents were complaining about them being on at all hours.

Instead of putting a timer on or closing the garage door, he went to each and every door in the neighborhood to find out who it was and then schmoozed the husband of the woman who complained.

They still play golf once a month, and I've heard him more than once on a phone call saying things like, *that bitch of a wife you have,* before laughing it off as some kind of silly joke. A man's joke, he told me when I informed him that was a rude thing to say. "You wouldn't understand, Olivia."

God.

Each day, I hate him more and more. I can't believe I spent so long with him, so long ignoring everything terrible about him. How did I almost marry such a fucking tool?

But I know how, of course.

It starts with the flush of new love, the excitement of it.

Everything is new and fun and he's on his best behavior. He's attentive and kind and schmoozes you until you're blinded, until the sharp edges blur and the red flags turn into a pretty pastel pink.

And who could find fault in a pretty pastel pink, right?

And slowly, it begins. Once you're so deep in, once you've convinced yourself he's the one, the true version starts to show.

First, he picked at my clothes. He didn't like this top or those shoes, and they became items I relegated to the back of my closet, hidden for girls' nights instead of date nights.

And then he would say things, call them jokes if I told him they hurt me.

You're too sensitive.

I think it was around the first year when I called him out the first time, and he spun and twirled it around masterfully to make me look insane, to make it seem like I was the one attacking him, gaslighting me into believing *I* was the issue, that I had to change, that I was the one not trying hard enough.

And, of course, I couldn't tell Cami, who would hold a grudge until the end of time, and I couldn't tell Cici because I didn't want her to think poorly of him, when really, *we're just having a bad day.*

Or a bad week.

Or a bad *month.*

I told my mother instead.

And, of course, she is always so twisted in her own life, holding her own messed-up idea of what's *normal* in a relationship, that she told me I was overreacting. *That's just how important men with high-pressure jobs are, Olivia, trust me.*

And I did.

I believed her.

I believed him.

And I was so confused and so gaslit, somehow, the wedding and the aftermath was a surprise to me.

Shaking my head, I reach for the handle of my car, stepping out and heading for the front door.

Bradley isn't here, of course, something I asked ahead of time so we wouldn't have an uncomfortable interaction.

Of course, I won't be there, Olivia, he had written. *Some of us have adult jobs that hold normal hours.* It was just another dig, one I had ignored so many times over the course of our relationship. He was nothing but a red flag, and I closed my eyes all along, trying to ignore it.

My mind recalls, though, with some pride, how over the past few months, those rose-colored glasses cleared.

Unfortunately, I brought it up to my mother again, instead of Cami or Cici.

She understood men like Bradley, after all.

"*Isn't it weird that he's not involved?*" *I asked my mother one day on our weekly call.*

"*That's just how it is with men like this, Olivia. They're busy. He doesn't have time to talk about little parties.*"

"*It's not a little party, though. It's our wedding. Isn't that different?*" *I couldn't fathom being so uninterested in something your partner considered important, but maybe I was being unreasonable.*

"*Not for a man like that, Olivia. You'll get used to it, I promise. It's just . . . different.*" *There was a kindness in her voice I wasn't expecting, one I hadn't heard in a while.*

"*We haven't figured out where we'll live when we marry yet,*" *I said, another concern that had been swimming through my mind.*

"*You'll probably buy a new place. I bet he has it all planned out. A surprise! Remember when Huxley bought the home in the Palisades? Didn't tell me about it, just walked me into that closet . . ."* She sighed a blissful sound, remembering the closet her husband had filled with designer clothes.

"I just don't know, Mom."

It was the first time I admitted it out loud to anyone. I trusted her with that small anxiety of mine.

"I know this isn't the easiest route; trust me, Olivia, I do. But it's going to be so worth it, being married to him."

I remember I felt a jab hit my chest, thinking maybe she saw me.

She understood how badly I wanted the relationship, the partner, how badly I wanted what Cami and my dad have, what Abbie and Damien have, and what, in their own way, my mom and Huxley have.

But now, I think when she was speaking about it *being worth it,* she meant the lifestyle.

Getting the *name* and everything that came with it.

And a part of me . . . a sick, crazy part wonders if she meant it would be great *for her.*

But I shut that part of me up quickly. The consequences of believing that truth are too painful to look at too closely. So, I don't, covering that up just like I do anything in my life that feels too uncomfortable, and move onto the task at hand.

Onto closing this chapter for *good.*

The small house on the outskirts of Hudson City is a ranch with three bedrooms, two bathrooms, and the cutest little front yard.

When we first started dating, I let myself envision one day moving in and adding a garden bed to the barren front of the house, maybe some planters or a vegetable garden in the back, a daydream I'd always had since I was little. That was quickly nipped when Bradley told me flowers attracted bees.

The man is *terrified* of bees.

If I were Kat, I would have gotten the ick when he told me that, realized this would never work out, and backed out before I could get hurt.

If I were Cami, I'd have told him to suck it up and planted flowers that same day.

If I were Cici, I would have shrugged, bought my own house, and planted as many gardens as humanly possible. Maybe even invested in a beehive.

But instead, I'm Olivia.

Sweet, non-problematic Olivia who never wants to make anyone's life difficult.

I could set my dream of a full, lush garden at my forever home aside if it meant I could spend every day with the man I loved, right?

God, I hate myself sometimes.

Pulling out the single key from my pocket, a key I took off the keyring earlier so I wouldn't have to struggle with it later, I slide it in the lock and turn it before stepping into what I once thought would be *our* place. But as I walk in, I'm amazed by just how deep I had gone into my delusion. I'd convinced myself everything here was a perfect fit, that I was excited to move in and become an *us*.

But it's cold.

It's somehow both incredibly boring and way too extravagant at the same time, everything chosen to be top of the line and in your face but still looking like every other rich home I've ever been to.

Everything with Bradley was a show, a way to impress the person next to him, and not in a way that told people he was insecure and wanted them to see him as an equal. In a way that he wanted to tower over them, prove himself as *better* than them.

As expected, my things are not collected in a neat space, not left with some kind of apology note (Okay, so a delusional part of me thought—no, I can admit it, if only to myself, *hoped*—he would have done the kind thing and collected my stuff, put it into a box, and wrote me some kind of letter explaining where we went wrong.) Instead, I need to rifle through drawers and cabinets across the house to get the few personal items I kept here. First, I go to the hall closet where he tosses all of the old cardboard boxes, too lazy to break them down himself and instead having his cleaning lady do it for him.

It's there—I see it—buried under a few brown cardboard boxes. The corner of a gilded frame hits the light just right, and even though I've been in this closet more than a few times, it's never been at noon when the light from the front window shines in and casts a glow. I've only ever stayed nights at Bradley's. I guess the midday sun is what I needed to find the photo.

I wish I had seen it a year ago, a month ago. Fuck, even if I saw it a week ago, I think it would have been enough to snap me out of my daze and, maybe, possibly make question this relationship just enough to save myself.

Because when I see it, I'm so pissed by it, I want to *scream*.

The photo is of us at the Beach Club the summer we met, me kissing his cheek and him looking directly into the camera, a sun-kissed arm around my waist.

I look absolutely enamored by him, and I was.

He looks so fucking handsome; I hate to admit it.

I remember blowing this photo up, buying the most gorgeous frame I could find, and wrapping it up perfectly to give him for our first anniversary. He told me he couldn't wait to hang it in his office so he could look at me every day and smile, knowing that was the day he found his lucky charm.

God, he called me his *lucky charm*.

He called me that because as soon as we got together, he landed a few big accounts. I never told him it was because my family started to recommend him, seeing as we were an item.

I never saw that frame again, not even when I went to his office. I never fucking asked because it seemed too needy, too clingy, too bitchy, nagging girlfriend. I was afraid to rock the boat, to upset him with the accusation he didn't adore my gift.

I thought for a moment maybe he had another woman, that he didn't want to hang it because she'd see, but there are other photos of us around the house. Plus, the paparazzi caught enough photos of the two of us, a quick google search would reveal he had a fiancée to any other woman he might be trying to trick.

Eventually, I convinced myself he broke or lost the frame and was too embarrassed to say anything. I could understand that because if it were me, I would be mortified. The guilt would eat at me indefinitely.

But here it is.

Not shattered into a million pieces or tucked safely in some box he can't remember where he placed.

Sitting in a storage closet where he keeps empty cardboard boxes and extra garbage bags and his vacuum tossed carelessly in the back.

I should ignore it. I should take my box and close the closet door and pretend I never saw it, grab my shit and close the *metaphorical* door once and for all.

But I can't.

I can't because anger and frustration and *injustice* course through my veins at the realization I meant as much to Bradley Reed as the photo sitting in the dark.

Absolutely nothing.

And just like this photo and the frame I agonized over, carefully choosing and wrapping and gifting to him with my heart full of love and adoration, I put effort into our relationship, carefully crafting my interactions with my former fiancé so as not to overwhelm him, to make sure I wasn't nagging him or being too much *work*.

And he tossed it in a corner to collect dust.

So I grab it.

I take the frame and the photo he never hung and throw it in the bottom of my box, tossing in the rest of my things, and when I realize it all fits into a box that I can balance on my hip, small enough to fit under my arm, I realize this is what I was always to Bradley.

A forgotten frame in a closet.

A tiny box of things.

A small inconvenience and a key left on the counter without a second thought.

I was nothing.

We were nothing, and somehow, I convinced myself otherwise for so long that when it ended—when he ended things with as little care and gentleness as he's ever shown—I was thrown.

I was *surprised,*

I shake my head, but I don't feel the all-consuming sorrow I think I should. Because really, there's no reason to be upset over a relationship that was always going to fail since only one of us was ever invested.

No, I don't need closure.

I need karma.

I need revenge.

I walk to my car with a small smile, despite the nerves in my belly.

Because now I have clarity.

TEN

THURSDAY, AUGUST 24

She's sitting in her car outside of Reed's house, and I'm 99% sure she's about to do something really stupid.

Really fucking stupid.

She walked in, and, based on her text conversation with Thompson, she had to rummage around and grab her things, hence why it took her a bit before she walked out with a golden frame and a brown cardboard box. Why the ass couldn't put her shit in a box, I don't know, but I'm not necessarily surprised—he did con thousands of people out of retirement funds, after all.

Based on her search history and her purchase at a hardware store on her way over using the credit card the bureau tracks, I'm pretty sure she's *not* just grabbing her belongings from an ex's house.

No, she's about to do something so stupid, it could fuck up not only *her* life but my career.

And it's not just stupid in the sense that cutting the brake lines of your ex's car is stupid and dangerous and could, oh, I don't know, *kill him*, but she's doing it with absolutely zero protection. Sure, the car is in a garage (with a door he leaves wide fucking open, which, if you ask me, is *asking* for someone to fuck with his vehicle), but it's fucking open and well lit, and the man has security cameras everywhere.

In fact, the man has so much security around his home, it should have been the first sign something was wrong.

No regular civilian who isn't doing some shifty shit has that many security cameras in a quiet suburb.

Shaking my head, my mind rioting as I try and figure out what to do, how to maintain the integrity of this investigation and still keep my subject out of prison so she'll be a reliable witness, I look out the windows once more.

This house is barely furnished, mostly because I didn't expect to be here very long. I am not a field agent. I am a behind-the-scenes tech guy, but when the opportunity to monitor surveillance and wire-taps from the newly vacant home across the street from our suspect arose, I raised my hand.

It got me out of the shitty apartment I shared with three other guys and gave me the opportunity to discover a lynchpin to close this case, to secure that promotion. Plus, since the house was wired for operations, so long as I locked the office door whenever I brought someone over, I could work remotely on occasion. Another opportunity to get the fuck away from Peterson.

And now, as I watch her from just a few yards away, I'm in a position I never pictured myself to be in.

The position where I feel the need to interfere.

I am not one to do that—in fact, I despise the idea of it, of interrupting in a case. I'm here for facts and figures and the truth. To bring people to justice and to do it with cold, hard proof. I'm on the side of letting humans be stupid humans, of letting them make their own bed and lie in it.

By going over to her ex's home and cutting his brake lines, Olivia is definitely *making her own bed.*

But if she does that and something happens and she gets caught, she can't be a witness.

Once I find the evidence I need to fully put this crime on Bradley

Reed, I'll need his meek little ex-fiancée to tell her tale of being taken advantage of, to tell the jury about how she trusted him, loved him, and he played her.

She won't be a reliable witness if she has charges of attempted manslaughter against her. And without her, I won't get that promotion.

It only takes a single heartbeat for me to decide *fuck it*.

Fuck it.

Fuck my own rules and standards because I need Olivia Anderson to keep her stupid, trust-fund-baby, spoiled-brat nose clean.

With a sigh, I stand, quickly moving to the door where I keep my running shoes, slipping them on, and taking my shirt off to complete the undercover look I didn't think I'd need.

Then, I wait.

ELEVEN

How to stay calm when you're breaking the law?

THURSDAY, AUGUST 24

Maybe this is a bad idea.

Maybe I should just turn on my car and drive off.

Let bygones be bygones.

Live and let live and all that.

But I remember the way my blood curdled when I saw that frame.

I remember the disappointment on my mother's face when the wedding was called off.

I remember how he didn't even give me the *dignity* of telling me to my face, of a meeting in a coffee shop to explain.

Nothing.

I remember how he couldn't be bothered to even gather my things for me.

And I remember telling the girls in the Jilted Brides Club that they need to *do* something to cut that tie, to get closure once and for all.

I remember the excitement that flowed through me when I decided to get my *own*.

Don't get mad; get even.

That's my new motto.

I'm no longer the Livi who allows people to walk all over her.

Or at least, I'm trying.

And this is the first step.

The way to turn the tide, so to speak.

But first, I need to calm myself the fuck down, to still my shaking hands.

I resort to old methods, ones I used back when I couldn't show my emotions, my fears or sadness or anxieties, outwardly because it was *not ladylike.*

Breathe in for ten, hold for ten, breathe out for ten.

Then repeat.

Repeat until you catch your breath, until the panic slows enough to slow the wheezing.

I was seven, sitting in an ambulance after an asthma attack that, when paired with my anxiety, made it so I could barely get a single breath in.

The EMS was a kind, late-middle-aged woman with blonde hair that was turning gracefully gray, her eyes kind as she held my hand.

My mother was standing outside, mad she was missing out on the horseback riding excursion her friends had planned but not that her daughter was in an ambulance, unable to take a breath because the fear of disappointing her mother was directly contradicting her unbearable fear of horses.

I remember thinking the woman was pretty, that she looked the way a mom should, and wondering what my mother would look like if she ever let her hair go gray, knowing even then it would never happen.

"Whether it's allergies or exercise or nerves, this will help, okay, honey?" she told me, patting my hand in time with the male EMS who was counting to ten. I nodded, holding my breath. "It slows down everything just enough so your body can do what it has to."

Nearly twenty years later and I still use the technique.

Ten in.

Hold for ten.

Out for ten.

Repeat until my brain and my lungs work again.

I used it when I got the text saying Bradley *couldn't do this* ten minutes before I was to walk down the aisle.

I used it when Cami and I had to sit in front of my grandfather and admit we purposely sabotaged my stepsisters because they're bitches.

I *didn't* have to use it the time I slammed my fist into Staceigh's face, but maybe if I did, I wouldn't have gotten arrested.

No regrets there, though.

And now, I'm doing it as I stare at my fiancé's house.

Ex-fiancé, I remind myself. *He's your ex, Liv.*

You're here to grab whatever you left here.

Looking at the small box sitting on my passenger seat, I try and see the bright side of things. I guess it's good we never moved in together, that I don't have to go through the process of moving all of my stuff out and finding a new place.

"That should have been red flag number one," I say out loud in the quiet of my car. The fact that after nearly three years of dating and an engagement, we never moved in together. Never spent longer than a night together. He was never even really willing to talk about how we'd manage things after the wedding, always saying something along the lines of, "We'll figure it out when the time comes. I just want to be married to you."

The idiot I am thought it was *romantic*.

Romantic!

What a fucking moron I was.

A quiet part of me has wondered lately if he ever planned on marrying me at all. If this was always his plan, to leave me at the altar, to humiliate me. Or if maybe it was just something that somehow went too far. Maybe he only ever intended for me to be a summer fling, something easy and short, but he got wrapped up in it.

A man doesn't accidentally propose and slip a ring on your finger,

Olivia, I remind myself. *It's time to stop giving people slack at the expense of yourself.*

> CAMI
>
> Please tell me if you need me, Liv. I'm
> serious. I can be there in no time at all.

I sigh, reading the message from my not-quiet stepmom, best friend, and business partner.

This is why I need to do this, something small and stupid as payback for what he not only put me through, but my friends— just look how worried they are for me.

I shake my head, grabbing my phone.

> I'm fine. I'm great even. Heading out in a
> few and then on to bigger and better things,
> right?"

> Emphasis on bigger

Then, she sends me a string of emojis, starting with a winky face and including an eggplant.

It makes me laugh, the sound almost strange to my ears as it ricochets around the car before I grab the brown paper bag on the floor, take the tool out, and slip it into my bag.

And then, I'm slamming my car door behind me, eyes fixed on that *stupid fucking car,* my strides sure.

Let's fucking go.

TWELVE

THURSDAY, AUGUST 24

From the front window of the home across from Bradley Reed's, I'm using binoculars to watch her close her eyes, still sitting in the car. She tips her head on the headrest and takes a deep breath while I wait to make a move. Maybe she'll back down. Maybe she's second-guessing her ridiculous plan and is going to just drive off without doing anything idiotic.

A man can wish.

But the wish is fruitless when her chest rises and falls once more in a deep, quick breath, when her dark hair sways as she nods then reaches for her door.

Fuck.

Fuck.

If she succeeds, she could kill Reed and ruin the investigation.

If she fails, she could get arrested, and my investigation will end before I find whatever it is I need to clear her name and pin it on her ex.

Why do I care? I think to myself. *Why do I care if some spoiled brat who has had everything handed to her in her picture-perfect life gets framed for some white-collar bullshit? We could still recover the funds and have a villain to show off to the American people. Isn't that what matters? Fuck, it would probably be even easier, seeing as everything is already in her name as it is.*

But it's not.

Because if that's how I work, if that's how I get the promotion, I'm no better than Peterson at the end of the day. I'm no better than any of the assholes at my work who value closed cases over justice, and I didn't get into this field for brownie points.

Fuck. I run through a plethora of options, but none make sense.

I have to intervene, don't I?

Reaching for the door, I kick back the voice in my head telling me not to step in and stop this woman's natural instinct for self-destruction.

Survival of the fittest can suck my dick.

Her door is opening as I jog across the street so I'll be on the same side as her, and as her dark hair pops out, I discreetly look to see if she notices me, trying to maintain my cover as *dude jogging and not paying attention.* Thankfully, she's lost in her own head, probably distracted by whatever psychotic revenge she's trying to carry out without thinking any aspect of it through.

Even more reason to intercept, she's not even watching her surroundings for witnesses.

Forcing my steps to seem natural and not like I'm trying to get to her before she's in that damned garage, I make wider strides, just a handful of them, cutting the distance between us in half. She's stepped out of the car and is moving toward the sidewalk by the time we're on the same block.

That's when I pull out my phone and start tapping it and touching my ear like I'm trying to get it to pair, caught up in the screen. And wouldn't you know, I just don't notice the woman barely five feet from me as I slow my strides.

Look natural, I tell myself.

Unfortunately, there is a reason I am not a field agent. I am a *behind-the-scenes* kind of guy. Yet here I am, trying to stop my target from committing fucking manslaughter.

Do it for the promotion, I tell myself when I start to wonder what I'm doing, start to wonder just how unethical this is.

I need this.

She's just a few feet away when I quickly glance up. There's some kind of canvas shopping bag slung over her shoulder, and I can only wonder what's in it, what else she brought to finish this stupid deed.

And then boom—I crash into her, her phone flying into the grass, the bag falling from her hand, and the contents spilling out, including a pair of what looks like bolt cutters.

From her internet search history, I know that's what some random forum suggested she use to cut Reed's brake lines.

"God, shit, I'm so sorry," I say, making a big show of apologizing for my *unintentional* faux pas, reminding myself to huff as if I've just run a mile instead of simply crossing the street. My own phone conveniently fell at the same time, so I have an excuse to start grabbing haphazardly.

"Crap," she says, and we both kneel to pick things up at the same time, causing her head to knock into mine. "Ow!"

"Fuck, I'm sorry," I say, and this time, the apology is more genuine as she falls to her ass, holding her head. I can't help the gratitude flowing through me as her eyes close and I get the opportunity to grab the bolt cutters and slip them into my loose pocket before ushering the rest of her shit into her bag.

And, of course, I take a moment to note there's nothing else in there that could be used to cut someone's brake lines.

Thank fuck.

"Are you okay?" I ask, kneeling in front of her.

"Uh, yeah, I just . . ." She shakes her head, and I move a hand toward her face, where she's still holding her forehead, but I don't actually touch her. When her hand falls away, I inspect the area from afar.

"I'm so sorry. Wasn't paying attention. Do you want me to call someone? It doesn't look too bad, but . . ."

"No, I'm fine," she says then stands. "I'm consistently covered in bumps and bruises. I was lost in my mind."

Planning vehicular manslaughter.

I stand as she steps to grab her phone then turns back to me, her eyes going wide. "Shit, you're bleeding," she says, looking at my forehead,

"What?"

It's then Olivia Anderson reaches forward, two fingers moving to touch a spot on my face gently, and a bolt of something runs through me.

It must be pain.

Or shock.

Her eyes are wide when she pulls her hand back, her fingertips dotted with red blood, her lips parted, but she's not staring at that.

She's not staring at some cut on my forehead.

She's staring at *me*.

Fuck.

Does she recognize me? Does she know me? Maybe she knows more than we thought. Maybe Reed said something—

"Sorry. Fuck, that was rude. It's just . . . you're bleeding."

I shake my head. "It's fine, I'm sure," I say then move to hand her the bag. "You dropped this."

"Oh, thanks." She looks in then starts digging, stopping to look around the area like she's missing something.

Which she is, of course.

"Missing something?" I ask as if I don't know. As if the weight in my pocket isn't the exact item she's searching for.

She looks around one last time before shaking her head and shrugging the bag onto her shoulder.

"Uh . . . no. No. Are you sure you're okay?" she asks, looking back at my head.

"I'll be fine, no problem. Is there—"

"Olivia! Is that you?" an elderly woman asks from behind me. Olivia's eyes close, and she takes a breath before plastering on a smile.

It's not completely fake but definitely exasperated.

"Edna! So nice to see you!" She steps around me to greet the elderly woman who I know to be Bradley Reed's next-door neighbor.

"I thought it was you, but I wasn't sure. I haven't seen you around lately! I thought for sure once Bradley made it legal, you two would be moving in together. Or did he move in with you? Haven't seen him around much, either."

Oof, god, lady. Bad timing.

I take careful note of Olivia's face before she answers, how her smile goes tight, how she bites her lip from the inside, and how she takes a deep breath before answering.

Even when she does, it's interesting how she guards her words. Not for her benefit, not because she's burying some kind of hurt, but almost like she's trying to soften the blow for the elderly woman instead.

"Oh, I'm so sorry. I, uh, you know. Bradley and I didn't end up going through with it." A silent beat passes before the woman yells loud enough I'm sure it can be heard a block or two down.

"What?!"

"Yeah, we, uh . . . decided it was best not to continue on together. It was mutual. I'm actually just here to pick up the last of my things." Her eyes shift from her to me.

"And you, young man? Are you here to help our Olivia grab her things or . . . Oh, goodness! What happened?" The shock on her face is extreme, and I wonder just how bad this cut actually is. My fingers move gently, and I fight hissing when I touch the cut.

Apparently, it's a lot worse than I thought.

"Just a bump, no big deal."

"No big deal, my ass, you come with me. Olivia, can you run ahead, open my front door? I've got a first-aid kit in the bathroom, under the sink. Big white box."

"Oh, that's very much not—" I try, but she shakes her head.

"Don't give me lip, young man. You're coming with me. I'll patch you up, and you'll have tea and some cookies before you scurry off."

"I really—"

"It's easier if you just go with it. Trust me," Olivia whispers from the corner of her mouth. "I'll go ahead. Can you walk her back to the house? It's the yellow one with the pink door." She points next to Reed's that absolutely does *not* meet HOA guidelines, with bright-yellow siding and a pink door and blue shutters with a colony of gnomes and flamingos out front.

This day keeps getting worse and worse and it's barely two.

THIRTEEN

How do you apologize for giving someone a scar?

THURSDAY, AUGUST 24

"So, what do you do, Mr. Valenti?" Edna asks, fluttering her eyelashes at the poor man I ran into during my failed attempt at revenge.

Abbie and Cami made it look so easy.

After Edna insisted Andre, the hot runner guy, come to her place, she made me find her first-aid kit so she could patch him up. "I'm a retired nurse, you know," she told us before fully ignoring his bleeding eyebrow and putting a hand on his firm, bare chest. "Let me check your heart rate." She gripped his pec with a mischievous smile and declared him *right as rain!* before cleaning the gash and applying a butterfly bandage.

When he tried to leave right after, she insisted he stay for a snack, making us glasses of cold iced tea and setting out a plate of cookies for us to pick at before she started bombarding the poor man. I felt bad, except I knew her badgering him meant she wasn't badgering me about my failed wedding and would buy me just a bit of time before my own interrogation.

"Our Olivia here helps promote events, runs a whole business, isn't that right, Livi?" I fight the urge to roll my eyes, knowing Edna will give me shit about it as if I'm not a grown woman with no relation to her, but one of her nine grandchildren.

"Yup," I say.

"I, uh—" There's a moment where he swallows a sip of iced tea, and I can't help but watch his fingers wrapped around the glass, slick with condensation.

He's got really nice hands.

Thick fingers, tanned skin, scars, and calluses like he does things with them often, and not just typing on his phone. "I'm a bodyguard," he says. "I work for a company over in Springbrook Hills." I blink a few times, shocked.

Springbrook Hills is a tiny town in western New Jersey that not many people know of. The kind of place you need to give bigger landmarks in order for people to understand where you're speaking of. *Ten minutes from Chester,* or *near Lake Hopatcong* is usually the best bet.

I'd never heard of it until I met Abbie Keller.

"No way. I have a good friend who grew up there." He blinks, and I might be imagining things, but it lasts just a millisecond too long, like he's calculating his response. I wonder if he's like me, if he evaluates all of his responses, going over them once in his head first before speaking them aloud, nervous about saying something wrong and sounding stupid.

When I was young, six or seven, my mother actually took me to a speech therapist one summer when she was in LBI. She noticed that after everything I said, I would slowly mouth the words, repeating them in my head to double-check if they sounded okay, praying I didn't embarrass myself by misspeaking.

She was sure I had some kind of issue.

The speech therapist told her it was normal, possibly related to some kind of anxiety (*ding ding ding*) but I'd probably grow out of it. I quickly did, never wanting to disappoint my mother, and I taught myself to do it in my head, hesitating only a moment to speak, just like Andre.

Is he an oddity like me?

"Yeah, I'm not from there. Just where my boss is headquartered. A buddy got me the job."

"Do you work that way often, or are you local?"

His shoulders seem to soften, relax with what seems to be an easier question for him to answer.

"I'm mostly headquartered over in Hudson City."

"Well, look at that! That's where my Livi lives!"

"You don't say." He looks at me with minimal interest and suddenly, I'm incredibly uncomfortable.

I know exactly what Edna is doing, and he not only doesn't seem interested, but disgusted, like I'm the last person on earth he would want to spend time with and he's annoyed he's stuck here.

"You two should hang out some time. She's single now, you know. Are you?" I want to slap my hand over Edna's mouth, but instead, I settle for wide eyes and trying to silently tell her to shut the fuck up. Unfortunately, I'm pretty sure she knows I would try and stop her so she's obediently keeping her eyes away from me.

"Single, I mean," she clarifies.

Even though I hate her at this moment, my eyes move to Andre and I watch the tips of his ears go the most interesting shade of pink.

"Uh, yeah. But intentionally. I like it that way."

"Now what does that mean, *intentionally?*" He coughs, looks at his cell, and then touches the butterfly bandage on his eyebrow.

He wants a way out.

He wants a way out *bad.*

"*Edna,*" I say, my tone a warning.

"What! He's a handsome boy. He should be looking for a good woman who could take care of him!" She pauses for dramatic effect, and I close my eyes and sigh, knowing what's coming. "Maybe you two would hit it off! You're a great girl, always taking care of everyone, including this old biddy."

"Edna, please."

"I'm just saying."

"And I'm just saying, leave the man alone." I glance at him again and he looks so . . . *uncomfortable*. God. I throw him a bone and hope he has the common sense to take it. "And really, we've taken enough of his time. You patched him up and got him a cold drink and I'm pretty sure there's no concussion—why don't we let him leave?"

"Oh, don't ruin my fun—"

"Actually." He looks at his phone, taking my lifeline. "I do have to run. I've got dinner with my mother tonight."

"And he has dinner with his mother! Olivia, if you don't snatch him up, I might have to," she says.

"Have at him," I say, rolling my eyes. "Let me walk you out, Andre." I feel like I've been here enough times to be the one to walk someone out of Edna's home. "You stay here and try not to make much trouble." I point at her with a falsely serious face and she smiles.

"Oh, I'm just going to sit here and prepare to interrogate you next." I knew that was my fate either way, so I don't even pause as I head to the door, Andre thanking Edna and grabbing one last cookie before he follows.

"Thank you," he says under his breath as I walk with him.

"No problem. I'm well versed in Edna. I'm surprised you avoided it this long, having been in the neighborhood for . . . a year?" I say, since we found out he moved here to be closer to his work.

"I work a lot," he says, not expanding.

He's clearly not a talker.

That's fine.

I don't need to talk with him.

"Anyway, thanks for enduring this for her. I'm really the only one who comes around so . . ."

"She's nice," he says, and I wonder if he knows things like compound sentences or, at the very least, sentences with more than four words.

"Sorry about your head," I say because, for some reason, I feel like I need to make him say more . . . anything.

And it has nothing to do with the tanned chest and the slight abs and the sprinkling of hair I couldn't stop staring at while sipping iced tea.

I need to get laid. It's been a while.

No, no, that's not fair. Bradley and I had sex every Saturday night like clockwork, skipping only the Saturdays when my period interrupted the schedule. That's when I would give him his monthly blow job.

No, I need to find a man to make me come. A one-night stand. A rebound.

That is what I need.

That's why I can't stop staring at Andre Valenti like he's a steak and I haven't eaten in weeks.

"All good. See you, Olivia," he says, brushing me off and walking out the door, leaving me watching his ass in those running shorts as if I weren't just left at the altar a week ago.

FOURTEEN

THURSDAY, AUGUST 24

I just spent a full hour with Olivia Anderson and I know two things for certain.

One, she is absolutely not guilty.

And two, I am so totally fucked.

FIFTEEN

How to tell your ornery neighbor your got dumped?

THURSDAY, AUGUST 24

"He's cute, Olivia," Edna says with a knowing smile as I walk back into her kitchen.

I fully anticipated something along these lines.

Edna *loves* love. Reading about it, watching it, talking about it— she's just in love with love.

She found her *one true love* when she was 15, married him when she was 18, and stayed with him until he was 72 and passed from lung cancer. Now, in her own words, she's watching all the young people fall in love while she waits until she "kicks the bucket" and sees him again.

"I just met him for the first time, like, an hour ago. When I walked into his head and gave him what will probably become a scar." She waves her hand like a head injury that could have used a stitch or two is nothing.

"Doesn't mean he's not cute."

"I will most likely never see the man again in my life," I say, standing and grabbing the plates and depositing them into the sink.

"And why not?"

"Uh, I just randomly ran into him. The chances of that

happening twice are slim to none," I say. I don't add *especially since I won't be living here* because I'd like to put off her the third degree of my failed relationship for as long as I can.

Even though I know it's *absolutely* coming.

"And I don't have his number or anything."

Wrong choice. Edna's face lights up with a smile.

"I do."

I sigh. "Why do you have his number?"

"I have a leaky faucet I mentioned while you were in the bathroom. He said he would come fix it." A cup of warmth spills over in my belly at the thought of him helping Edna.

Sweet.

It's fucking sweet.

"Well, then you can enjoy his cuteness. I will be back in Hudson City since I have absolutely no need to be over here anymore." Edna perks up like a chihuahua who heard the treat bag move a solid inch into the cabinet while you were looking for the salt.

"So you admit it? He's cute?" I *really* need to remember to watch my words around Edna. She is a dog with a goddamn bone.

"No, he's just . . . He's a man. That is all. A man who isn't horribly unattractive." She opens her mouth to continue, to grab that vague statement and run with it, but I stop her, using my trauma as a distraction. "And right now, men are fully and completely off the table for me." That does it, piquing her interest enough for a subject change.

I will not be addressing why I would rather talk about the train wreck that is my failed relationship with Bradley instead of the cute stranger, *thank you very much.*

She folds her hands overtop of one another and leans in like she can't wait to hear whatever tea I'm about to spill.

"Ah, yes, I didn't want to badger you while the cute bodyguard was here. What happened?"

I sigh.

There's no way I can avoid this conversation. I had a molecule of hope before she saw Andre's face and insisted we come for tea, since I was pretty sure she wasn't going to quiz me about my failed marriage in front of a stranger, but now that her grandmotherly radar is on, she's not going to back down at all.

I also know there is going to be some guilt on her part for bringing it up, but there was no way for her to know.

"It just . . . It didn't work out," I say, fruitlessly hoping we can just skim right on over the whole mess.

"Bullshit," she says. I will never not find this adorable old woman cursing hilarious.

"I'm serious, Edna. It was . . . That was it. It didn't work out." She leans over the small table between us and grabs my chin, forcing me to look at her. I swear to God, her gaze is like an X-ray, scanning my body and face for lies and deceit, and I have no choice but to respond.

She's worse than Cami.

"He broke it off," I say low, and she gasps, leaning back and crossing her arms over her chest as she shakes her head.

"I knew he was no good. What else? What aren't you telling me?"

I bite my lip and try to think of a good lie, but that *fucking* X-ray gaze . . . I have no choice. Plus, a quick google would tell her everything, and through a much more distorted lens.

"He dumped me ten minutes before I was supposed to walk down the aisle."

The gasp she lets out this time is almost comical. If this were a cartoon, you'd be able to see smoke coming from her ears.

"Are you fucking kidding me?" I'm a glutton for punishment so I continue. She'd find out eventually.

"With a text."

Finally, Edna stands up, her chair making an ear-splitting screeching sound on the linoleum, and turns away from me.

"Where are my shoes?" she asks, looking around the little kitchen.

"What?"

"I said, *where are my shoes?*" The words come out like I'm an idiot, and I fight a smile. Smiling at her antics is never a good idea when it comes to Edna.

"Okay, why? Why are you looking for your shoes?"

"So I can walk next door and tell that boy how I feel!"

"He's not even home; calm down. You're going to give yourself a coronary."

"Someone's gotta knock some sense into him!" She's moving around her kitchen in her house slippers, looking for what she calls her outside slippers before she looks down at her feet, mumbles, "Fuck it," and starts for the door.

"Edna!"

"Who needs shoes?! I'm only going a couple feet! Gonna take my cane and bash his windows in!"

"Edna, please. I'm begging you to stop for a moment. He is not worth going to prison for. Trust me."

Maybe I should take my own advice.

Or not. Definitely not.

Because I, unlike Edna, won't get caught. And I won't brag about my successful revenge plot to everyone and their mother.

"Well, I *know that*," she says, like I'm telling her something obvious. "He wasn't even worth spending. Friday night with, Olivia. But you? You're worth going to prison for."

She has a very strange sense of justice, that much is for sure.

"Then who would talk sense into me on the regular?" I ask with a smile,

That distracts her just enough, Edna straightening her shoulders a bit.

"Does that mean you'll start listening to this old lady when I give you advice?" I roll my eyes, and she widens hers in a, *hmm?* kind of way, and I know exactly why.

Edna Cohen was the only person in my life who flat-out told me they didn't like Bradley Reed. I thought it was because she very badly wanted to set me up with her grandson, but maybe she knew more than I did.

"It's fine. I, uh . . . I found a support group of sorts." She turns and looks at me with her hands on her hips.

"A *support* group?" I laugh because every time I talk about this, it sounds stupider and stupider.

"A group of jilted brides."

"Jilted brides."

"Yes. Stop looking at me like that," I say. The look on her face can best be described as . . . skeptical.

Maybe a bit concerned.

"I just . . . It doesn't seem like your thing, Liv," she says.

It doesn't.

It *isn't*.

But . . .

"Yes, but they don't look at me like you are right now. Or like Cami and Cici and my dad are." She raises an eyebrow and I groan. "Everyone is treating me like I'm about to shatter into a million pieces and they'll have to schedule me a grippy sock vacation. And I'm *fine*. It sounds stupid and like a lie, but I am."

The great part about Edna is she's seen a lot of shit in her life, and that's made her learn a lot. I'm grateful for that when she somehow knows to give me space to think about how to put words together in order to further explain myself.

"I think I knew for a long time, maybe from the beginning, that it wasn't going to work, that it was a bad choice." I remember the way I would get anxious going to his house for a night, having to pick which clothes to pack.

Compared to my friends in long-term, loving relationships with the least toxic men on the planet, it was out of place. They could wear a muumuu and have a rat's nest on top of their heads and their partners would still find them to be the most gorgeous women on the planet.

And I was getting a blowout every Friday morning so I would look good for Bradley.

"Why didn't you stop it?"

And that's the question, isn't it? It's also why this is the first time I'm admitting this out loud. If I knew in my gut, whether I would admit it or not, that something was off, why was I going through with the wedding?

"I think a part of me hoped it was cold feet. Or maybe that it was normal. My mom—" Edna scoffs.

Edna hates my mom.

Edna has not *met* my mom, but she still hates her.

I ignore the noise and continue. "My mom told me it was normal for men in power, men in money. That it's just the way it is. She was . . . so excited for me to marry him. I think it rubbed off on me. I started to convince myself it would work." Her face shows genuine shock, a first for this woman, I think.

"Are you telling me you were going to marry that jackass who can't even close his damn garage door because it would have made your mother happy?"

"No," I argue quickly, but we both know the truth.

Maybe.

Yes?

I don't know for sure anymore. I thought it was just a bonus, her being content with my choice, but now that I've broken free from the hold he had on me?

I'm not sure.

Edna doesn't argue with me, though, knowing which battles to fight and which to let die.

"You deserve to be happy, Olivia. You weren't put on this earth just to make the people in your life happy."

This is not Edna.

Edna is not pep talks and deep conversations. It's why I love her.

"Edna," I mumble because I have no idea what else to say. My throat aches with emotion I refuse to give life to.

"I'm just saying. Life is both painfully short and dreadfully long, and you only get the one. Live it for you."

I don't respond.

I can't.

Instead, I focus on the emotions I've committed to not giving into, slowly gathering the tethers and slipping them back into the bottle until I can find that stupid cork, sealing them away.

"It's okay. You don't have to respond. Just couldn't live with myself if I croaked and didn't tell you that." Tension cut, I roll my eyes and she leans in conspiratorially again. "Now, tell me all about this support group of yours."

SIXTEEN

MONDAY, AUGUST 28

"You should call him," the woman says, and even though I can't see her, even though I'm not even technically involved in this conversation and I'm listening as a government entity, my head moves back.

You should call him.

It's Olivia Anderson's mother speaking, on what I've found over the past few months to be her weekly call with her daughter. While they are never very cordial or loving, the calls often peppered with jabs and discreet dismissals, this, somehow, is throwing me the most.

It's been barely over a week since her fiancé broke it off, and her mother is . . . telling her to call him?

"I should call him? Who?" Olivia sounds just as confused as I am, even though, like me, I'm pretty sure she knows who her mother is speaking of.

"Bradley, of course. God, Olivia, I swear, sometimes I think if it wasn't for me, you'd be completely clueless about life."

Silence fills the line as she tries to think of what to say, how to respond.

She doesn't argue like she should, though.

She doesn't question her mother's sanity or mental health.

"Why?" Olivia asks, her voice somehow smaller.

"Why? What do you mean why?"

"I mean, why should I call Bradley, the man who sent me a text ten minutes before our wedding to call it off? And who never even attempted to explain, never offered to meet up since then to talk things over?"

There she is, I think. *There's her backbone.*

As I've slowly learned is her way, Melanie St. George sighs like her daughter is stupid or exhausting.

"Because he's a *Reed,* Olivia." There's a pregnant pause before she continues. "And because it's an *embarrassment.*"

"I'm an Anderson. What does that matter?" Olivia clearly brushed past the second part of her statement.

"Don't be silly. Anderson doesn't *mean* anything. I so wish you would have just taken my last name as I told you. It would have been so much easier to make *connections.* It's not too late, you know."

"I'm not changing my last name, Mom." This argument actually comes up often, with Melanie telling her daughter to change her last name to Melanie's maiden name of *Kincaid* for the boost in value, despite Olivia being nearly twenty-seven years old.

"Then call Bradley," she insists, her voice going from annoyed and creeping into angry.

"I'm not doing that either. He broke up with me. I'm not going back to that, no matter what."

You'd think a woman so pinned to her image would think crawling back to a man who left you would be social suicide.

But I guess when money and status are involved, all bets are off.

"God, Olivia. You're always so stubborn. No wonder he was afraid to commit. All you do is *argue.* A man like that needs a *docile* woman. Someone he can come home to and be *soothed* by."

My teeth grind at her words.

Nothing sounds worse than coming home each day to a fucking wet blanket that bends to my every whim.

What would be the fun in that?

"I don't want to do this, Mom. It's been a very long week for me."

"For *you?*" Melanie asks, her voice indignant. "For you."

"Yes, Mother. I would have been coming home from my honeymoon yesterday if everything went . . . differently. I've been rearranging my entire life and trying to put it back together."

"Olivia, do you know how it's been for *me* this past week? How many calls I've gotten? How many questions from friends? I've been fielding calls all week! And don't even get me *started* on the press!"

The press that you call every time you leave your home in order to have them follow you and feed your ego? I wish I could say, though they wouldn't hear me through the bugged line.

Watching Olivia Anderson for the past six months has been the most painful experience. Her life is inexplicably *boring*, mostly promoting the extravagant events her business partner plans and kissing the ass of every person in her life.

She is a goddamn pushover of the *worst* type.

But watching her has also meant keeping an eye on those around her, including her parents. While Zachary Anderson and his partner, Camile Thompson, seem relatively normal, if not for their extensive collection of, should I say, home movies, her mother is a piece of work.

I've never encountered someone who so badly craved fame and fortune more than this woman. Though, I suppose when you grow up with access to money and anything materialistic thing you could ever desire, you need some other kind of goal.

For Melanie St. George, that's having the press and adoring fans hang on her every word.

I've also learned how she has trained her daughter to treat her *just like* one of her adoring fans and social climbers who ache to be on her good side, so I'm not surprised when Olivia responds with an apology.

"I'm sorry, Mom. You're right. I wasn't thinking."

"I just don't understand why you can't reach out. It was probably a misunderstanding. Maybe you did something to hurt his feelings."

"How's it goin', Valenti?" Peterson asks, interrupting the call, and I close my eyes, breathing in deeply. I turn to him and point at the headphones I'm wearing. Even though this conversation is going absolutely nowhere, listening to Melanie St. George berate her daughter for something that wasn't her fault at all is still better than talking to my boss.

He, of course, ignores me, moving into my little cubicle and sitting on the edge of my desk, leaving me feeling cornered by the man.

"Listening to a call now," I say, trying to get him to leave.

"Who is it?" I sigh.

I just know there's no getting out of this. "Olivia Anderson and Melanie St. George."

"Record it. It won't be much more than her yelling at her daughter from some weird rich-bitch shit."

The true sign that Melanie St. George is the worst is when even Peterson thinks she's a bitch to her daughter. Still, he's not leaving, so I take off my headphones and set them aside, the audio already set to record.

"You got something for me?" I ask. Since this is the FBI, one would assume if you're interrupting an investigation actively in progress, you have something important regarding the case being worked on.

But I know Peterson.

I know there is a reason I want to leave this department.

"Huh? Oh, nah. I mean, not about this. I just wanted to see if you saw . . ."

I zone out the rest as he begins to gossip about which agents are hitting their numbers and which are fucking and which he *thinks* are fucking instead of letting me do my actual job.

Any pity or sympathy I feel for Olivia Anderson evaporates.

I can't have sympathy for the spoiled nepo baby who got caught up in some bullshit because she trusted another idiotic nepo baby. I need to focus on myself, on closing this goddamn case and getting the right people behind bars. On crafting airtight evidence.

Because if I have to spend another fucking year in this godforsaken office listening to Peterson belittle everyone around us, letting him interrupt my work and be expected to do fieldwork instead of what I really enjoy, I'm going to *lose my fucking mind.*

SEVENTEEN

How do you convince your friends you're okay after a breakup?

TUESDAY, AUGUST 29

When I pull into the lot of our Hudson City office on the day that would have been my first day back to work after my honeymoon had I gone, Cami's car is parked out front, and I know she's here not to work, but to investigate.

Whether she's here of her own volition or because my dad sent her, I know she's only here to make sure I'm not completely falling apart. I sigh, staring at the building and thinking about running the other way.

I don't want to do this.

I want to work.

I want to get *lost* in it and forget that I've apparently joined a support group for jilted brides, forget that I am, in fact, a jilted fucking bride.

I want to forget I wasted two years of my life on a man who didn't even bother to look me in the eyes when he dumped me.

I want to forget about revenge and *failed* revenge and how disappointed my mother is in me.

I want to work.

But seeing Cami's car in the lot, I'm questioning that.

Maybe I should go home and put my giant noise-canceling head-phones on so I can't hear anything but the sound of the blood in my ears while I work from my couch. And when my thoughts become too loud, I can turn on Noah Kahan until I forget how depressing my life is.

You can't be depressed while listening to Noah Kahan.

I think they're doing a study about it, about how a mix of folk music and heartfelt lyrics that break your soul somehow counterbalance your own internal emotions until you're at some kind of equi-librium.

Or maybe they shouldn't because I don't need any scientist to tell me it's all in my head.

I like living in my delusion, *thank you very much.*

Staring at the brick building, I know in all actuality, I can't turn around.

That would cause too much of a commotion, would raise suspi-cions, make people worry, and that's the last thing I want. Fuck, the guilt from that alone has been keeping me up late each night, as evidenced by the circles under my eyes.

What does it say about my relationship that I'm angrier about how it's impacting my friends, how they now feel the need to worry about me, than I am knowing I was left at the altar?

Probably nothing good.

Probably nothing I didn't know long ago.

Last night, while I tried to make my own one *Mississippis* match the rhythm of the second hand on my clock in order to perfect the length of a second, I came to the conclusion that I knew things were no good long before August 19.

I think I knew the night of the Labor Day party at the Fishery the very first summer we were together. Bradley stayed for a full ten minutes before leaving to go to some house party that was much more *beneficial to his career*—his words, not mine.

The next morning, I was prepared to end things until my mother called to have brunch.

That was when, for the first time in my memory, she told me she was proud of me.

She was proud of me for landing Bradley.

Now let's see if you can keep him. She'd said it with a smile and a wink and a conspiratorial nudge that was meant to feel friendly, girlish, but it felt like a challenge.

One I'm fighting with myself not to feel like I *lost.*

I didn't lose.

He did.

Right?

Last night was the first time since my wedding day that I cried.

I cried not for my relationship with Bradley, for those wasted years, but for the light it shone on me.

On who and what I am.

I cried for the fact that I stayed in a relationship for two years despite all of the red flags and the side eyes from my family and friends because I wanted to please my mother.

Because I was afraid of being a disappointment to her.

I thought I was over this.

I thought I was over it when I deserted my best friend since elementary school in favor of pleasing her latest target's daughters.

I thought I was over it when I nearly sabotaged her wedding to get revenge on Cami.

I thought I was over it when I sacrificed any hope of getting my trust early in favor of starting my own business, of making a name for myself.

But I'm not better than I was then, and I don't know *how to move forward.*

The call with her was the eye-opener, the moment when I realized something had to change, that we had to change or I'd lose myself completely.

But who am I if I'm not working to make everyone in my life happy?

Is this what a midlife crisis feels like?

I don't have *time* for a crisis of any kind.

I'll have to wait until I get home from work because even though I can't see her yet, I know Cami is watching my car from the window of our office, waiting for me to get out to assess my mental state and report to my dad.

So, I take a deep breath.

I pull down the mirror, making sure my makeup is impeccable, that it's covering the dark circles and the zit on my chin I can't help but stress pick at, smile once, twice, three times to make sure I still know how to make it look believable, before reaching for my bag and heading into the lion's den.

I'm in the kitchenette when she ambushes me.

She wasn't waiting at the front door, wasn't sitting at Cici's desk in reception when I walked in, and Cici did nothing more than smile and say good morning.

Cami didn't come to my office as I took off the light jacket I put on to fight the slight chill in the late-summer air or placed my bag on the spare seat.

She wasn't there as I hooked my computer up to the monitor or as I logged in.

She didn't come in as I started my intricate coffee routine, as I ground the beans (it's truly not as good if you grind them ahead of time and I'll die on that hill), or as I scooped them carefully into the French press. Not as I frothed my milk or added my syrups into the cup.

Instead, she came as I was scooping the foam on top, as I was starting to think she was going to, at the very least, let me get settled with my coffee before bugging me too much.

"Good morning, Cami," I say, my back to the door, my soul somehow in tune with the person who I've built this business with. I know Cami is my dad's soulmate, but I think she's also partly mine. Like a friend or an older sister soulmate, or a not-quite-mom.

She was always meant to come into my life when I need her most, whether I want her here or not in the moment. Spoiler: I would much prefer if she *wasn't* here, ready to break through my walls and check in on me.

"Morning, Liv. I see you're already back at it with your intense coffee routine." There's a friendly smile on her face that's hiding her concern, but I play it off with a roll of my eyes.

"You know that as soon as the pumpkin spice comes out, I move to hot lattes, and there is a very specific way to make the perfect drink."

"I know you're so neurotic that we had to stop getting coffee from the shop down the road because you kept trying to give them tips on how to improve."

"I just think if you have coffee shop, you should know the art of foaming milk. And if you're advertising a flat white, you better know how to make it right and not just hand me a shitty latte."

"Liv, it's a chain coffee store, not a specialty boutique." I roll my eyes, grab my coffee, and head to my office, Cami following. I'm happy it seems like we're not jumping right into the hard stuff and that, at the very least, she's not treating me with kid gloves and coddling me.

Instead, she's teasing me like normal, which is what I *want*.

I want to pretend the last week . . . the last month . . . fuck, the last few *years* didn't happen and I'm just Livi.

Normal old Olivia.

Not Olivia who was left at the altar. Not Olivia who had a mental breakdown, who was so blinded by pleasing everyone around her that she missed all of the signs that things were going to fall apart even after they cracked.

"Whatever, what do you know about good coffee? You drink whatever my dad gives you." Cami smiles, a smile reserved for people in love—the kind that people in love don't even realize they make but the people who aren't always see it.

I fight off a hint of jealousy.

I convinced myself I had that once and it was all a lie.

Sitting at my desk, I shake my mouse to wake up my computer

before logging in and opening my email, trying to ignore my business partner.

Cami leans on my doorway before finally asking what she has wanted to since I walked in. There's no other reason she's in this office today when she could be at the Beach Club, within arm's reach of my dad.

"So, how was getting your things?" she asks.

"Fine," I say, leaving it at that.

"Just . . . fine?"

"Yeah. I grabbed my things then had tea and cookies with Edna."

"Oh. Oh, well . . ." She pauses like she isn't sure what to think of this news, isn't sure if it's good or bad. "That's good. How is she?"

"A pain as always. I actually ran into one of Bradley's neighbors, busted his eyebrow open. Edna patched him up and forced us to stay." I can hear the smile in Cami's voice when she speaks next.

"Now *that* sounds like Edna." It's important to note how Edna has somehow weaseled herself into my life beyond the occasional neighborly snack, making friends with Cici and Cami and forcing her way into an invite to more than a few of our events.

Everyone loves Edna. It's hard not to.

Though, thinking back, Bradley didn't.

Another red flag I ignored.

Note to self: run next potential boyfriend by Cami *and* Edna.

Not that I plan on ever giving a man any power over me again.

No thanks.

"She hit on the poor guy the whole time. So, he got a battle wound from me because I can't even pay attention to where I'm walking and got harassed by Edna."

"Was he hot?"

I roll my eyes and shake my head before looking over my shoulder at her.

"You're just as bad as she is, you know."

"You said she was hitting on him! I like knowing Edna's taste in men." With a sigh, I turn back to my computer, deleting an email about a sale on boxes from one of our suppliers.

"He's a bodyguard over in Springbrook Hills."

"Wow, the town Abbie's from? Small world."

"Yup," I say, popping the "p" and hoping she'll leave me be soon. No such luck.

A silent moment passes before she speaks again.

"So . . . you're good? You look good, I guess."

"Gee, thanks, Cam."

"You know what I mean. You don't look like a train wreck. You're avoiding eye contact with me, but you don't look like you've been crying yourself to sleep every night."

"I told you I was done crying."

"Yeah, but you'll say absolutely anything to get us off your ass."

"It is a good ass," I say, and Cami laughs. Then she sighs, and I know I didn't make it out of this conversation yet. I glance over my shoulder at her, and her face has transformed from happy and joking to . . . concerned.

"Your dad is worried," she says. "That's why I'm here, which I'm sure you guessed."

"You don't say," I say with an eye roll.

"He wants me to find an excuse to stay with you, to keep tabs to make sure you're not having a meltdown." It will never not be funny to me how Cami takes my side and rats out my dad regularly. It kind of helps the burn of knowing one of my best friends and business partners is boning my dad on the regular.

"Jesus, he must really be worried about me if he's sacrificing time with you," I joke, but Cami doesn't.

"Of course he is. He loves you, Liv. I love you. We're all worried about you." I move back to my computer screen, trying to look super interested in an email about influencer advertising.

"It's not a big deal, really."

"Not a big deal," she scoffs. "Olivia, you were *left at the altar* a week ago. That's a big deal. You're allowed to be upset, to be angry.

To be hurt." My mind goes blank in an effort to deflect her words, to put on an air of *I don't give a fuck. Can we end this boring conversation?*

"And I was. Now I'm not. I'll be fine, Cami." My words are firmer, and I know she can feel how badly I want to end this conversation. It must be radiating off me.

"You really should take more time. Reflect, cry. Be hurt. Go away for a few weeks. Avoid the media." That reminder stings, knowing they're also coming for me. "Get out of the city." That's a big no.

"I can't. Work is here."

"Work can wait. Your mental health is more important." For the first time, I give her the truth and not fragmented versions of it. The whole truth.

"The only thing saving my mental health right now is work, Cami." I turn to her, and there's concern on her face which has deepened. *Goddammit.* "I need this, the distraction. I need to feel productive. I don't need to sit around my place being reminded of how dumb I am, how I fell for his shit."

I don't need to focus on any of it: the wedding, the marriage, the photo in his junk closet. I don't need to dig into how a week ago, I was ready to commit to him, that I was so head over heels for him and now he's . . . nothing. I don't need to think about how rapidly I fell out of love with him or feel concerned for how I feel *no guilt*, no pain. All I feel when I think of Bradley Reed now is anger that he dragged my family through this shit alongside me, how they're all worried because of *him*.

And how I want him to feel that pain and feel it deeply—by my own hand.

Cami sighs, knowing this is a lost cause. "Okay, well, keep me updated," she says then starts to leave. My shoulders drop, a hint of relaxation creeping in, but then I hear her heels turn like she has more to say.

And she does.

"Just to let you know so you're not blindsided by it, Cici told me we've gotten two calls already today," she says with hesitation in her voice. I look over my shoulder at her, furrowing my brow like I'm confused. I know what she's talking about, but I play dumb anyway.

Maybe if I don't speak it into existence, it won't be.

"Calls? What kind of calls?" She sighs, and I know my effort was wasted.

"Reporters. Tabloids. People looking for some kind of scoop or information on the breakup."

Now it's my turn to sigh as I turn back to my desk, trying to pretend like I don't care.

And I don't, not really.

This has been the norm more or less since my mom married Huxley and joined the reality show, but after the first year or so when they realized I was as boring as toast, it quieted down.

Unfortunately, my mother used *my* wedding preparation as her main storyline this season, meaning so many people were invested.

The wedding that never happened.

Before the big day, calls would come in once a day, most filtered through the automated system before they got to Cici, but I should have known it would only get worse. With the promise of a tasty scoop, they would be relentless.

"It's no big, Liv, just want you to know so you don't pick up your office line and get blindsided, you know?"

I don't face her when I ask my next question. "Have they been calling you? Cici?" She doesn't respond, and I don't *need* to look at her to know the answer. "Dad?"

"It's fine, Liv, seriously."

That's also a yes.

I don't say anything, closing my eyes despite facing my computer screen, trying to evaporate.

It's one thing for my stupidity, my trusting in Bradley and letting my mother turn it into a circus, to impact me. It's a whole other for it to impact my friends and my father, who never wanted to ever be in the limelight.

"No worries, Cami. Thanks for the heads-up," I say, my throat feeling closed. She waits a beat, her eyes burning on the back of my head, attempting to decode me, trying to decide what to do, but whether she admits it or not, we're a lot alike. We both deal with our issues internally, taking on a lot of guilt and responsibility for those we love.

So when she sighs, I know I'm in the clear.

"Alright, Liv. Love you. Let me know if you need anything, okay?" It's not a question that requires an answer, so she starts to walk off. I take a deep breath, knowing she's going to leave me be, that I survived this interaction.

Until I fuck up.

"I'm sorry, Cami," I say as an impulse, the sound barely a whisper, weighing me down. Strange how five syllables can feel so damned heavy on my soul.

Her heels stop clicking on the tile, and I turn in my chair to look at her. Then she's facing me, confused, her mahogany skin stunning against a lavender shirt.

"What?"

Might as well get this done now.

"I'm sorry you have to deal with this." She steps forward, and I regret saying anything at all.

God, why can't I just keep my mouth shut sometimes? I'm reminded of years when I was younger and my mom would tell me under her breath through gritted teeth that *children are to be seen and not heard.*

"Olivia, no."

"I just—"

"You just *nothing.*"

And then she's in front of me, grabbing my hands and moving to one knee so she's eye to eye with me where I'm sitting, like I'm a small child and she needs to be on my level in order to speak with me, to make me understand. The new angle forces me to look at her, to take her in.

Concern and worry cover her face.

Fuck.

I should have stayed home.

Noah Kahan and those noise-canceling headphones are sounding mighty fine right now.

"Olivia. You never apologize for things out of your control. And really, you never apologize for things *within* your control that aren't done with malicious intent. You are human. Things happen, and you are my *friend*. You're my business partner, my partner's daughter. You're *family*."

God, that word.

Family.

It rips at me for some reason I can't pinpoint.

Won't pinpoint maybe.

"That doesn't mean—"

"Your mom fucked you up. One day, you'll talk about it more and we'll cry over wine and pizza about it. But until then, until you're ready to come to terms with it, I need you to know nothing you do or say is a burden to me, Livi."

The lump in my throat throbs painfully.

"I know what it's like to feel like that, and I also know what it's like to find someone—to find people who not only don't believe it but want to banish the word from your vocabulary. And you, Liv? You have those people. They might not know how to handle it, how to handle you with kid gloves, especially when you're putting on a brave face because you don't want us to feel bad for you, don't want your shit to impact us, but know that we *all are here, Olivia*. We all want to help you. We all love you, no matter what."

It takes everything in me to fight the single tear begging to drop, but I don't let it.

I won't.

Not now.

Not for this.

"So, you can keep your brave face and pretend everything is fine, and I'll let that go. But you are not going to apologize because of that asshat and because of your mother, who tried to capitalize on your life for her benefit. Not on my watch, Liv." Her hand comes up and pushes some of my hair behind my ear, a move that is so motherly, I again wonder if she was sent to my dad just for me.

"Love you, babe. That's all that matters."

I don't respond.

I can't.

I can't because the lump in my throat is so big, so painful, the wrong move will make it break like an overfilled water balloon.

It doesn't matter, though. Somehow, she knows, leaning forward to press her lips to my forehead and standing before moving out the door again.

"I'll be back at noon for lunch, yeah?" she asks, but she doesn't wait for the response I'm unable to give.

At noon, she and Cici bring takeout from my favorite ramen place down the road into my office, and all three of us joke and laugh and catch up as if last week didn't happen, as if this morning hadn't happened.

And I love her for that.

But by the time I get home, tired from having to keep up the facade of having it all together, my desire for revenge is even further strengthened.

He deserves to pay.

EIGHTEEN

THURSDAY, AUGUST 31

When I die, I have about a million fucking questions for whoever is running this whole show. The very first will be what I did to make him hate me so much that I was assigned to Olivia Anderson. I don't know what I did to deserve this case, but right now, the fact that my entire career relies on her using her fucking head and staying *out of prison* seems unbearably unfair.

Because it's an average Thursday afternoon and she's currently hiring an assassin.

Or attempting to, at least.

The woman is *hiring a fucking assassin*.

Somehow, she's managed to find some kind of website where you can hire contract workers to do your nefarious deeds on your behalf. The woman who looks more like Snow White than The Bride from *Kill Bill* is accessing the Dark Web on a surprisingly small learning curve.

And she's doing it out in the open in a *goddamn coffee shop*.

To be fair, from what I can tell, she's just looking for someone to scare the living hell out of Reed, which, in theory, would be hilarious, but also, there are *so many ways* this could go wrong. Like, say, how the person she's currently messaging has a criminal record for, you guessed it, *murder*.

This case is going to be the death of me. I'm sure of it.

If getting out from Peterson's thumb wasn't my all-consuming goal right now, I'd let her do it. I'd let her follow through with this bullshit, let her get caught and imprison our one solid lead, making her an unreliable witness if we ever are able to pin this shit on Reed.

But that promotion is the only hope I have right now, the only thing that has me willing to roll out of bed and go to work every day instead of just quitting on the spot and trying to figure something else out.

But fuck, Olivia Anderson is really making this shit hard.

It only takes a few clicks on my end before I have her location. She's a few towns over from her townhouse, I'm assuming to try and keep a low profile. Through some stroke of luck, which makes me wonder if maybe the big man *doesn't* hate my guts, it's just a few blocks from the fed office where I am.

I spend a full sixty seconds staring at the blinking dot that is Olivia.

And then I make my decision.

NINETEEN

> Hire someone to scare your ex 🔍

THURSDAY, AUGUST 31

I'm sitting at a coffee shop three towns over from my apartment and one over from my work, doing something I most definitely shouldn't be doing, when I almost pee my pants.

A voice beside me makes me jump, both from being so lost in my own world and because I'm not one hundred percent sure, but what I'm doing might just be incredibly illegal.

Okay, that's a lie.

Googling how to hire someone to break into your ex's house while he sleeps to scare the shit out of him is most *definitely illegal*.

Who's counting, though, you know?

"Sorry, I didn't mean to scare you," the familiar, low voice says as I slam my computer shut, questioning all of my life choices.

Even more so when I look up to see Andre, the man I bumped into outside of Bradley's house.

No way.

No *way*.

"Hey, this is so weird, but didn't I run into you a few weeks ago?" I roll my lips into my mouth, turning a bit to face him, my manners kicking in.

"Uh, yeah. Yes, that was me," I say, then my eyes zero onto his eyebrow, where a red line shows a healing cut.

"Oh my *god*. Is that from me?" I ask, my fingers moving out on instinct to touch the split in his eyebrow. Thankfully, my brain kicks in and I pull back quickly.

"I mean, I was the one who wasn't looking where I was going," he says, which is a total lie, then takes a step back, tipping his chin at my table. "Are you here with anyone?"

I stumble on my words, unsure of how to answer because, for whatever reason, my brain goes squiggly when he is near.

It has to be because he always scares the shit out of me.

"I, uh. No. I'm here by myself, just working."

"Oh, sorry, I didn't mean to—"

I should let him think he's interrupting.

I should let him think he's a nuisance.

I should let him walk away.

I don't.

I'm a glutton for punishment, it seems, these days.

"No, no. I work for myself. Nothing . . ." I think of the deep dive I did last night to figure out how to find the right person to scare Bradley. "Nothing important."

"Good to hear," he says, but the happy expression doesn't meet his face or his eyes.

I wonder for a moment if he's just perpetually grumpy or if his face is stuck like that, as if he might be the happiest person alive and I'm being a judgmental ass.

"Let me buy you a cup of coffee," he says, interrupting my thoughts. "For interrupting you."

"Oh, you really don't have to—"

"What if I said it was a slightly selfish move since there are no open tables at this place and I'd like to steal this one?" he asks, tipping his chin to the empty seat across from me. I look around and confirm he's correct. I'm at a small rectangular table meant for two and every other table is full.

"Oh. You don't have to do that, buy me coffee." I lift my half-full cup to show I'm good before, flustered, I start moving my things from the table until it's just my closed laptop taking up one-third of the space. "But you're more than welcome to sit here."

He nods then sits, dropping a nondescript, worn leather bag before digging inside it.

The same feeling I felt last time I was around this stranger hits, even though this time, he's fully dressed and not bleeding from his head. A tightening of my chest, a nervousness I refuse to admit, and full-blown attraction that I *wish* I could just ignore are so consuming.

Because Andre Valenti is fucking *hot*: tanned skin and a white smile and dark eyes, a small, thin gold chain on his neck that makes my fingers twitch with an unprecedented desire to touch it. He's in a white tee today, and it stretches across his broad chest and is tight around his thick arms. His dark hair has a bit of a curl to it, longer on top and barely styled, like he goes through the trouble of using some kind of gel or wax but gets bored after one pass through of his hands.

It's all very modern-day Danny Zuko in the best way possible.

Except even now, when he looks up from what he's doing and catches me watching him, he gives me a look like he's irritated or frustrated. Like he's here but annoyed he has to be and for some reason, I'm at the core of his irritation.

It makes me want to leave, to pack up and run off and get out of his airspace so he isn't annoyed by me anymore.

"I can . . . ," I start, looking around and once again seeing no tables as he pulls out a notebook and a pen. I'm dying to know what is in that notepad, to interrogate him because I'm nosy and he intrigues me, but I fight the urge. "I can leave if you need privacy or something. I've been hogging this table for a while."

Or if you just want me far, far away from you, I think.

He shakes his head.

"No, that's not necessary. I don't mind the company."

"Even if it's me?" The words fly out without me being able to fight them back, and it's interesting to watch his brows furrow, to watch them come together in confusion.

"You?"

"Well . . ." Fuck. Now I have to explain.

I feel stupid, like a schoolgirl getting called out on the playground. "I just . . . I kind of thought you were super annoyed by me. Deservedly, but . . ." Oh god, this is so embarrassing.

"Why would I be annoyed by you?" His face shows genuine confusion, which is both a relief and a cause for panic because now I just sound *ridiculous*.

"Well . . . the whole eyebrow thing." I tip my head to where there's now a healing cut splitting his dark brow. "And I'm kind of a pain. And I forced Edna on you. Is she really making you fix her sink?" I remember our conversation the day I got my things and her telling me she had gotten Andre's number for her leaky pipe.

"Her sink," he says, confirming. "And I'm hanging a few things on the walls around her house." I groan.

The poor man.

He wanted to go for a peaceful run and I couldn't watch where I was going, and now he's saddled with Edna.

"God, I'm sorry. I totally can do that: hang things. And maybe the faucet. I don't know. I'm pretty good at googling things and watching videos. I'll call her and—"

"It's fine. She's nice. I like her."

"I mean, everyone likes Edna in their own way, but you don't have to do anything for her. You're busy, I'm sure—"

He groans then cuts me off, and I think I have an out-of-body experience when he does, the sound deep and frustrated and traveling to places it *absolutely should not go*. "Jesus, are you always like this?" he asks.

"What?" I ask, thrown off in more than one way.

"Apologizing for shit out of your control."

"Well . . . it's kind of—" He shakes his head like he somehow knows what I'm going to say, and I shut my mouth.

"I'm a grown man. You are not to blame for me going to an elderly woman's house to help her out. No idea how you're twisting that to be your fault, but you can stop. If I don't want to do something, I just don't do it."

That makes sense.

And that seems to be his vibe. He doesn't seem the kind of man who would do *anything* unless he genuinely wanted to.

"And you . . . You want to help Edna?"

"I want to help my neighbor, yes." He says it like it's the obvious answer.

"I just . . . I feel bad, you know?"

"Don't," is all he says, and that's so much easier said than done. But then, he's staring at me the way Cami does, like he's reading my mind and my thoughts and digging below a surface I intentionally don't let people near. He's getting too close to truths and guilts I haven't quite unpacked yet, and I am so not doing it in front of this stranger.

No fucking way.

So instead, I nod, smile, and open my computer to go back to my work.

I promptly slam it shut once more, a different kind of guilt suffusing me as I remember I was trying to figure out the best way to terrorize Bradley and my search is downright *unhinged*. Though I have a screen protector to prevent anyone from reading over my shoulder, the guilt of feeling "caught" burns on my cheeks.

"You okay?" he asks, his voice gruff.

"Oh, uh, yeah! Totally fine. I just realized I finished all of my work today so . . . no reason to, you know, keep it open." He looks at me like I'm insane, which is fair because I'm acting *like an insane person.*

"So, you're a bodyguard, huh?" I ask, putting an elbow on top of my computer and leaning my chin into my hand like some kind of 'oos sitcom character scrambling to hide something and act cool.

"Yup."

"What's that like?" He leans back in the chair and crosses his arms on his chest and god*damn,* he looks good.

Nope.

NO.

No way, Liv.

"A job." I stare at him. "A job where I get paid to follow people around, occasionally have to protect them." I raise an eyebrow because that is the most bullshit answer I've ever heard. "I can't give too many details. Confidentiality and all."

"Oh, shit, yes, of course. I'm sorry, that . . . should have been obvious."

God, why am I such a fuckup? What kind of power does he hold that has my mind erasing and turning me into a total mess of a human?

Also, what is the proper amount of time to sit here trying to make small talk before I can stand up and leave without looking rude? Strangely enough, the etiquette classes my mom sent me to didn't cover what to do when a hot bodyguard interrupts your revenge attempt for a second time and now you want to escape, but he's sitting at the same table with you and wouldn't that look *rude?* Just getting up to leave even though you were clearly here for a reason just five minutes ago?

I'm lost in my mind when the rumble of his voice registers, causing me to snap out of it.

"I'm sorry, what? I was lost in my head."

Get it the *fuck* together, Olivia.

"You're not a coffee drinker?"

"What? No, coffee is my favorite beverage of all time," I say, confused. He tips his chin to my cup, an iced green tea leaving a puddle of condensation on the table.

"Oh. That. No, I don't trust them to make a good drink for me here."

And for the first time, he smiles.

It's the kind of smile that could change a day from horrible to

THE FALL OF BRADLEY REED   131

wonderful. The kind that, if you saw it every morning, you'd be the luckiest person alive. It makes me want to go buy a lottery ticket on my way home because fuck, being able to see this, something I somehow know is so rare, in person, means my luck is at peak levels.

"Then why are you here?"

I absolutely cannot tell him I'm here to use public Wi-Fi to pull off some devious deed to get revenge on my ex.

Instead, I tell him a different version of the truth.

"Because everyone in my office is driving me insane and hovering to see if I'll totally crack today. I think there's a good chance they have a bet going on."

"Are you?"

"Am I what?"

"Going to crack." My impulse is to say no, of course not, but instead, something about Andre makes me want to tell him the truth.

"Not . . . exactly. Not in the way they think, at least. Not in the *going to burst into tears randomly* way. More in a *might cut all my hair off with kitchen shears and carve my name in his leather seats* kind of way." I don't get a full smile this time, but the corners of his lips tip again.

Warmth slides through me.

"You'd look good with short hair," he says.

It's a shock to the system, a compliment from him.

"My mom would murder me," I say without thinking and watch his brows furrow.

"How old are you?" he asks.

"Twenty-six. I'll be twenty-seven in December." He lets out a hmmm kind of sound, noncommittal, but his face says everything.

Twenty-six and won't cut her hair because of her mother.

"So, you're hiding from your coworkers?" he asks, changing the subject.

I almost say no.

Almost tell him I was joking, that they're totally fine and we never have any issues. I was lying, after all, about being here to get work done. What's one more on the pile?

But instead, I tell him something else.

Instead, I shrug my shoulders and play with the straw on my drink, stirring it so the ice makes that satisfying scraping sound before speaking. "They mean well, but I'm tired of them worrying about me. If one more person asks me how I'm doing, I might go full-on Tonya Harding on someone." His eyes go wide, and I can't help but smile.

"Wow, intense."

"Try having every single person in your life waiting with bated breath for you to have a mental breakdown. That's intense."

"Got it, don't ask you how you're doing." Guilt fills me.

"It's not . . . It's not that. I've come to a realization."

I shouldn't tell this relative stranger this. It's too personal. Too intimate.

But also . . . he's a stranger.

I can't tell Cami because she'll want to help, and I love her but I don't want her to.

I can't tell Cici because she loves me and she'll encourage me, pressure I don't want or need.

I definitely can't tell my mom, who will absolutely tell me I'm being overdramatic or selfish.

But I can tell this stranger because no matter *what* he tells me, it won't matter.

He's a stranger.

He won't bring it up in conversation later or ask me how it's going.

"I've come to a realization that, to my detriment, I'm a people pleaser," I say like it's a huge earth-shattering confession instead of a very basic-bitch problem.

"To your detriment? How so?" He leans back in the small chair he is *way* too big for and crosses his arms over his broad chest, the white tee he's wearing stretching around his shoulders and biceps in a way I really need to stop looking at.

Jesus Christ, he has *arm veins*. Not normal arm veins but the kind that flex and bulge and make you want to run your tou—

Get a fucking grip, Olivia.

Get a motherfucking grip.

"I don't know who I am," I say, keeping it simple. I kind of want this conversation to be over. But he doesn't add to it, doesn't do anything more than sit back in that chair and stare at me, waiting for me to speak, so I fill in the silence.

"I've spent a good chunk of my life morphing to be what my mother or my father or my friends want. I like the people around me to be happy."

"Even if you aren't?" The question twists in my gut and immediately, I jump in to correct him.

"It's not that I'm *not* happy," I say, but I stop when I start to really hear his words, to process them and pick them apart.

Is that the truth? Am I happy?

I just don't know.

"It's just, I've changed so much to make others happy, taken their advice and their wants and desires so much into consideration that I don't know what I want. The only thing I've done even slightly selfish is my business and even that—someone else had to push me into it." I think about how Cami made it a contingency for me to work with her in order to get the contract with my grandfather. "I was so blinded by everything, by others' expectations, I didn't even see my own doomed relationship."

"Who wanted that?" he asks, somehow hitting the nail on the head. I grab my drink, swirling it a few times and refusing to make eye contact before confessing.

There must be something in the air, some kind of pheromone coming from him that's twisting my mind and forcing me to expose myself to him.

"My mother. She liked his family, the prestige of it. We met at my family's beach club and were dating casually, nothing big, but my mom, god, was so excited. So, I got excited and I became so into him.

But now, I think . . . I was less excited about the relationship and more excited about pleasing my mother. I had fucked up big the summer before in her eyes, and this seemed like a surefire way to win her over."

"But you weren't into him?" He looks at me like if he could, he would be taking notes, like he's taking in my every word intently.

"I mean . . . I was at first. But there were *so many signs* that he just wasn't for me, that it wouldn't work, and I ignored them all. Which led to my mom being embarrassed in front of all of her friends when the wedding was canceled. He left me ten minutes before we were supposed to get married."

His brows draw together and he leans forward on his forearms, and I take the opportunity to look at them again.

God, he's got really great arms—a wonderful distraction.

"Led to your mom being embarrassed?"

"Well yeah. She invited all of her friends, had planned it all, sent out press inquiries—the whole nine. It was pretty much all she talked about. It became her whole personality."

"But you—you weren't embarrassed? That he left you like that?" I shake my head.

"No. Not really. I mean, a little, mostly because I felt stupid, but it didn't take long to realize I wasn't that into him. Into the relationship. And I surely didn't really love him like I had convinced myself I did. That was what hurt the most, I think. Realizing I had conned myself into something that would have changed my life. Being so dumb and pliant and persuaded." I shrug. "I don't know if that makes sense."

It does to me, but to this man who clearly has his shit together, who obviously doesn't get attached to anything or anyone? This man who has probably never pleased anyone other than, from what I can guess, in bed in his entire life?

It probably sounds extreme.

"Were you two connected in another way? Money, business?"

I frown and shake my head.

"No, we didn't even live together," I say with a laugh. "My business is tied with only Cami, really, and my money is all my own. That's probably the one thing my mother taught me that was valuable. Always keep your own money separate from whatever man you're with. Take his, of course," I say with a roll of my eyes. "But keep your money safe. Oh, and make sure the prenup benefits you."

When I look up from his arms, his eyes are brooding and confused.

"God, I'm so sorry. This is so dumb. I didn't mean to ramble on about my life bullshit. You just needed a table to sit at, and here I am, spilling all of my trauma."

TWENTY

THURSDAY, AUGUST 31

"Shit," Olivia says, looking at the sidewalk and breaking whatever chain of thought she had. Her face goes from introspective to panicked and instantly, I'm on alert. "*Shit.*"

"What?" I move my head around, inspecting the coffee shop to try and figure out what has her so anxious. She shakes her head quickly and sighs before tipping my head to the sidewalk outside, where a few people are standing, waiting, taking photos through the glass.

"The sidewalk," she says in a stage whisper, not turning her head but moving her eyes in the direction.

"What—" I turn fully to look, but I'm stopped in my tracks when the entire universe tilts on its axis in the worst way possible.

She puts a soft, warm hand on my cheek, the cheek with a five o'clock shadow because I was too lazy to shave this morning, and pushes on it gently until I'm facing her again.

The problem isn't that she moves my head, breaking some kind of code and forcing me to do something, but it's the way her hand feels on my skin.

The astronomically horrible part is the electricity snapping when her hand meets my cheek, in knowing what her soft, warm hand feels like there.

And when I look at her, I'm pretty sure she feels it, too, the forbidden charge.

I know it instantly, somewhere deep in my gut, whether I acknowledge it then or not.

Fucked.

I am so fucked.

"Don't look," she says, her voice breathy now, impacting me in a way I force myself to ignore. "Don't let them know we know they're there."

"I don't understand," I say, even though I kind of do. It's just a much better thing to focus on than the feel of her hand on my cheek. The hand she still hasn't dropped, like my skin is metal and she's a magnet.

"It's paparazzi."

"Paparazzi? For you? Why would there be paparazzi for you?" Another deep sigh exits her lungs, and she drops her hand, running it through her hair as she does her best to ignore the cameras.

"My ex . . . our breakup was a big to-do. My mom is . . . God, it sounds so dumb. She's on one of those housewives shows." I nod and take in the blatant anxiety on her face, the way she absolutely does not want those cameras, that attention.

It's interesting.

It's also a direct contrast to what I thought I knew about this woman.

The whole afternoon has been, in fact.

Whenever she was out with Bradley, on his arm at events or going out to expensive dinners around the city, she never looked uncomfortable.

She never looked out of place.

The few times she's been on her mother's show other than for those weekly calls, she didn't seem like she wanted to hide, like the fame or exposure wasn't something she craved.

But here she is, trying to avoid being seen at a coffee shop. Is it because not ten minutes ago, she was attempting to hire a goddamn assassin? Is it because she's here with me?

Or is it something more?

Something that, in the past few weeks of seeing Olivia Anderson through a new lens, I've started to pick up on, pieces I've started to put together.

Olivia Anderson has no idea what she likes or wants for herself, instead living to make everyone in her life content, to make their lives easier. It's clear enough through her calls with Melanie that she's always trying to keep her mother happy, but does it go deeper than that?

"And they're here because . . . ?" I ask because I'm not supposed to know much of anything about her. She pauses before shrugging and giving me an answer.

"I don't know why. Sometimes they follow me, but not too often. More since the breakup, but I also haven't been out as much." She looks to the sidewalk again, noticing at the same time I do a long-lens camera pointed our way.

"Fuck. Fuck, fuck, fuck," she whispers, the expletives laced with increasing panic and her head swiveling around. She's looking for something, possibly a door or some alternate exit, but nothing is glaringly obvious. It's safe to assume the only customer entrance and exit is the one up front, though most establishments like this also have a rear entrance for staff.

"What should I do?" She says the words to herself, and it is clear to anyone paying attention that with each passing second, her panic rises. "They're going to see us. They're going to take pictures. I don't even . . ." She looks around again, once more confirming there is only one door. "Why are they here? I don't understand." Her breathing is quickening, and uncontrolled fear is starting to win.

Watching it happen hurts something.

I tell myself it's just because I don't like to see women in fear.

I tell myself that it's because I've been watching her for so long, it's like I know her.

I tell myself it's because I know what a piece of scum her ex and her mother are, and I hate that they've put her in this type of state.

But it doesn't matter because even though I also tell myself to stay professional, to stay away, I do it anyway.

I place my hand overtop of hers, pressing it down onto the cool tabletop.

I'm not sure if the photographers can see this far into the café since we're in a dark back corner, and I don't know if anyone will be able to tell who I am from here, but at the moment, I don't take any of that into consideration.

None of it.

Because that touch, my hand on her soft skin, the pressure, it slows her breathing. It takes some of that panic out of her face. It causes her eyes to float back to this plane of existence, to calm and steady, like my hand is bringing her down to earth.

Like this small gesture is a grounding presence.

Her eyes move up to mine, and she speaks again.

"They'll see you here, too."

I should figure out her first issue.

I should ignore that and get her out of here.

But for some reason, a thought bubbles up from my gut and leaves my lips without permission.

"Do you mind?" I ask. I tell myself it's good research for the case, figuring out how deep she still is in with Reed and how much she still cares about him the same way I let her vent to me for the past twenty minutes, let her spill her concerns about who she is to me. But for some reason I can't dig into right now, the thought of her answering yes and it being because of him cuts deep.

"Do I mind?"

"Being seen with me?" The question seems to rattle her brain, like she can't quite wrap her mind around it.

"Being seen with you?" she echoes. I wonder if it's the situation, the press right outside following her that has her discombobulated.

"Here. At this coffee shop." Her brow furrows deeper.

It's definitely not cute.

No fucking way is Olivia cute.

My thumb moves against her hand without my mind telling it to and her eyes drop there.

"Why would I—"

"You just got out of a relationship." Her eyes move up and look at me and the honesty there, it fucking guts me. It's the first time I've looked at her and really seen her, and something tells me it's not because I usually look at her through a lens or a screen or some other filter.

It's because, for whatever reason, a curtain dropped, and I think for the very first time, I'm looking at the real Olivia, the core version untouched by the desires and hopes of others.

"I'm realizing it wasn't much of a relationship at all. I've spent the last few weeks trying to plan revenge to get back at him." There's a small smile on her lips when she says the words.

I stare at her, trying not to make it obvious *I know* about her revenge. I was not trained to be a field agent and I have not in any way mastered making my face blank. It must work because she interprets it not as an accusation, but . . . "No. Not because I'm not over it or because I'm hurt or anything like that." She pauses, then she tips her head left then right before correcting herself. "I mean, I am hurt, in a way, but it's more . . . complicated than that. I want revenge on him because I'm pissed and he's a piece of shit and he doesn't deserve to leave this . . . unscathed."

I smile.

That's my fucking girl, I think.

Wow, where the fuck did that come from? She is so very much *not* my girl by any stretch of the imagination. She's a spoiled rich brat who has never had anyone tell her no in her life. She also is incredibly delusional and irresponsible, forcing me to chase her ass around the city to keep her out of fucking *prison* in order to save this shitshow of a case.

The only reason my mind would even go there, obviously, is because I've been watching her for so long, I've created some kind of bond with her in my mind. After watching Reed use her and fuck her over, even if she *is* a spoiled brat . . . it's nice to see her get her own.

It's essentially Stockholm syndrome.

Right?

Except, I've talked to her only two times and those opinions are shifting quickly. Is she really a spoiled brat? Is she really what I assumed from the start?

"I just want to do something for me," she says, breaking through my thoughts with a little self-deprecating laugh. "It would be the first and only time in our relationship."

As I stare at her, that truth is clear. She doesn't want this so-called revenge because she's some kind of woman scorned.

She wants it for *herself*.

She might even need it to move on, in order to close this chapter of her life.

Suddenly, I wish I could tell her about the investigation, about how the best revenge she could get would be to work with us and put him behind bars, but of course, that's not a viable option.

So instead, I offer to help in the only way I feel equipped to.

"I'll help you get out of here," I say, standing.

Like this, I tower over her, and I wonder how tall she is and why that was excluded from her file. Or why the file just says brown when her hair is a warm chocolate color with light caramel highlights, not from the salon but from the sun, like she spent days out in its rays, probably at her dad's house or her grandfather's club.

Or why it's stated her eyes are green when—

"What? How?" she asks, breaking into my thoughts.

Thank god for that. Clearly, I need to go home and sleep because my mind is not working well.

"Stay here," I say, eager to get out of her stratosphere. "I'll go talk to the employees."

TWENTY-ONE

THURSDAY, AUGUST 31

She's parked in a secluded parking area that I insist on walking her to once we get out through the back of the coffee shop.

"Let me walk you to your car," I say, and once again, I try not to let myself think about the *why* of it.

Why am I insisting on walking her to her car? She's a big girl. There's no paparazzi out here, so what does it matter? It can't be that far.

I tell myself it's because she's a subject.

Because if anything happens to her, our case is fucked.

"That's really not necess—" she attempts to argue.

"Can you humor me? My mother would absolutely murder me if she found out I had coffee with a woman and just let her walk off." She waits a moment before trying to argue again.

"I—"

"Please. She's got eyes and ears everywhere. Chances are one of her minions is watching right now." She stares at me, and her face goes a little anxious as she looks left then right like she's worried one of my mother's minions will, in fact, pop out at any time. "I'm kidding. She doesn't actually have people watching us."

She relaxes, and I fight a smile.

"You're really bad at that, you know?"

"What?"

"Telling jokes. Being funny. You're too . . . serious." I roll my eyes because it's not something new. I've heard it my whole life.

Andre, the serious one.

Andre can never take a joke.

Andre, always ready to bring everyone down with reality.

As if that is a *bad* thing.

"Life is serious," I counter.

"Not *that* serious," she says with another roll of her eyes and a shake of her head. "But fine. You can walk me to my car if you insist. It's"—she looks around, trying to get her bearing—"that way." In silence, we start to move toward the parking garage. September in New Jersey is hit or miss, but today is one of the cooler ones, and Olivia rubs her hands on her arms, trying to warm up. I also regret not wearing a thicker sweater or a jacket but, in my defense, I left the office in a bit of a rush to intervene.

"Fuck, it's getting cold, isn't it?"

"Yup, it's my favorite time of year," she says with a smile in her voice.

"Ah, you're a fall girl?"

"Very much. I love sweater weather and cozy drinks and the falling leaves. Pumpkin picking. All of it."

"Pumpkin picking is the most ridiculous scam ever," I grumble. She looks at me like I just told her I drown puppies for a living.

"What!? It's an American pastime! A childhood right of passage!"

"And if you buy a pumpkin from the big bin at the grocery store, they are a third of the price and you don't have to get stabbed in the ass by hay bales."

"It's about the *experience!*" She clearly feels strongly about this, and even though she's an obnoxious, spoiled brat, it's cute.

"Maybe for children."

She stops walking altogether, and I'm forced to turn around. Her mouth is dropped open and her arms are crossed on her chest.

"What?"

"Oh my god, you're one of *those*, aren't you?"

"Uh, maybe?"

"One of those people who thinks fun stuff is only for kids and adults should be stuck with boring old-people things."

"Well, I don't know about—"

"Adults can enjoy pumpkin picking! And hayrides! And cider! They can enjoy the fun of *fall!*" Her face is going red and her tone is going higher, like the indignation of my not enjoying pumpkin picking is a personal attack on her.

"Adults get plaid and Oktoberfest; isn't that enough?"

"Oktoberfest is *barely* even fall, and it's usually filled with a bunch of frat boys," she says with an exasperated groan.

"I would think that's your type, no? You're what, 22? Frat boys are your demographic."

"I'm 26, thank you very much." I knew that, of course, but hearing her say it out loud hits my gut. Unintentionally, I do the math, realizing she's a full seven years younger than I am.

"So, no frat boys, then?" She rolls her eyes and starts walking again. I follow.

"No boys at *all*. No men. They're all terrible."

"Ah, yes, the ex-fiancé."

"How much has Edna and her big mouth spilled?" she asks.

Not much, more like I've been essentially stalking you for nearly a year, but that works more in my favor so lots.

"Don't know exactly, but she loves you so she talks about you a lot." A smile graces her lips.

"She's a pain, but I love her too. Let me guess, she's trying to convince you to call me, to let me cry on your shoulder, and then fuck the pain away?" I nearly choke on air at her words and she laughs. "It's nothing personal. It's just Edna. She's old and horny and wants me to get the good stuff."

I should not ask my next question.

Not at all.

There is no universe, no plane of existence where I should ask this.

It sure as fuck doesn't help the investigation.

But still . . .

"You weren't, uh, getting the good stuff from your ex?"

She *laughs.*

"God, no. I faked it for the first six months, but after that, I didn't even bother. Faking it is a lot more exhausting than it sounds, believe it or not, especially when it doesn't really matter one way or another to your partner."

Well.

I guess that's . . . insight on Reed. I can call this a fact-finding mission. I'm not sure how it could benefit an embezzlement case, but I'm going to pretend I can use it to justify this afternoon in my mind.

"That was a lot," she says when I don't answer, mostly because I'm trying not to let myself think about what a crime it is for a man not to worry about a woman who looks like her in his bed. "I'm sorry. I must be a little frazzled from the paparazzi. I'm not totally sure why they were outside the coffee shop, trying to take pictures of me. My mom's show gets me a little attention, and the wedding was a mess, but that . . . was unexpected."

"No, you're good," I say, trying to assuage her.

"You're a stranger mostly. There is no reason to be telling you about my sex life. It was a step too far."

"You're allowed to vent. Sex and orgasms are a normal part of life."

Do not think about Olivia having sex or an orgasm, no matter how fucking normal it is, I tell myself.

"Well. Thank you then. For not holding it against me," she says with a laugh, her steps slowing. "And thank you for this. I needed it." She reaches into her bag and bleeps the locks for the car we're stopped in front of, which I recognize as hers.

"Needed what?" I can't help but ask. My fingers fidget with my own nondescript keys, my car not far from where she parked.

"A confirmation all men aren't trash." *Oh fuck, she thinks . . .*

"Oh, look, I'm sorry. I'm not—"

"I know. I just . . . It's good to know, you know? That there's someone out there who is a gentleman. That listens to me verbal vomit and doesn't hold it against me. Much." She smiles with that last word, a self-deprecating kind of smile she seems to do a lot.

It makes me feel *uneasy*, and I don't like it.

"Anyway, thanks. For helping me get out of there and for walking me to my car." I nod, snapping back to reality and putting a hand out.

"Give me your phone and I'll put my number in. In case you're in a spot and you don't feel safe. You never know what could happen."

"Oh, I don't—"

"Humor me," I say, and I don't know why I do, why I insist on giving her my number in case of an emergency. "I'm a bodyguard, remember? If things get worse, if they keep following you around, I can recommend some things."

She stares at my outstretched hand for a few minutes before nodding to herself, grabbing her phone, and unlocking it. I create a new contact, labeling it "Andre - Garden State Security," and hand it back.

Guilt floods me as I do, that lie feeling worse than normal, even though if you look me up, it does, in fact, look like I work for Garden State. I'm close with the owner and the men who work there, and when I needed a cover, they offered their help openly.

"Just in case," I say as she takes it, and she nods, slipping it back into her bag. Her hand moves to the door then opens it, and I hold it for her as she steps in.

"Thanks again, Andre. Really." I nod without saying a word then close her door and watch her drive off, and I can't help wondering if she'd be saying thank you if she knew the truth of who I am.

TWENTY-TWO

Bradley Reed new girlfriend

WEDNESDAY, SEPTEMBER 6

After another failed attempt, I had come to the conclusion revenge—for closure or otherwise—might just not be in my DNA.

I'm okay with that, mostly.

The universe has spoken and intercepted both of my attempts and that is that.

That is, until Cici calls me the morning after the coffee shop disaster.

"Hey, babe," she says, and her voice is what scares me.

"What happened?" I ask instantly, panic swirling in my veins.

"What?"

"What happened? Who died? Did we lose a big account?" I stand to pace in my townhouse, where I was planning to work from home today, my mind running to all of the worst-case scenarios.

"No, no, Liv, calm down."

"I can't calm down. You have your *I'm going to let her down easy* voice on." She sighs and it's then I know I wasn't *wrong*. She called with her "let me down easy" voice because there is something to let me down easy about.

"Are you sitting?" she asks, and nausea starts to brew.

"Ci—"

"No one's dead, Liv. It's about Bradley," she says, cutting me off.

"Oh. Is . . . Is he dead?" *God, am I going to hell because I felt even a modicum of relief at that thought?*

"Unfortunately, no." Well, if I am, at least my best friend will be joining me, I suppose. I'll be in good company and all. "He was photographed at an event on Monday."

"Ohhhkay?" I say, drawing the word out. My mind moves through my mental calendar, and I remember there was some kind of fundraiser for his firm this month. I assume that was where he was.

"He brought another woman."

It's not that my gut drops; that wouldn't be accurate.

It's more like my head starts to swim, like I can't see clearly. It's not jealousy but a . . . fury. A haze of irritation I suddenly can't see through.

"He brought another woman?" My voice is calm and cool, ice cold, like the feeling taking over my veins.

"I'm sorry—"

"He brought another woman to a press event just a few weeks after he left me at the altar?" Cici sighs.

"He's a piece of shit. He also . . . Shit. He was *with* another woman. They were kissing for the cameras and everything. Some socialite. I don't know her, but the press has been eating it up." There's another pause before she continues. "There's a lot of speculation. About them. About you. Articles are popping up. I just . . . I wanted to be the one to tell you so you weren't blindsided."

The haze gets thicker.

It's not that he's moving on.

Even after everything, I want that for him. Go on, go off, whatever.

It's that he's flaunting it like we never happened, like he didn't leave me with little more than a text and no explanation.

He's also throwing me under the bus, I realize.

"That's why there were paparazzi," I say.

"What?"

"I was at that coffee shop in Montclair—" She cuts me off.

"Why? You hate it there. You say the coffee tastes like asshole."

"It does but I got an iced green tea. It was fine. I just needed to get out of my house. I . . ." I can't tell her I was attempting to figure out probably illegal things on a public Wi-Fi. "I needed to get out."

"Why not go to the office?"

God, I hate my friends, I swear. I tell her the truth because I can only keep so many of my emotions bottled up at one given time and I have too many secrets piling up.

"Because you and Cami are smothering me, waiting to see if I'm going to have a mental breakdown or not." Guilt twists because I just know she's going to feel bad and I don't want that for her.

That's why I wasn't going to say anything, but . . .

"We don't—" Cici starts, but I stop her.

"You do and it's fine because it's done out of love, but this is my formal request for you to stop. I'm not just saying it when I tell you I'm totally fine."

She's not sold, not in the least. And I guarantee once I get off the phone with her, she'll be calling Cami up and comparing notes on my mental state. But I would do the same for them, so I can't hold it against them.

She sighs. "Okay. I'll tell Cami we have to back off. We just love you, Liv. You've been through a lot in the past few weeks, and now this?"

"This is just dumb, selfish Bradley stuff. We both know he's not above this kind of behavior, and it's not like he ever put my emotional well-being first, so why would he now?" She doesn't respond for a long moment.

"I'm relieved, you know, in a twisted way," she admits.

"Why?"

"I thought . . . When it first happened, I thought you'd dwell on him, convince yourself it was some kind of a fairy tale. God, Cami and I have an emergency plan on standby if you ever listen to your mom and try and win him back." I smile.

I love my friends.

My chosen family.

"I would expect nothing less."

"But it's good to know you see it for what it was now. It's like you stepped out of some kind of daze or something, you know?" That's a good way to explain how I feel, how the past few weeks have felt. Losing Bradley, finding myself, it's a journey of self-discovery.

"It's been good to find me again," I say. "But you don't have to worry about me. I don't care about his bullshit. He can go fuck every Barbie on the East Coast. I'm the one who dodged a bullet." There's a smile and relief in Cici's voice when she speaks.

"Good. I'm glad. Are you coming into the office today?" I shake my head then answer.

"No, I'm having a lazy sweats day, working from home."

"Good for you." A phone rings in the background. "Shit, gotta get that. Love you, Liv," she says.

"Love you more."

Then, the line goes silent and I'm free to feel my real feelings.

I'm *annoyed.*

And when I stupidly take to searching his then my name, then *our* names together, I'm overwhelmed by all of the articles, the photos, the speculation. It's like I'm a reality star myself, a person of public interest instead of just the daughter of one.

It seems, at least right now, the tabloids are leaning in *his* favor, speculating why he dumped me, why he already has a new woman.

The best guesses are I was a terrible girlfriend who never loved him, as if I weren't the one who took care of everything for him, who literally held our relationship together. I know damn well now if one day I had stopped reaching out to Bradley, stopped setting up dates and coming to his house on Fridays and bothering him about wedding details and our *future* together, he wouldn't have chased me.

The relationship would have fizzled.

And that might be embarrassing, but that's a private embarrassment for me to wrestle with.

This? This is fucking war.

How *dare* he!

How dare he go out and flaunt some new side piece and act like *I* was the problem.

Again, it registers in my mind somewhere that I'm not mad he's moving on.

I'm not hurt he has someone new, or, at least, not because our relationship meant so much to me. And I'm not hurt he's chasing someone else. It just proves I never really meant anything to him and not a single part of him cared about me, my feelings, and my reputation.

I'm pissed about the way he's using the media to spin a narrative to save face.

Not on my fucking watch, Bradley Reed.

That's when I pull up my document.

That's when I scroll to find which to try next.

Because the third time's a charm, right?

TWENTY-THREE

> How to send a tip to a tabloid   🔍

FRIDAY, SEPTEMBER 8

I should be required to put my phone in a safe when I take an edible. Or at least when I take the whole dose instead of my normal night-time quarter. I can't sleep at night without it because my brain won't stop replaying every embarrassing moment in my life and the people I've wronged over the years.

Sue me.

But on Friday night, with all of my work done almost two weeks out because I've been using it to keep my mind busy, I decide to order too much junk food via a delivery app and take the whole damn thing. I think back on the call from Cici today and the fact that Bradley is already flaunting some new woman like we never happened.

An hour later, I open my phone because I already have an email opened on my laptop and I have some questions to ask before I can hit send.

See?

Someone should take my phone away.

Maybe my entire access to the internet. Do I know anyone smart enough to code some kind of test where in order to open it, I have to answer questions only sober Livi would know?

Probably not.

And since I don't, I find myself texting Andre "Hot Bodyguard with the Fine Ass Arms" Valenti on a Friday night.

> If your ex were to leak something to a tabloid, what would hurt the most?

What?

> It's Olivia Anderson.

Got that.

> So, let's say you have an ex.

> Do you have an ex?

I'm 33.

> I don't judge.

Jesus, yes, I have an ex. Multiple exes even.

My belly churns at that.

Moving on because I will not read into that, thank you very much.

> Okay, so let's say you fucked your ex over and she wants to make you pay for it.

This is hypothetical?

> Incredibly.

> What would she leak in order to really piss you off?

I have no reason for any kind of media to be interested in me.

HYPOTHETICALLY, ANDRE.

Jesus.

Are you always this boring?

Yes.

Are you sober?

What do you consider sober?

Able to drive a car.

I mean, I COULD drive a car. It might not be advisable though.

Let me rephrase: legally able to drive a car.

Oh.

Then no.

You're very well-spoken while drunk

Oh, I'm not drunk. I'm a different kind of impaired. A sillier kind.

Got it.

Do you partake?

Drug tests in my line of work.

It's legal in New Jersey.

Doesn't have to be illegal to get you fired.

Got it.

Anyway. Revenge. Leaked information.

Is this the best idea?

If you don't tell me, I'm headed to Reddit.

Have you been on Reddit lately?

The girlies over there are feral.

I love them.

I want to be them when I grow up.

Don't go to Reddit.

Then tell me what kind of juicy details I could leak.

This doesn't seem very hypothetical.

Oh, it's very hypothetical.

I would never leak information about my ex to a tabloid.

Never.

Never ever.

Scout's honor.

The best thing you could do would be to move on, Olivia.

That's boring.

I also hate men right now.

Odd conversation to have with a man.

Maybe not you.

You seem cool.

A little grumpy.

I'm not grumpy. I'm serious.

You're grumpy.

It's fine. Being grumpy. Some people find that hot.

Go to bed, Olivia.

Can't. Got stuff to do.

You should really go to sleep.

And you should really mind your business.

You texted me.

Good night, Mr. Valenti.

Olivia.

Olivia, don't do anything dumb.

Olivia?

Look, can you just let me know you're alive and well?

I'm alive. Good night, Andre.

Tip sent to *Starlight Publications* at 2:13 EST from an anonymous source.

Olivia Anderson wasn't dumped—she let Bradley Reed tell the world he was leaving her because she wanted to end things.

Turns out she'd been having a months-long affair with another man because Reed couldn't keep it up.

Olivia allowed her once lover to save face by appearing to be the one to break it off. Now, she is being kept up all hours of the night with the new love of her life, blissfully unaware of whatever stunts Bradley is pulling.

●●●

The next morning, when my phone is ringing off the hook with journalists wanting to get a quote from me on the subject of Bradley and my relationship, I don't regret it.

After all, Andre did imply the best way to get back at my ex was to get over him with another man.

He didn't say the other man had to be *real*.

And when I answer a call from one of the biggest publications, best known for only printing articles with substantial proof behind them, I tell them what they want to hear.

"It's all true, but I would like to remain anonymous. If you need a quote from my team, use: at this time, Ms. Anderson would appreciate it if the press and the public respected her privacy."

"But it's all true?" the woman with a thick New York accent asks, seeming surprised.

"He couldn't keep it up long enough to get me there, that's for sure," I confirm.

At least that was mostly the truth.

I smile through the rest of the day.

My first day with a real, true smile.

Revenge might not be the best answer, but fuck does it feel good.

TWENTY-FOUR

How long before dating after failed wedding?

SUNDAY, SEPTEMBER 10

"Wait, so you gave him a scar?" Julie asks with a shocked expression, and I smile.

It's my second meeting with the group and just like last time, I slide right in like we're old friends trading war stories. All of these women are so fun and open to talking about their own issues and how they've learned to get over things; it gives me so much hope and makes me feel a bit normal.

And most importantly, they don't look at me like I'm about to break and they're going to have to piece me together.

We're all perfectly happy being damaged goods and letting each other live our lives.

I love Cici and Cami, but I'm so tired of them looking at me like I'm three seconds away from another mental breakdown. I'm tired of being handled with kid gloves. I don't hold it against my friends—I know they mean the absolute best—but these women don't do that because they've been here and they know how it feels.

"I mean, it's not a scar yet, but possibly. It's just a cut now." I think back to the pink line in Andre's eyebrow, such a clean cut from our messy collision, and know somewhere in my gut he'll be left with that reminder for a long time.

"Jesus, Olivia," Chrissie says with a smile. "You have the absolute *best* stories."

I just told them about my failed attempt at getting back at Bradley when I picked up his things. Though, when I saw their own revenge lists, which were full of things like *send him a letter* and *call his mother* and *put fish in his air conditioner* (okay, that one was a good one I might want to borrow, but still), I decided telling them I attempted to cut my ex's brake lines or hire someone to break into his house and scare him might . . . scare them off.

And, okay, *reasonably so.*

Regardless of the fact that I just wanted to *scare* him or simply make him crash his *stupid car,* it doesn't necessarily sound great.

So instead, I just told them I tried to get back at him by *messing with his house* but lost my nerve when I ran into Andre.

Of course, telling them about the disaster of picking my things up and how it turned into teatime with Bradley's elderly neighbor and causing bodily harm to a hot bodyguard led to talking about Andre. And despite how I'm at a support group for jilted brides, barely three weeks from my failed wedding, I can't fight the silly, girlish smile and butterflies I get thinking of him.

"So, is he hot?" Simone asks.

I blush and hide a smile.

"Oh my god!"

"No, no, it's not . . . It's not like that."

"I bet it could be. A girl like you? Any man would be stupid not to." They really know how to hype a girl up.

Still, I shake my head and sigh. "I'm not ready for that."

"For what?"

"A relationship."

Nina gives me a face that says, *Girl, be so fucking for real.*

Cami would absolutely *adore* her.

"Babe, you don't need a relationship. You need a booty call." This also sounds like something Cami would say.

"I don't know—"

"The best way to get over a man is to get under another."

We're all shocked that sweet Julie is the one to say that, and all of us laugh until I'm wiping tears from my eyes.

"I'm pretty sure he isn't even remotely interested," I say with a sigh because that's the truth.

I'm actually not entirely convinced the man doesn't hate me, full stop.

"He walked you to your car, right? When the paparazzi were at the coffee shop?" I tilt my head from left to right before answering.

"Yes, but he's a bodyguard. He was just being nice. I bet some-where deep in his DNA, *keeping women safe* is encoded there."

"Nice, my ass," Nina says with an eye roll, and there is a round of murmured agreements.

"Really, I'm serious. And when I thanked him, he straight up told me that he wasn't interested in that."

Somehow, I left out the part where I texted him while high and flirted with him shamelessly all while releasing an exclusive to the tabloids that I had a secret boyfriend.

"But you also told him that you were dumped recently after a long-term relationship, right?" Technically, Edna did, but still.

"Yes, but as I said, our relationship was . . . flawed. I'm seeing that now." I already told them how I'm feeling immense guilt over the fact I don't *miss* Bradley the way I think I should. I don't turn at night and wish he were lying next to me, don't look at my ring finger and mourn how there isn't a wedding band there.

I'm just . . . mad he let it get so far, that it impacted everyone so much, and that he embarrassed me by playing me along the way.

I'm also mad at myself for not seeing it sooner, but the women have also confirmed that being gaslit for two years to think all of my concerns were in my head meant it was harder for me to be realistic.

Somehow, it's a comfort to know it's not just me and my absolutely terrible decision-making to blame, but also Bradley just being a shitty person.

"So what you're saying is, if the hot bodyguard came to his senses and tried something, you'd be open to it?"

I should say no.

It should be an impulse, an easy explanation.

Of course not! I'm not ready for that! should be the first thing from my lips.

But . . .

If Andre offered, I don't think I would refuse.

I definitely wouldn't feel guilty about moving on so quickly, that's for sure.

Unsure of how to answer, I put on my inner Cami and give them a coy, man-eating smile.

"It's been almost three years since a man has made me come, so . . ." I let them figure out the rest.

And when they all laugh uproariously, I know I did my job of changing the subject.

But that doesn't mean I don't think about Andre making me come for the rest of the day and well into the night.

TWENTY-FIVE

FRIDAY, SEPTEMBER 15

It's a week after the tabloid tip when I do something really fucking stupid.

So fucking stupid, it not only puts the investigation and my career at risk, but it puts Olivia Anderson at risk.

And no matter what I keep telling myself, no matter how many times I remind myself she's just a spoiled brat and nothing but trouble, I can't find it in me to fully believe that anymore.

Lately, when I worry she's going to be hurt, it's not because it would put my best witness for this case at risk.

It's because it would put *Olivia* at risk.

It happens when I turn on my monitor at the office and I notice a conversation taking place between her and a beekeeper via personal messages on a social media app.

How would I go about paying you? she asks.

I accept digital payments through multiple platforms, whichever you're most comfortable with. We simply require you to pay in full and don't offer refunds if anything happens to the hive.

The hive?

THE FALL OF BRADLEY REED   163

What the—but then, I look at who she's messaging.

QUEEN BEE BEEKEEPERS—YOUR SOURCE FOR ALL THINGS AT-HOME BEEKEEPING.

My mind flicks back to Reed's file, which covers everything from his hair color to the records of the time he broke his arm when he was eight to his allergens.

Peanuts

Bees.

No fucking way.

What *is* it with this woman and her desire to kill her ex?

Moving to her psychotic search tab, I notice it's changed, and I look at the search history.

NJ BEEKEEPERS.

WHERE TO GET BEES IN *NJ*.

HOW DO YOU GET A BEEHIVE?

CAN YOU PUT A BEEHIVE IN YOUR HOUSE?

DO EXTERMINATORS KILL BEES?

HOW MANY BEE STINGS CAN YOU GET BEFORE YOU GET SICK?

Jesus fucking Christ, this woman is unhinged.

Does that temper your fucking hard-on for her? the devil on my shoulder asks.

I refuse to even *address* such an outrageous claim, and not because talking to myself would make me a potentially insane person.

Definitely not because I refuse even to acknowledge I do, in fact, have an unwanted hard-on for Olivia Anderson. No fucking way, not that little menace.

Whoever ends up with her better wear a jockstrap and sleep with one eye open at all times.

You are so totally fucked, that stupid fucking devil whispers.

The angel who is supposed to counterbalance him is nowhere to be found.

Clicking back to the conversation with the beekeeper, I sigh when I see her next question.

CAN I PAY IN CASH?

At least she's using her brain enough to attempt to make it harder to track her by paying in cash, I suppose. If she pays with a card, that's like a neon sign screaming *it was me!* if something happens to him. With cash, it will muddy the waters, even if it's just a bit. Though, if Reed gets killed by a mysterious beehive, someone is going to backtrack to the person who delivered it. It wouldn't take much research to find a simple social media direct message exchange.

God, if she were mine, I'd put her over my knee for being such an idiot.

Jesus fucking Christ, Valenti, get it the fuck together.

THAT'S FINE. WHEN ARE YOU AVAILABLE? she replies.

I hope not soon because I need time to—

NOW? I'M AVAILABLE ALL AFTERNOON.

Goddammit.

I slam my fist onto my desk, running a hand through my thick hair before looking at the ceiling, closing my eyes, and wondering who assigned me this psychotic woman and what sick fuck up there decided keeping her *out of prison* would be what my entire career hinges on.

When I open my eyes, they're already arranging a meeting location (the beekeeper's small farm a few towns over) and exchanging phone numbers.

I sit for five whole minutes, trying to decide how best to stop Olivia from paying a man to drop a beehive off at her ex's house. A beehive that could very well put him into anaphylactic shock with just one sting and, if she's lucky, or, in my opinion, unlucky, could kill the man in mere minutes.

All of the options I run through don't work to both keep her safe and the investigation hidden.

There's only one option I can think of, and I don't like it much.

But still, I open a search tab and look for the number I need to call to save this investigation.

TWENTY-SIX

What to do if paparazzi are following you?

SUNDAY, SEPTEMBER 17

I think $264 plus tax is a reasonable price for the ultimate revenge on my shitty ex.

Right?

Right.

The perk of being a business owner with what Cami would call *more money than sense* is occasionally, you can waste it on simple pleasures.

Some women get designer bags.

Some get expensive, shitty chain coffees every morning.

I, apparently, spend my *fuck you* money to get a beehive delivered to my ex's house.

The only bummer is that I won't be able to stake out Bradley's place indefinitely while I wait for him to get home, find the buzzing box on his front step, and then freak the *fuck out* when he realizes it's one of his biggest fears.

Hundreds of them.

Sweet little bumblebees buzzing around merrily, taunting this trash human.

Flies would be more poetic, since he's a piece of shit, but bees are more impactful, you know?

I'm smiling just thinking of it as I drive to the small farm. I'll have to ask Edna if I can borrow the passwords to her security cameras so I can try and watch it remotely. She would absolutely *love* this plan.

I always thought it was such a stupid fear of his, bees. He was so scared he wouldn't even have flowers outside his house, and once last summer, he paid to have his entire front lawn redone in sod because the clover mixed in the grass kept flowering and the bees would come.

I almost *married* that little bitch.

Whatever. All's well that ends in perfect revenge, or however that saying goes.

The GPS on my phone tells me to turn left then another right on twisted backroads you could easily get lost on, but it's then I realize there's a small black car following me. It's probably just a coincidence, but . . .

I make a left instead of a right to see if I'm wrong, and my heart beats just a bit faster when I realize I'm *not*. They are most definitely following me.

Panic starts to build, taking over the excitement I felt just a few moments ago.

What do I do?

This has never happened to me.

What are you supposed to do if someone is following you? I don't recognize the car as someone I know, so I can't convince myself it's a friend who happened to recognize me in this less populated area and is trying to flag me down.

I continue making haphazard turns, trying to convince myself that maybe it's just someone who happens to live around here and I'm the one headed to their house or something, but they are *definitely* following me. So instead, I follow the GPS to the little farm, hoping once I'm there, I'll be able to hide out and call someone.

Except . . . as I start to get closer, I'm confused by the number of cars in the area—way more than should be in this small country town.

There's no . . .

My gut drops to the floorboard as an idea builds.

There's no way.

But as I pull up to my original destination, my fears are confirmed.

I have no idea how or who or when, but somehow, the paparazzi got wind of where I was going and a dozen of them are on the street outside the farm, some out of their cars with cameras.

Who the fuck do these people think I am? Taylor fucking Swift out with some new, controversial boy toy?

I am a nobody. I'm barely even interesting enough to be related to my mother, and Bradley is *always boring*. We never had issues with paparazzi while we dated, and I—

It's just then I remember the tip I sent in on Friday and the swirling press coverage it received.

The one about Bradley having a small dick and me leaving *him* instead of the other way around, and I remember I was a *liiiiittle* high, but maybe . . . Did I add . . . ?

Yes. I added I had a new secret beau who was keeping me up *all hours of the day*. And that I was madly in love with him.

Fuck.

My windows are cracked a bit in the comfy September air, so I hear someone call from the crowd:

"Olivia! Who's the new man?"

Another voice jumps in too.

"Why did you stay with Bradley so long if he couldn't satisfy you!?"

Oh *god*.

I fucked up so big, and now I'm dealing with the consequences of my own actions.

Fuck this revenge plan.

Why the fuck did I think I could do this? I'm not Cami. I'm not Abbie. I should have stopped when the first attempt when so awry.

I keep driving past the small crowd, that black car following me and then two more joining in, and I can barely breathe through the panic coursing in my veins.

I need a plan.

I need to call someone, tell them where I am and what's happening, figure out a solution.

I should call Cami.

I should call my dad.

I should call the *police*.

Even my mother might not be the worst idea, since she's dealt with this before.

But for some reason I can't quite look at straight at, my finger scrolls to another name in my contacts while I drive right past the little bee farm, that same car following me as I do.

"Andre? It's Olivia Anderson. Can you meet me at my townhouse?"

TWENTY-SEVEN

SUNDAY, SEPTEMBER 17

"Are you going to tell me why you called me, or are you going to continue to put off this conversation by going through the most extensive coffee-making process I've ever seen?" I ask an hour later.

I told myself I came here for the case.

It's another chance to ask her questions, to keep her off her stupid fucking revenge plans.

I answered and showed up because it's part of my job.

Because of my promotion.

Definitely not because the edge of fear in her voice made me sick to my stomach. Definitely not because I felt an unavoidable need to check in on her, make sure she was okay, in one piece.

It was for work.

That's why I got to her townhouse before she even got there, why I drove in circles for ten minutes making sure her place was safe from paparazzi who might try and ambush her, then another ten minutes after she got there to ensure it was still clear.

For work.

There's a hint of guilt because I'm the one putting her through this. After all, I'm the one who tipped off the press.

If I want to *really* take on the guilt, I also was the one who didn't stop her from sending that email to the paparazzi, fueling their interest in her and her relationship.

"This isn't me putting it off. This is me making coffee," she argues.

"There's been six steps already, and you haven't even gotten a cup."

"Coffee is an art form."

"Coffee is something you chug on the way out the door in order to get caffeine into your bloodstream." She stops at the seventh step and stares at me.

"Why do I feel like you drink instant coffee?"

I can't help it.

I smile.

"Oh! He smiles!" she exclaims, and I can't help but feel it widen.

Her eyes go warm in a way I should not be taking note of, like seeing it brings her some kind of joy. "I'll drink instant if it's the only option," I admit, and she scowls.

"That should be illegal."

"Know what should be illegal? Calling a relative stranger to your place on a Sunday and not telling them why."

"You're not a relative stranger."

I raise an eyebrow.

"We've had lunch together at Edna's, and coffee at the coffee shop, and we texted." Her cheeks go an adorable shade of pink and it twinges in my gut.

Nope.

No way.

It's probably just the ulcer that has surely been slowly forming, the stress of my job and dealing with Peterson, and, now, Olivia.

"Yeah, I guess we're not quite strangers, are we?" She bites her lip, and I force myself to ignore it. "So what's this about, Olivia?"

"You can call me Liv. Or Livi." I blink at her.

I don't tell her shortening her name is too familiar, that being familiar is the last thing I should be doing, even if I know more about her than her closest friends.

"I'll stick to Olivia," I say. "That's your name. It's a sign of respect to your parents." She scoffs before she can stop herself and then quickly shakes her head and rolls her eyes.

"You're a pain, you know?" I don't respond because it's not a question requiring a response and because I'm still stuck on that scoff, on the idea of her not believing her parents deserve respect.

Or maybe just her mother.

It makes me contemplate once more all the conversations with Melanie St. George I've overheard in the past year, the way her daughter caters to her despite Melanie not deserving it. It's looking like Olivia Anderson has finally started to come to her senses and sees her for what she truly is.

"I need help," she says, slicing through my thoughts.

"I figured as much. Not really any other reason to call me over here," I respond, crossing my arms on my chest.

"Oh. Yes." She stops, staring at me for long moments, lost in her head.

I'm not sure if it's because she's trying to figure out what to say or nerves, but either way, I give her a push.

"You need help . . ."

"Oh. Yes," she repeats, and it's cute.

No, I scold. Not cute.

Olivia Anderson cannot be cute.

Not to me.

To some normal, boring man who works a normal, boring 9-5 and would come home and expect dinner on the table at six on the dot and who would put the kids to bed before fucking her missionary and falling asleep with her tucked into his side, she can be cute.

To the man who is pretending he isn't investigating her and can't stop getting in her way when she nearly self-sabotages?

No.

I cannot find her cute.

"So, if you couldn't tell, I've got a bit of a . . . press problem."

Of your own making, I don't say because even if she didn't leak to a tabloid her ex was terrible in bed and she was actually the one who left him for her long-time boy toy, the press would eventually be on her.

"Got that."

"And as much as I just *love* being stuck in my apartment all day, every day until the end of time, I do occasionally have to leave. Except . . . God, this is so embarrassing." She runs her hand through her dark hair, and for the first time since I got here, she looks serious.

"With them on me like this, I'm not . . . comfortable. I don't like having them in my life like this, following me, talking to me, speculating. It's not for me."

"Why would that be embarrassing?" It seems like a very normal reaction. Maybe a bit surprising based on my initial impression of Olivia, but as I'm beginning to understand her more? It tracks.

"Because I asked for this. This is my life. I should be used to it."

"Did you?"

"Did I?" She doesn't understand the question.

"Ask for this?"

"I dated Bradley and not in a low-profile way. I don't live in seclusion. I . . . was on my mother's show a few times."

This might hold weight, except I know the few times Olivia appeared on the show, it was after weeks of guilt trips and bugging from her mother and of her saying how she very much did not want to live a public life.

"That does not mean you asked for your life to be put under a microscope, for people to take photos of you as you try and work from a coffee shop or walk into your townhouse. That does not mean you told them it was okay."

Guilt plays across her face. "I did something really, really dumb and now I need your help," she says.

My gut twists. I know the dumb thing she did, and there is no way I could be involved in helping her that wouldn't be the most terrible idea ever.

Not just because despite her being a pain and my subject, a part of me I refuse to look at too closely can't stop thinking about her, can't stop checking her recordings to see what she's up to, if she's staying out of trouble. If her mother is giving her a hard time.

Involving myself further would be detrimental to everything.

"Does this have to do with you texting me the other day?" That text exchange was both hilarious and alarming, especially when I watched her write up a tip for a tabloid and hit send.

And when she confirmed it all the next morning, fully sober.

"Maybe."

"Does it have to do with the tabloids saying your ex couldn't keep it up to, ahem, satisfy you?" She has a catlike smile now and I have to fight one of my own, fight to not look proud when I most definitely should be annoyed or, at the very least, disappointed.

"I don't know what you're talking about." I raise my eyebrow at her. She rolls her eyes. "Fine, yes. Yes! I sent a tip to a tabloid saying I had a secret boyfriend all along and I left Bradley because he couldn't keep his dick hard. Okay? Sue me."

"Well, I won't, but he might. Slander and all that."

"It's airtight. I did it anonymously." She waves her hand at me like it's no big deal, like I'm being a nuisance by bringing logic to the table. "Plus, he never made me come. I faked it every time. So, kind of the truth." I force my brain to skate *right* over that one.

"Yeah, that's not exactly how that works, Olivia."

"God, I don't need a lecture!" She huffs.

Annoying, I remind myself. *She's annoying and bratty.*

"Then what do you need, Olivia?" Might as well cut to the chase before I take this opportunity to look through her home and learn more about her.

And not for the case.

For purely selfish reasons.

I'm going to hell. Absolutely and irrefutably *going to hell*.

"I need your *help*."

"Yeah, I got that. How?"

"I need . . . your services." My eyes widen with shock. I don't mean to show on my face that my mind is going somewhere it *absolutely* should not, but she shakes her head and rolls her eyes. "No, you creep, not that kind." There's a pause, then she tips her head from left to right like she's contemplating something. "Well, I mean, not exactly."

"Olivia—"

"I need a bodyguard. But I don't want you to be a *bodyguard*." My gut drops.

"I'm not following. I am a bodyguard."

I am *absolutely* following, and I do not like where she's going.

Don't you? the little fucking asshole on my shoulder asks. *Don't you like it? Even just a little.*

I punch him.

"I need a bodyguard because it seems like every time I'm out and about, they're on me. But I also . . . I also need a lover." I ignore the way my dick responds to that and jump in with the logical response.

"Wow, not my field of—" She rolls her eyes.

"Calm down, buddy. A fake one."

"Look, I don't think—"

"Whatever your fee, I'll double it." I pause like any normal human would, even though I don't *have* a fucking fee. "I'll double your fee and we won't even have to do much. Just a few . . . outings. I'll work from home and keep a low profile, and you can accompany me to the grocery store, the coffee shop. Maybe a date or two?"

I remain silent.

She thinks it's because I'm contemplating her offer, but I'm silent because Peterson put a deadline on her innocence and that deadline is approaching.

Quickly.

An opportunity like this—the chance to bum around with her, be seen with her, to *talk* with her—could benefit the case.

I could get that promotion.

We could pin this on Reed once and for all.

And you could spend time with Olivia.

The little devil is somehow climbing back up to my shoulder, and I wonder if maybe talking to this insane woman is actually detrimental to my health.

Possibly.

But to my career . . .

"We wouldn't have to do much more than go out a few times," she says, continuing to attempt to sell me on the idea.

"Much more?"

"Well . . ."

"Well?" I don't like the way that *well* sounds. "Olivia?"

"Look, a kiss for the cameras wouldn't be the worst idea."

It would.

It would be *catastrophic*.

"It absolutely would. That's not what I do."

"Maybe just one! A peck. Or not. We can see how things shake out if the opportunity arises. And then we'll . . . conveniently break up on Halloween." She's clearly thought about this quite a bit, pondering ideas and solutions.

"Halloween?"

"I have a party to go to. A fundraiser. We could go, be seen, have a fight . . . end it then."

Damien Martinez's firm throws a big Halloween party that, a few years ago, he turned into a fundraising event for their charity that provides legal counsel for women in abusive relationships and helps them get on their feet.

That's the event, without a doubt in my mind.

And she's right.

While there won't be press inside the party, there is lots of press coverage at the event and even a red carpet of sorts. We could, in theory, have a public breakup—a solid end date.

And even more important, I would have an excuse to be with Olivia.

I kick the part of me that says *for my own benefit* and add *so when I need to stop her chaotic plans, I don't have to make a scene.* It would be the perfect excuse to talk to her more, to try and understand her, and maybe figure out this fucking case before Thanksgiving.

"Come on, Andre. Would it really be that much of a pain to go out with me?" The way her eyes sparkle both with mischief and nerves twists my gut.

It's like there are two people in there, the old version who would never ask anyone for anything that might inconvenience them and this new one she's trying to create, battling to see who will win.

One is a little menace, causing trouble, who I'm pretty sure wants me to break.

The other is self-conscious, the one who thinks she's a burden, the people pleaser.

Even if I want to keep this shit professional, even if there is nothing in me that would say looking at Olivia Anderson sideways is a good idea, I know which side I want to win.

The little menace.

That's the one the world needs.

"Fine. I'll do it."

TWENTY-EIGHT

How to deal with a meddling old lady 🔍

SUNDAY, SEPTEMBER 24

On our first official fake date, we take his car.

"If someone follows us, I'm trained in evasion," he said, and I rolled my eyes because clearly, his bodyguard instincts are much too strong.

"No one is going to—"

"But they did, Olivia, and you called me having a panic attack in the middle of nowhere," he reminded me, and I shut my mouth.

Oh. Yeah. Somehow, I had let myself forget about that part.

"Fine," I grumbled and let him drive, engaging in polite small talk but fully in my own head, not paying attention to the familiar turns we take.

Which leads us here.

Outside of Edna's house.

"What are we doing here?" I ask, looking at him sitting in the driver's seat. He sighs.

"She called this morning, told me her hot water wasn't getting hot. I offered to help."

I think about her check-in call yesterday and how I let it slip I was going out with Andre. I'd done it so she would stop texting me *every single day* asking if I'd had rebound sex yet. It was a bad decision I made in a last-ditch effort, thinking that if I was going to be paying Andre to date me, might as well get everything I could out of it.

She'd never see us in person together to use her X-ray vision and decode I was totally full of shit, so what would it hurt?

A lot, apparently, because you forgot how fucking sneaky the old hag can be.

"She's going to be a pain in the ass, you know," I say. He nods.

"I know. That's why I figured I'd bring you. I'm going to hide and fix whatever she needs and you can keep her from staring at my ass while I'm bent under her sink or wherever."

"Why do I feel like you're speaking from experience?"

"So far, I've fixed a leaky pipe that was mysteriously dry, a garbage disposal someone had unplugged, and about a dozen squeaky hinges I couldn't hear a thing from but Edna told me kept her up *all night long.*"

I laugh.

"That sounds like Edna. You never should have told her you lived nearby."

"To be fair, when I did, I was bleeding from my head and a pretty girl was standing in front of me."

We both pause.

We both stare.

Then we both try and talk over each other.

"I'm sorry—"

"I didn't mean—"

This is so uncomfortable.

But also . . .

Pretty girl.

The word runs through me like warm maple syrup and I fight a sigh.

Unfortunately, or fortunately, depending on how you look at it, neither of us have time to say anything else because there's a knock at the window. When I turn, Edna's face is right there.

"You two gonna sit in here giving each other googly eyes forever, or are you gonna come fix my pipes?" I shake my head, looking at the roof of the car like God is going to come and give me some kind of reprieve.

It never comes.

"Come on, menace. Let's go before we send her to an early grave."

"If only," Edna says.

● ● ●

I'm alone with Edna while Andre checks her shower, which is dangerous in and of itself, when she leans into me.

"Have you fucked him yet?"

"Jesus Christ, Edna! No!"

"You're telling me you're with that hot piece of ass and you haven't tapped it yet? Good lord, you're a waste of youth, Olivia Anderson." I roll my eyes and fight a laugh.

"Was your shower really not getting hot enough?" I ask with a raised eyebrow. "Or did you just need him to leave so you could interrogate me."

Her smile is the answer.

"So why aren't you two making whoopee? You're hot; he's hot. You should be hot together."

"Oh my fucking god, Edna! Stop it! We're not even really dating!" The words spill out before I can stop them and her head moves back a bit in surprise. "I did something dumb so he's helping me out."

"Sure looks like you're dating. You know, going on a date together and all."

"I fucked up and told the paparazzi that I was with a boy toy the entire time I was with Bradley because he couldn't make me . . ."

God, this is so weird. "*You know*, and that I had left him for my boyfriend."

"And Andre agreed to be your boy to—" I cut her off and continue my story before she can finish.

"And then I had paparazzi on my ass, following me everywhere, asking where my *boyfriend* was. Andre's a bodyguard. He agreed to let me hire him but to pretend he was . . . not my bodyguard." She claps her hands in excitement.

"Oooh, so it's like one of those fake dating romances! Where they start as pretend and then before you know it, they're boning!"

"Edna! Can you please stop? He's *in this house!*" I say through gritted teeth. "No, that is not going to happen. He's so very much *not* into me. And I'm . . . still getting over my breakup," I lie because other than the stupid press stuff and my desire for payback, there nothing to *get over* between Bradley and me.

"Oh bullshit. You were never even into that man so there's nothing to get over."

I don't argue.

It's not worth it.

Though I am intrigued with how Edna even knew that.

"Either way, I am a job for Andre. And that's fine. As soon as this all quiets down, we're going to pretend to break up and that will be it."

"He looks at you like he wants to eat you alive, Olivia. That's not how a man looks at someone he views as a *job*."

"I know you love love and you want what's best for me, but that's not what this is, Edna."

"You said you're playing it up for the cameras—has he kissed you?" A thin, penciled-in eyebrow is raised, and I shake my head but feel a blush burn on my face.

Like always seems to happen when I'm around Edna, her X-ray eyes pull the truth from me.

"From that blush alone, I know you're into him. It'll happen and soon, and I'm telling you right now, if you try and convince yourself it was all some kind of publicity stunt, I'm going to haunt you when I finally die. That man is *into* you, Olivia, and not in a platonic work way. You should fuck him."

"Edna—"

"He asks me about you, you know." I pause. "When he's here, helping me out, he asks about you. About your relationship, your family. Your job."

I don't know how to process this new information that Andre is asking my ex's neighbor about me.

"You told me you wanted to break free from the Bradley bullshit, from the cage your mom puts you in? He'd be a good way to do it. You can think you're a job to him all you want but that man wants in your pants."

"I don't know—"

"I know enough for the both of us. He'd make a great rebound, Olivia. Just don't count it out just yet, you know?" I open my mouth to respond but Andre is coming into the kitchen, holding a small towel he's wiping his hands on, a scowl on his face.

God, he's fucking handsome in a resting bitch face kind of way.

I start to tell myself to shut up, this isn't that, like I do every other time I see him, but I remember what Edna told me.

And this time, I take him in.

His eyes move right to me and scan my body, not like he's a robot without feeling but like he's a man who wants to see what's beneath my shirt and jeans.

When I bite my lip, his eyes move right there, and I can see it.

The struggle.

Holy shit.

Edna smiles, not at Andre but at me.

She knows.

He'd make a great rebound, Olivia. Her words ricochet in my mind and I wonder if she isn't right. It would work for both me and Andre, who said himself that he doesn't want a relationship of any kind with me.

"What aren't we counting out?" he asks. I panic, opening my mouth to spew something random and incriminating, I'm sure, but Edna saves the day.

Kind of.

"Olivia becoming a cat lady. There's some charm to it. I think she could easily grow into being an old cat lady." I roll my eyes and Andre looks me over, this time without the heat.

Maybe I imagined it?

"I could see it."

"You're an ass," I say, smacking his chest, and for the third time in his presence, I get to experience an Andre smile.

It's good. That smile alone could convince me to try and make him into something more.

"Yeah," is all he says in response.

"Well, did you fix it?" Edna asks Andre.

"Yeah, but funny story." He raises a dark eyebrow at her. "The hot water switch was just off. Took me so long because I had to dig through a very precarious tower of junk in order to get to it. You know anything about that?" he asks. I stare at Edna and shake my head before snorting a laugh.

Andre turns his attention to me.

"What are you laughing at, little menace? Like you wouldn't do the same, the one who told the press she had a perfect lover and her ex couldn't keep it up." I roll my lips into my mouth and momentarily panic that he's mad at me before I get my fourth smile.

He's not mad.

He's *teasing me.*

"Little menace! God, it's just too perfect, isn't it? His little menace." Edna practically has hearts in her eyes. "Can you imagine him saying that during—"

"Edna!" I scold even though I don't think she knows how *not* to be fully out of pocket. Then, I turn to Andre, moving a hand to smack him for calling me a fucking *menace.*

I fail when he grabs my wrist, his thumb brushing the soft spot.

It sends a chill down my spine, one I try to ignore.

"You're an ass," I say, but there's no fire behind it.

How could there be when he's looking at me with those eyes?

They hold a fire that shouldn't be there, not if I'm just a job to him.

"Told you," Edna says with a gleeful smile, breaking the moment. Andre lets go of my wrist, but the spot where his thumb rubbed burns. I look to see if he left a mark, but it's just fair skin and faint bluish veins.

"Alright. It's been . . . something, Edna, but we gotta head out," Andre says, twirling his keys on a finger.

"Oh, don't let this old lady hold you two back!" she says then stands from her seat and starts shuffling toward us, using her hands in a shooing motion to get us out the door.

"Call me tomorrow, Olivia!" she shouts as we walk toward Andre's car.

I flip her off, and her laugh follows us as we drive out of the small neighborhood.

TWENTY-NINE

| How to make people think your relationship is real |

SUNDAY, SEPTEMBER 24

"Where are we going?" I ask for the third time since we left Edna's as we drive on unfamiliar roads toward a destination I don't know.

It makes me itchy, the not knowing.

"Do you trust me?" he asks, probably so very much over my questions, he's rethinking agreeing to be my bodyguard slash fake boyfriend.

I still can't believe that's a sentence running through my head.

"No," I lie because I'm starting to think I would trust this man with my life and it has absolutely nothing to do with his career path.

It has to do with how he called me the day after I somehow got him to agree with going along with this charade and told me he was taking me out on a date.

And how, when I told him that wasn't necessary, he told me he doesn't half ass things and if he's my fake boyfriend, we're going to make sure "that shit hits that idiot square between the eyes sooner rather than later."

It also has to do with Edna and how he's apparently humoring her, letting her call him over for small handyman projects, knowing she's probably lonely and likes having people in her house.

It's why I started going there so regularly after all.

But most of all, it's how, even though he never smiles and he tells me I'm a menace and he always looks so fucking mad and he *carries around a gun* like it's the Wild West or something, I feel safe.

Somewhere in my gut, I know nothing bad will ever come to me in his presence.

Still, I will never tell him that.

No, sir.

"You're a shitty liar, you know that?" he says, completely straight-faced.

"I'm actually a very good liar," I say without thinking. "I've honed the skill my entire life."

"Yeah? Why's that?"

This?

This would be why I *don't* trust him.

Because he sees through my bullshit better than anyone ever has been able to. I thought Cami and Edna were bad, that they were too good at seeing what I was hiding, but they don't hold a candle to Andre Valenti.

And even worse, he doesn't *drop things*. Not only can he read through my bullshit like an expert, but he doesn't let me get off easy with my normal, brushed-off answers.

Instead, he digs.

And digging is dangerous when your entire personality is a carefully created veneer.

I have to remind myself that even though it doesn't feel this way, this man is a stranger. I don't *know him*.

He doesn't need to know that I've lied my entire life because I feel out how people feel about me, about situations, and I change my answers to better suit their expectations.

Somehow, though, it seems like he knows already, like he has insight into me I can't fib my way around.

"I'm an only child of parents who aren't together. I got very good at telling them each what they wanted to hear when I was a child."

Then, I add on as a second thought, to cover up *that* truth a bit, "You know, to get better stuff or stay out of trouble."

He gives a noncommittal hum. And even though he doesn't actually *say* anything, it's like he knows I'm lying.

"What about you?" I ask. "Any siblings?" *Any kind of conversation we can have to steer the topic as far away from me as humanly possible?*

"A younger brother."

"And your parents? Are they together?"

"Just my mom." I stare at him, waiting for more, for him to expand, to put an effort into our small talk.

Nope. No such luck.

"Parents divorced or . . ."

"My dad left right after my brother was born. It was just us three." I sigh and roll my head back, staring at the roof of his car.

"God, you're a really bad conversationalist." I groan.

"I don't like talking about myself."

"Why not?"

"Because I'm boring."

"I doubt that," I say without thinking. His cheek twitches like his instinct is to smile but he doesn't want to.

"What's up with that?" I ask, turning in my seat to better stare at him. His eyes are fixed on the road, the traffic slowing down ahead of us.

"It's traffic. We're almost there," he says, and I roll my eyes.

"Not that. You. With the smiles."

"What about it?"

"You never do it."

"Yes, I do."

"Okay, fine. You try your best *not to* smile," I say, and he doesn't argue. "Is it a bodyguard thing? Or are you just grumpy all the time and don't want the occasional smile to fuck with your bad ass image?"

The car is quiet as he pays someone for parking then moves

through a bumpy grass lot, following directions from men in yellow safety vests waving around orange flags until we're parked.

"A little bit of both maybe," he says, finally, before unbuckling. "Come on, we're here."

●●●

Here turns out to be an Oktoberfest on a mountain and the vibes, even though I will never be a beer girlie, are immaculate. The German outfits, the people all kinds of excited, the music, the food . . . it's absolutely magical.

And from what I understand, so *very not Andre*.

"So, this is an Oktoberfest," I say, looking around as Andre walks toward a booth that reads, *Tickets*.

"Yup."

"Is this a tradition of yours or something?"

"Nope."

"God, you're insufferable."

"Why?"

"Because you literally talk in single syllables. We're on a *date*, right?" I ask, raising my eyebrow.

He turns to me and glares.

"I'm just saying, you said you wanted to hit him"—I lower my voice despite not seeing a single paparazzi or journalist nearby—"*right between the eyes*. Looking like I'm a puppy following you around and you giving one-word answers doesn't exactly scream *happy couple*, you know?"

His steps slow and I catch up to him, finally able to walk along-side him toward the line.

I must have hit some kind of mark because his hand reaches out and before my brain can process it, he twines his fingers with mine then pulls our hands, and by association me, closer before pressing his lips to my fingers.

I can't stop staring as he does, my eyes glued to the movement like I'm making a recording and I know damn well I'll be replaying it late into the night.

The feel of his lips, the way the omnipresent scruff scratches my fingers, the short puff of breath from his nose, all of them somehow change something about me, about us. And most ground-shaking, the way his eyes lock onto mine, it's like I'm the only thing in this universe.

But a moment later, I'm brought back to reality.

"Don't look, but behind you is a man in all black, a camera in hand, taking a picture."

"Oh," I whisper.

"So don't punch me for touching you, okay?" he whispers, a small smile on his lips.

Fuck.

It's a good thing he doesn't smile often.

I couldn't handle seeing it more than once in a blue moon.

"Got it," I whisper.

"Show's on," he says, lowering our hands then releasing mine. But he moves next to me, hooking a hand around my waist and tugging me close.

My body prickles where it touches his and I shiver.

He must think that it's nerves, that the shiver is from anxiety instead of anticipation.

"You're safe with me, Olivia," he says, so low only I can hear.

I nod, but I don't tell him the truth. I don't tell him that somehow with Andre, I don't feel terrified the way I did that afternoon when I called him, or even the first time they found me when I was in the café.

I feel safe because his arm is around me and he's got me.

And that's a dangerous feeling, considering I'm just a job to him.

THIRTY

SUNDAY, SEPTEMBER 24

"Here," I say, handing her one of the two cups in my hand. "Supposed to be the best light beer here." She grabs it and looks at the cup, reading the logo. "You're a light-beer girl, right?"

She gives the vibe.

"Oh, uh, yeah! Much better than dark."

"Cheers," I say.

"To keeping me safe both from paparazzi and from being embarrassed by my own terrible actions." There's a pause before the smile on her lips becomes more genuine. "I really appreciate it, Andre. I know I kind of guilted you into this, but really, you're saving my ass."

Guilt twists in my stomach because she means that.

She feels like she forced herself onto me, forced me into this situation, but I had my own selfish reasons for agreeing.

That guilt turns into nausea when I imagine her reaction when she finds out who I really am.

Still, I clink my cup—some cheesy souvenir mug she wouldn't stop giggling about when she was walking around so I bought two—and take a sip.

She follows suit and it's small, but it's noticeable.

A cringe.

"No?" I ask. Her face moves quickly, too quickly, like she's covering something, but I already caught it.

"What?" Even that, a single, simple word, comes too quickly. I tip my chin to her cup.

"You don't like it?"

"Oh. No! It's wonderful! So good." Her smile is so fake, it's almost humorous.

It's almost as if, if I didn't know she was only giving it to me to protect my feelings, she's forever afraid to insult someone or be an inconvenience.

"You hate it."

"No! Not at all. It's great! Beer at an Oktoberfest in the mountains? What else could you ask for?" I have to fight a full-out laugh when she attempts a second sip, a smile on her lips but a look of panic in her eyes.

"Olivia, give it to me."

"What? No! Why?" She moves the cup over, like she's attempting to hide it from me, like she's not half my size and I can't just reach over and grab it.

"We'll get you something you like. Dark beer? Cider? Apple juice?" She scoffs.

"I'm not a *child,* Andre. I can drink."

"Then give me the fuckin cup and tell me what you want to drink." She moves again, trying to stay out of my reach.

"No! This is fine!"

I sigh and stare at the blue sky, trying not to let the frustration take over me.

"Menace, give it to me."

"Stop calling me that!" She steps back again.

"Then stop being a fucking menace and give me the damn cup so I can get you something you'll actually *like.*"

"You spent money on this! It's fine!"

Fine.

It's fine.

You spent money on this.

There is it. Her reasoning.

"I don't give a shit. It was a waste of money if you don't like it."

"You don't have to waste money on me, Andre. This is great." She takes a third sip, this one seeming to go down a bit easier now that she's had one, before smiling at me. "See?" Pride is on her face, and I shake my head at her before stepping closer and wrapping my arm around her waist.

She feels good there, pressed against me.

It must cloud my mind.

Or maybe it's the two sips of alcohol I had.

Or maybe it's the sun.

Or maybe it's the short fucking skirt she's wearing that swishes against her upper thighs with each step.

Either way, I speak, and the words absolutely do *not* pass through a filter before leaving my mouth.

"If you were mine, I'd fuck 'fine' out of your vocabulary. A woman like you? Deserves nothing but fucking perfection." It comes out low and quiet, but I know she heard me. Her mouth is dropped open, and even though all I can seem to do is the exact opposite of what I should do, I manage not to kiss her.

Instead, my free hand reaches behind her, grabbing the glass from her hand and stepping back before pouring it into mine.

"Now, what the fuck do you want to drink, Olivia?"

Her mouth is still open, she's still standing there frozen, but she answers.

"Cider, please."

I smile.

"That's a good girl. Now go sit and wait for me to bring your drink."

* * *

"Shit," Olivia whispers an hour later as we sit at a small table, picking at a pile of fries. The day has been a surprise, not because the place was nice or particularly entertaining (it wasn't, though Olivia seems to think so), but because, to my surprise, Olivia Anderson is good company. She likes to talk, but not just about herself. In fact, I've come to notice if you encourage her, she has a story for everything under the sun.

And though she's been giggling and smiling the whole time we've been here, when I look at her now, her eyes are down and her face is a bit pale. She puts down her second cider of the day and drops her head a bit.

"What?"

"Photographers." I scan the area, and it only takes a moment to peg him. A scrawny-looking dude in all black is headed our way, a camera in hand, taking photos even as he walks.

Jesus.

"You stay here," I say, moving to stand, but I'm stopped by a small hand on my thigh.

"Andre—"

I lean in even though I shouldn't.

I use a hand on her chin to tilt it my way, even though I shouldn't.

I brush my hand down her neck, using it to push her hair over her shoulder, even though I shouldn't.

And I lean my forehead against hers, even though I *absolutely shouldn't*.

I'm in such dangerous territory, playing with fire.

Let me burn.

"I'm here to keep you safe, Olivia. You sit here, you look fucking gorgeous, and I'll talk to him. Get you your space."

"You don't—"

"You let everyone think you don't need their help, Olivia, but you're getting mine no matter what, okay?"

I don't give her a chance to answer as I stand and do one more ridiculously stupid thing.

Because she's looking up at me, eyes wide with wonder and confusion, and she looks so pretty like that, so far out of her head, I can't help it. I lean down and I press my lips to her forehead before I make my way toward the man.

I tell myself the move was for the pictures.

For the press.

And it's not that far off—when I look up, I don't miss how he's stopped, how the camera is to his eye, how he clearly captured those moments.

But I can admit—if only to myself—that the move was completely selfish. Fully motivated by nothing more than wanting to put my lips on her skin, by wanting to comfort her.

And I repeat: I am so fucked.

"What?" the camera man says as I approach, and as gently as I can so as not to make a scene, I grab his elbow.

"You follow me," I say.

"Look, man—"

"Shut up and make this easy on both of us."

I'm a big guy, so I shouldn't be shocked when he does just that, following me to a quieter part of the field.

"Are you snapping pictures of Olivia Anderson?" I ask once there isn't anyone around, and the man, a full foot shorter than me and holding a camera in his hands, cowers. Still, I'm impressed when he straightens his shoulders and answers.

"Yes. I'm with *Starlight*. My boss assigned me to Oktoberfest, but I know who Olivia Anderson is. I know people are talking about her, and I know . . ." He bites his lip like he's losing some of his bravery. "I know if I get something good, I might get a raise."

At least he tells the truth.

At least he doesn't spin it or act like an asshole.

And considering I'm with Olivia right now for the same reason, to get my own promotion, I can't be too mad.

"I'm sorry. I swear I wasn't trying to be intrusive. I was just going to ask for a photo, I swear. My partner . . . I want to ask him to marry me but I need a ring. A raise would really help right now, and—" He's rambling but I cut him off.

I've heard enough.

I'm a relatively good judge of character, so I believe him. He didn't mean harm. He wasn't trying to crowd or sell out Olivia.

I also don't even let myself harp much on the fact that, in theory, Olivia and I are here *for this reason,* for the press to catch wind and spread the news.

But the way she looked when she noticed the cameras . . .

I sigh.

"Look. If I give you a quote, can you agree to stay the fuck away? Take your pictures or whatever the fuck but from a distance. Do *not* get in my woman's face." He thinks for barely a second, probably realizing this is a good deal, and nods.

"Man to man, we've got a deal?" I put out a hand and he takes it. I shake it harder than necessary and look him in the eye, hoping to get my point across. "I'm not the kind of man you cross." His breathing stutters before he nods.

"Here's what I'll say." He scrambles for a pen and paper and then clearly decides I will not be slowing for him at all and grabs his phone instead. I assume he's either recording my words or using a voice-to-text app, but that doesn't matter.

"Olivia Anderson is a gorgeous woman inside and out who has been dealt a shit hand. I'm absolutely honored to have her on my arm, to be her man. Anyone tries to get in her fucking way, though, they're going to get my wrath." The color drains from his face and I smile.

I don't know where this version of myself is being dragged from, but there's no time to argue.

"Got it?" I ask, and he nods. I turn, ready to walk off, but the guy's voice cuts through the sound of the crowd and I stop.

"Sir?"

"What?" I look over my shoulder at him and he hasn't moved.

"Is there a name?"

"What?"

"A name I could attribute to the quote?" I shake my head.

"All that matters is Liv. Worry about her." Then, I turn to head back once more.

"Ready?" I ask as I approach. Her eyes have been locked on me the whole time.

"What happened?"

"Nothing. He's going to give us space," I say. "You ready? I saw some kind of carnival games over that way." I tilt my head in the direction I saw them.

"I, uh, Andre?"

I ignore her.

I put my hand out, silently telling her to take it.

She looks at it, then at me, then over my shoulder to where I left the reporter, then back at my hand.

And then she grabs it.

THIRTY-ONE

What to do when your bodyguard kisses the life out of you?

SUNDAY, SEPTEMBER 24

We spend the entire afternoon at the Oktoberfest, eating junk food and playing games and watching a few bands play. The ski mountain where it's hosted even turned its chair lifts on, so we were able to take a ride and watch the trees, which are starting to change colors already, to get away from the chaos.

And even though this is all fake, all a setup, I'm having a blast.

This is definitely the best date I've ever been on, hands down, which, depending on how you look at it, could be really depressing.

I'm choosing to look on the bright side.

We're heading out after an afternoon of being left alone once Andre said *whatever he did* to that reporter when his hand reaches out and grabs mine, slowing our steps as we near the car in the grass parking lot.

"There are cameras on us again," Andre says, and I follow where his eyes are shifting gently, spotting some people a few yards away holding phones up directed right at us.

"Shit," I whisper, reaching for his car door, but his hand stops mine.

The tender spot on my wrist is burning from his touch, and

slowly, so slowly, he moves me until my back is to the car and his front is against mine. The cooling air moves against my heated skin, my shoes slowly crunch leaves as we move, the smell of early autumn air fills my nose, and I think . . .

I think there's a reason my brain is committing each sense to memory.

I know in my gut actually.

And really, this is a terrible idea.

Maybe the worst.

It could fuck up everything, twist my mind in ways it can't afford to be twisted.

But really, it's the best *idea,* I try and convince myself.

"Do you have anyone who's gonna come for my throat if they get a shot of you and me together?" he asks. His voice is low and rumbles on my chest, but I can't shuffle his words in the haze.

"What?"

"Those people. They're taking pictures, probably going to be online in no time. You said you wanted to make it look real." My heart skips a beat.

"Yes . . ." His hand lifts, pushing hair behind my head, using his thumb to tip up my chin, hand wrapping around my neck.

"If you were once mine and I fumbled that, I'd be furious, seeing you out and about with some man." He waits for a beat before I answer, taking a breath and licking my lips, swallowing to bide my time.

But he waits me out.

He's always so fucking patient with me, like nothing else in the world matters.

"Oh," is all I can muster up.

"You said we wouldn't kiss for the cameras unless the opportunity arose." I wonder if he can feel my heartbeat beneath his hand, if he can feel it going insane, feel how his words affect me. "I think the opportunity has risen, Olivia."

I don't respond.

At least not with words.

Instead, my eyes drift shut, my head tips up a bit, and my lips part.

And I wait.

He doesn't make me wait long before his breath is playing along my lips.

And then those lips are on mine.

The universe stops turning.

It might implode for all I know.

The entire festival behind us could burn down, oceans could come and swallow up the entire state of New Jersey, an earthquake could crack this parking lot in half and I wouldn't notice.

Because Andre Valenti is kissing me.

His lips glide along mine at first, gentle and smooth, making my pulse quicken even more, and my hands move as he does, one to the nape of his neck to twirl the hair there, the other going to his chest, where his heart is beating as quickly as mine is.

His hand on my neck has moved to cup my jaw, the other trailing to my waist to pull me in closer as he continues the kiss, slow and lazy like he doesn't have a care.

Like the world as we know it isn't changing completely.

He doesn't take it far, but it lasts longer than needed for a simple *prove ourselves to the media* kiss, and when he does finally break it, resting his forehead on mine, he does so with half a dozen small kisses, like he can't bear for it to be over either.

We stare at each other, chests rising and falling quickly, before I break the silence.

"That was a really, really good kiss," I whisper without meaning to. For some stupid reason, when he's around, the filter between my head and my mouth evaporates.

"Olivia," he says in a growl against my lips, and it's low and travels straight to my belly, making it warm.

It was meant to be a warning, but instead, it's a turn-on.

A dangerous, dangerous turn-on.

"Andre." My own voice is breathy, and his name on my lips has his hand tightening on my waist.

"This isn't that," he warns, and it sounds like he's reminding himself too.

"I know." He moves back a tiny bit, just enough to look at me, but I don't miss how he's still holding on to me, and I'm almost certain it's not for any cameras.

"Why do I feel like there is most definitely a *but* there?" I can't fight the smile.

"*But,* it was a really good kiss. And kisses that good should never be held to a standard of never being replicated." There's a tease in my voice and I don't know who she is, this woman talking, but I really like her.

"Olivia."

"Kiss me again," I whisper. He shifts then, and *I feel it.*

He's hard.

Not rock hard, but he's definitely stiff beneath his jeans, and if that's just from one silly, nonconsequential kiss, one *fake* kiss . . .

"No."

"Andre, it doesn't have to be anything. We—"

His hand moves to my throat, tipping my head back again so I have no choice but to look him in the eyes.

"I am not the kind of man who does *it doesn't have to be anything,* Olivia. I am all or nothing. And if I gave in, if I had you, I'd need it all. We can't be all so we have to be nothing. Does that kill me? Absolutely. Do I want to drag you out of this godforsaken place and take you home and fuck you until the only word you remember is my fucking name? Absolutely. Am I going to? No. This is not that, Olivia. We are not that."

He keeps a hold on my neck, and my lips part with annoyance and lust and a million other emotions, and I wonder if he can feel it, how chaotic my heart is beating.

I can't tell for sure, but in his eyes, there are swirling thoughts and longing, a look I know is reflected over my own face.

And then he groans, just low enough for me to hear.

"Little menace," he says before dipping his head forward once more, pressing his lips gently to mine, and I decide I'm going to take his advice after all.

I'm going to get my revenge in the form of thriving post-Bradley.

And I'm going to do it with this man who is consuming me as we stand here.

THIRTY-TWO

SUNDAY, SEPTEMBER 24

I made a mistake when I kissed her. I knew it immediately.

I was a fool to think kissing Olivia Anderson once would be enough, would sate me. If Olivia is a spark then I am a forest, and I don't know how I'll be able to stop her flame from consuming me now that she's set fire to my world.

THIRTY-THREE

SUNDAY, SEPTEMBER 24

When we drive past Olivia's place, I realize I also fucked up by kissing her where I did, in front of everyone, the festival, the paparazzi . . . the world.

Because four paparazzi are parked outside her apartment, waiting.

She reaches over when she sees them, grabbing my hand in a panic, and I feel it.

She's shaking.

She plays a good game and pretends she doesn't care, that it's all part of being her mother's daughter or maybe her own fault for sending in that tip, but she hates this.

She hates being in the public eye. The scrutiny. The need to show outward perfection.

It makes me wonder how the fuck a mother could intentionally put her daughter through something like this, put her into the lime-light and expect her to thrive—to perform, really—where she doesn't belong.

But of course, I remember Melanie St. George does nothing for the benefit of others, and Olivia being in the press and causing a stir, be it by dating a wealthy socialite or by standing at her mother's side, helps her own image become more omnipresent.

"Andre," she whispers, and I know.

I know.

There's no way into her building where we could avoid those cameras. The parking area is right next to the entrance and I would bet that even the back is being watched like a hawk.

My mind works through a dozen options.

There's quite a few after all.

We could go to her friend's apartment—I know Cici wouldn't mind.

We could go to her office building until things settle.

I could even drive her down to Cami's or have her father meet us halfway.

We could also just go in, use me as a shield or call the police and enter her townhouse, then come up with a better plan.

But I don't.

I don't do any of those very reasonable plans because, it seems, I am not a reasonable man.

I have lost my goddamn mind. It's so obvious. It started with interrupting her stupid fucking revenge then agreeing to be her . . . bodyguard slash fake boyfriend.

And it peaked when I made the mistake of kissing her.

Now, my entire body can only focus on protecting her, on keeping that waver out of her voice, on keeping her safe and happy and . . . mine.

No, not mine, I remind myself, because that line of thinking isn't just stupid—it's dangerous.

Still, I make my decision and turn left instead of right.

"Where are we going?" she asks, her voice still a shaky mess, her hand still having a slight tremor of panic. I fuck up again when I keep my eyes on the road but lift her hand, pressing it to my lips.

"My place," I say against her skin.

And when her entire body relaxes, when she becomes quiet once more but not in a worrisome way, I should be concerned by how my body also relaxes.

But I'm too far gone to.

THIRTY-FOUR

How do you get your fake boyfriend to fuck you?

SUNDAY, SEPTEMBER 24

I've showered in Andre Valenti's shower.

I've sat at his kitchen island in his tee, that fits like a freaking dress, with wet hair and eaten takeout and talked to him about nothing that held any real importance.

And I've sat on the opposite side of the couch from him while we binged nearly an entire season of *The Office*.

I even watched him crack a few *almost smiles*.

And not once has he tried something.

Not once has he kissed or touched me, even when his eyes roamed my body when he thought I wasn't looking.

Stupid fucking gentleman.

And now we're standing in the small hallway that connects the primary bedroom to the rest of the home and he's holding my hand.

It swipes against the base of my thumb, and my mind can think of nothing except what that gentle touch could feel like elsewhere. My mind, so twisted and unhinged from a kiss that happened *hours ago* and the way he likes to protect me and the way he treats me with both kindness and like I'm unbreakable, wants that.

And so does my body.

I'm so lost in my need and my attraction to him, I somehow lose any sense of propriety and self-consciousness.

"Come with me," I say in a whisper, my fingers grazing his hand and a plea in my voice.

"I can't, Olivia," he tells me, his voice just as low, the rumble doing amazing things to me.

Just talking to him like this, his eyes burning, his voice gravelly, is the best fucking foreplay I've ever had.

"You can. It won't . . . It doesn't have to be a big thing." He shakes his head slowly.

"We already had this talk, menace," he says, and something about the way he says that word, like I'm a torment to him, puts butterflies in my belly.

The hallway we're in is small, so small there's barely a foot between us as we stand facing each other, me in his shirt and little else, him fully clothed even though I wish he weren't.

"Maybe we should have it again," I say, placing a hand on his chest. "This all-important talk." He breathes in deep, closing his eyes for just a moment before his hand moves, tipping my chin up.

"Fine. I don't do quick. I don't do easy. I don't do *just this once*, and that's good because somehow, I *know* with you, it would never be *just this once*. You would be an addiction I couldn't quit, a distraction I'd never want to come back from. And right now, my job is protecting you." Something flashes in his deep eyes, like that means something more to him, and it pools, warm and liquid, in my belly.

I step forward, closing the gap between us.

"I'm fine with that."

He groans, and it hits me right between my legs as my hand moves up his chest until it's in the hair at the back of his neck.

"A menace," he whispers, lips brushing mine as his head tips down, and then he's stepping, moving me until my back is to the wall, until I'm pinned in place with his body, and he's kissing me.

He's *kissing me*.

Holy fucking shit.

This isn't like at the festival when there were cameras and eyes recording us. This isn't proof for the world that we are together. This isn't controlled and concise, a specific impact he's trying to make.

This is a man *breaking*.

A man who is giving into something he desperately wants but won't let himself have.

This is lips and teeth and tongues clashing.

His teeth nip my bottom lip, and I groan into his mouth, the sound igniting something in him until he's bending his knees, never breaking our kiss, and grabbing my thighs to hoist me up.

I wrap my legs around his waist, my fingers moving to tangle in his hair as our kiss continues, pinned against the wall. His lips then move, and he's kissing and nipping my jaw, tugging my ear between his teeth, hot breath sounding there. The feeling lands right between my legs, making my pussy clench, making my panties drenched.

I need more.

I need him.

I need *everything*.

I moan, rocking my hips, trying to get friction, holding his head to my neck where it's licking and sucking.

"Andre," I moan, and that has him unlatching from the mark that's probably going to be left there, lust-filled eyes meeting mine before he's kissing my lips once more, tasting me, his tongue fucking my mouth like he wishes it were something else.

Shifting, I grind myself, finding his hard, thick cock, moving so it's right over my clit, rubbing where I need him most in this moment. As I whimper, though, his body stiffens with a groan, and he breaks our kiss, pulling back and pressing his forehead to mine.

"Andre," I whisper, the sound pained even to my own ears.

"No, Olivia. Not today. Not now. There's too much . . . It's too messy," he says.

"I happen to love mess," I say with a smile, and he shakes his head, forehead rolling against mine before he slowly—painfully slowly, like he doesn't want to do it—sets me down.

But not before he brushes his lips against mine once more, as if he can't help it.

"Go," he says, the growl in his voice low. "Go to bed."

"I want you to take care of me," I whine.

It's the most honest thing I've said aloud in some time, the most blatant acknowledgment of my own needs.

"I'm starting to think all I want to do these days is take care of you, Olivia," he says, and the way he says it, like it's a confession pulled from the deepest depths of his soul, shakes me.

"Then do it," I say, moving to my tip toes, my nipples, peaked, beneath his oversized tee brushing his chest. "Do it, Andre."

"You don't know what you're asking me, Olivia. You've had a long day, an emotional month. You—"

I groan and lean back against the wall, widening the gap between us. "God. I'm so tired of this."

"Olivia—" I lift a hand to him, stopping his excuses.

"No. Everyone thinks they know what I need most, what I should be doing, how long I should be *mourning*, and what's *best* for me. But you know what? All of you are wrong. I don't need to do anything any of you say. I don't need to follow ridiculous rules and expectations. All that's gotten me is turning into someone I don't recognize, almost marrying a man who was so, *so* wrong for me."

He lifts a hand like he wants to touch me, to comfort me, then drops it. I roll my eyes.

"You're just as bad as them, thinking you know best. I like you, but I know you aren't looking for anything major, much less from me. I'm a 26-year-old woman who hasn't had a man make her come in over three years. And I know my panties are soaked from a single kiss and you're hard because even though you're trying to be all gentlemanly and professional, you want me just as bad as I want you."

The pupils in his eyes flare and his mouth opens a bit, just enough to let me know my words impact him.

"But whatever. I'm turned on because I've been around you all fucking day, teasing me just by *existing*. Because even though it's dumb, I am wildly attracted to you. So, I'm going to go lie in your bed and take care of myself since you refuse to step up and do the job." I step closer to the door, eyes locked on his so I can see the way the fire burns there.

"Olivia—"

"What, am I not allowed to do that either?" I'm annoyed, and it's clear in my voice.

But I'm *tired*. I'm so tired of everyone thinking they know what's best and never standing up for what *I* want.

"Of course not. I—" I smile.

"Good. Feel free to listen. I'm not exactly quiet."

And then I close the door on him.

And I run to his bed, getting under the covers with a gleeful squeal because I can't quite believe I did that.

I can't believe I *said* that. To his face!

I can't believe I challenged him.

I can't believe I told him I was going to touch myself in his bed.

And I told him to *listen!*

Who am I?

This is you, a voice says. *This is who you were always supposed to be. Loud and outlandish and brash and* fun.

I smile to myself as I kick off my underwear, losing them somewhere among the blankets, but I leave on his shirt. It's soft and cozy and smells like Andre, perfect for . . .

I brush a hand over my breast, the tee adding delicious texture to my tight nipple, and sigh. My hand moves to my other breast, tweaking the nipple there and eliciting a small moan from my lips.

I wasn't lying when I told him I was turned on. The entire day, no matter that it was some kind of fake tabloid fodder of a date, felt like endless foreplay. There's something about the way Andre smells, the way his eyes burn on me, the way he touches me, even though he tries to avoid it.

My hand moves back to the first nipple, tweaking it as well, while my other hand moves beneath the blanket, pushing the shirt up over my belly. Starting right below my breast, I brush my hand down, circling my belly button with a single light finger while my other hand works my breasts.

My breath catches as I imagine it's Andre's hand touching me. He'd be tentative and teasing, partly because he's unsure and partly because something tells me that man would play with me for hours, until I beg for more, delighting in the way I moan and writhe without him doing much of anything.

That thought alone pulls a moan from my chest.

It's unintentional, fully natural, based on how keyed up I am and my daydream of Andre that has me on the edge already.

But it does double duty, it seems, when from the other side of the door in the small room, I hear a groan.

A deep, manly, pained groan.

"Olivia, come on."

It fuels me.

Something takes over me, a personality I've never encountered before, a braveness that is so foreign to me, it throws me for a moment.

"I'm touching my breasts, Andre. I'm imagining it's you, that you're pulling on my nipples over your shirt, hiking it up, sliding a hand down my belly." I do as I've described, my free hand sliding down, down, down until the tips of my fingers touch the trimmed curls between my legs.

"Should I circle my clit?"

"Olivia."

I smile at the pain and frustration in his voice. I bet he's hard. From what I can tell from the quick glances through his pants and the way it has pressed into me on occasion, he's thick.

I bet he would fill me *divinely*.

"Feel free to intervene at any time."

The thought that he's still outside the door, listening and frustrated, drives me more.

Makes me wetter.

Makes me move my hand down another inch until the tip of my middle finger touches my clit, already swollen with the need for release.

"Oh god," I groan. My finger circles my clit, not touching the neediest spot, my pussy throbbing.

In my head, it's Andre's thick, rough finger teasing and torturing.

"Oh god, fuck, should I put a finger in, Andre?" I moan as my finger brushes softly over my clit before returning to the torturous circles. I dip down once to my entrance, gathering the wet there and moving back to my circles. My other hand continues to work my sensitive nipples.

I arch into my hand when he responds, his voice pained with barely controlled restraint.

"If I were in there with you, I'd be torturing you for being such a naughty fucking girl and playing with me like this."

Somehow, I knew he would want to dominate me, punish me for not listening, for not obeying him, the opposite of how he's encouraging me to do things for *me* out in the real world.

"Then come do it." I groan, my finger dipping down again, this time sliding in just one knuckle deep before moving back to my clit. "God, I'm so fucking wet. Fuck. I don't know the last time I was this turned on."

The door jostles from the outside. He snaps, I think, in the only way he'll let himself.

He wants me.

That much is clear.

But he doesn't *want* to want me for whatever reason. Because he's working for me, or he thinks it's too close to my breakup, or he's got some issues of his own he needs to tackle first, I don't know.

But I do know Andre Valenti *wants me*.

And he makes that abundantly clear with his next words.

THIRTY-FIVE

SUNDAY, SEPTEMBER 24

"Who is it all for, little menace?" I ask, and my voice is so gravelly and raw, I almost don't recognize it as my own.

I sure as fuck didn't *mean* to say it, didn't plan to do anything other than listen with my head against the wood door while Olivia tortured me from my bed.

I should have walked the fuck off when she closed the door in my face.

I should have gone straight to the bathroom for a cold fucking shower.

I should have hopped in my car and run to fucking Mexico to get as far away from her as humanly possible.

Instead, I stood outside my bedroom door like a fucking chump while I listened to her moan. I didn't think she'd actually do it, sweet Olivia who doesn't want to ruffle any feathers, who would never want to make anyone uncomfortable even to her own disadvantage, but I should have known.

There's a little menace hiding underneath it all, begging to be let out. Lucky me, I'm the one it seems most comfortable showing itself to.

My words seem to egg her on because she moans again before speaking. "Come in and find out."

I groan.

It's an involuntary response to this unique brand of torture.

"No, I'm staying here where you're safe. When you have a clear fucking head, we can talk about this like adults. But for now, you're going to do what I say."

Why? Why the fuck am I doing this?

I hear her breath stutter even through the door, and the thought of her—in my bed, mouth open, eyes wide, my shirt lifted over her perfect fucking tits, nipples I want to wrap my lips around —has my hand moving to my cock through my jeans and adjusting myself.

I groan at the feel.

"What?" she asks.

"You want to play this game? We're playing it my way. One finger in your cunt, Olivia."

"What?" Her voice is breathy and confused and turned on.

"Do as I fucking say, menace."

That's what she is.

A menace in all regards. To her ex, to me. To herself.

And I'm fucking enthralled by it.

Silence comes from her side of the door.

Did I push her too far? Was that too much?

I guess that it's for the best if we find out she can't handle this side of me, if it's too much, if we figure it out before I even put a finger on her—

A low moan fills my house.

I'm not sure if it's loud or if I'm so fucking in tune with the noises coming through that godforsaken door that it's overtaking my entire subconscious, but it fills my ears like nothing before.

"What do you feel?"

I want that to be my hand.

"Fuck, I'm soaking. It's tight, Andre. It's . . ." Another moan, and I picture her sliding the finger out, it glistening in the low lighting of my room, then pushing it back in. "It's been a while."

My cock throbs.

"It's mine now, Olivia."

I don't know where it comes from.

I shouldn't think like that, possessive, controlling.

I can't think like that.

But I do all the same.

And when she replies, "God, I'm yours, Andre. Tell me what to do," I know I'm really fucked.

Because not only can she handle that, but the moan in her voice tells me she likes it just as much as I do.

"Two fingers inside, fuck yourself and rub your clit with the heel of your palm." A moan and then *god-fucking-dammit*. If I hold my breath and listen, I hear it.

The wet of her fucking her cunt.

Of her riding her fingers.

For me.

Because I told her to.

"Fuck, Olivia. I can hear how wet you are. Roll your nipples, baby, and keep riding those fingers for me."

"Yes. God. I'm close." Her voice is almost confused. "How am I close?"

"Because I'm in control. Imagine how close you'd be if it were my fingers? My cock stretching you."

Said cock throbs, and I rub it through my jeans.

I won't jack off in the hallway, not when I need all of my focus to be on Olivia, but I sure as fuck am cataloging this for later.

"I want your cock, Andre. Please, god, come in here."

"Not this time." It's a dangerous thing to say, even at the moment, because Olivia misses nothing.

But I don't know if I can deny there will be a *next time.*

"This time, you're going to ride your fingers in my bed and come saying my name." Another frantic moan and I dig the hole deeper.

"When you're done, Olivia, I'm going in the shower, and I'm going to jack myself off thinking of fucking you. I'm going to come thinking about filling your tight cunt." She mewls at my words, panting. "Do you like that, Olivia? The idea of me claiming you with my cum? And when I'm done, I'd go down to your cunt and stuff it back in when it slides out, make sure you get all of me, that you keep it inside for as long as possible."

I'm sick.

I'm a sick fuck and I'm going to Hell.

But she doesn't seem to care.

"Oh god, oh god." She moans, and I picture her hips rocking, her fingers fucking herself as her back arches in my bed, naked expect for that shirt pulled up to her armpits, her full tits bouncing with each movement.

"My name," I growl. "My fucking name is what you say when you come, you hear me, little menace?"

"I'm . . . I'm so close." She moans again, and I can hear it in her voice, the edge she's riding.

"That's it, Olivia. Come for your man. You're mine, and I'm telling you to come; now do it."

She doesn't speak for long moments, moments where I think I overstepped, but then . . .

"Andre!" she shouts, a scream of epic proportions filling the house as she comes, as she shatters. "Fuck, Andre, oh god, fuck!"

It feels never-ending.

It feels like she comes and comes and comes, and I would give anything to watch her writhing on my bed, to watch her tightly wound good-girl facade fall apart for me.

By me.

Eventually, she quiets, nothing but labored breathing coming through the door.

I wait patiently.

Then she speaks.

"Are you still there?"

Her voice is nervous now, like she can't believe she did that, that we did that.

My cock throbs as I readjust it in my jeans.

"Yeah, menace. I'm here."

Silence once more, then I hear her soft voice.

"Thank you for that," she whispers. It travels through the door all the same.

"Go to bed, Liv," I say, then I turn and walk straight to the bathroom, undressing in haste.

It only takes four tugs of my cock under the hot spray of the shower before I'm coming, moaning her name loud and low, and my balls tighten at the idea of her hearing that.

We are so fucked.

THIRTY-SIX

MONDAY, SEPTEMBER 25

In the middle of the night, she comes into the living room where I'm sleeping.

Her toes on the hardwood wake me up, causing me to open an eye and look for her, search her out. I sit up when she comes into view, my vision cloudy still from sleep.

"Olivia?" She comes closer, looking almost like a ghost in the dark room. "Is everything okay?"

"Please come sleep in your bed, Andre," she whispers, her voice hoarse and low.

"Olivia—"

"I won't try anything, I promise. Your bed is huge. We can even put pillows between us if that helps. But the guilt of taking your bed is eating at me and I'm never going to be able to sleep if you're out here. So, either suck it up and come sleep in the same bed as me, let me sleep out here, or let me take a cab home," I stare at her in the dark, her fair skin the only thing I can really see, her brown hair and my black shirt melting into the shadows.

Temptress, I want to say. *You're a damn temptress.*

But her face tells a different story.

She's telling the truth. She won't sleep well knowing I'm sleeping on the couch because she's in my bed.

I hate that face.

I think I would give up everything so she never makes it again.

I sigh.

"Get back in bed, Olivia," I say. She opens her mouth to protest but I continue, "Get in bed. I'll be there in a minute." Her face transforms into a gorgeous sleepy smile before she nods and walks back to my room. I sit there for a full minute, wondering what the fuck I've gotten myself into, how on earth I'm going to continue with this woman, who I know now will always get her way when it comes to me.

When I crawl into my bed, she's lying on the very edge, facing away from me. Looking over her shoulder, she says, "Promise. I won't even leave this spot." She smiles again, and it must be that smile or the exhaustion or the chaos of the day that has me doing it, but I reach over, hook my arm on her waist, and tug.

She lets out a little OOF! of surprise before she settles, her back melting into my bare chest in just a moment. A few minutes pass, her breathing evening out. She's not asleep, but she's close when I whisper into her hair:

"You're a menace, you know that?" She lets out a tired laugh.

"But am I your menace? Because I think I want to be your menace, Andre," she whispers.

The words coat me like a balm, smoothing out the rough edges of the world, and though I don't respond—I can't really—her words run through my mind, driving through my dreams, a sentence said in the honesty of near sleep.

I think I want to be your menace, Andre.

The next morning, I slip out of bed before Olivia wakes and pace my kitchen.

I don't have the fancy shit she needs to make her coffee, but it *is* the right season for her fancy fall drink, so I tap it into an app and get her order delivered, hoping it will be here before she wakes up.

And then I start to mentally unpack what happened between us and how badly I fucked up.

Last night was a mistake.

Not the kind of mistake where I regret holding Olivia all night or talking her through a fucking orgasm.

The kind of mistake where I've decided I need to have her. I need Olivia in my life, but the timing is so unbearably fucked because I cannot have her with these secrets between us. In order to salvage this, to give myself any kind of chance to have her as mine when this shit show is over, I need to put space between us.

She can't be mine and not even know who I am. I can't surveil her day in and day out and then pick her up for dinner. She's been lied to enough her whole fucking life, her trust in other people so tattered and mended and patchy. I don't want to add to her list of traitors who have lied to her.

So this needs to stop.

And I need to close this case.

I am now determined because it fucks up me having even a modicum of a shot with her, and I don't want to fuck something up that could be good. Decision made, I answer the door to grab the coffee, and as I turn, Olvia is shuffling out, hair a mess and my shirt grazing her upper thighs.

Jesus.

A fucking dream.

I am so fucked.

"Hey," she murmurs, and I step to her, handing her the coffee. "Is this . . . ?"

"Your fall drink. I don't have any of the shit to make your normal coffee, but it's fall season so this passes, I think. Or did I fuck it up?" I ask, referencing the time she told me she only goes to this coffee shop to get a drink in fall, the *only time she can trust them to make a good one.* She looks from it to me and back, then to the paper-wrapped straw in my hand. She unwraps it, slides it in, and takes a sip.

Pure bliss takes over her face.

I want to give her that bliss in a very non-coffee-related way.

"It's perfect. You're a gem," she says, shuffling to the kitchen table and sitting down with it, still mostly asleep.

I should give her time, but I don't.

"We need to talk," I say, and she groans.

"I barely woke up."

"Then just listen." She pouts.

It's too fucking cute, which strengthens my need to say my piece before I lose my nerve and bring her back to my room and peel that tee off her.

"I don't want to."

"Too bad." She rolls her eyes at me, and I fight a smile, sitting on the edge of my kitchen table. "Look. Last night—"

"I'm sorry I made you sleep with me," she says, cutting me off with a guilty look.

"That was the best part of my night, Olivia," I tell her truthfully. She pauses and looks at me, and I wonder if her filter works less this early in the morning.

"Then why are we having the 'about last night' talk?" I sigh.

"The kiss. The . . . other thing." Her eyes widen.

"Oh," she says, and again, I fight a smile.

"Yeah. That . . . unfortunately can't happen again." Her brows draw together in confusion.

"But . . . But you want it to?" She says it like a question, like she's trying to piece things together.

I sigh. "I'd be a liar if I said I didn't. But things are too complicated with me being your . . . bodyguard. We can't do that again."

"For now or forever?" she asks, and goddamn.

It's like she's reading through every carefully chosen word I'm saying to find the truth.

"We can revisit this conversation at another date." She nods like it makes sense to her, even though it doesn't actually make *any* sense. Not without the whole story at least, one I can't give her yet.

"So . . . friends," she says, taking another sip.

"Friends," I agree. The word tastes sour.

"For now?" she asks.

"While this chaos is happening, while I'm technically working for you, yes."

"Because you . . . don't want to confuse things."

"Yes," I say. And even though it's not the full truth, I feel a semblance of relief because it's almost like, even though I can't *tell* her, she gets it.

Wheels spin in her sleepy mind.

I know those wheels are dangerous.

Dangerous to me and my sanity, for sure.

Then she nods.

"Okay."

"Okay?" I ask, shocked.

"Well, yeah. I'm not going to force myself on a man who doesn't want me."

"I didn't say—" She cuts me off by standing and turning her back to me before looking over her shoulder.

"All good, Andre. I'm gonna go take a shower, okay?" She lifts her hands to fix her hair, piling it on top of her head before wrapping a hair tie around it expertly.

But I don't take note of that technique.

I'm lost on the way my shirt rides up with the movement, revealing the bottom half of her ass in a thong.

Jesus.

Fucking.

Christ.

"And don't worry. I won't throw myself at you anymore. When you're ready to want me, you'll have to make the first move."

And even though I've loved watching this more confident, zero fucks given menace of hers come out, I know I am so totally fucked.

THIRTY-SEVEN

MONDAY, SEPTEMBER 25

Her sleepy words from last night ring through my head as I walk to Peterson's office.

I think I want to be your menace.

Olivia Anderson is so much more than I initially thought or assumed. She's kind and sweet and funny as fuck, but beneath all of that, she's strong and vulnerable and wants so badly to be the kind of person who just doesn't give a fuck.

But any version of *us* really has to wait until this fucking case is settled. The goddamn bane of my existence. Then, there won't be anything between us if and when we're together. I won't have to worry about that black cloud when I'm with her.

So, it has to stay professional, even if, as of this morning, my face is splashed on tabloids all over.

"Olivia's New Boy Toy," one headline read.

"Bradley Who? Melanie St. George's Daughter Out with Hot New Lover."

Or, my favorite: "Drunk in Love? Olivia and Her New Man Go to Oktoberfest."

The photos of us kissing against the car are mostly blurred face shots; a few more professional shots show me pushing her hair back or kissing her hand, but even those didn't capture my full face.

Still, it's why I'm headed to Peterson's office, just in case.

I knock on the doorframe and he lifts his gaze, a jelly donut halfway to his face.

I hate him more with every moment.

"Hey, Peterson, you got a moment?" I ask, looking around his office as if I'm interrupting actual work instead of a love affair with a donut. He shakes his head, takes a bite, jelly squeezing out to land on his desk, and waves me in. As he chews, a finger swipes the jelly from his desk, and then he pops it into his mouth.

God, this man is horrific.

"What can I do for you, Valenti?" he asks, food still in his mouth.

I try not to cringe.

"I, uh, I have to talk to you about my case. Olivia Anderson?"

"You got her?" he asks, his face going a bit excited. "It was her all along?" I screw up my face in confusion, still unsure how he could reach that conclusion seeing as every bit of evidence we have points to Reed and not Olivia.

"No," I say, shaking my head. "No, it's something else."

"Well, what is it? I don't have all day." I look at him, wondering not for the first time who he is related to or who he has blackmail on in order to have this fucking job. I'm also reminded that if I close this case and clear Olivia's name, I not only get a promotion and don't have to work under this jackass, but I also can get Olivia.

"I, uh . . . I took it upon myself to do some more research." I'd been thinking all morning about how to spin this so Peterson would think it was either his idea or not of interest to him. "Remember when you told me to do whatever it took to get you at press conferences before Thanksgiving?" He smiles like I've already done the job.

"Can't wait to rub that shit in my cousin Roddy's face, the asshole. Always talking about his boring fucking corporate job. He should try a real job like us, you know, Valenti?" I blink at him.

"Yeah, sure. So anyway, I saw something on the computer and

was able to"—how to phrase it—"intercept her at a coffee shop. Make friends. The press has been on her cause of her mother, and we have me listed as an employee at Garden State Security."

He takes another bite of his donut and nods.

"Anyway, she needed security and a cover from the press. I've been taking her around to get back at Reed and . . ." This part aches.

Even though it was how I convinced myself to start this shit, I feel wrong saying it out loud to Peterson, of all people.

"Use the access as an opportunity to try and get more intel from her."

"Ah, smart. Good move, agent."

A small weight lifts from my chest.

"Anyway, I just wanted to, you know, give you a heads-up. There was some press where I took her last weekend and a few photos with me in them. Undercover, of course."

He nods like he understands. "Of course."

"Just . . . wanted to keep you in the loop," I say." He nods again.

He's a fucking useless human.

"You fuck her yet?" he asks with a lascivious grin, leaning forward.

My fingers twitch with the desire to punch him square in the face.

"What?"

"You fuck her? I've seen the reports from when she was with Reed. Hot piece. I'd hit that."

You cannot hit your boss at the FBI in a federal building. You cannot hit your boss at the FBI in a federal building.

I repeat this to myself over and over until I start to believe it, until I drown out Peterson.

"Uh, no. That seems a bit unethical," is all I say.

"I don't give a fuck if you fuck her every day from now until kingdom come. I don't give a fuck if you have a threesome with her mother. I just want her locked up, no matter the method."

My brow furrows.

"We all agree it's not her."

"I want *someone* locked up, Valenti. Right now, it's looking like the person we have the most on is the Anderson girl. The public is getting restless." I blink at him, trying once more to convince myself not to lose my cool.

"The public has no clue this investigation is ongoing," I say without thinking.

"They will once it all comes out. I told you, no matter what, I'm standing at a podium on the Wednesday before Thanksgiving and speaking in front of the people." He shakes his head at me like he thinks I'm being stupid. "I don't care who it is that takes the brunt of this."

"We need more time. Just became her name is on everything—"

"You have until November before she's getting charged. We don't have anything concrete to tie him to this shit, but we've got a lot to tie it to her."

"I just need time—"

"Then what the fuck are you doing here, Valenti? Wasting time is what you're doing. Get out of my office and do your job," he says, his mood swinging from jovial frat boy to asshole boss.

I nod and stand then head out to continue researching.

And to be totally honest, it didn't go nearly as poorly as I anticipated, telling him about Olivia.

But now the pressure is on to solve this stupid fucking case.

THIRTY-EIGHT

How do realize your worth?

SUNDAY, OCTOBER 1

"I met someone," I say, sipping my coffee and refusing to look at the girls at our first meeting in October. As seems to be the way with these, we go around and give updates on our lives.

It's been an interesting experience since we all "joined" this group, for lack of a better word, after we were dumped right before our respective weddings. When I was first invited, I thought it would be an hour of us all sitting around and bitching about our exes, but it's not that.

It's a group of women, with really only one thing in common, coming together to talk about their lives—the joys and the pains and the mundane—but we don't actually talk about our exes that often.

Instead, we end up talking about moments of grief, guilt, and, it seems, moving on.

"What?" Naomi says with a wide smile. "No way! Tell us everything!"

The blush taking over my face feels good. I couldn't tell you the last time I *blushed* over a *boy*. I fill them in on Andre, on how he's the guy I literally ran into, how he agreed to help me with my press issue, how he's helping Edna, how we went on a date, and how we . . . kissed.

I leave out the part that happened in his house, though. I might combust into flames if I didn't.

"So you're into him?" Julie asks, and my instinct is to shake my head and say no, but that's not fair.

It's not the truth, either.

"Yes, but . . ." I hesitate, trying to find the right words. "But he is incredibly *responsible,* so we haven't . . . done anything more." A lie to a degree, but—

"Why not? Has he seen you? You're a fucking smoke show."

The girls nod, agreeing with Chrissie, and I smile at them.

God, I'm so glad I met them. So *lucky.*

"He's *responsible.* This is work for him. He doesn't want to blur lines, which I guess I respect, but—"

"So fire him," Naomi says, and we all laugh while I shake my head.

"You guys are ridiculous. We have another date next weekend so we'll see."

"A date?"

"A fake date. For the press," I say.

But I'm beginning to wonder how much of that is true. Our "coffee date" ended up completely undocumented, both of us sitting and chatting while we worked—or, in my case, gleefully tormented my ex—for hours. It wasn't planned ahead, and his reaching out randomly like that didn't feel . . . like work for him. But still, when he walked me to my car, he didn't touch me, not even a handhold, and he surely didn't kiss me. He simply helped me into my car, tapping the hood twice and watching me drive off.

"Would you be . . . open to him?" Julie asks. "So close to everything that happened?" It's not said with judgment or accusation, but it's still something that's been playing in my mind: the fear of being judged.

What will everyone else think?

Still, if anyone would understand, it's these women, so I tell them the truth.

"I don't . . ." I pause, unsure. "I don't think it matters anymore. That he matters. The further I get from him, from that relationship, the more I see it was a train wreck, totally one-sided. It was . . . I had convinced myself of a lot of things in order to keep the relationship going, but now that it's over . . . I see it wasn't anything. At all. It was over well before that day, you know?" Guilt fills me from admitting that out loud, but Julie nods.

"We get that."

"My relationship was the same, you know. I gaslit myself into believing he was the one, that everything was perfect because I wanted to get married *so badly*. Sometimes, I'm grateful for him breaking it off when he did. I don't know if or when I would have been brave enough to."

Heads nod, and it's a relief, once again, to have this group—these women who understand me, who don't judge.

"So the revenge is off?" Chrissie asks.

It takes me aback.

"What?"

"These revenge plans." She digs in her bag and pulls out a piece of paper. "I've been adding to mine." Other heads nod, all moving to grab papers, and *holy shit.*

They all have their lists.

I thought for sure it had scared them off, that they weren't interested, but . . .

"We thought it sounded like a great way to close a chapter," Naomi says with a smile, and something warms in me.

I did this.

I brought the idea of revenge, of getting even, of taking your own back to these women, whether it was sound personal advice or not, and they took it. They *ran* with it.

Of course, I can't leave them hanging, so I shake my head.

"No. We deserve closure," I say with a smile.

"But only if it doesn't mess with your new guy," Julie says, her face stern.

The mother of our little group.

"What?" I ask, confused.

"You look happier talking about that guy than you have since you joined the group. You know how to put a face on, Olivia, but even you can't hide how much you like him."

"Oh, I, uh—" I start, ready to cover it up, to play it off.

"Not with us," Chrissie says. "You can do that with your friends and family you don't want to worry about you but not us. How do you really feel?"

For a moment, I almost lie again.

Almost.

But I decide she's right.

I promised I'd be more honest with myself, with my friends and my family, and I'd stop putting everyone else first.

Maybe that starts with being honest here.

"I . . ." I take a deep breath and look at the ceiling of Naomi's apartment, trying to find the words to say what I'm feeling. Oddly, looking at the ceiling feels easier, so I speak. "I deserve a Zachary Anderson."

"What?"

"I deserve a Zachary Anderson."

"You . . ." There's a worried pause before Naomi finishes her concerned sentence. "That's . . . your dad's name, right? You want your dad?"

"Jesus Christ, no. God, I just mean . . ." I stay looking toward the ceiling as I try and piece the right words together. "I deserve a man who loves me—no, who adores me. I deserve a man who would try and figure out how to stop the world from spinning if I mentioned it one time in passing. I deserve . . . I deserve seven flavors of ice cream and a man who isn't afraid to get caught in the tampon aisle."

They look confused.

That's fine.

"My dad spent my entire life taking care of me. Even when I was a bitch to him—and it happened often—he still loved me more than anything in the world. Still worked until his fingers bled to give me whatever I wanted. But not just that, he worked hard so I would know I was so fucking loved and worthy of love. Never—and I mean *never*—did he make me feel like I needed to prove myself. Like I needed to change who I was in order to make him more comfortable." I shake my head, mentally comparing him to my mother.

"I deserve that in my life. I had convinced myself . . . Fuck, I had convinced myself that I didn't. That Bradley was *good enough.* So what if he acted like a high school boy when I was on my period? What did it matter if he could never remember my coffee order? He said he loved me, and in a world where people would kill for that, who was I to be picky? But I know now that I deserve the world."

"You do, you know. Deserve the world. We all do. I think that hope is why we keep coming back here. To heal so we can try again."

It makes sense, and it makes me smile.

"My dad met Cami and he knew then. I know he did. I can guarantee that very first night, he knew somewhere he wanted to make her his. And they had bumps, and she didn't trust *anyone,* and I made shit harder, but he worked through that. Fought for her. I watched it happen in real time, and it was amazing to see." I don't add how, at the time, she and I were at utter odds and I couldn't stand her.

"I just . . . I want to find that. I deserve that. I once thought wanting that—asking for a man who was so unbearably into me, he would try and stop the world from turning—was selfish. That it made me self-centered." I shrug. "I don't know. Maybe it is. But I also don't think I care anymore. I want it."

There it is, laid out on the table, with no opportunity to explain it away.

Nerves bite at me while I wait for the girls to reply, to tell me if I am, in fact, selfish or not.

And you know what?

I don't care. I don't care if they think that's selfish or anything.

Because I'm done with putting myself—my wants and needs and desires—second to others' feelings.

But I don't have to worry, not when Julie smiles wide and the others follow suit.

"I'm proud of you, Olivia," she says, grabbing my hand.

"That's not selfish, Liv. That's life. That's human. You're allowed to want someone to fall in love with *you,* not just to fall in love with someone else."

That shift changes everything, I think.

I'm allowed to want someone to fall in love with me as well.

I'm allowed not to have a one-sided relationship.

And maybe most of all, I'm allowed to leave if I'm not getting that.

"Of course, you deserve that, Liv. Of *course* you do. Why would you think otherwise," Simone says.

I give her a face because she knows.

They might not have known me for too long, but they know who and how I am.

"You can tell your people pleaser to go fuck off," Naomi says, and I laugh. "Move over, at least until you get laid by the hot bodyguard."

It is enough to break the tension, to cut through everything, and we laugh, but when I leave, I don't let that fade into the back of my consciousness.

I let that live in the front with me, my need to beat back the people pleaser, and I learn to be comfortable without her.

THIRTY-NINE

SUNDAY, OCTOBER 8

> What are you doing?

Working, unfortunately.

> Wanna get coffee? I'm working from the
> shop down the road from you; you can work
> here. Get out of your office and get a
> tabloid shot.

I text her at noon when she's in the office and I'm watching her
change the password for Reed's fantasy football league. Last night, I
noticed his calendar was blocked off for his team's draft that would
happen today at one, and now, at noon, she's logging in, changing his
information so he can't get in. Wreaking havoc, as usual, it seems.

The woman never stops; that much is for sure.

I don't really have any reason to do it, to text her and set up a
coffee date. Screwing with his fantasy league isn't something I'm
going to intervene in, considering it won't land her in prison, and I do
have a bunch of work I could be doing in the office, but . . .

An opportunity to watch her in action?

A chance to spend an afternoon with her, even though I have to be strictly professional?

I'm fucked in the head but I'll take it.

Thirty minutes later, she's sitting across from me, both of us with laptops open and drinks in front of us, when she asks, "So, how does fantasy football work?" I want to smile at how obvious she is, but I also have to remember I don't know what she's doing.

For all she knows, I don't know anything other than the fact she has a shithead ex and he's part of the reason the press is all over her. So instead of smiling because it's fucking cute, her trying to be sly, I furrow my brow and look at her in confusion before answering.

"What?"

"Fantasy football. Do you play it?"

"I do a league with my buddies every year, yeah." Her eyes go cat-like, like she's found an in and she's happy about it. She leans forward, her forearms on her table.

"How does it work? How do you win? Or is it like . . . all a guessing game and you get lucky?"

"I mean, there's a skill to it, but . . ." I pause, looking at her, her laptop open in front of her. "Why do you ask?" I'm intrigued to hear what she'll say, though I doubt she'll tell me she's breaking into her ex's account in order to trash it. She shrugs, and you can almost see the wheels turning in her head.

What I would give to be in there, to watch how it works. To watch her balance her people pleaser with the little menace.

"Bradley was in one every year. He would always get bent out of shape about it, about his draft being good or bad or whatever, but he never taught me. I thought it would be funny to . . . make one of my own, try and see if I could do better than him." She's lying, of course. It's cute to me because even though she thinks otherwise, Olivia is a terrible fucking liar. At least in the eyes of someone who knows what to look for.

"You're making a team?" I ask, clicking around on my laptop to find the program I need.

"I'm thinking about it," she says, sipping her drink.

It only takes a few clicks before I can see it. She has the fantasy site Reed uses open, and she's logged in and changing the default email address to a burner one.

I watch, enamored, as she goes through his account, not quite sure of her goal, of what her plan is.

Well, that's a lie.

I know, at the very core, it's revenge, even if it's small and insignificant in the grand scheme.

I would love to know her reaction, though, when she realizes just how much money he has hidden away in that account, how much he's playing silly games with. When I see her eyes go wide, her chin dip back in shock, I bet that's it. My screen confirms that she's seeing the thousands of dollars he has on the platform to bet with.

After a few minutes of trying to figure out how the site works, she begins her work: removing players, adding others, and thoroughly destroying any chance of him having a winning team. Occasionally, she asks me about players, about who is the best and then who is the worst for each round, and I'm sure to tell her which players would hurt him most. She's nearly giddy as she works.

It's clear what she's doing—she's getting even—and when I move to the monitoring software I have on Reed, it's actually pretty hilarious watching him have a mental breakdown over not being able to log in. It seems that even though he got a confirmation email saying his email was changed, Olivia also knows how to get into *that* email and deleted it before he could see. So, he's floundering, calling everyone he knows, and flipping out when they tell him he's active on his team, accepting picks each round.

I do find it interesting, though, how he attempts to play it off. He doesn't tell his teammates playing with him that he's not in control, that he's been hacked or anything like that.

Afraid to show his weakness, maybe? Afraid to let others know he doesn't have full control? Afraid for others to find out he *has* a weakness?

I guess that's what happens when you allow a woman access to things, take advantage of her kindness, and then fuck her over. Karma always comes back around, and this time it's in the shape of a short brunette from Long Beach Island.

It's not as big as, say, attempted murder, but it sure as fuck is going to piss him off and ruin his fantasy season.

For a moment, I wonder if I should try and interrupt her, try to stop it . . . but it's not worth it.

I leave her be, let her have this one.

Fuck, all things considered, fucking with his fantasy league is best-case scenario. He also was pretty fucking terrible with it so who knows—maybe she's doing him a favor. Honestly, it's no wonder the man couldn't just make money gambling and instead had to resort to stealing from vulnerable people. He's shit at it.

This is the least of his concerns.

That list Olivia made is damn near terrifying and *absolutely* deadly.

I'm still sitting across from her, both doing minor clerical work on my laptop and watching her and Reed work, when a notification pops up on my screen.

Another text from Reed.

> Do you have any idea what email I used for my fantasy team?

He's reached out a few times since she got her belongings from his place, and each time, I do the same unethical thing.

I tell myself it's for the case or that it's for Olivia's sanity and mental health.

Sometimes, I believe myself.

But I always know the truth deep down.

I block every text and call that jackass makes because I want Olivia for myself. And somehow, along the way, I've taken it as my job to protect her sanity and mental health and her goddamn peace.

And every single day, I've realized more and more I'm not working for this goddamn promotion anymore.

I'm working to clear her from this mess because as soon as I do, she's mine.

I may have made a mistake the last time we met up, letting things get too far, kissing her in my house and the whole . . . bedroom thing, but everything makes sense now. In order to make it so when she's clear and I can make her mine, she doesn't have as much room to question everything, we need to stay platonic.

And when I look over my computer screen to where she's sitting across from me, a blissfully glee-filled face on as she destroys this man's fantasy league, I'm further convinced.

Olivia Anderson is going to be mine at the end of this.

I just need to make sure I don't fuck this up before I can make it official.

FORTY

Where is the best pumpkin picking in New Jersey?

SATURDAY, OCTOBER 14

When Andre picks me up for our next date, we don't go to Edna's house.

We do pull up to another bumpy road, and just like our last little date, we're guided along by some man waving an orange flag, directing us where to park, but it's not an adult beer event this time.

In fact, nothing here seems very adult at all, with a bounce house on one side, little photo ops to stick your head in and smile, and, of course, a dozen or so families dragging small children around, some happy and excited and some so clearly miserable.

"We're going pumpkin picking?" I ask, and he nods, eyes never leaving the car in front of us as we drive onto the property of the crowded farm.

"But . . . you hate pumpkin picking." Confusion and a hint of guilt run through me. "You told me it's a scam."

"And you said it was your favorite." My mind goes back over that conversation.

"And you said it was stupid. I think you said *only an idiot would want to spend an afternoon at a smelly fucking farm.*" He parks smoothly, turning the car off, but we both sit there, not speaking.

"I stand by that. Pumpkins are cheaper at the grocery store, and you don't get your ass poked by fucking hay bales on a bumpy hayride with squealing kids."

"You don't like kids?" I will be ignoring the way that twists my stomach, thank you very much.

"I love kids. I don't love other people's kids hyped up on excitement and candy apples and parents who don't know how to control said kids." Fair. That's fair.

"Okay . . . but why don't we just go to ShopRite and buy pumpkins there?"

"Because you like it this way," he says like it's that simple. Like he knows it's something I enjoy so we are, of course, going to do that thing even if he is miserable.

"Yeah, but, it's fine. I can drag Cici or—"

"Get out of the car," he says then unbuckles himself, opens the door, and steps out, slamming it behind him.

I don't move. Instead, I sit there, confused.

So confused.

Andre bends down to look through the driver's-side window and gives me an *Are you coming?* kind of look. I have no choice but to unbuckle and walk around the car to him.

"Come here," he says when I stop at the trunk. I'm still confused, but I've also learned if Andre says we're doing something, we're doing it.

My body doesn't know how to do anything but listen to him, it seems. Exhibit A: the time I was in his bed and he coached me through the door.

"Come *here,* Olivia," he says when I don't move as quickly as he would like.

"Why would I—"

"Jesus fucking Christ, do you think there will ever be a day when you don't give me a hard time after I ask something of you?" he asks then leans forward, his long arm grabbing my waist and tugging me close.

I land on him, his back against his car, and he catches then settles me with a hand on my hip.

It would be innocent, so perfect for keeping the distance but maintaining the image that he's my fake boyfriend, except for when I try to shift, to put some more space between us after I fell onto him, he wraps an arm around my waist, keeping me there.

We could kiss like this. The way he's tipping his head down, the way I'm looking up, probably with awe and adoration and confusion written all over my face, he could bend a few inches and press his lips to mine.

I could move to my tip toes and take a kiss from him so easily.

But he wants to keep things professional, I remind myself. *Strictly professional, despite that night in his house.*

A night I've taken to thinking about in my own bed.

But his firm words that morning remind me no. The guilt on his face was a mirror of my own, more than enough to convince me to hold steady.

"You have to stop that," he says, quiet enough for just me to hear.

"What?"

"Trying to think ahead to what people want from you. Trying to be what they want at the expense of *what you want.*"

I hate how he does that.

Reads me.

Knows me.

But also . . . I can't help but wonder what exactly he means.

Going pumpkin picking when he told me he didn't want to or . . .

Or how I wanted to move to my toes and kiss him.

"I don't . . . I don't know what you mean," I say with full honesty.

"All of it," he says. I open my mouth to say something, anything, but he speaks first, all while his free hand moves to brush a stray hair behind my ear.

"I'm going to make it my mission that you, Olivia Anderson, only do what *you* want to do. That you start living your life by putting yourself first."

Once more, I open my mouth to speak, to tell him I'm confused because he told me there was a line we weren't to cross, so how was I supposed to balance that? But I watch his eyes shift just a hair before moving back to me and speaking once again.

"There's a camera—paparazzi—at 3 o'clock. My three, your nine," he says in a whisper. "Ready to give them a show?" he asks.

There's a smile there in his voice.

Is he happy because we're about to kiss again?

Because we're about to check another box on this fake boyfriend schtick?

Or something else? Maybe he's teaching me?

Either way, there's only one answer. I have only one way to answer this man that follows the guidelines he's giving me, does things for me, things *I want*.

And I really, really want him to kiss me.

"Yeah," I whisper.

It was so quiet, I move to say it again, louder this time, but it's unnecessary. He's dipping his head down in a heartbeat and his lips are on mine, always so much softer than I expect for this man with his prickly exterior, and I melt against him, his arm going tighter to keep me safe as my arms wrap around his neck.

His other arm goes into my hair, scratching at my scalp, and I let out a little sigh because fuck that feels so good, giving me all-over body chills. My mouth opens just a bit with the sigh, and he takes advantage with a small groan I feel in my chest because it's against his more than I hear. His hand tightens, and he pulls me in deeper as his tongue takes the opportunity of my open mouth and slides in against my own.

It's so much better than I remember every single time, like somehow my mind took that moment that shouldn't be recreated and shouldn't be desired and downgraded it so it wasn't as amazing, not as memorable.

But this . . . the way he tastes and smells and how his lips and tongue glide along mine, guiding mine to obey the rules of this kiss, his hand tightening in my hair and his arm pulling me impossibly closer . . .

It is amazing, and it is memorable. Unfortunately, like all of the best things, it must end, and this one does when I hear a bit of a commotion near where the cameras were, bringing me back to reality.

Andre slows the kiss, giving me one, then two quick kisses before he steals a third like he can't help himself, like I'm irresistible and he needs this as much as I do, before he rests his forehead on mine.

His face is stoic as always, and I know the tiniest smile is playing at the corner of my lips.

"So, was that you making the first move or was that your version of professional?" I whisper with a tease in my voice once I catch my breath, once I realize my feet are back on solid ground.

He shakes his head, his forehead moving against mine. Not in a *no* gesture but like he doesn't understand something.

Doesn't understand me.

"I never do anything I don't want to do, Olivia," he says.

That reply raises more questions than it answers. "So that means you . . ." I can't even finish the sentence, afraid to embarrass myself by even insinuating something like that. It makes no sense, not after he told me so outright we shouldn't have kissed in his house, that we need to keep this perfectly professional.

"It means I've been thinking about kissing you since last time, and before that, I was stuck on our first kiss, and before that, I spent every minute in your presence staring at your lips, wondering what they would taste like."

"So that wasn't for the cameras?" I ask, and he sighs.

"It was and it very much was not." He's speaking in code, walking circles around the point.

"You said this isn't a good idea," I say, trying to remember all the reasons he told me and all the reasons I listed for myself, all the reasons that Andre Valenti and I just won't work right now.

He's not my boyfriend, and he's not a rebound, and he's not a fuck buddy.

He's my bodyguard, an employee, a friend doing me a favor.

But fuck if I don't want him to keep doing that, to keep kissing me like his life depends on it, like he can't go another moment without being reminded how his lips feel on mine.

"Kissing you might be my downfall, Olivia, but I'm going to be doing it anyway. If I'm going to hell, might as well taste heaven along the way."

It makes no sense, his words, the direness they imply, but I don't have time to think or ask or anything because he's pressing his lips to mine once more, quickly this time, before speaking.

"Come on. We've got a pumpkin to go find."

And then we're headed toward the entrance, an arch of fake pumpkins and corn stalks, and I'm so much more confused than before.

But also, so much more excited.

●●

A few hours later, we're sitting inside of a barn that the farm has turned into a makeshift café, eating cider donuts and drinking apple cider and living the damn dream, in my opinion. Our pumpkins have already been safely transported to the car by Andre while I perused the little bakery area. He inevitably needed to make another drop off to the car when I bought a container of pumpkin butter, decorative gourds I definitely didn't need, a dozen donuts, and a gallon of cider.

I cannot control myself in places like this.

Even more, the entire time, Andre has been such a good sport, taking the hayride to the pumpkin patch instead of the walking trail offered, carrying my giant pumpkin for me instead of telling me to grab a smaller one, not even blinking when I begged to go to the little petting zoo, and taking pictures with me in nearly every ludicrous, stupid photo op.

But now, he's sitting across from me with a scowl.

Not his normal grumpy scowl I've come to realize is just *part of him*, but a deeper one, his eyes consistently scanning the room but never really looking at me. And no matter how many conversations I attempt, he gives short, simple answers before clamming back up.

My stomach churns more with each second.

You did this, my anxiety tells me. *You told him you like this cheesy shit and he is a gentleman, so of course he took you. And now, he's counting down the minutes until he can take you home.*

Forcing down the last bite of my still-warm donut, I use a thin food service napkin to wipe my fingers before finally asking.

I might not have lived up to my goal of not being a full-out people pleaser anymore, of living fully and completely with myself in mind, but I'll do this.

I won't sit on my feelings anymore for the benefit of others.

"Are you . . . Are you mad at me? Did I do something wrong?" I ask, biting my lip. Even though I'm determined to be a bigger, better version of myself, anxiety and panic bubble in my gut. I wish I were more like Cami, with her self-assured *fuck everyone, if they don't like me, they can suck a dick* attitude.

Instead, I'm me: a people pleaser who instantly assumes the problem is *me*, that other people's emotions and moods are mine to fix.

His head moves from the door entrance of the barn, where he's been angrily staring for the last five minutes, to me.

His brow furrows like he doesn't understand.

"No. Why?"

"You just . . . You keep staring at the door like you want to run out of it, and you look . . . well, pissed."

"I am pissed," he says instantly. My gut drops to the floor.

"Oh."

"But not at you." . . . *oh.*

"Oh."

"I'm pissed you have a fuckwad of an ex, and because he was born into some fancy family, that means you have to deal with paparazzi swarming like vultures, trying to get your opinion on some new girlfriend of his."

"Well . . . to be fair, part of it is because of who my family is—"

"Did you ask for this?" I pause, confused.

"What?"

"Did you ask for this? For your ex to leave you at the altar, to cause a scene?"

"I mean, I did send in a tip—" I start to say under my breath.

"As a way to salvage your dignity and because you were hurt. But Olivia, did you ask to be followed by the press and have every date documented?" I don't answer, but I don't have to. "Have you asked them to stop ever?"

"I did a few times, in the beginning. But—"

"Let me guess, your mother told you you had to keep up the facade."

I don't reply.

He knows why, of course, so what's the point?

"I'm sorry, Andre. I don't want you to be upset—"

His chair scrapes as he turns to me, moving to get closer, grabbing my hand, and leaning into me.

"I need you to hear this now. You are not responsible for my moods, Olivia. Not at all."

"But I am; the whole reason we're here—you're here—*is because of me.*"

"Why do you feel like you are responsible for how I am responding to things?" he asks. It's clearly a challenge.

"I just . . . You were quiet. I thought maybe . . . I mean, I know you told me at your place"—I lower my voice in case anyone is listening—"we need to keep things professional. So, you're stuck here with me on this date that you would never choose to be on and you don't even get the . . . perk of it."

For the first time, a smile tips the edge of his lips, and fuck, he's handsome.

"Is this a date?" His smile spreads as the panic surges through my system, electric and consuming, making me light-headed.

"Well, it's, you know." I make wide eyes at him. "Not a *date, date*."

"Why isn't it?"

"Because this is . . . you know. And you said we can't."

"What if I said I wanted this to be a date, date." I stare at him, so fucking confused. "What if I'm tired of pretending this isn't what it is and I want to say fuck it to the consequences? What if that's the root of my shitty attitude?"

Our eyes meet and hold for a full thirty seconds of silence, my pulse beating wildly in a way I can't fully explain before he grabs my hand and stands.

"Andre—" He cuts me off with a tug of my hand until I'm on my feet.

"Come on," he says, heading straight for the parking area. I can barely keep up with him as he speeds toward his car, unlocking it as we approach and opening my door.

"Andre, what—"

"Get in the car, Olivia."

"Andre—"

Jesus, fuck, fine, I'll do it," he says then bends, lifts me, and tosses me into the passenger seat before leaning over and buckling me in. I open my mouth to argue, but before I can, he's moving, pressing his lips hard to mine just once before stepping out and slamming the door.

I sit in stunned silence as he backs out, as we leave the little farm, speeding nearly the whole way back to Hudson City. It's not until we start to turn into his neighborhood that I recognize he isn't taking me to my place, but his.

"What are we doing?" I ask, excitement and butterflies in my belly that I refuse to acknowledge.

"Don't worry about it," he says, his face as stoic as ever, his voice grumpy.

"Of course, I'm going to worry about it. That's what I do. I worry about things."

"Well, maybe that's your problem," he says, turning onto his street.

"I have a lot of problems."

"You *are* a problem, Olivia," he says, pulling into his driveway and putting his car into park. Neither of us move.

"Am I your problem though?" I ask, and my voice sounds flirty and fun and not the version of me I'm used to hearing. Andre doesn't respond, though. Instead, he opens his door, steps out, and slams it, a man on a mission, before he walks around the front of the car to me. Then he opens my car door, dipping in to unbuckle me and then grabbing my hand to tug me out of the vehicle.

It's then he moves toward his front door, unlocking it, pulling me in, and slamming it shut. Somehow, he both locks the door and moves me until my back is against the wood, and he's holding me in place, one hand against the door, propping himself up, the other sliding up my neck until it's cupping my chin and forcing me to look at him.

"You're my biggest problem these days." The words are said not with anger or frustration but with awe and reverence, and my body goes weak.

He's staring at me like he wants to devour me, and I *want* that.

I want him to *consume* me.

Except he's told me . . . we're not that, right? There was the kiss in his house, and then later that night, there was the whole making myself come thing, but he was incredibly clear that was a mistake.

Today has been all light touches and handholds and kindness and sweetness for the cameras, but it hasn't been . . . lust and want and need, despite what *I* might feel for him.

Because I want Andre Valenti in a way that is neither fake nor vengeful but equally as dangerous. Because if I give myself to this man who doesn't want me, if I subject myself to the risk of falling once more and I let myself get lost in it, what happens then?

What happens when I've spent the last month and a half digging myself out from under Bradley's influence, finding who I am without the pressure of my mom and my family and everyone else, only to lose myself again?

"I am a careful man, Olivia. I do not do anything without extensive thought, rationalizing. Without mapping out all of the potential outcomes and figuring out how things could go wrong. But no matter how many times I tell myself this can't happen, we can't happen, it always comes back to how I cannot stop thinking about you, how I fucking crave you, how I want nothing more than your skin on mine at all times," he says, his voice low and rumbling.

He could be a rebound, a voice in my head tells me. *Simple as that.*

It makes sense to me.

I kick back the little voice screaming I will never be a no-strings girl, that my emotions run too deep for friends with benefits or a rebound with no expectations.

And instead, I sigh, tipping my head back before meeting his burning eyes.

"What now? You said this wouldn't work, not now. What do we do? Because I'm telling you, Andre, I want you. Badly," I whisper.

And then, with no cameras watching to impress, no audience to put a show on for, just Andre and me and the quiet of his home, he growls two words that change everything.

"Fuck it."

FORTY-ONE

Can too many orgasms kill you?

SATURDAY, OCTOBER 14

The kiss that follows is all-consuming.

Soul shattering.

Breathtaking.

His lips are on mine, capturing my gasp that escapes and stealing any remaining common sense. His tongue moves out, tangling with mine, forcing it into submission as his hands move to my face, and he's kissing me like his life depends on it.

And it feels that way.

It feels like some part of my life, my future, my joy, and my happiness all depend on this kiss. It's life-changing, the kind of thing you look back on and say, *Yes, that was the moment things changed.*

My hand moves to tangle in his hair, loving having the thick strands between my fingers, and I moan as I think about having my fingers in his hair in a different way and how that's not necessarily even out of reach anymore.

The moan pulls a groan from him, and again, the kiss changes. His lips stay on mine as he bends his knees, his hands moving to my thighs and sliding, lifting me up until my legs wrap around his waist, and he pins me to the door, groaning as his cock grinds into my thin leggings.

"Oh god," I whisper.

"Weeks watching you be so fucking pretty, so fucking sweet." His lips move down my neck, and my head tips back to give him room, rolling along the door. "A menace. Teasing and taunting me, showing me what I couldn't have." He moves his hips, grinding into me like he's already fucking me, like he can't wait until we've left this space, can't wait to take off my clothes and touch me.

I groan, tipping my hips to get more.

I would give anything to get more.

"It's yours," I whisper. His lips move up my neck, nipping my jaw and my ear before they're at mine once more, brushing against me with his words.

"What is?"

"Everything. God, whatever you want."

"Fuck, you're perfect," he murmurs, and then he's kissing me again, except my back is no longer against the door and we're moving through the living room, down the hall to his bedroom. There's a noise, I assume from him kicking the door open, but I'm kissing Andre Valenti so what the fuck do I even care?

He breaks the kiss before tossing me on the bed like I weigh absolutely nothing, and I bounce once before settling. My eyes are heavy with lust as he watches me, crossing his arms on his chest and leaning on the wall opposite the bed. I hold myself up with my hands, leaning back and staring at him.

"Off."

"What?" I ask.

"Off. Take your clothes off."

"I—" I start to object.

"And do it slow."

My body goes warm.

Not from his words but from the heat in his eyes, the way they burn on me, the way it feels like he can already see what's behind my clothes and likes it a fuck of a lot.

I smile wantonly.

This is not me.

I am not confidence and undressing for a man and doing it *slow*.

But the way he's looking at me?

Yeah. I think I could be that.

I kick off my boots, knocking them off the side of the bed before sliding down my leggings, leaving me in a small pair of underwear, before sitting up. He's in just his pants, his shirt having been tossed off while I was distracted. I start on the tiny buttons on my shirt, moving slowly and not because I'm following his instruction.

Because now, the nerves are kicking in.

I look down to watch my fingers fumble, breaking my contact with a fully-clothed Andre.

I get one free from its hole finally right before warm hands take over mine.

"I got this," he whispers, pressing his lips to my temple, slowly unbuttoning my shirt, sure fingers grazing my skin as he does in a way that both eases my nerves and fires up my arousal. "There is nothing —I mean nothing, Liv—to be nervous about when it's you and me. This? This thing between us is as natural as breathing. Always has been." Ironically, his words stop my breath, it only starting again as he pushes my shirt off my arms.

"God, you're so fucking perfect," he whispers, pressing his lips to my shoulder then reaching around to my bra, unclasping it and tossing it wherever the shirt went.

Finally, I'm naked in front of him, other than my blue tiny panties. His hand moves from my collarbone, resting where my jaw meets my neck before his thumb presses into my chin, tipping my head until I'm forced to look at him. "Perfect, Olivia," he says.

The sweet words are such a contrast to who he is, brash and frustrating and gloomy, but maybe that's just him with me: sweet as sugar and as comfortable as being wrapped in a soft blanket. A shield from the world, hard as can be on the outside, safe and secure on the inside.

"Back," he whispers, and I shift, leaning back. He moves, grabbing thick pillows and propping me up just enough so I can stare down my body. His hands move to his jeans, undoing the button and fly, pushing both his underwear and pants down, his cock bobbing out. But I don't have time to take him in too long because he's speaking once more.

"These—" His finger hooks under the waist of my panties, sliding back and forth, over and over. "These are driving me fucking wild, Olivia. You, in my bed, panting for me and wearing nothing but these? Fuck. I'll think about this until I die, jack myself off remembering it when I'm fucking eighty." He presses his mouth to the spot right over my underwear and under my belly button, then he runs his tongue along the fabric.

"Oh fuck." His lips purse as he breathes cool air on the wet spot, my pussy clenching at the feeling before he takes a finger and runs it down the center.

"God, you're so wet even like this. These panties? Fucking soaked, Olivia. I can feel it from here."

His finger keeps running up and down the front of my pussy over my panties, and I can't get *air* into my lungs.

How will I handle him touching my skin for real?

"Andre," I whisper.

"I know what you need. I'll give it to you when I'm ready." He moves on the bed so his feet are on the floor, his body bent over the foot of it and his face inches from where I need him most.

"But tell me. What do you *want?*"

"What?"

"I know what you need, Olivia. I know what your body needs, but tell me what you want." His finger moves again over those fucking panties, but this time, it stops over my clit, pressing and rolling.

"Oh fuck."

"Fuck? That's what you want?" I moan as his thumb moves down and presses my panties into my soaked core. "Right here?"

"Ah!" He slowly mimics fucking me, his thumb pressing in barely, then off, then repeating as I squirm.

"Use your big-girl words, little menace. Tell me what you want from me."

My breath stutters before I speak, the words coming out in breathy whispers. My hooded eyes never leave his as I stare at him.

"I want you to fuck me, Andre." I swallow, watching the heat in his eyes burn like he wants to consume me. "Please."

"Fuck you? So you don't want me to finger this pretty pussy first?" The pointer finger of his free hand moves, hooking beneath the fabric and tugging my panties aside gently. "God, look at that. So fucking drenched for me."

"Yes," I say, this time a bit louder. "Finger me. Oh, fuck, please finger me." His finger teases me again in the same way, moving up and down my slit but this time with no barrier. My head falls back with a moan before I look into his eyes again, not wanting to miss a moment of this.

"What about eating you? Do you want that?"

"Yes," I moan, my voice firm now.

I'll take anything he will give me. Anything but this dreadful, spectacular *teasing*.

"Use your manners, Olivia."

"*Please*," I moan, my hips moving infinitesimally.

The hand holding my panties pushes firmly. "Stay. Do not move while I play."

While he plays.

While. He. *Plays.*

And then he leans forward, his tongue swiping my entrance and up, sliding through before wrapping his lips around my clit and sucking.

"Ah!" I shout, a shockwave of pleasure and lust cracking through me before his head is up, his eyes burning, his lips wet.

"Fuck, you taste better than I thought. Goddammit, it should be fucking illegal to be as perfect as you."

"Andre, please." I groan.

I'm already tearing over a precipice, begging to fall, my body a live wire.

"Patience, baby. Patience." His finger moves again, sliding up and down through my wet, lightly circling my clit and moving back down.

Then sliding in slowly, finally.

Just one finger, but the feeling of being filled is exquisite, and I moan loud.

My hips try to move, to get more, but his hand holds me down, holds me still.

"Such a needy fucking girl," he says, and my pussy clenches around the single finger he has in me, unmoving, torturing.

"Andre, please."

"Yes. Beg, baby. Beg for me. Beg for me to give you what you want, and if you do it really, *really* well, I'll give you everything you need."

I moan because his words are wrapped around my throat and my body and my soul. Maybe that's all that can come out.

A desperate moan.

"Come on, my little menace. You won't tell anyone what you want ever, but you sure as fuck will when you're in my bed." His finger is a taunt I clamp around again, dying for more, for movement, but stunned into silence.

Then it crooks.

His finger crooks so barely, so briefly, but it sends a shockwave through me.

"Fuck, fuck, fuck." My hips buck to get more, to force him to give me more or maybe take it, but again, the finger stops.

Then, it slides out, leaving me so fucking empty. It makes slow, soft circles around my entrance, so slow I almost wonder if he's moving at all. "What do you want?" he asks.

"You! I want you. God, Andre, please."

"How do you want me? How should I make you come this first time?" His finger continues with the slow circles, sending me spiraling in panic.

But I don't miss the promise.

This first time.

God, he's going to be the death of me.

"I won't be doing anything until you tell me exactly what you want."

Somehow, I know that's the truth. He won't do anything beyond this nearly painful teasing until I tell him exactly what I want.

In explicit detail.

And I'm shocked when I *want* to do it. When my legs spread farther to give him room, I say, "Fuck me with two fingers, Andre."

When they slide in, stretching and filling me, I groan with both satisfaction and gratification, a strange pride welling in me. He starts to move, sliding them in and out, and heat starts to bloom in the small of my back.

"Fuck, it's so good." I moan, gripping the comforter in my hands, arching my back in pleasure.

"Jesus Christ, you're a goddess, Olivia. Tell me what else you need," he says on his knees, naked before me, two fingers in my pussy.

Serving me.

At my will.

Never in my life have I felt so fucking powerful. So sexy, so *wanted.*

And somehow, I know this is what he wanted. This is why he pushed me past my discomfort and made me tell him what I want, want I need. Because he wanted me to feel this.

It's beautiful, really, if you think about it.

"Finger fuck me and rub my clit and make me come," I say, the demand firm and so unlike me.

"Goddamn," he murmurs to himself, but then he does just that. His fingers start moving, crooking to swipe my G-spot with each and every thrust, pressing me perfectly, his thumb rounding my clit over and over and over until I'm so close to the edge, I have to let my eyes drift shut, my head tip back, my back arch just a bit. My fingers move, ghosting over my belly before landing on my nipples, gripping them between my pointer and thumb and twisting and pulling, trying to relieve the way I'm so oversensitized, so on edge, trying to find the right movement to tip the scale and make me break.

"God, look at you, playing with your tits. I know I'm serving you right now, but fuck if it doesn't feel good to know it's all for me. You're all for me. Aren't you, little menace?" His warm voice rolls through me, my pussy clenching as I tiptoe closer to the edge but not dropping off.

When a sharp crack hits my inner thigh, his free hand slapping me there, my eyes open, meeting his.

I pulse with my need for release.

"Tell me you're mine, Olivia. Tell me I rule your body, rule this cunt."

That's what it takes.

A mix of his words and the slap that is now hot and warm and so close to my core and the look in his eyes—I fall.

"I'm yours!" I shout, then my back arches off the bed as I shatter for him, as I come apart, falling into a million little pieces, some I don't think I'll ever get back.

Pieces that will be Andre's forever.

"That's it, baby, ride my fingers like a good girl." He groans, his eyes leaving mine to look to where his fingers have stopped fucking me because my hips have taken over, moving with a mind of their own. His thumb still continues its torture of swiping, and even though the orgasm faded, it starts right back up.

"Fuck, fuck me, Andre, please, holy shit." I can't function.

I can't think.

I surely can't come again, that's for sure.

"Not yet," he says. "Again."

Again?

I'll cease to exist.

But it's in my belly already, building and swirling, the ball of tension growing quicker now that the first orgasm is out of the way, like it was a reminder to my body of the glory of a good orgasm and how to get there.

"Andre, I—"

"Again, Olivia," he says, his voice firm, and then he slides in a third finger.

The stretch.

The fullness.

The way his eyes droop just a bit and his mouth opens as he watches me take his fingers.

It builds.

Fuck, it *builds*.

"That's it. There you go," he says, his voice a rough growl, and I could come like this right now, nothing more, and I almost do, but then . . .

His free hand moves to his cock, and he starts to pump himself in time with the thrusts on his fingers, watching me take him, and I hold off.

I need to experience this for a moment longer.

"Fuck, you like that, don't you. Watching me jack myself off while I try and get you off. Fuck. You were made for me, my menace."

"Oh god, Oh god. Fuck. This is . . . Oh shit," I ramble, and then the wave hits again, slamming into my belly, my mouth opening in a silent scream as he continues to move his fingers.

"So fucking tight, Jesus. God. Need to fuck you, Liv." He groans, and as I fall down from my high, as I go limp, he removes his fingers from me.

"Clean these," he orders, putting his fingers in front of my mouth, and though I haven't even caught my breath, I clench again with need already. My head moves, my eyes locking with his as I stick out my tongue and begin to lick my wetness off his fingers. "That's my girl," he says to himself. I continue my work as he moves closer to me, spreading my thighs farther, making room for himself.

And then he's there, his cock bumping against me, my hips moving to try and get something, anything.

His wet fingers move, and he grabs his cock with a groan before he's running the head along my pussy. My hips buck, my body trying to get him where I need him.

"You're on something, yeah?"

"What?" I ask, confused and lost and not understanding. Words don't work when he's hovering over me, cock in hand, it seems.

"Birth control, Olivia. You're on it?"

"I, uh, yeah."

"I'm tested regularly, haven't been with anyone since my last a few months ago." I pause, trying to get my brain to wire correctly to have this conversation.

"I, uh. After the breakup. I'm good."

"So I can fuck you bare?" he asks, his cock running up and down my slit. "Because I really want to come in this cunt, Olivia."

Oh my fucking god, I think.

"Is that a yes?" he asks, and I guess I said that out loud.

"Yes, god, please." I moan.

And then I get a smile.

An Andre Valenti smile, and I would take the time to appreciate a *naked Andre Valenti* smile, except then he's sliding into me and my head is tipping back as I moan out his name.

"Holy fuck," he groans, the words shaking me to my bones as he slides in until his hips are against mine, and he stops, leaving me full of him.

I'm *so fucking full.* His cock is thick, stretching me in the most delicious, heart-pounding way, and I can't think past the throbbing in my cunt, past the way he fits so fucking perfectly inside of me.

"Fuck, you feel good, Olivia," he says again.

I can't answer.

I can barely open my eyes.

Until, of course, his hand moves, taking my leg by the knee and sliding it up, up, up until it's over his shoulder, letting him in even deeper, the angle even better.

"Holy fuck, oh god." I moan.

My entire body starts to spiral again as I go light-headed with pleasure, as he slowly slides out of me and then slams back, body shaking with the movement.

"Look at this, Olivia. Right fucking now. Watch me fuck you." I can't ignore his words so I do, forcing my eyes to open and stare where we're joined. The way I'm positioned, one leg spread wide, the other over his shoulder, means I get the most impeccable view of his cock sliding in then back out coated in me. With each thrust, I can both see and hear his balls slap against my ass, can feel the way he slams in deep.

He's splitting me in two, and I wish I could stay here, teetering on this edge for fucking ever.

I let my eyes roll, let them watch his body, all tan skin and muscles and sweat glistening from his efforts. I watch his face, his firm jaw, the way his head is tipped to stare at where we're joined, his hair falling over his forehead, and goddamn.

"That's it, Liv, fall. Fuck. Fall for me."

"I can't. I want—"

I try to tell him I want to watch.

Or maybe I want him to come, too.

I don't know.

Because his hand moves to my knee not over his shoulder, gripping it firmly in a way that will absolutely leave bruises and tugging to the side, opening me farther, letting him get even deeper.

Then his free hand grabs my hand roughly, placing it over where he's fucking me.

"For the love of fuck, Olivia, make yourself come for me."

I have no choice.

None at all.

First, I slide my hand down, my pointer and middle fingers splitting so I can feel his cock sliding there as it enters me, and I groan at the feel, at his thickness, his throbbing. Then I slide back up and rub my clit, hard.

It doesn't take long, just a few rough swipes as he pounds into me before I'm screaming his name, coming apart harder than anything I've ever experienced.

My vision goes black with small specks of white as I do, like when you stand up too quickly and get light-headed, but when I come back, I realize he stopped.

He waited for me to come back to earth so that I can watch his head tip back, his neck go long and lean, so I can see every corded muscle on his body as he groans my name, pumps in deep, and comes inside, throbbing as he fills me, just like he promised.

Long moments pass as he comes back down, my pussy still clamping on him, my body no longer in my control.

Finally, he pulls out, breathing heavily, breaths mirroring my own, and I can't help but think that my life will never be the same after tonight.

Not because I slept with Andre, which, yes, was life-changing, but because I came so fucking hard and so fucking often, my pussy still throbbing with the need for just *one more release*.

There's no way to recreate that.

For the rest of my life, every other person on this planet will never live up to this experience.

I expect Andre to roll over, to wait for our breathing to regulate, for both of us to come down from this high, but as seems to be his way, he surprises me.

He moves down the bed, crawling, then uses a finger to run through my wet, swollen pussy, groaning as he does.

"Jesus fuck, just look at this. You're full of me, aren't you?" He's not really talking to me, mostly to himself like he's proud of his handiwork, and as his finger circles my swollen clit, my entire body reacts, flinching before melting, the ball of tension building in my belly again almost instantly.

"Shit," I whisper under my breath.

"One more, Olivia."

One more? How?

"Andre, I can't—"

"You can," he insists, and he sounds so fucking sure of himself. A finger slides into me, and I moan at the feeling.

He groans as he feels me, feels himself inside me. I lift my hips, and his finger moves back to my clit. "Come on, babe. Let's go. Come for me one more fuckin' time." His fingers start to move back and forth, on a mission of sorts, until my hips are lifting, the tension in my belly building and building and *building* until I'm almost there, the feeling taking over me again.

It's then I wonder if you can die like this.

Death by orgasm.

I wonder if I even care.

"Let go, Olivia," he says, his voice firm, and that's it. That's what takes me over the edge.

Not his fingers and not the speed or the pressure or the look of utter fascination on his face.

His fucking words have me tumbling over the cliff, moaning his name as my eyes drift shut, as the wave crashes over me and warmth overtakes me.

It's not as big as the last one but no less sweet, no less all-consuming.

I'm smiling as I come back down, my eyes opening in search of him.

But he's not looking at me.

Instead, he's staring at my pussy, his eyes intense and burning.

"God, just look at that. Look at you, wet as hell and dripping with my cum." He tsks like I'm a naughty schoolgirl who broke the rules. "That just won't do. Not at all."

And then a thick finger is pressing inside me again.

"Oh god, fuck, no, Andre—"

"I'm done with you for now, menace." The finger moves out and then presses in, seeming to collect something as he does.

It's then, I know.

"This time—the first time I have you, you're keeping all of me in you."

A thrill runs through me, and Andre smiles when he watches me get it, watches it click for me.

He's pushing his cum back into me.

"Mmm, much better," he says then leans down, pressing his lips to my clit one last time before crawling back up my body.

Holy.

Fucking.

Shit.

I was right.

I will never *ever* be the same.

FORTY-TWO

What happens when you like-like your fake boyfriend?

SATURDAY, OCTOBER 14

He's quiet for long, long minutes after I clean up and get back into the bed with him, and despite how languid and loose my body feels, old habits build in my gut, thoughts and second-guessing and panic swirling and swirling.

Because even though he's so fucking grumpy, sometimes I look over him to check if there's a rain cloud following him overhead, and even though we are so very different, it doesn't make any sense, I like Andre.

I like him as a person.

I like him as a friend.

I like how he forces me to look at things both within myself and within my relationships and friendships and question them. He makes me want to be a better version of myself *for* myself.

He's made me believe I deserve that.

So as I lie on his chest overthinking, listening to his slow, steady heartbeat, his fingers gently brushing up and down my back in a way I wish he would do until I died, I let my anxieties win and speak.

"This doesn't . . . This doesn't have to change everything," I say, my voice shaky even to my own ears.

I'm terrified he'll use this as a reason to put distance between us, to step away from a friendship I'm coming to value greatly.

Or maybe this was all he needed to sate some curiosity, and then he'll disappear as quickly as he came into my life.

"What?" The word is a low rumble on my ear I feel more than I hear.

"This. Us. It doesn't have to change anything. We can still . . ." God, this sounds stupid and desperate and annoying even in my head, but I know Andre and I've started, so now I need to continue. "Be friends. You can still be my bodyguard. This doesn't have to change that. This can be just . . . you know. A one-time thing."

A rebound, I almost say before that rumble comes back, filling the room with the dark cloud that follows him. His irritation and anger feel like they're everywhere, taking over, and my panic builds with them.

"This isn't one time, Livi."

Livi.

God.

Sweet.

It's the first time he's said it, my nickname everyone else uses for me, the name he has never said coming out for the first time in this intimate space after what we just shared.

But his words . . .

"What?"

"Do you really think I'd let you get away?" My brows come together. I'm confused and unsure of how to respond.

"I don't . . . I don't understand."

"Fought this, I fought *you* for a long fucking time, my little menace. Did that because I knew." He makes a noise that is half sigh, half chuckle. "Fuck, I knew if I had you, there was no way in hell I would be satisfied with once."

My mind tries to process his words, his fingers still working their lulling magic on my back.

"I originally convinced myself you're a spoiled brat, silver spoon and all that." I open my mouth to argue, but he continues, his free hand now moving to my hair, pushing it over and aside repeatedly. "Then I thought you were still wrapped in Reed. I told myself it was too soon. Then I told myself even if you *were* over him, even if you were never really *in* with him, that this was work, that I needed to separate the two."

Suddenly, he moves us so I'm forced to look at him, his eyes dark and meaningful.

"And then I kissed you at that mountain and I knew then. I knew I would do anything, tell myself any kind of lies I needed to, to make you mine."

"Andre—"

"This is going to be complicated, Olivia. I won't lie and tell you that it won't. The press, the bodyguard shit, your mom. But now that I've had you, I'm not letting you go." Time passes as I try and remember how to argue, how to make common sense win.

I can't.

Because with him, all I can think about is *my happiness*.

How when I'm with him, I'm closer to the version of me I'm chasing, the version of me that's been hidden for so long.

Because not only does Andre put me first—but he teaches me to put myself first, too.

"I have a lot of baggage," I whisper, my fingers reaching up to touch the line in his eyebrow, proof of how my baggage could hurt him.

"Good thing I'm strong," is all he says.

"My mom's going to hate you," I admit."

"Good thing I'm not dating your mother then, right?" I smile wide.

My entire chest feels like it's filled with Champagne, bubbles rising and popping with joy, the effervescence of it making me light-headed.

"I'm going to make you cut down a Christmas tree. And go to strawberry festivals and probably plant a garden in your yard. Which, of course, means you'll have to lug around dirt and dig holes because as much as I like the idea of a garden, I don't like the idea of manual labor."

"You're a pain in my ass, you know that?"

"Sorry, I am what I am."

His fingers move from my back to my hair, using a light grip to force me to look at him.

"God, look at how far you've come. I am so fucking proud of you. The Olivia I met in August would have apologized and felt bad. This one? The one who says *I am who I am* and expects me to either deal or move on? God. You can be a pain in my ass every fucking day if this is the woman I get."

My heart beats, and my mouth opens and closes as I try and figure out how to respond, but I don't get the chance because his eyes go teasing, breaking the tension.

"Plus, this ass?" There's a smile in his voice now as his hand reaches down and grabs my butt. "Definitely need to fuck that eventually. So, I'll return the favor at some point. Be a pain in *your* ass." I gasp, moving to get away from him, but he doesn't let me, instead rolling until I'm pinned under him, his grin wide and handsome, his hair falling forward as he stares at me.

"Uh, no. I would like to be able to sit, thank you very much." He moves to stroke a thumb over my cheek.

"Oh, don't worry. We'll prep you good and well before that happens. You, my little menace, will absolutely love it. Having my cock deep inside you, my chest on your back, my fingers on your clit . . ." His voice goes rough before he trails off, and my heart stutters, my pussy clenches despite the fact I came not long ago.

I never ever thought that would be something I would even consider, but with Andre? The way he's speaking, the way he's looking at me?

"I'd never hurt you, Olivia."

There's a promise there that has nothing to do with anal sex or ass pain but something so much more.

I'd never hurt you, Olivia.

I know in my heart of hearts, down to my toes, to the depths of my soul, he means that.

Andre Valenti would rather take a bullet than hurt me.

My hand lifts, moving up and up and up before I brush my thumb over the split in his eyebrow, the area definitely going to scar.

A forever reminder of me coming into his life and making things difficult for him.

"I'd take a million cuts and bruises and run-ins, and I'd do it over and over again if I got this one moment with you, Olivia. You are so, so worth it."

And you know what?

For the first time in my life, I'm starting to believe it.

FORTY-THREE

SATURDAY, OCTOBER 28

She's off.

I can't tell if it's because she's nervous because I'm going to meet her friends or because this is our first official outing without the guise between us that I'm her bodyguard, but either way, she's off.

It's been two weeks since I gave into the pull Olivia has on me, gave into the unreliable connection. Two weeks since I said *fuck it*. I don't regret it. Not in the least.

I'm shocked I lasted as long as I did, shocked I was strong enough for so long without giving in to her.

I do regret that in two weeks, the only progress we've made on Liv's case is, I think, nailing down all of the countries and *potentially* the bank names of the overseas accounts Reed opened in Liv's name. Unfortunately, without the account numbers or an ironclad warrant, there's no chance of us accessing and recovering those funds.

"You make a good Pink Lady," I say, stepping up behind her in the bathroom mirror. She's leaned forward, carefully applying a bright-red lipstick that I know will be on me by the end of the night.

I can't find it in me to care.

Last week, she spent an hour on the couch with me, her legs

draped over my lap while I watched a game, scrolling through her phone to find what she deemed the perfect couples costume for a guy who wouldn't be caught dead in a couples costume.

A fair assessment.

I didn't tell her I would have worn whatever the fuck she asked me to if it meant it made her happy.

But it worked because after scrapping some old couple from a Disney movie, an officer and an inmate (that one hit way too close to home), and a dog and cat, we landed on a Pink Lady and a T-Bird.

Now, she's in a pair of shiny black pants (*"Pleather,* Andre," she had said in her voice that makes it clear she thinks I'm just a stupid, silly man) hugging every part of her ass and a black top that leaves her shoulders bare and a scarf around her neck. There's a little pink jacket as well, draped over the couch. I lucked out with just a black tee and a pair of jeans and a gallon of junk in my hair, but I'll take it.

"Thank you," she says, her voice low and quiet, still so unlike her, as she caps the lipstick and then stands straight. "You ready to head out?"

We're on our way to Schmidt and Martinez's Halloween party slash fundraiser, and while a week ago she was ecstatic about the event, now she's ho-hum at best.

"What's wrong?" I ask finally.

She doesn't even look confused when she asks, "What? Nothing."

"Olivia, what's wrong?" She shakes her head and moves to walk around me.

"Nothing's wrong, Andre, but we do have to go so we're not late. I *hate* being late," she says, and that's true at least. God forbid Olivia ever feels like she's being a nuisance to someone else, ever feels like she'd be letting someone down.

I grab her wrist before she can get far, tugging her until my arm can wrap around her waist.

"Don't kiss me; you'll smudge my lipstick," she whispers.

"Like I care."

"I do."

"And I care about how you're quiet and shifty and avoiding my eyes." She rolls those big hazel eyes I can never stop looking in, trying to brush me off, and I groan. "Olivia, what is *wrong*?"

"Andre—"

"Something is wrong. You can trick your friends and your mom and your dad all you want, tell them until you're blue in the face nothing is wrong when something clearly is, but you won't do it with me. I see through your bullshit, Liv. Now tell me, what has you so far into your own head?" A few beats pass, and I'm sure she's going to move right past it, lie again and say nothing, so it's a surprise when she speaks.

"It's Halloween," she says. The words don't make any sense to me. I mean, yes, it's Halloween, but that's not . . .

And then I remember.

We can break up at the Halloween party.

Back when this wasn't real, back when I was playing bodyguard and fake boyfriend to help with her self-made paparazzi issues, we were supposed to end tonight. It was all supposed to be pretend, and now . . .

"This was our original last day."

That lip she was so worried about smudging goes into her mouth, little white teeth leaving indents there. She doesn't say anything, but she doesn't have to.

My girl.

My fucking girl, so good and kind and sweet, has probably been worried about this day for a week. Longer, if I know her the way I think I do, but she never wanted to ask because that would make her look needy. Would make her a burden, a nuisance.

God, we have so much work to do to get her head on straight.

I sigh then use my hands, moving them both to her waist before lifting her up, turning, and placing her on the bathroom countertop. Her pleather pants squeak on the quartz, but I ignore that as my hand moves to her chin, gripping it and tipping it up so she has to look at me again.

"How long?"

"What?" she asks, confused.

"How long have you been stressed about this?"

She doesn't answer, trying to divert her eyes, and I give my head a small shake.

"You gotta learn to talk to me, Olivia. We'll work on it, but you have to *learn* to *talk to me*. If you're anxious about something, tell me. If you're worried about our relationship, *tell me*."

"I didn't want to seem like a crazy girlfriend, and he—" Her eyes water, and it cuts me somewhere I don't think will heal, tiny lacerations given to me as a constant reminder of the people who have hurt my girl.

"He?" I say, and she knows who I mean. Reed. "He was a jackass. If he gave you shit for speaking with him about your concerns, your worries, your stress then fuck him even more. I thought I hated him, but it gets worse every day, Olivia. You and me? The way we work is you *talk to me*. The way you heal is you let the people who care about you help you through things."

"You—"

"Don't play dumb," I say, knowing her question before she asks it. "You know I care for you. You know that. But this? This is not over tonight. Tomorrow, I'm going to wake up with you in my bed, and I'm going to eat your sweet pussy and then fuck you senseless, and then I'm going to watch you sway your ass into my kitchen and make some wildly convoluted coffee drink—"

"It's not—"

"It is, but I like it. I like *you*, Liv. That's it. I would be crazy to end things right now. We stopped being that a long time ago."

"I don't want you to feel obligated. To feel locked into something you don't—"

"I wouldn't have had you if I wanted anything other than this. I would never have fucked you, Olivia. You wouldn't be waking up in my bed most mornings. I wouldn't be keeping the crazy oat milk bullshit you like if I were just holding out for Halloween so we could make some kind of scene and end things. No way."

It happens then.

Her body relaxes.

Her mind eases.

It's like the words finally go through and she sees it, understands it.

Thank fuck.

"Do you understand?" I ask, pushing her hair over her bare shoulders, my hands skimming down her arms until I'm twining our fingers together.

"You . . . You want to be my boyfriend for real?"

"I hate the word boyfriend, but for you? Yeah. I'll be whatever you want me to be."

Then, she smiles.

And it's one of her rare ones, the kind she does when she's totally free, when she's not worried about anything, about anyone—not their feelings or their judgment or anything, when she's fully and completely the version of Livi that is *all Olivia.*

They seem to be coming more and more often, and they never stop taking my breath away.

"Oh. Okay," she says, and I shake my head.

"You're a pain in my ass, you know."

That makes her smile widen.

"Tell me about it, stud," she says in a breathy voice, and I stare at her for a full minute, trying to figure out what the fuck kind of malfunction she just had, watching her face slowly contort with confusion, a reaction to mine.

"You know. *Grease?* At the end, where Sandy . . ." She stares at me. "Oh my god, you've never seen *Grease.*"

"Do I look like the kind of man who watches 70s musicals?"

"We are *so* watching it tomorrow."

"We are so not."

"We are," she says with a smile.

And it's clear then that we both know the truth.

We are watching *Grease* tomorrow, even if I might gouge my eyes out while it happens.

Because what Olivia Anderson wants, I'm going to give her.

So if Olivia wants to watch *Grease* together, that's what we'll be watching.

FORTY-FOUR

How do you avoid getting the ick?

SATURDAY, OCTOBER 28

"Oh my god," Kat says, watching her newest boyfriend over at the self-serve bar on the other side of the room.

The party is, as ever, absolutely stunning, Cami and her team planning it spectacularly, from decor to music to the specialty food and drinks being walked around. My end of this job, alerting the press, sending invites to the right influential people, and making it *the place to be seen,* means tomorrow morning, everything about this party will be plastered *everywhere,* giving quite a boost to the Schmidt and Martinez Foundation.

"What?" I ask, but I should know by now. I've known Kat for almost three years, and I've heard of this phenomenon but never witnessed it. Cami and Abbie give each other a knowing look.

"Goddammit," she says under her breath, and it's weird to watch what I've been told about happen right in front of me. To watch any molecule of attraction to the man she'd been dating for about a month leave her body.

"No! One more date!" Abbie says, irritation in her voice.

"Ten dollars, Abs," Cami says with a smile, putting her hand out.

"Did you guys *bet* on how long my relationship would last?" Kat asks with exasperation.

"Not—" Abbie starts.

"Yes," Cami says outright.

"Are you guys kidding me?" Her shoulders drop, a deep sigh leaves her chest, and a look of sadness, or maybe frustration, passes over her face.

"What was it this time?" Abbie asks. Kat scrunches her nose, looking over at the man again and shaking her head with a final sigh.

"He put the drink in first, *then* added ice." I look to Cami, confused. "With his *hands*." Confusion turns to a cringe.

"Oh, gross," Cami says.

"Goddammit, now I'll have to switch the ice out," Abbie says.

"Don't worry about it. He didn't grab it from the ice bucket. He grabbed it from the cooler with the drinks," Kat says with a shake of her head. "Dammit. I thought he had . . . potential."

"Wasn't he wearing socks with sandals when you met him?"

"I thought it was quirky!"

"What was quirky?" Damien asks, coming to the group once more with Andre, who walks over, wrapping an arm around my waist.

"Kat's ick kicked in," Abbie says as if that explains everything, and it does in a way.

"Ahh, got it."

"Ick?" Andre asks, and I lean farther into him.

"Kat never dates a guy for more than seven dates."

"Never?" His brow furrows, that spot on his eyebrow that hasn't grown back catching my eye and making me smile.

"Never. She gets the ick before then."

"The ick." He clearly doesn't understand what I'm saying.

"You know, something really random that makes her instantly unattracted to a guy."

"Like . . ."

He waits for me to fill in, but Cami jumps in first. I'm pretty sure talking about Kat's ick factor is one of her favorite pastimes. "Like, once it was a guy who sang the girl's part of a Broadway song in the car."

"Look, if you're having a sing-along and you have one guy and one girl, obviously you should *take turns*," Kat says in an attempt to justify.

"And one time, there was a guy who only drank hot coffee." That's Abbie, a small smile of her own on her lips.

"It was, like, a hundred degrees out!"

"And the guy who called her *little girl* in bed." Believe it or not, this time, it's Damien jumping in.

"It just isn't my thing!" Kat says, hands on her hips.

"You literally made him stop mid-thrust and walk out of your apartment," Cami says, not bothering to fight her laugh anymore. My dad is by her side, and if you had told me a few years ago I'd be at a party with my dad talking about sex and not instantly cringing, I would never have believed you.

But life has a way of surprising you, and here we are.

"I wasn't going to let him finish. I surely wasn't going to get off, so why should he?"

Cici's date makes a face, and before I can stop him, before I can give Cici a look of warning, he opens his mouth and speaks as men are wont to do.

Unfortunately.

"I don't know. Sounds like maybe your standards are too high, you know?"

Heads turn to the man who is, at best, *mildly* good-looking but not good-looking enough to justify being a douche.

"What?" Cami says.

My dad's arm wraps her waist and I fight a smile, knowing he's preparing to hold her back if needed.

"It's just . . . you know. You're not perfect." Cami's mouth drops open, her eyes closing and opening in a slow blink, clearly unsure of what to say.

"Did that just happen?" Abbie says in a stage whisper.

"I think so," Kat says. Shock is on both of their faces, rightfully so.

"You know, Cici. Maybe this would be a good time for *you* to get . . . the ick." The way Andre says the word ick kills me, like he's not fully sure he's using it correctly, but I don't have time to sit on it when the guy speaks *again*.

"Fuck off, man. Come on, Cici. Let's go dance or something."

"I think," Cici says, stepping over toward me. "I think I'm going to take Danny Zuko's advice."

"What the fuck?"

"You should probably head out," she says, "You were my plus one, and I . . . am happy to be a 'one' right now."

"Are you kidding me?"

"I think she was extremely clear," Andre says, stepping forward and in front of me and Cici.

"Who the fuck do you think you are? Look, get out of my way so I can talk to my date."

He looks from the douche to Damien, who shrugs, some kind of unspoken man conversation happening between them.

"I think I'm the guy who's about to see you out, man."

"The fuck you—"

And then Andre is grabbing him by the back of his shirt and tugging, leading him toward the exit. Damien and my dad move as well, following behind in case he needs help, but it becomes increasingly clear Andre does *not*.

His arms flex as he moves, barely using any strength, it seems, despite the man trying to stop him from escorting him out.

"Oh my god, that is so hot," Cami whispers.

"Definitely *not* an ick," Kat says.

"Yeah," is all I can say, my eyes fixed on the group of men until they're out of our view.

"Holy shit," I whisper finally, staring at the door they disappeared through.

"I need a drink," Abbie says, fanning herself. "Anyone else?"

"Me!" Cici says, and then we go about our night like the douche canoe never even interrupted it at all.

●●●

Two hours later, I'm three drinks in and already ready to leave. Not because I don't absolutely adore my friends and family, but mostly because the way Andre looks in his costume and the way his hands keep brushing my ass, the way his rough thumb keeps swiping the spot where my pants don't quite meet my shirt . . .

I need to get out of here.

And the opportunity to head out without disappointing anyone comes, whether I like it or not, when Abbie and Damien walk over to us, Damien's face firm, Abbie chewing her bottom lip.

"Hey, what's up?" I ask.

"The front entrance has a dozen or so paparazzi. Expected, but unexpected is . . ." Damien starts before pausing. "They're out there for you two."

"For us?" I ask, confused.

Of course, Andre gets it.

"That scumbag reached out to someone?" I roll my eyes when Damien nods.

"What a fucking douche. He gets his ass handed to him so he *calls the paparazzi?*" I say.

"It doesn't matter," Andre says with a shake of his head and a squeeze of my hand. "All that matters is getting you out of here safely.

"There's a back entrance we can show you, but unfortunately, the parking garage only has one main exit." I sigh.

"That's fine. Menace, you go say your goodbyes. I'll talk to Damien." I open my mouth to argue. "Not now, Liv. Please. Go say your goodbyes."

With the look on his face, I don't even bother to argue, instead moving to my tiptoes, pressing a kiss to his lips, and doing as he asked.

When we get back to his place after taking the most contrived way home to try and make sure no one followed us, he walks me to the door.

"Get inside, lock this door. I'm going to go make sure the area is safe, that no one followed us," he says as he walks me inside.

"It's not that serious, Andre. Honestly." My hands move to his chest, sliding up and looping around his neck.

"Humor me, okay?" he says then bows his head, pressing his lips to the spot beneath my ear. "And when I come back, I want you naked."

A shiver runs down my back.

"Deal."

FORTY-FIVE

What do you do when you realize your boyfriend is stalking you?

SATURDAY, OCTOBER 28

The door slams behind him, and I only have time to take one step before it opens again, Andre's stern face peeking in.

"Lock this door, Liv."

"I was working on it! I can't move at the speed of light like some people." I give him a chiding look, and he rolls his eyes at me before shaking his head.

"Lock it," he says. I smile. And then, like he can't stop himself, he shakes his head once more, steps inside, grabs me by the back of my neck, and pulls me in closer, pressing his lips to mine. "You drive me out of my mind, you know?"

"I know," I whisper, words barely working before he steps back, leaving me dazed as usual.

"Door. Lock it."

"Got it."

"Now, Liv."

"You're kind of still in the house, babe." He shakes his head.

"Menace." The word makes me smile. Finally, he steps back, closing the door, and I slide the lock on the knob and then the dead-bolt right after he steps out.

●●●

Looking around his living room, I decide a drink would be good, especially if I'm expected to be naked when he walks back into his house. Unfortunately, I've never actually served myself here, so that requires me opening and closing a million and seven cabinets until I give up and move to the fridge, where I find a cider.

Four hard ciders, to be more specific, a variety, like he went to a liquor store and bought them individually. And they're next to a six-pack of beer.

It makes me smile, the way he does this kind of stuff, little moments telling me he pays attention.

Unfortunately, it's not a screw top, so once again, I start opening drawers, looking for a bottle opener. Considering I grew up in a bar, technically, I could manage without, but I also don't need to be denting and dinging Andre's countertops. Once I find one and take off the top, I give into my Cami-esque desire to snoop because how often do you get left alone at your new boyfriend's place.

Opening the first door I see, I come face-to-face with a clothes closet, two jackets hung on a rail and a few pairs of shoes scattered at the bottom. Nothing interesting.

Closing the door, I move to the one I've always wondered about, the one that is *always* closed, mostly because this time, it's gently cracked open, like he meant to close it but was in a rush or something. I enter, seeing a desk on one side with multiple computer monitors, all blacked out, and a few filing cabinets.

Walking to the desk, though, I forget all about snooping in them.

Because on top of the desk is a navy folder.

A navy folder with my name scrawled across it.

I stare at it for a long moment, blinking once, then twice, trying to decide if I'm just so full of myself I'm starting to see things or if there's really a folder on his desk with *Olivia Anderson* written on it.

I place my hand on my chest, trying to see if my heart is fully outside of my body with the way it's beating.

But no, it's still safely inside.

My hand is trembling when I reach for it.

Somehow, I know this is bad.

Well, obviously, your name on a folder on a desk at the guy you're dating's house isn't a *good* thing, but still.

I contemplate leaving it, walking out and running, for a millisecond before lifting the cover of the folder with shaky hands. When I do, I immediately want to throw up.

A photo of me is paper-clipped to an info sheet with . . . everything about me written on it.

My full name.

My address.

My parents' names, Huxley's, even Cami's.

My school history, my fucking social security number.

Nausea climbs up my throat, sharp nails digging as I take out the top page and flip it.

Photos.

Photos of me.

Walking into work, into my apartment building. At lunch with Cami and Cici.

With Bradley.

Some of these—stealthy surveillance photos in black and white—are six, eight months old.

Long before I met Andre, that's for sure.

There goes any hope of justifying it away, of saying it was something he got from Garden State when I hired him. I flip to the next pages, bank statements with my name on them, lists of banks in different countries. Accounts I've never seen or heard of.

My trust, maybe?

Scanning, I try and find my mom's or my grandfather's name on it to understand where this money is, whose it is, where it came from.

And there's more.

More bank accounts, all with substantial amounts of money, all with my name on them. But looking closer, I notice they aren't actually bank statements but something else. Assumed bank accounts with estimated amounts of money in each.

What the fuck is this?

Flipping again, nausea grows for a third time, this time all-consuming, and I move quickly out of the room before throwing up into the kitchen garbage can. I heave and heave, trying to catch my breath, trying to understand reality. I go back and grab the folder, bringing it into the light of the kitchen as I continue my reading.

The next page is all me.

Screenshots from social media, from my computer. My search history.

All of it goes back months. Some almost a full year ago.

Moving back to the folder once I catch my breath, I slowly and meticulously move each paper, lining them up on the table so I can see everything, the invasion of privacy, the . . .

The *accusations*.

Slowly, I start to understand, though not completely.

Bradley isn't just an asshole, isn't just a gaslighting ass who never gave a shit about me.

No, he's a thief.

He's been slowly siphoning off money from the investments he makes for clients, scattering the funds across bank accounts, both domestic and international.

And quite a fucking bit of them are in my name.

How?

When?

And *who the fuck is Andre?*

So many moments hit me, moments that, with this new context, start to make more sense.

Him living across the street from Bradley, us *running into* each other that day.

It wasn't some great kismet, that's for sure.

Andre showing up when I was at the coffee shop, the way he fit so well into my life and accepted me so easily. His underlying, unexplained hatred for Bradley. I thought it was an exaggeration, it was just because he was so into me and hated I had been put through that, but . . .

That's not it. It's not that at all.

It was all a lie, and just like with Bradley, I was too stupid and wrapped up in him to realize.

And with that realization, the door opens.

FORTY-SIX

how to delete your search history 🔍

SATURDAY, OCTOBER 28

I think about leaving, about running home and not looking back, about ignoring his calls and avoiding him for all eternity, but what would be the point of that?

Apparently, he'll find me no matter where I go.

"Liv?" he asks, his voice genuinely confused, my back to the door as I face his kitchen table.

I turn, and I know there's venom on my face, that it's laced in my words. I feel it in my veins, coursing, burning, dying to get out.

"Oh, so I'm Liv now?" His brow furrows as he locks the door behind him, walking closer to me. His eyes move to the table behind me, and he gets it then.

He understands.

"Olivia—"

"Ah, there it is. The full name. Because we're not *friends,* right?"

"Olivia—" I cut him off again.

"No, I'm just a subject, an investigation." I shake my head, the venom turning into a hard, painful lump in my throat. "God, I'm so fucking stupid."

He walks closer to me, and I shout:

"No. No! You do not come closer to me. I don't need you in my space." I'm appeased when he stops, but also shocked, if I'm being honest.

"Please, let me explain." God, it sounds so cliché, such an expected statement that I actually laugh.

It's better than the alternate reaction.

"Fuck explaining, Andre." Then I pause, thinking. "Oh my god. If that's your name!" The panic takes over as I try and come to terms with everything in this short span of time.

"It's my name. My name is Andre Valenti. Nothing is . . . Nothing is different. Please, just talk to me." His eyes are soft, pleading, even, but the betrayal cuts through that.

"*Nothing is different?!* Everything is different, Andre!"

"If you would just—"

"No," I say, my words final before I look around.

I need to move. I need my bag, my phone.

I need to get out.

I need to get a cab, to go somewhere.

I need to reevaluate my *entire fucking life*. I need a cat, maybe.

A cat is safer than a man, for sure.

"Olivia, talk to me," he says, his voice exasperated, like I'm a pain for not giving in and having some kind of conversation with him.

I stop, whirling on my foot and staring at him. "Shouldn't we be in some kind of special room for this? I should be read my rights and all that." He doesn't respond, so I ask more questions. "FBI, right? You don't work as a bodyguard?" I cross my arms on my chest, staring at him.

He sighs before answering, "While I have friends who work for Garden State Security and they help provide my cover, no. I do not work for them. I'm in the white-collar crime division of the Federal Bureau of Investigation."

My vision goes a bit blurry with the confirmation.

"White-collar crime. Because . . ." The words stop in my throat.

"Because Bradley Reed has been embezzling funds from his firm and he's tied you up in it." A moment passes before I realize I've stopped breathing. "Liv, please. Sit down and we can talk about this," he says, stepping forward, concern on his face.

Concern.

As if that's his place. As if he has a *right.*

Slowly, more and more pieces come back to me and start coming together.

"All of those times you ran into me, none of them were acciden-tal. It was all planned." Here I was, thinking it was some kind of romantic kismet, the universe rewarding me, apologizing for the bull-shit it's put me through, when really it was a *fucking investigation.* "I was just a suspect to you." My voice cracks, but I ignore it.

"Running into you had nothing to do with your case, with the bureau, Olivia. It wasn't part of my assignment. That was on me." His face holds honesty, but not the whole story.

"Then what was it? Were you just *so enamored* by the idiot who got played you had to meet me?" I can't believe this is my life, that I'm here arguing about this. I can't understand what I did to make the universe hate me so fucking much.

He steps forward, but I take a step back.

"I was stopping you from getting *arrested,* Olivia. That's what I was doing." He shakes his head, a humorless laugh leaving his lips. "I have been risking my career and intervening because if you did half of that vengeance shit, you were going to be booked for fucking *attempted murder* at best."

I think about arguing, telling him I wasn't trying to *murder* Bradley, that I just wanted to get some small sense of revenge on him, but something else piques in my mind.

"How did you know?" I ask, and his thick brows furrow.

"What?"

"You said you ran into me because I was about to do something unhinged that would put me in jail. How did you know?"

A look comes over his face, and *fuck, fuck, fuck.* Before he speaks, I know. It's the only thing that makes sense.

"You were my subject. I've been keeping tabs on you for the better part of a year." He throws his hands up like he gives up. "There's no point in hiding it now."

"Keeping tabs . . ."

"I was assigned to watch your movements, your computer, your texts, calls, searches to see how much you knew about what Reed was doing, make sure you wouldn't try and flee the state. It was clear pretty quickly you knew nothing, but—" One of those has my heart stopping.

"Wait, my searches?"

His face stays stoic.

"Oh my god, you've been watching my searches. My recent ones, too?"

"Livi—"

"Oh, fuck, you've seen my search history." The reality hits me with an alarming slap, panic filling me completely.

I bend forward, hands on my knees as I start to hyperventilate.

No.

No.

"I mean—"

"You saw when I researched *anal sex!*" A quick look of confusion crosses his face before he shakes his head and speaks.

"Liv, I—" I don't give him time to respond or finish because I am *spiraling.*

"You mentioned it, and then I searched it because I had questions and . . . Oh my fucking *god,* is that in some kind of fucking *database?!* 'Olivia Anderson researched anal sex and the proper way to prepare for such action on October 14 at 8:19 pm.'" I feel lightheaded as all blood seems to leave my body with my panic and embarrassment. "Is it *on my permanent record?!*"

Is that a thing? Does the FBI have a permanent record, a file of all the unhinged shit I've done and searched? Do they have a copy of that slideshow I made for my mother's wedding? What about the boob pic I sent my high school boyfriend before I realized what a shitty idea that was?

"Honestly, you should be more concerned with the fact that you searched how many bee stings it takes to cause anaphylactic shock and then researched how to get a beehive delivered to your ex-boyfriend's home. Who is allergic to bees."

I shake my head and wave him off. "He's not allergic to bees. He's just *afraid* of them, like a little bitch," I say.

"No, he's definitely afraid of them because he's allergic, Olivia." I wait, trying to weigh the consequences of that in my mind before I shrug.

"Whatever, I stand by my decision there." I also stand by my decision that I *need to get out of here.* My mind continues to move, anger and frustration still so fresh on the surface, thankfully covering up the hurt that's brewing right beneath it. I move to grab my bag.

"Olivia, please, please let me explain."

"No," I say, my voice calmer than any other part of me. It's like I've completely dissociated from what's happening.

"What?" He looks genuinely confused.

"I said no. I don't want you to explain. I want to go home and pretend the last two months didn't happen. I should never have . . ." I sigh, shaking my head.

"Never have what?" Finally, I stop and face him, really look at him.

"I should never have tried to move on."

And strangely, that's what hurts. I thought I was being brave by moving on, by trusting so soon after everything blew up. I thought he was helping me be a newer, better version of myself, but . . .

It was all a lie.

Because all along, all Andre wanted from me was information.

"Was it a fun little bonus, getting to fuck me? To play with me? Was it so boring watching Bradley, you decided to spice it up, see if you could make me fall for you too?" A knife turns at the betrayal.

"Olivia, you can't really think—" Anger surges.

"You do not get to tell me what I can and can't think."

"Can't we just—" He tries to step closer to me and I panic, stepping back again and raising my voice, letting it all spill out.

"No! Do not get closer to me." I shake my head and look at the ceiling, fighting the tears that are inevitable. "I trusted you! I trusted you with *everything*. And god. God! I thought you were my *prize*," I admit, and it happens. A tear falls as I confess my truths to him, to myself. "I thought I'd dealt with *him*." I thrust my hand to point across the street, the situation comical now. "I'd dealt with him and endured my mom and the press and all the bullshit because, at the end of it all, I got *you*. This kind man who put me first and wanted *more* from me. Who was teaching me to stand up for myself."

"Olivia, I do—"

"Except you didn't want *me*. You wanted *information*. Well, the joke's on you, Andre! I have none. I'm just a dumb little girl who apparently has the *worst* taste in men. A dumb—"

"Enough." His voice cuts through the room, angry, as if he has the right. "Enough. You don't talk about yourself like that, not in front of me." He's closer now, and I back up until my back hits a wall. There is nowhere else to go.

"Why is that, Andre? What was the goal there? So I'd be a good witness? Help me find my backbone so when you needed to use me, I wouldn't crumble under the pressure?" His jaw ticks, and he gets closer to me.

"You're hurt and that's *fair*. You have every right to be."

"Oh, wow, thank you *so much* for telling me what I can feel, *agent*." He ignores me and keeps talking. "And you can spew your venom at me. I'll take it. You let it out, baby. But you need to know I was in a shitty position. I'm here for a year, hitting dead end after dead end in this job I *hate,* and all I want is to wrap this case up." He steps to me, putting a hand on the wall beside my head.

Trapping me as he weaves his tale of deception.

"One day, I'm monitoring the *one person* we have who, if we tie the right pieces together, can lock him up for good. And you start searching for how to cut brake lines. You go buy a fucking bolt cutter and start walking to his house. So I bump into you, and I stop you because you're right, Olivia. You're no good to this case if you're *locked up for manslaughter.*"

"I wasn't going to kill him," I say, my voice annoyed and low. His face is so close to mine, I have to fight to remember why I'm so livid with him, why I can't let him kiss this pain away.

"You were trying to *cut his brake lines!*"

"So he would crash that ugly fucking car! He wasn't going to make it far!" He sighs and shakes his head, and even though I've got fury running in my veins, it's kind of funny.

Not that I'll laugh or smile.

More like in a few years, when I trauma-dump this on someone, I'll laugh and use this funny little tidbit to convince them it wasn't that big of a deal—just silly girl things.

He sighs and then continues his story. "I spend an afternoon with you and an old woman, and you're *nothing* like I thought. You're not a spoiled rich brat who thinks the world revolves around them. You're not some dumb broad who was too self-centered to realize her man was playing her. Instead, you're kind, and you're caring, and you put everyone before you." His breath plays with mine, and his hand moves up to brush aside a piece of hair. I hold my breath, waiting for his skin to touch mine, but it doesn't. He pulls back before he does.

"And a week later, I'm watching you try to hire a psychopath, and you're just a few blocks from me, and it felt like a sign. So I sat with you and distracted you and watched fear fill your damn eyes when you saw the press. A new piece of the puzzle then snapped in. You don't like this life. And I walk you to your car, and you thanked me for not being a piece of shit, and I swear to fuck, Olivia. I almost told you then. Almost told you and asked you out because you deserved that, a good man."

"But . . . ," I say, knowing it's coming.

"But that wasn't my place. You were just dumped, and you were my job, and it wasn't . . . It wasn't right."

"What happened then? You changed your mind obviously."

"You happened, Olivia. I don't think a man on this earth could be in your presence for long, watch you fight for everyone but yourself, and not want to save you. So my goal changed from wanting to close this case to get a promotion to wanting to close this case so I could get *you*. And I told you it was too messy, that the time wasn't right because I wouldn't lie to you and tell you I didn't want you. I could see myself falling for you, Liv, but I wanted the slate clean before I did."

My heart stops, but he keeps on talking.

"But I don't know a man who could resist you, either, Olivia— spending time with you, watching you grow, watching you get your confidence back? Fuck, it's been beautiful. And then we changed, and I've spent the last few weeks with this shit eating at me, but I couldn't *do anything*. I need you to know that, to believe that."

"You lied to me, and then you kept lying and kept lying until there is no way for me to know what the truth is. You said it yourself; you wanted a promotion."

"I was trying to *save you*, Olivia! Yes, this is my job. And if I get a grand slam on this case, I get a promotion, which I want because I work under a man who makes me fucking miserable. But you know what would be the easy answer? Case closed? *Letting you take the fall.*"

The world stops.

"Everything points to you, Olivia. That's the easy hole-in-one. I'm sure you saw it on those documents, documents I pour over every fucking morning trying to find something to get the finger off you. That's what my boss wants these days. For us to pin it on you and give him a closed case."

"But I didn't . . . I never—"

"I know. I know that, Olivia, and your ex is a dumbass, but he covered those bases. There's enough reasonable doubt to get him off if he went to trial and enough evidence to charge you."

I don't know what to say.

My mind is reeling as I try and piece this together, try and understand how my ex-fiancé is a white-collar criminal with the FBI on his ass and somehow, he framed me for his crime.

"I'm . . . I'm innocent, though," I whisper, trying not to break completely.

How did this shit get so messy?

"I know you're innocent, Olivia. I know, but it's not as easy as that. You could probably get off, but not without years and years in court and lawyers' fees and the media bashing you."

Something in that registers in my mind.

"How do you know?" I ask, my voice low. The question throws him off, and I cross my arms on my chest, brushing his with his closeness.

"What?"

"How do you know I'm innocent? How do you know I didn't tell him to put those accounts in my name, that I'm not in on it." His brow comes together in confusion, like he can't even fathom that question.

"Because . . . you're good. Because you're you. You're . . . You're Olivia."

"You don't even know me," I say, and it comes out like a fractured whisper.

It sounds how I feel right now.

"Yes, I do." His words are so sure, and I shake my head.

"No. You know me at surface level. You know what I do in the day-to-day. Who I talk to and what I search, but you don't *know* me, Andre."

It's then he looks at me, gives a small laugh, runs his hand through his hair, and shakes his head.

"I know you, Olivia, a lot better than you think I do, and it has *nothing* to do with watching you. Nothing to do with this investigation and *everything* to do with *you*." He looks around the room like he's trying to figure something out before he starts speaking like he's given up.

Putting all of his cards on the table.

"You spend time with Edna, letting her annoy the fuck out of you because you know she's lonely. You endure your dad and Cami, even if it makes you uncomfortable because they're happiest together. You have a weekly call with your mother, who does *nothing* but berate you, because you want to make sure she's okay. You almost *married a man* because you thought it was what was expected of you. You never put yourself first, always think about how the smallest action you make will impact someone else. You could never hurt hundreds of people like this. It's not in your nature."

I stare at him and take shaky breaths at his words. The world is spinning around me, and I don't know what to do.

"I just need you to believe me, Olivia. To believe in me and us, and then we can figure the rest out."

"I just . . . I don't know how I'm supposed to, Andre. How do I know you aren't saying this to save your ass? Because you want to have your cake and eat it too?" His head dips, his nose barely grazing my neck, and I fight a shiver.

"Because if I didn't care about you believing me, I would just fuck you until you shut up about this shit." My head moves back, hitting the wall he still has me pinned to in irritation.

"What, do you think you can just fuck me into submission?"

"I think we both know the answer to that, menace," he says, and his voice is low and raspy and *goddammit.* I need out of here.

Now.

I duck under his arm to get away.

"This is useless. This is . . . I need to go home," I say, grabbing my bag.

"Olivia, please."

"This is too much. I can't . . . I can't trust you. And if I can't trust you, what's the point, Andre?" I throw my arms in the air before letting them fall to my sides.

"I hated lying to you. Each and every day, each and every lie tore at me."

"What a lovely lie, Andre. And so conveniently unprovable," I say.

Because I'm done with pretty words covering ugly lies, and I'm tired of men who think I'm too stupid to see them for what they are.

"My journal," he says, his voice low.

"What?"

"If I could prove to you I hated lying to you from the start, would it help?"

"I don't—"

"Stay there," he says without letting me finish, turning toward his bedroom quickly. Then he turns *back* to me and puts a finger up. "Please, Liv. Don't leave. Five minutes."

"Five minutes?"

"If I don't convince you, you can leave. I won't even chase you." I'm an idiot, and I know it when my stomach drops when he says that.

I won't even chase you.

"Five minutes, menace. Give me five minutes." And then he's out of the room.

I contemplate leaving, running while I can, never looking back unless it's with a court order or a warrant or something. But I don't.

Maybe it's because I'm weak.

Maybe it's because I want this all to be a joke.

Maybe it's because a part of me is holding onto hope I very much need to let go of.

Either way, I stand in his stupid, boring living room, my arms crossed on my chest while I wait for him to return.

FORTY-SEVEN

How do you trust someone who has lied to you from the start?

SATURDAY, OCTOBER 28

"Here." Andre throws something at me when he walks back into the room, stark relief on his face when he sees me still standing there. I catch it by some miracle, a small spiral-bound book you'd get in the dollar store, battered and barely the size of my hand.

"What is it?"

"When I was ten, I couldn't keep a secret to save my life." I raise an eyebrow and he smiles. "Ironic, I know. Trust me. Anyway, my mom was throwing this big surprise party for my dad. She got me this because I told her secrets felt like lies and I'd been taught not to lie." I, again, raise an eyebrow. He ignores me. "She told me to write it down every time I wanted to tell her secret, every time I wanted to talk about it. Every night, she'd come into my room and have me tell her them all, share my secrets." A part of my belly flips at how sweet that is.

"I never stopped. It sounds ridiculous and you can call me a momma's boy, but I did it through high school, writing it down and sharing shit with her—things friends told me about others I wasn't supposed to share, white lies I told so I wouldn't hurt someone's feelings. It was a bonding experience and she's a vault, so it felt safe. I stopped talking to my mom about it, obviously, but . . . in this job . . . the secrets pile up. So I started doing it again a few years back. I have dozens of these, but this one . . ." His voice trails off as he walks over and grabs it, flipping to a date.

"This one starts the day I met you, Olivia. I know some of the other ones have some things about you, times I felt like I was intruding on your life when I didn't have to. You can read those, too, but this is the one that matters.

And I see it.

August 24.

The day I met him.

"I ran into Olivia Anderson today on purpose. She was trying to cut her ex's brake lines. Had lunch with her and Edna. Felt bad I couldn't tell her who I am."

I flip a page to until I see my name again.

September 4.

"Went to Edna's house to fix her sink and she kept talking about Olivia. She wants to set me up with her."

I flip a few more and see other things—told Peterson he didn't have anything in his teeth—he did. Told Mom I fell asleep and missed her call but I ignored it.

"Told Olivia I was there to get coffee. I was there to stop her from being dumb."

"Being dumb?" I say, slightly annoyed with a raised eyebrow.

"You were hiring an assassin, Olivia," he says.

"What?"

"That guy? You were trying to hire him online?"

"He was just going to scare Bradley."

"He has a history of breaking into houses and killing people." My gut drops into my stomach.

I keep flipping.

Moving on from that because I will not be touching it with a ten-foot pole.

September 17.

"I called the paparazzi on Olivia."

My eyes go wide and I look lip at him. "That was *you?!*"

"You were going to kill him with that beehive."

"Jesus Christ," I mumble. He moves away from me, like he's less worried I'll run, and sits on the couch, watching me.

I keep flipping pages.

"I told Olivia we can't be together," I read out loud.

"I almost called my mom for that one," he says low. "It felt like drinking battery acid." I have so many things I want to ask him, but I don't. I don't even look at him. I can't. I keep reading instead.

It's all here: every time he lied to me or had to manipulate the truth in big or small ways. The extent of his guilt is here, on lined paper, scrawled in black pen in messy handwriting.

"I hated it, lying to you. But I didn't really have a choice." His voice is hoarse and shoots through me painfully.

I don't reply, instead moving to the front of the little journal, reading it over again, finding little things I missed—pen changes, how some days were scribbled quickly and others he took his time. The day I spent the night at his house has an entry.

"I told Liv we couldn't be together because it was too close to her breakup, but it's because of work."

He wrote Liv, not Olivia.

My heart breaks then.

The position we're in is so messy, so contrived, so many other people involved that even though I want this—and I think it's safe to admit I *want this*—it just . . . will never work.

How could it?

"Please, Olivia," he says. "Come here." He's still on the couch, but now his legs are wide, his arms out. "Please. Let me hold you. Just for a minute."

My body wants to go to him.

My heart wants me to go to him.

My mind . . . battles.

Because he lied.

He lied and I feel stupid. It's not the first time this has happened —not from him, but from others, and he had to have known how that would make me feel.

But it was his work.

He had no choice.

He's trying to help you.

He risked his job.

But I'm hurt.

"One minute," he says in a whisper, one that travels across the room to me. "Sit with me for one minute. I'm begging you, Liv. Please."

It's the Liv that does it.

The nickname he doesn't use often, but he is now.

A few steps bring me to him, and I stand right in front of him.

His arms wrap around the backs of my legs, pulling me in tight. I expected him to tug me into his lap, to make me *sit* with him. But he's somehow okay with just this, his head on my stomach, his arms around my body.

"I don't know what to do," I whisper. His head tips up and he looks at me.

"Neither do I. All I know is I don't want to lose you, Olivia." I stare at him and I break.

I break in my firmness, in my anger, and I run my hand through his long hair, watching it shift as I do, watching as sweet relief enters his eyes.

"There are things I want to tell you, Olivia, that aren't appropriate to tell you right now. Things I want to tell you when we're both happy, when shit is good. Things I want to tell you without any clouds of doubt over us." My heart skips a beat. "But I'll tell you this: say the word and I'm off your case. I'd absolutely rather have you than a promotion. I've already made that decision."

I continue running my fingers through his hair, breaking up the light clumps of gel, breaking apart the strands meticulously. I don't look into his eyes.

"Is this . . . Is this case important to you?" He doesn't hesitate.

"You're more important to me, Olivia."

I don't know if I've had that before, not from anyone other than my father at least.

"That wasn't my question, Andre."

"The answer is more complicated than yes or no."

"So, yes. The case is important to you." He sighs then presses his lips to my belly like he needs that, needs the connection even while we're in this tumultuous place.

"I want you safe. This case is messy, and my boss is a fucking ass, and I don't trust him."

"Don't trust him?" I ask, trying to understand. He sighs, letting go of me. I instantly miss it.

"Can you . . . Can you sit down?" He pats the couch next to him. I should sit there.

I don't, though, and I don't know why I do it.

That's a lie.

I do it because I want to be close to Andre, want to feel him, to have this conversation touching him.

Just in case, I tell myself.

Just in case this ends shitty and this is the last memory I have.

I sit in his lap.

His hands shake with nerves as he moves my hair behind my neck, and the lump in my throat that was soothed by anger and a few answers throbs again as his face goes into my neck, breathing there for a few moments.

Like he's doing the same thing, soaking me in just in case.

A part of me decides then. Decides no man who was fucking me as a fun perk of the job would mourn the potential loss of me. No man who was playing me would hand me a journal his mom encouraged him to make over twenty years ago.

Or maybe I'm delusional.

Maybe he would. Maybe I'll leave this with a broken heart.

Or worse, a broken heart *and* a jail sentence.

But it's time for me to trust my gut. It's time for me to believe in myself and do things for me and listen to the voice in my head. I ignored it for so long and look where that got me.

"I believe in you, Andre," I whisper, the fear taking over, and his hands on my hips tighten. "I believe you and I'm terrified, and I need you to know if you're lying, this will break me in a way I'll never come back from. I'm giving you everything. Please," I whisper, my face in his neck as well because I can't bear to look at him. "Please take care of me."

I've never asked that of anyone.

I've never trusted anyone with *me*.

And here I am, in the lap of a man who lied to me since the day we met, trusting him more than I've ever trusted another person.

And somehow, I know I made the right choice.

FORTY-EIGHT

How soon is too soon to talk about marriage? 🔍

SUNDAY, OCTOBER 29

\"So, Cami is your dad's . . ."

"Partner. But you know that already, you psycho stalker," I say with a smile. It's hours after everything, long after we kept talking things through, long after I've had multiple crying jags about . . . well . . . everything.

Andre investigating me.

Being investigated.

How fucked this situation is.

How I'm falling for a man who, in theory, could put me in prison.

It's nearly four in the morning and I'm exhausted, but we've spent the last two hours playing some strange version of *getting to know you* games, trying to fill in gaps, letting Andre admit just how much he knows about me, and trying to catch up to him.

He pinches the skin on my side, making me giggle before he rolls me until I'm sprawled on top of him.

He's been like this since I stood in front of him, when he laid his head on my stomach, trying to get every inch of my body on his, as much contact as possible, like he's nervous I'll run off or that this is all in his head.

"Yes, I know the absolute basics of your family, little menace. But not everything. Like, do they plan on ever getting married?" I shake my head.

"No. It's not important to them." He hums in understanding. Every time I tell him something, he does this, like he's filing it away for later.

"And you?" His hand brushes my hair back and over my shoulders.

"Me?"

"Do you want to get married, or did you evade it once and saw the light or something?"

I smile because I've thought of this before, if a wedding and marriage are ruined for me.

"I do. I like the idea of it, of being tied to someone, of there being something holding us together beyond feelings and admiration and a common friend group. I like the . . . certainty of it. The surety."

"Because your little people pleaser would twist up anything but a declaration and a promise of forever into something else."

He's joking, but my smile drops just a hair. Enough for him, the ever-present, ever investigating Andre Santino Valenti to see.

"I want that too, you know. The surety. If I'm tying you to me, I want to know if I fuck it up, I've got time to fix it before you pack your things and start searching how to cut my brake lines." I roll my eyes and slap his chest, but he grabs my wrist, pressing a kiss to my pulse point.

"I'm joking, Liv."

"Are you ever going to let that go?"

"Never. Sorry." I roll my eyes, but he grabs my chin, forcing me to look at him. "But in all seriousness, I'm telling you now. A year, two, three down the road, if I manage to convince you to be mine for that long, I want my ring on your finger. A big fucking thing so no man can miss it from a mile away."

"Manage to convince me, huh?" He just smiles, and it's boyish and light. The smile I only ever see when we're alone, making it my favorite ever. "A whole, what? Two months and you're already planning our wedding?"

His face goes serious, and I'm confused for a moment before he speaks.

"Olivia, I've been falling for you for almost a year at this point. I've watched you be kind—too unbearably kind—to people who don't deserve it. I've watched you shift and move to make everyone in your life happy. I've watched you continue to build your business. I've watched you make new friends and help that group of friends find small ways to overcome their own trauma. I've watched you be completely un-fucking-hinged because someone wronged you." I'm not sure if my heart is beating.

I'm not sure if I'm *breathing*.

Instead, I'm taking careful note of every crease, every freckle, every scar on Andre's face, committing it and this moment to memory.

"So yeah. In my head, you're it for me, Liv. But I know you're a good year behind me. We've got time." His thumb brushes my cheek like he's committing it to memory, too. "So a wedding. A big one?"

I take a moment to catch my breath before answering, before I shake my head.

"No. Last time . . . God, it was the worst. So much planning, and I do that shit for a living. Too many people. If I ever . . . If I ever try it again, I want it small. Friends and family and no one else," I say with a smile.

"Small is good." His smile reflects my own.

"If I could, I'd hand it all off to Cami, let her have fun. I wouldn't touch any of it. Too stressful. Too many opinions. Too many people to please and keep happy." He keeps staring at me, reading me, trying to decide if I'm telling him the truth or saying that because I think it's what he wants to hear.

Then he speaks.

"Alright. Small wedding it is."

It's like there's no doubt in his mind that in one, two, three years down the road, we'll be doing that: having a small wedding with just friends and family.

My mind takes this moment to remind me of the mess we're in, of all the obstacles we'll have to jump before that can happen.

Reality sets in.

"What happens next?" I whisper.

"What do you mean?"

"Where does this leave us? You're a literal FBI agent who is supposed to be investigating me." His jaw goes tight.

"And I'll keep doing that."

I know there's no right answer here, but I can't help but look at him incredulously.

"Olivia, I told you—you are very tied up in this." Worry overcomes me, and he rolls until he's holding himself up and hovering over me.

I want to argue with his statement but I can't. I also can't tell him how to do his job, how to live his life. This will never work if we start that now.

"What about my support group?" I ask.

"Ah, yes, your support group." I shouldn't be shocked that he knows about them, but all of this is so new.

"I told them I'd help them get closure." I tip my chin up, knowing he's going to try and argue, to tell me that's not my responsibility.

"And why is that *your* job?" he asks, confirming my assumption.

"Because I told them I'd help, and they deserve that." He sighs, doing a small push-up to press a kiss to my forehead.

"You know what your problem is?"

"I have terrible taste in men and apparently no red-flag system? You included." He lets out a sound that is half laugh, half groan before giving me his answer.

"You're a people pleaser." I roll my eyes.

"No shit, tell me something I don't already know."

"It's not your job to help them get closure, Olivia, even if it was your idea, even if you want to make them happy." I glare at him. "And

even if you want to ignore that, you should at the very least understand that you need to lie low right now. Wreaking havoc and causing
an issue with Reed is not good for your case."

"I don't care about the stupid case. I want revenge. More now
than when I thought he was just a gaslighting asshole who broke up
with me at the worst time ever."

And it's true. I'm angrier with that man than I could have ever
fathomed. Not only did he fuck with my life and make me look like a
fool, but he's apparently trying to *frame me* for a fucking *crime*.
Andre sighs and swipes his thumb on my cheek.

"The best revenge you can get on him is to help me put him in
prison. To testify against him. To sit across from him when he
thought you were too dumb and silly to know better and put him on
blast." My eyes go wide and my stomach drops at his words.

"Wow, wow, wow. Testify?" He must see the panic on my face
because he rushes to answer.

"Not right now, but eventually, sorry to say, you'll be called as a
witness. We need to pin everything to him, where it belongs, first. But
you . . . You'll probably be the best witness we have. That's why I
need you to keep your nose clean."

I file away the whole testify in court thing because I am not in the
right mental state for that.

No fucking way.

Instead, I go back to him ruining my revenge plans.

"It's not just me. There are other girls—"

"And there are *victims*, Liv. People who lost money, their savings,
because of his greed."

"Why can't I do both? Help these people when the time comes
and help these women? And get closure for me?" He opens his mouth
to argue, but I speak over him. "I told them they'd get their revenge
and that I would help." He opens his mouth, but I keep talking. "I
can't just . . . back off my own vision."

"Olivia, you shouldn't be doing it yourself *or* encouraging a group
of women either. The best revenge is moving on."

I know the right answer is to agree. To do whatever I have to make this issue right, to lie low as needed in order to keep myself safe. But . . .

He sighs, rolling next to me and looking at the ceiling before running a hand through his dark hair, and somehow, I know he knows what I'm thinking, what I'm feeling.

"Why do I feel like you're never going to be content until you get your own on Reed?" he asks, confirming my thoughts.

I smile.

"Because I'm not." His eyes drift shut, and a deep breath enters and leaves his lungs.

"Jesus Christ. If I help you do some dumb shit, make sure you don't get caught, will that be enough?" A smile spreads on my face.

"What do you mean by dumb shit?"

"Stupid revenge. Not a fucking beehive or cutting his brake lines so he crashes his car and fuckin' dies—"

"I told you, he wouldn't have died. He would just have crashed into a fire hydrant and made a big mess and had to pay for it all." He stares at me with a look of confusion mixed with awe on his face.

"A menace. You're a fucking menace."

"You like it. So this revenge . . . "

"If I help you, will you stop trying to be so fucking unhinged all the time?"

"Can I bring the girls?" I ask, thinking they'd get such a kick out of coming on some big, petty revenge day. He groans then rolls to his side and presses a kiss to my neck.

It sends a shiver down my spine.

"Fine, but everyone follows my lead. If I say we're done, we're done." My smile goes wide with triumph.

"You're a good one, you know that?"

"What does being a *good one* get me?" he asks with a smug smile, rolling again until I'm on my back beneath him.

"I'm starting to think whatever you want."

FORTY-NINE

How to tell your friends about your new boyfriend?

WEDNESDAY, NOVEMBER 1

Walking into the Jilted Brides Club on Wednesday feels a bit like cheating. I, of course, texted the group chat ahead of time to check in and make sure it was okay, promising I had a reason, but it still feels . . . wrong.

Like I'm bringing a lion to a group of gazelles.

Or a boy where there are *no boys allowed.*

On the bright side, Andre doesn't seem phased in the least, standing next to me in the hall as we wait for Naomi to open the door. "I'm not sure if we're going to do actual group today," I say. "But if we do, you'll have to sit in the hall or something until we're ready to go." I assume he'll argue or groan or anything, really, but I forgot this is Andre we're talking about.

Instead, he nods, reaching over for my hand and squeezing it.

"Of course. That's private. I'll go sit in the car." Warmth runs through me because not only does Andre *get it,* but he's understanding and good and kind.

I don't have time to express my gratitude, though, because the door is opening, and all of the girls stand behind it, looking anxious.

"Hey, guys." It's funny to watch the girls' eyes move from me to him and back, still not fully sure of what's happening. "This is Andre." He smiles his wide, white smile and it happens.

I watch it in real time, how Andre's smile impacts women when he uses it with his panty-dropping power.

Thank God he never used that power on me. In the beginning, I had started to keep count of his few and far between smiles, and they were never megawatt like that.

I would have folded like a chair before I ever had a chance.

Still, I look at him and roll my eyes. "Ignore him. He doesn't know how to act in front of people and doesn't know the power of a good smile," I say. "Can we come in?" They nod, leading us in and to the living room area.

We get settled, Andre sitting on the loveseat and me on the arm of it, the girls on a large sectional after Naomi offers us snacks and drinks, and everyone declines before I finally speak.

"Okay, so I know boyfriends"—a gasp sounds and I roll my eyes, fighting a laugh—"are kind of the opposite of the point here, but I promise there's a good reason." Chrissie raises an eyebrow like she doesn't quite believe me.

"I came here, and you all welcomed me with open arms, and I am forever grateful I found you all. You're so kind and caring and generous. The best thing that came from all of . . . the mess was you guys. Seriously, I'm so thankful." They smile in turn, nodding and relaxing a bit.

"When I came here, I told you we should be doing something for revenge, something to get our own back. You all are normal, sane humans who made lists with things like, writing a letter or glitter in his vents." Andre snorts out a laugh.

"And Liv wrote *cut his brake lines* and *deliver a beehive to his home*." Julie gasps, and I roll my eyes, hitting him in the chest.

"Can you stop? I didn't *do* any of it!" I say to Andre, who shakes his head.

"You didn't *succeed* at any of it. Mostly in thanks to me." I roll my eyes again and shake my head.

"I promise if there wasn't a good reason to have him here, he would *not* be here." I sigh but don't miss the way the girls' eyes are lighting up with laughter and the little looks they're giving one another.

Whatever.

"Anyway, so all of my . . . unhinged revenge didn't work. And honestly, most of you are so past your exes, you shouldn't even bother being toxic like me."

"But it sounded so fun!" Simone says with a small pout. I laugh.

"This is where Andre comes in," I say with a proud smile. "I've got this plan to help us all get a little taste of revenge, and he's our . . ." I look at him and my smile grows.

His disappears, which makes me laugh.

"Lookout."

"Is it . . ." Julie looks from left to right before speaking a bit quieter. "Is it safe?"

Andre takes that one.

"Livi told you I'm a, uh . . . a bodyguard, right?" he lies, and they all nod.

They don't need to know he's an FBI agent and we met because he's investigating my ties to my shitty ex's entrenched embezzlement scheme.

"I also live near her ex. I can keep watch while you guys do . . . Well, you tell them, Liv." I smile, excited now, fighting the urge to rub my hands together like some kind of villain.

"I have a list. An Andre-approved list, so it's not nearly as chaotic as it could be—"

"Thank God," Andre murmurs, and I ignore him.

"—of revenge we can all pull off together."

"Together?" Naomi asks, and I smile.

"Together. You guys will come with me. I have all of the supplies, but if you guys have anything . . . more to add, we can stop to buy more."

"When is this happening?" Julie, the most realistic of us all, asks.

"On Monday night. If you guys are interested. We're calling it petty revenge day, where the jilted brides are getting our own on one of the worst men on this planet," I say with a wide smile.

"Alright, menace, maybe bring it down a notch," Andre says.

"Maybe not the worst, but he really, really sucks, okay?" Andre smiles but doesn't argue with me more. "So basically, you guys get to feel like you got that sweet revenge without having to risk yourselves or even think about your exes again."

Naomi opens her mouth to speak, but I keep talking.

"If you want to, though, I'm your girl. If you want to do your revenge on whoever, I'm there, buying the materials and delivering them to you and being your getaway car."

Julie opens her mouth to speak, but again, I step in.

"And if you don't want to, I will *not* be offended. At all. I just . . . I started this, so I wanted to end it with . . . all of you." Simone tries to speak again, but I need to cover my bases. "Oh, and if you think I'm insane now and want to kick me out of the group, I get it. I'll head out as soon as you tell me to."

"Can I say something?" Julie asks with a small smile, and I realize I haven't let any of them speak, lost in my excitement and nerves.

"Of course," I say, and I sit on my hands to try and stop my jittering. Andre, of course, notices and grabs the hand closest to him, holding it and rubbing his thumb over my pulse point.

My body eases instantly, the magic only Andre seems to possess filling my bones.

"First, I can only speak for myself, but we're *so* happy you found someone, Liv," Naomi says. There are murmurs of agreement, and about a third of the tightness in my shoulders relaxes.

I'd been worried about this part specifically, of them being mad I have a new boyfriend, of them questioning it, of me not being accepted into this group anymore because of it.

"And he seems absolutely enamored by you," Simone says, and again, they all agree.

"Love that for you, Livi," Chrissie says.

"And this revenge idea . . . it won't be anything that would . . . send us to prison, right?" Julie asks.

Clearly, they know me well, and Andre laughs before answering for me. "Not at all. I pre-approved Livi's ideas and, no offense, will have to approve any you guys add." She nods then turns to the girls and then back to me.

Julie is the ringleader of this group, and I think that means good things for me.

And for this day.

"I want to put a pile of glitter on his ceiling fan," she says. "You know, so when he turns it on . . . boom! Glitter. Everywhere."

And I know then these girls were put in my life for a reason.

FIFTY

MONDAY, NOVEMBER 6

We're across the street from my place in front of Edna's house when I glance at Liv.

"Are they ready?"

She nods, looking at her phone. The support group girls piled into Julie's car, parking a block down so as not to bring any unwanted attention.

"They're walking this way now," she says, then she looks up and down the street, stopping when she sees four women walking this way.

"What's the rule?" I ask for the fifth time, at least. She rolls her eyes and god, she's such a fucking brat sometimes.

In a good way, in a way I'm obsessed with, but a brat nonetheless.

"If you say we have to leave, we have to leave immediately." Her voice is an annoyed drone.

"And?"

"And I can't do anything that could hurt him physically."

"And?" She looks confused this time, a bit annoyed.

"That was it. I had two restrictions."

I lean forward, grabbing her chin in my hands, pressing my

thumb underneath to tip it up, and pulling her close until our lips are almost touching but not quite.

"And you remember that no matter what, Olivia, you came out on top. He's a piece of shit who is one day going to look back and realize you were the best thing he ever had and he fucking *squandered that*. You remember that you're a goddamn queen and you're doing this for you and your friends. Not for him." She stares at me, her eyes wide and frozen, before she whispers a single word.

"Shit." My heart drops, and I think I did something wrong, said something wrong.

"What?"

"You say shit like that, and I'm wondering if I even need revenge as closure." A smile breaks out on my face, and her eyes go soft.

"Then I'm doing my job. Let's go, little menace."

Hours later, we're back at my place, Liv's head in my lap and my hands raking through her hair as she watches some movie I'm not paying attention to. The day was a long one, and I think, in a way, it closed that door for her. We, of course, will have one final revenge, but until then, this will do.

The women did all the things on Olivia's list that weren't absolutely illegal and I approved of, and all of them made me promise to never let Olivia go—if only because when she's got the scent of revenge, she goes all out.

And I mean *all out*.

Putting pieces of shrimp in the curtain rods.

Taking all of his left shoes.

Putting glitter on the ceiling fan.

Superglueing all of his containers, like his deodorant and his condiments, closed.

Took the microwave turntable and all of the racks in his oven.

Flipped the batteries in the remote and superglued it shut.

Cutting all the seams in all of his pants pockets.

Poking holes in every container in his fridge so they would slowly leak everywhere.

None of it was anything disastrous, just frustrating and inconvenient and will probably result in a bit of a cost, but it made Liv happy.

And the way she and her friends giggled the whole time, like they were kids getting away with a prank on their parents, made it worth it.

After, we all went to a restaurant in town and ate and laughed, a few of the women telling me their own stories, making me feel like a welcomed part of the group.

But most of all, it was clear *Liv* is a welcome—and cherished—member. She might even be the ringleader. She thinks it's Julie because she's the one who formed the group and, from what Liv told me, she's the one who runs the meetings, but it's her.

And like always, Olivia doesn't see it—doesn't see her own value, how much people around her love her.

Of course, I know the source—her mother and her need to please everyone and her stupid fucking ex—but that just makes my mission to show her how precious and worthy she is even more tangible.

Even more important.

We just need to get past this stupid fucking case.

Suddenly, she moves her head in my lap, turning to look at me, her eyes soft and comfortable, a little sleepy.

This is *my* Olivia.

The comfortable one.

The sated one.

She's turned off, isn't ready to jump in and find solutions, doesn't have her armor on, and has packed her little people pleaser away for the night.

It might be selfish, and I know there's more to it—work she's done on herself in the past few months, work that's been hard and draining and effective—but I know to a degree, I give her this.

This freedom to just be herself and not worry about everyone else.

Pride swells when I think of that.

She stares at me for a few moments, and I brush her hair back a few more times, soaking this in before she smiles her sweet smile and speaks.

"Thank you," she says.

"What?"

"Thank you. For today." I continue running my fingers through her hair, waiting to see if she has more. "For helping me do all of that. Helping the girls. It felt good, a chapter closed, you know?"

That warmth in my gut blooms anew. "You needed that, didn't you?"

She doesn't reply immediately, staring at me as I watch her, the TV low in the background, but we're in a little bubble; this moment a little bubble of us, of understanding.

And somehow, I know it's a step forward she doesn't realize we're taking.

"I really did," she admits. A hint of darkness crosses her face. "I'm over him, you know. It wasn't like that. To be totally honest, I'm not sure I was really *into* him beyond feeling like the match made sense in my life, in what . . . in what my mom wanted and who the world wanted me to be and be with." She shrugs, something I feel against my side rather than see.

"You're saying the world doesn't want you to be with some grumpy FBI agent?" She smiles.

"You're not grumpy anymore."

"Yes, I am." She rolls her eyes.

"Not to me, you aren't. At least, not when it matters." And I guess that's the important part, right? "But anyway. I didn't need to do it because I'm still hurt, not in that way at least. It was just . . . the closing of that book so I can start another."

She's staring at me, nerves creeping into her eyes like she's worried I might react poorly, like I might take her words the wrong way.

"Liv, if you have to do something petty to that jackass every day for the next three years to account for all of the time he took from you, I'll be your backup every single time. I do not care."

"Well, I don't think I need three years . . ."

"I'm just trying to tell you, whatever you need in order to feel good, to be the happiest version of you, I'll give it to you so long as every night, you come cuddle up to me in bed and fall asleep on my chest." Her smile widens, and fuck, she's so sweet.

What did I do to win this, this sweetness?

It feels that way, too. A prize I won, I earned.

"Every night, huh?" she asks, moving until she's straddling me in my lap, her chest pressed against mine. My hand goes into her hair, pulling her to me so I can kiss her, long and slow, to show her exactly how I feel about that.

"Fuck yeah. Every night for as long as you'll stay." Her eyes are hazy with a mix of joy and lust, and her lips tip a bit with a smile.

"Don't tempt me, Agent Valenti. You might never be able to get rid of me."

I shake my head and move, rolling over her until she's under me on the couch, letting out a squealed laugh as she does.

"That's my plan," I whisper against her lips, and then I proceed to show her just how much I mean that.

FIFTY-ONE

TUESDAY, NOVEMBER 14

The front light is on at my house, and for the first time since she started spending more and more time here, I wish it weren't.

I wish I were walking home to a dark, empty, lonely house. Not because I don't want to see my girl—fuck, I spend every moment of every day anticipating getting out of the office to see her, trying to find ways to spend more time with her—but because I'm in a foul fucking mood.

We're two weeks out from Thanksgiving, and I had hoped Peterson had forgotten his arbitrary deadline. There's no way the man, despite his lack of experience with an actual *investigation*, expects this case to just wrap up out of nowhere.

Right?

Except over the past month or so, I've learned while doing some research in my downtime that Peterson only got this job through a friend of a friend, and if I'm being totally frank, I'm not sure why. When I dug to find his resume, there was nothing exemplary that would have made him a shoo-in for the position, either.

But none of that matters because today, not long before I was

about to leave the office after another fruitless day of trying to clear
Liv and pin this mess wholly on Reed, he came to my cubicle.

"How's the Reed/Anderson case going?"

His body was barely six inches from my face, and the way he
crowded my space, I had to wheel my chair back a bit before turning
to look at him.

"The Reed case, you mean."

"I said what I meant, and I'm getting really fucking tired of you
correcting me, Valenti."

I took a deep breath and chose my next words carefully to ensure
I didn't say anything that would get me fired.

"I just mean Reed is the culprit."

"And Anderson is the dumb broad who let him use her. What
of it?"

I remind myself that in this building, Olivia is not my woman.

She is not mine at all.

She is just a victim I need to work to exonerate.

Who could have foreseen this entire case would get so messy, so
intertwined?

*Probably everyone, Andre. You're the only idiot who was too blind
to see you were going to fall for her.*

"Got it. It's going."

"Am I going to be charging her or Reed the Wednesday before
Thanksgiving?"

My pulse slowed, and my hands went clammy.

"What?"

"Told you I want to go to Thanksgiving and rub it in my brother's
face that I closed this case." *You didn't do fucking anything for this
case, you jackass.* "No matter what, I'm standing at a podium in two
weeks and announcing the investigation."

"I just need time, Peterson."

"And I can hand this case off to any other idiot on this team.
You're all interchangeable." My jaw tightened because I know while

other agents are phenomenal with fieldwork, I'm the best under Peterson's supervision with computers, tech, and analyzing.

"Bet a bunch of them would love that promotion you've been offered." He said it like he knows it's a carrot dangling, and he's been using it all along.

I also knew if I argued, it wouldn't help my situation. I breathed in deep through my nose, closed my eyes, and nodded.

"Got it. I'll make sure I've got everything before then." His face went from annoyed and accusing to cordial and friendly before doing that thing that makes my skin crawl, knocking twice on the side of the flimsy cubicle like we're good old buds instead of me wanting to rip his eyeballs out.

"Great, that's what I love to hear. Talk to you soon, Valenti."

And then I stayed later than anticipated, knowing Liv was getting a cab to my place right after work so her car wouldn't be spotted by Reed and cause an issue, knowing I could have left and gone right home to her.

But knowing that I still don't have a solution to her problem.

To *our* problem because what ails Liv now ails me, and I've taken it upon myself to become her panacea.

And it's killing me that I can't *fix* this.

I walk into my house, the one the bureau pays for so I can watch that scumbag but has become just another constant reminder of how twisted this all is, and lock the door behind me. Liv turns toward me on the couch, a sweet smile on her lips because she's always so fucking ecstatic to see me, like a little corgi who hasn't seen its owner all day.

She's already cozy in a little pajama set with an oversized button-down shirt that's so big, it dips a bit off her shoulder. If I wasn't drowning in frustration and stress, I'd walk over, lean down, and press my lips to that exposed skin, missing her after a full twelve hours of not touching her, and her hand would move up, her blunt nails running through my hair and scratching at my scalp in a way I've come to crave.

"Hey, you," she says, and her voice is so sweet, it almost cuts through the cloud of my shitty mood, but not quite.

"Hey, Liv," I say, hanging my bag on the hook next to the door then moving to the kitchen to grab a drink.

I need to figure this out. I need to clear this shit up so we can have this: easy nights where I come home to her smile and her soft words and I don't have to stress about what's going to happen to her in two, three weeks. It's all on me, and I'm fucking this up.

The sound of her soft feet on hardwood hits my ears as I crack open a soda, but I don't turn to her. Her hand touches the small of my back, soft and kind—more so than I deserve right now.

"How was your day?" she asks, and I turn and look at her.

I need space.

I need room to breathe when she's not right here, reminding me of how much I'm failing her.

"Fine. I'm gonna go in my office, work some more," I say.

Try and look over everything again and figure out what to do in order to save this, save us.

"Oh, uh, okay . . . ," she says, and the way her eyebrows draw together in confusion, the way hurt flashes on her face almost does me in.

But I remember Peterson's threat.

So I move to walk past her, to brush her off and grab the key for my office and stay in there, not leaving until I've found a solution.

I almost do, too, almost escape,

And then her frail, nervous voice hits my ears.

FIFTY-TWO

Can you fuck someone out of a bad mood?

TUESDAY, NOVEMBER 14

In another life, I'd let him walk into that room, mad and ignoring and brushing me off.

I'd let him go, and I'd stay up all night on the couch, watching that door like a hawk but pretending I wasn't, dissecting every word and movement I'd made in the last ten minutes, the last day. I'd twist myself in knots, sure I was the problem and I was the only one who could fix it and if I really, truly cared, I would do it without further burdening him.

But I'm not her anymore.

Or at least, I'm really *trying* not to be.

So instead, I speak before he's out of my line of sight, before he's locked away and inaccessible.

"Did I . . ." I breathe, biting my lip as I watch him pause with his wide back to me. "Did I do something wrong?"

He turns and his face . . . He looks like he might snap at any moment, like he might lose his mind.

"What?" Something like concern crosses his eyes but is gone before I can recognize it.

"You're clearly mad. Angry. Did I . . . Did I do something?" Acid churns in my stomach as I watch softness take over his face for the blink of an eye before it's shuttered and replaced by something colder.

"This is how I am sometimes. If it's too much for you, we should end this now." His jaw ticks as it tightens, as his hands curl into fists like he has some kind of bottled-up energy he needs to release and isn't sure how, hasn't found the right outlet.

That takes me aback but also adds clarity to the conversation.

It's not about me.

Relief pours in.

A part of me recognizes with shallow pride this is also growth for *me,* to hear his words and accept it's not about me, it's not something I did.

"It's work?" I ask.

"It's none of your business, Olivia. Go watch your show, relax. Go to bed."

I fight the urge to do as he says, to put my head down and go to the couch and overthink every interaction, to fall back into old habits he helped me climb out of.

Every molecule in my body is telling me this is somehow my fault. That even though he said it's not me, even though I'm pretty sure it's work, it's something *I* need to fix.

"No," I say, my voice firm. He looks at me with confusion. "I won't do that because we're both going to stay here and figure this out. If it's not something I did then we can talk it out, figure out a way to fix it."

"Olivia—"

"I was with a man who treated me like shit and told me things were my fault, even when they were out of my control. You are not him, but I'm telling you right now, I'm feeling that. In my gut, I'm feeling it, and I'm *fighting* it." I'd feel pride for having this conversation, for admitting this right now, but I'm too worried about him.

His face softens.

"This isn't about you, Livi. I promise. I'm just . . . I'm just in my head. I gotta go sort it out."

"If you can tell me a single good reason for me not to be here, for me not to help, I'll leave, Andre." A battle crosses his features, like he's fighting with himself and isn't sure what to do.

"This isn't your job." His voice is softer now, less unmoving.

I'm telling him the truth: if he tells me he needs space, that he really doesn't want me here, and says it with conviction, I'll leave.

But by now, I know Andre Valenti. This isn't how he would act if he wanted me gone. He wouldn't play games, wouldn't be cruel and uncaring.

This is a man who is struggling with something out of his control. And for a man who loves control, that is unbearable for him.

"I know that," I assure him. "I know your emotions are not my job, not my fault. I'm a recovering people pleaser, though. I want to help you. When I see people I care about struggling, I want to fix it. You are people I care about. Please. Let me help. Tell me what's wrong."

He sighs, and it sounds like bone-deep exhaustion, but not in the sense that he needs to sleep.

"Things aren't going well at work. Like I said, this happens. The job I have . . . It happens. I'm angry and frustrated and I have no way to channel it. That is not your job, though, Olivia. Your job is not to fix me, and this is *not* your responsibility."

"I want it to be, though."

And then his truth comes out. "If I put my shit on you, make it your shit, then I'm no better than he is."

There it is.

He doesn't want to give it to me because he doesn't want me to feel like it's my job, my responsibility. "You are so much better than he ever was simply because you're asking—no, begging me to put myself first. That means more than anything ever could. But you and me, Andre? We're a team. Every time I've struggled, you've lifted me up and coached me through it. Let me do the same for you." I take a step forward, no longer willing or able to have this space between us, wanting a physical connection in order to fuel my emotional one to him.

FIFTY-THREE

TUESDAY, NOVEMBER 14

She steps forward, and the pull I always feel to her intensifies, intoxicating and undeniable.

"Stay there, Olivia," I say, watching her battle the need to come here, to take care of me like she loves to do to. To fix the sour mood that isn't her fault, isn't her responsibility.

My little people pleaser.

My menace.

Mine.

"Andre, there's something wrong. Please, let me help."

"Why don't you go home tonight, stay at your place? I'm not good company." She visibly flinches and I fucking hate it. Hate seeing it, her fear of rejection making itself known. I attempt to soften the blow. "Or if you don't mind waiting for me to let off some steam, go in my room, go to bed. Maybe I'll just go for a run or . . ." She steps forward, and my body freezes because her face has changed.

Gone are her nerves, the sharp pain of rejection.

In their place is determination.

Fuck.

"You need to let off steam?" she asks, and her steps closing the gap between us turn sultry as her hands move up to the top button of her pajama shirt, slowly undoing it. She's braless underneath, like she always is for bed. "Use me. However you need, I'm here."

The emotion bubbling under my skin transforms from frustration over my work and circumstances to a different kind.

"Fuck, Liv." I groan, watching her fingers work.

"Tell me what you need, Andre." Her fingers move on little buttons, slowly undoing them and revealing creamy skin, and my eyes are completely transfixed on the movement.

Still, I give her an out.

"I'm not in a good place, Liv." My voice is low and gravelly, and she's barely a foot from me now, no longer approaching me as she undresses but instead waiting for me to give her my demands.

For me to take what I need from her.

For her to give me all the good that is *Olivia*.

"I know. Take me there with you." I groan at her words and her implication, watching as her hands finish on the buttons of her shirt.

"I can't. I can't, Olivia."

"You'd never hurt me. I know that. You know that even if you're lost in your head."

"Menace," I say in a whisper, but I can't help it as my hand reaches out, wraps her waist, and pulls her into me.

"What do you *need*, Andre," she whispers, her head tipped back, her lips brushing my own. I didn't even realize I had dipped my head, letting her soft lips graze mine.

"I need to let off some steam," I repeat, but this time my words aren't a warning; they're a request.

"Okay. Tell me where you need me." I stare at her, trying to comprehend what she said, what she means. "Do you want me on the bed? Do you want me on my knees?" Her voice gets breathier with each word, and if I wasn't watching it happen with my own eyes, I wouldn't believe it.

Olivia is getting turned on by this.

By the idea of me using her to overcome my frustration.

By the idea of . . . serving me.

My little people pleaser.

My fucking *menace*.

God.

I don't think there could be a more perfect woman for me.

I don't answer her question, instead turning my back to her and walking to the bedroom.

She follows, and as she approaches the door, I'm leaning against the bedframe, starting to take off my work shirt.

"Stop," I say as she starts to step into the room. She does of course. "Undress."

The shirt is unbuttoned already, so she simply pushes it off her shoulders before stepping out of her shorts. I finish unbuttoning my dress shirt, tossing it into a pile in the corner, leaving me in just an undershirt, before I start on my belt.

Liv's eyes watch as I work on it, undoing the clasp then slipping it from the loops and tossing it with my shirt. Then, I start on the button of my pants, slowly undoing the zipper. Her tongue peeks out, licking her lips, and my cock jumps to attention.

"On your knees in front of me, little menace," I say. My voice is so low, I barely recognize it, but I can't help it between the way she's looking at me, what I have planned for her, and the frustration still boiling in my veins.

She does as I ask, too, moving quickly and kneeling before me. I use a hand to rake her hair back, my other to tip her chin up. "You look so pretty like this," I murmur. "Take my cock out."

Her hands move to where my pants are unzipped but not down, and she pushes my boxer briefs down a bit and pulls my cock out. Her hand moves along the length, jacking me, but her eyes stay on me.

"Before we do anything, Olivia," I say, my hand still moving through her hair. "Before anything, I need you to know two things. One, you are not responsible for my emotions." She nods. Her hand doesn't leave my cock, and it takes everything in me not to ignore talking to her and just get on with it.

"Two, you're on your knees for me not to serve me, not for any reason other than you want to be. Do you understand me?" She nods. "If you're done, you're done. Understand?"

This is important to me, for her to understand this.

"Yes, Andre. I understand." She moves her head closer to where my head is and licks the precum off my dick. "I really, really want to do this."

"Jesus Christ," I groan, and then I take over.

I grab her hair in my hand, tugging it back hard until her eyes meet mine, wide and turned on, my cock in her mouth. I pull out, leaning back just a bit so there's more room.

"Open," I say, and she knows exactly what I want, opening her mouth and sticking out her tongue. Then, I tap the head of cock there, one, two, three times.

This visual?

I absolutely will remember it for the rest of my life.

I know she likes it, too, when she moans.

"Do you like this, menace? Being on your knees, ready to suck me off?" She nods and I smile. Slowly, I rub my cock along her open mouth, her tongue out, like I'm fucking it. "The only time you're a people pleaser anymore is when you're on your knees for me, you hear me?"

I back off and look at her so she has room to answer.

"Yes, Andre. I understand."

"Good girl. Now suck me, Liv," I say.

I don't have to ask her twice before one hand goes to the base of my cock, the other moving to my thigh to steady herself. She starts slow, sucking on the end, licking me, torturing me, before she slowly slides the entirety of me in her mouth then out again. The slow movements drive me fucking wild. My hand in her hair directs her gently, showing her what I like, the depth I want, the speed I need right now. When I tap the back of her throat for the first time, I moan.

"Play with yourself," I order, and she does, spreading her legs and touching herself. She moans, the vibrations running up my cock and into my balls almost instantly. When she lets out another moan as I slide into her mouth, it allows me to go even farther, sliding down her throat as her eyes go wide.

"Are you wet? Does sucking my cock turn you on, Olivia?" She moans her agreement, her eyes slipping closed.

"Keep your fucking eyes on me, Olivia. When my cock is in your mouth, you look at me." Another moan, but her eyes stay open this time.

"Such a good girl you are," I murmur, gathering her hair in my hands once more, creating a hold for myself. "Now, I want to fuck your face. Are you okay with that?"

Letting off steam or not, I won't do anything she doesn't want.

But Olivia moans, nodding with my cock in her mouth as she continues to slide over it, her fingers working faster at her clit.

The wet sounds coming from her pussy are a clear indication she's fucking loving this.

"Okay. If I need to stop, slap my leg," I tell her, but her free hand moves to my ass, pulling me deeper.

"Such a little menace," I say. "Loosen your jaw. Let me use that pretty little mouth of yours." There's another moan from her, a deep one that comes from her chest, before her jaw goes slack around me. The visual—Liv on her knees for me, serving me, eyes wide, playing with her pussy, jaw loose and ready for me to fuck her face . . . I groan.

And then I begin.

Using her hair as leverage, I piston my hips and start fucking her mouth, going as far back as she'll let me. She starts to moan, her eyes fighting to stay open, her hand working faster at her clit. Her tongue plays with the underside of my cock as best as she can while I thrust into her, the head slipping down the back of her throat with each movement.

"Fuck, Olivia. Goddammit. You should see yourself like this." I wrap my hand around her hair again, tightening the grip, and she moans.

Sweet Olivia secretly likes it rough, and I fucking love that about her.

Mine. Made to be mine.

And she makes it explicitly clear in the next moment.

"Stop, I'm gonna come," I say, tugging her hair to pull her off me. Her hand tightens on my ass, trying to get me to come in her mouth, I assume, but I slow my thrusts.

"No. I wanna see my cum on you, Liv. Claim you as mine." She moans because she loves that, too, when I get possessive and fucking caveman on her like a lunatic.

I've never been into that, into marking my territory, until Olivia Anderson.

Finally, I step back, and the hand that was holding me drops, moving to her tits and pinching a nipple.

"Don't stop," I murmur, watching her and slowly tugging my aching cock. "Keep playing with that pussy, baby. Widen your legs so I can see better." She does as she's told, and I see she's fucking *dripping.*

Jesus fucking Christ.

"Andre," she moans, and my name on her swollen lips will never not do it for me.

"I'm gonna come on your tits, Liv. Then I want you to get on that bed, ass to the edge, legs spread wide. I'm gonna make a mess of you."

She mewls, now riding her fingers, her legs spread so I can see everything. But her hand on her tit drops, giving me full access.

"Come on me, Andre," she murmurs.

I don't even need to wait a moment longer.

Two strokes of my cock and I'm groaning, forcing my eyes to stay open as I paint her chest with my cum. Liv moans as well, as if she's getting just as much pleasure out of this as I am. When I'm completely spent, I steal a moment to take in the vision before me, a moaning, panting Olivia on the edge of her own orgasm, covered in me, before I tip my chin to the bed.

I catch my breath and tuck my cock back in my pants as I watch her move quickly to her feet, then she gets onto the bed, scooting her ass to the edge as instructed and spreading her legs wide, her feet at the edge of the mattress as well.

Walking over, I take her in.

Fucking stunning.

Dark hair spilling on the light-gray comforter, her lips swollen from sucking me, cheeks flushed with desire, chest heaving and covered in my cum . . .

And her cunt, soaking wet, desperate for my attention.

I don't waste time once I stand in front of her.

"How close are you?" I ask.

"So close. Please, Andre. Please."

I smile before I slide two fingers into her, and she moans. Unlike normal, I don't fuck her with the digits, instead leaving them in deep and moving in short, quick circles on the swollen spot on the front of her.

"FUCK!" she shouts, her hips moving. I put a hand to her belly, pressing there, a thumb moving right above her clit and pulling so the hood moves back before putting my mouth on her.

"Jesus, fuck, Andre, oh my god." Her hand moves to my hair to hold me in place, and my teeth scrape against her clit. I keep working until I hear the wet sound I'm looking for then pull back. "What? No!"

"I told you, you're gonna make a mess for me, Liv," I say, then I use my fingers on her clit, leaving the hand on her belly to keep pressing, rubbing quick and hard.

"Holy shit," she screams.

She's so fucking close.

She's going to gush for me, and if I hadn't just come hard, my cock would be *painful.*

I put my fingers back inside, pressing on that spot that keeps swelling.

"Andre, no, what the fuck?" She moans, her head moving from left to right in anguish.

"Trust me, menace," I say before lowering my head again, sucking on her clit like she needs, giving her both relief and building her painful pleasure higher.

"Yes, yes, yes," she chants, hips moving in time with my fingers.

I stop again.

I move to her clit and start to rub.

Olivia *shrieks*.

"Oh god, fuck . . . No, Andre, I don't—"

"Trust me, baby. Make a mess for me, my menace."

The wet sound continues as she begins to convulse, Liv no longer in control of her own body as I continue my assault.

And then it happens.

She *screams*.

Olivia screams, and as I rub her clit, a gush of liquid comes from her.

"There it is. Jesus, fuck, the hottest thing I've ever seen." I moan, continuing to rub as she cries and moans and comes, her hips bucking before another gush follows.

"Holy fuck! Oh my god, oh my god!" As her body begins to jolt, as her clit becomes painfully sensitive, I slow my strokes before removing my touch altogether and, finally, running my tongue from entrance to clit, cleaning her.

I can't resist.

Then, I step back to examine my handiwork.

There's a wet spot on the comforter, and her tits are covered in my cum.

I've never seen anything more spectacular in my life.

Slowly, she comes back to, then she leans up on her elbows, surveilling the mess before looking at me.

"Did that, uh . . ." She smiles. "Blow off some steam for you?"

All I can do is laugh before pulling her up to me and kissing her.

FIFTY-FOUR

> Is it illegal to look at government documents about you?

TUESDAY, NOVEMBER 14

"We hit a dead end," he says into the quiet room. It's after we showered to clean up together and Andre ate a quick peanut butter and jelly, and we're lying in his bed once more.

"What?"

"With your case. I'm stuck. No idea where to go now. I'm trying . . ." He sighs, his chest rising and falling. "I'm trying to find the ties. Right now, we go after Reed, he gets a good lawyer, and with everything in your name, it's reasonable doubt. He gets free, we probably never get those funds back, they never go to where they need to go."

"Or . . . ?" I can hear the single word in his words.

"Or they pin it on you."

"But I didn't *do* anything," I say. Andre sighs, his fingers running through my hair.

"My boss is an ass."

"And wants to pin this on me?" I try not to show him the panic I'm feeling now.

"He wants to pin it on *anyone* that will get him the biggest gold star. He wants to *stand at a podium and tell the world someone is guilty so he can brag about it at Thanksgiving.*"

I just . . . This is *insanity*.

An entire criminal case based on bragging rights?

"That's why I was mad. It's frustrating. I want you free of this shit and right now, it's looking like . . ."

"Like I'll be guilty?" I squeak.

"Guilty, no. But you'll be stuck in court and put through the wringer. I have the proof you never went anywhere out of the country to open accounts—"

"You know where I've been?" I ask, cutting him off.

"I know everything about you, Olivia. If you ever ran, I could chase you. There's nowhere in this world you could hide from me, menace."

That should feel bad.

Should feel icky.

It should make me uncomfy.

But instead . . .

Heat.

I smile.

He rolls his eyes.

Then, slowly, an idea forms.

"What can you show me?" I ask.

"What?"

"Your files. What can you show me? I'm technically a suspect—"

"No, you're not." I try not to roll my eyes at his firm voice.

"I mean, it *sounds* like I am, but you know what I mean either way. How much of what you have can you show me?" He shakes his head.

"Legally? Nothing."

"I've already seen half of it," I say, thinking of that folder.

"That was not half of it. Not even close." I cringe, realizing how many documents there must be. "Plus, that's just because I was too much of an idiot to lock it back up."

"What about off the record?"

"Olivia—" But I'm excited now. My mind is stuck on this idea.

"I won't tell anyone. And who knows, maybe for once in my life, I'll be useful," I say with a little laugh and a smile, but he doesn't return it. Instead, his rough hand grabs my face, pulling it to him so he can look at me, his expression stern.

"No more of that, Olivia." My brow crinkles in confusion and I try to jerk my head back, but his hand on my jaw tightens. "I'm serious."

"What?"

"That self-deprecating bullshit, making it seem like you're not helpful, not worthy, not smart. Stop. It ends now."

"I don't understand." My voice is low now, as I'm in a panic.

"One day, I'll crack through that shell of yours and show you just how fucking beautiful and worthy and kind you are, but until then, I meant what I said before." He leans forward like he can't help it, pressing his lips to mine gently before pulling back. "You are no longer that people-pleaser version of yourself. You work only to make yourself feel all-encompassing joy at any given moment, no matter who else is in the picture."

"Andre—"

"Unless, of course, we're alone and you're naked. Then you're my little people pleaser." My pussy clenches even though it was sated not an hour ago.

"You do not laugh off your usefulness. You do not act like you are not the most incredible, amazing human on this planet. You've sacrificed enough."

"Andre, I was just joking."

"It's a joke you believe, so it's one I won't tolerate. Most mean jokes hold a modicum of truth, and yours about yourself are not fucking excluded from that."

I can barely catch my breath; it feels like I've been punched in the chest.

"Andre, I—"

He lets go of my chin, wrapping a thick arm around my waist and pulling me close before burying his face in my neck. "It's fine. We're fine, Liv."

As always, he knows I need that, that this conversation is making my stomach churn, that my brain started to twist it into me doing something wrong, him being mad at me, so I needed that reassurance. "I just am so fucking enamored with you, think you're so fucking amazing, and it kills me you don't think it too. But don't worry, we'll get you there." He presses a kiss to my neck then stands, reaching out for my hand. I grab it, and he tugs me until I'm up before he grabs my hand and leads me toward the room with the locked door.

"Come on," he says. Let's go do some illegal shit."

FIFTY-FIVE

What do you do if your ex is framing you for a crime?

TUESDAY, NOVEMBER 14

The illegal shit, if you couldn't tell, was looking through Bradley Reed's extensive file that Andre and the FBI put together. It showcases the calls he's made, and connections he's created, money that's going into and out of bank accounts, purchases that were made and are in one way or another untraceable.

That Chevy Nova? Paid for in cash, and neither his savings nor his checking ever saw a hit.

Same with the house which, to my horror, is deeded in *my name.*

Funny how the house I never lived in is in *my fucking name.*

"Where are the accounts?" I ask, trying to understand the gravity and span of his scheme.

Bradley has spent the last five years working for Hanson Finance Group, slowly siphoning funds and investments off his clients into shell accounts, charging fake interest and account management fees until the money finally makes it back to the original account with just a bit less than it started or the same amount, depending on the original interest rates. He also has fake clients that are under a million layers of fake names, many *ending* in my identity that he puts money into and then withdraws.

It's like one big shell game, trying to figure out what's going where. Apparently, his boss contacted the SEC when he noticed that while Bradley has the largest number of accounts with the group, he has the lowest percentage of return.

Also, of his over 400 accounts, about 2 percent of them are holding large amounts of money and collecting the full investment interest but attached to fake names and dead social security numbers.

"That's what we're trying to figure out," Andre says. "None of the typical strongholds have anything that we could trace to Reed, and of course, the offshore accounts won't let us just ask around without raising suspicion. From what we can tell, he hasn't spent all of it—he doesn't have a shit ton of real estate or investments or anything like that. He lives low-key, a few nice things here, a few there, but nothing extreme."

"He's cheap," I say under my breath, which makes Andre laugh out loud.

"Yeah, I've picked up on that."

"So, how can I help?" I ask, fighting the urge to tell him I'm of no help instantly because I'm stupid or I'm no good with numbers or whatever lie my brain tries to tell me.

"Just . . . look through these. I'm pretty sure it will be a bust, but maybe . . . You never know," he says, running his hand through his thick hair. It's chaotic from my grabbing it while he ate me, and the memory has my heart beating, my core throbbing all over again.

He notices, of course.

My agent notices *everything*.

"Or we can say fuck it and lock the door behind us and I can eat you out again before I fuck you."

Tempting.

So fucking tempting.

I lick my lips, and his devilish smile widens.

"No," I say like he's a naughty dog. "Later. I want to see if I can help at all. If not then you can fuck me until I can't see straight." I smile now and he shakes his head, pulling me onto his lap, where he sits at the desk, and kissing my neck.

"Jesus, what are you, 15? How are you hard already!" I say with a laugh, feeling him on my ass.

"Menace, I'm never far from being hard when you're around." He shifts me in an attempt to make me more comfortable before his hand lands on my upper thigh.

"Andre," I warn. His hand moves to open the manila folder.

"Go on. Get to work so we can leave this room."

"Or we could stay . . . ," I say, wiggling in his lap. His hand tightens on my thigh, and I laugh at the groan that leaves his throat before I start flipping through the pages.

I've almost given up on being of any real help to Andre about fifteen minutes later, when I've flipped through nearly half of the stack of manila folders and have nothing valuable to add.

There were a few times my heart raced when I got excited thinking I could be useful because I saw a name or a face I recognized. Inevitably, though, Andre already had the information, the little sneak.

Okay, so, it's his literal *job* to know that stuff, but still.

I'm starting to feel defeated, ready to tell him it isn't worth it and we should do what he promised, lock the door behind us and go fuck him into an even *better* mood, and then it happens.

There's a list of numbers under the word *Locations?* scrawled in what I'm learning is Andre's messy handwriting.

I almost moved to the next page but I don't, stopping to move a finger down the list, trying to pull out why they look so familiar from the recesses of my brain.

Why are these numbers so familiar?

They're two to three-digit numbers until the bottom, where there are five-digit numbers.

Five-digit numbers I've seen before.

Numbers I've *searched* before.

"You recognize this?" Andre asks, breaking into my mental deep dive.

"I . . . I think so. Have I searched any of these before?" His face displays clear confusion when I look over my shoulder at him. "On my computer."

"I don't know."

"Haven't you been watching me?"

"I mean, yeah, but I don't watch each and every thing you do. And . . ." He hesitates before continuing, "I stopped." My head moves back in confusion.

"Were you taken off the case?" He shakes his head.

"No, I stopped checking your search. It was after, uh. After we, you know. After we got together." A smile starts to pull on my lips as a blush comes over his cheeks. "It started to feel weird, okay? We were . . . And you didn't know. It was an invasion of privacy. I set a flag to your stupid Google doc so if you opened that revenge plan, I could stop you from doing something really dumb, but that's it."

My smile widens farther as his blush deepens, and I put a hand on his cheek.

"You are too sweet, you know that? You're a good man." He turns his head and nips my thumb.

"Well, that's actually a lie. There's one thing I never stopped monitoring." I raise an eyebrow and he sighs. "You gotta promise not to get mad."

"Andre—"

"It was part for your own good, part really fuckin' bad jealousy." That confuses me.

"Jealousy?" He sighs, closing his eyes before he speaks, but his words come out in a hurried rush that I can't understand.

"What?"

The next time, they're slower but mumbled.

"Andre, speak like a normal human. You're worrying me." I try to stand, worried I might be about to get *really* mad at him, but his arm tightens like a vice grip and he turns me somehow so I'm straddling him, facing him.

"I've been blocking some of your calls." Silence fills the room. "Well. Just one caller. Reed's tried to call you at least a dozen times since you went to his house the first time."

A long beat passes before I speak.

"What?"

"Your ex-fiancé has tried to call you, and I intercepted and rejected all of the calls." When I don't respond, he continues. "Mostly to your cell, occasionally to your work number."

"I'm . . ."

"One time, he called your mother. I diverted that one too. I don't have access to her line, but I do have access to his." He bites his lip.

I think about what he's telling me.

Bradley has tried to contact me and Andre stopped him.

"I know that's a lot. It's intrusive, and it honestly could fuck the case. Maybe even would have *helped* the case if you had just talked to him, but . . . I don't know. I did it before we were even an us and I didn't know why."

"And now?"

"And now what?" He doesn't understand what I'm asking.

"Do you know why you did it now?"

"Oh. Fuck yeah." He smiles a half smile, and his smile and his words make *me* smile. "I'm head over heels for you, Olivia Anderson, and I'm pretty sure I was even before I knew you. When this all started, I thought you were a spoiled brat who was too caught up in herself to notice, but even then, even before I knew you were caught up in wanting everyone to *like* you and keeping everyone happy, I *knew* you. I saw you going to Edna to keep her company and saw you doing free work for nonprofits without having to rope in Cami. And, of course, I saw you were so fucking beautiful, it hurt. I tried, Liv, tried not to like you, tried not to be pulled in by how sweet and kind and beautiful you are, and I failed." My jaw has dropped, and my eyes are wide on Andre as I try to process what he's telling me. His hand moves, brushing my hair back.

"So when I saw that first call come through, I looked at it and redirected it. He didn't deserve any more of your time, and you were thriving without him. You weren't even sad, weren't missing him, none of that. It's like you knew it was never right and reverted to a time before him, and I didn't want that asshole to fuck it up."

His thumb swipes my cheek, catching a tear I didn't realize had fallen,

"I kind of need you to say something, Liv, or I'm going to lose it thinking I fucked this up so bad."

I nod then sit still there for a moment, trying to collect my thoughts, trying to tell him something beautiful and meaningful and consuming like he just gave me.

"These numbers are zip codes," is what I come up with. His face screws up in confusion. "And country codes."

The man confesses his love, tells me he probably broke a law or two because he was jealous of my shitty ex, and I tell him that a bunch of random numbers are zip codes.

Dear Lord.

"Oh. And I love you too."

Another moment passes before he tips back his head, his long neck flexing with the movement, and laughs.

A deep, full-belly laugh that vibrates through my whole body.

The kind of laugh that's so contagious, I start to laugh as well.

His arm tightens on me, and when his laugh dwindles, he buries his face in my neck.

"God, that felt good," he whispers there. My hand moves to run through his hair before his head moves back up, his lips against mine. "I've been dreading this conversation."

"You're lucky it came with a very, very sweet declaration." His smile falters.

"You know that wasn't just talk, right? It wasn't so you would forget about me blocking him. You can scream; you can be mad. You want space, I'll give it to you." His arm loosens, and I grab at his wrist, keeping it where it is.

"You let go, I'll kill you."

His smile widens. "You're insane, you know that?"

"So are you. We're quite the pair." He shakes his head, but he's still smiling, so it's a win.

And then, he sighs, the smile faltering but his free hand moving to play with my hair, tuck the strands behind my ear.

"Hate to tell you this because you looked so excited, but I know those are zip codes and country codes." He says it gently, like he's afraid I'll be upset, but the reminder has me smiling.

"What are they for? It says locations."

He sighs before turning the desk chair so both of our sides are facing the table. "Locations for where we think Reed is keeping his money. These are cities in those countries." His fingers touch the longer numbers then the shorter ones. "But without any account numbers, we can't do anything. The countries are known safe havens for money laundering and offshore banking, so it's already going to be more difficult to recover those funds, but without the accounts numbers?" He lets out a soul-deep tired sigh. "We're shit out of luck."

I smile.

I smile so big, my fucking face hurts.

"What if I had the numbers? The account numbers, I mean." He freezes.

"What?"

"Would it help? If I could get you the account numbers?"

"Well, yeah. Then we could trace them to find the funds and link them to Reed. It wouldn't fix everything, but also . . ."

"But what?"

"We still have the issue of your name being on everything, Olivia."

"But I didn't *do* anything. What if I give your boss the numbers myself?" He sighs.

"I mean, it might help for sure. But your name is attached to all of the American ghost accounts." My stomach churns.

"But it *wasn't me.*"

"I know that. The bureau knows that. But if Reed got a really fuckin' good lawyer, he could claim you manipulated him, that it was all you and he was blinded by love."

"But I didn't—"

"And he could claim that he found out and that's why he called off the wedding."

My blood runs cold.

"I . . ." I don't know what to say.

"I haven't brought it to Peterson yet, but I think that was his plan. He was either thinking ahead or got scared and wanted a sure bet, a way out if he got caught. Who knows, he could have had a lawyer advise him. There could be a million reasons, but . . ."

"But it would work," I say quietly.

"And my boss wants an ironclad case."

"I hate him," I say, a wobble in my voice I know Andre can hear.

I know he definitely heard it when he wraps me in his arms. "I know, baby."

"Why me?"

"Honestly? I'm not sure. Probably your mother, your family. Enough exposure to make it seem legit, but not too much where you were hounded."

I think of all the times we'd have dates and go to premiers or fancy dinners.

Places we'd be *seen* together instead of at home, hanging out.

I was *so stupid.*

My mind keeps working, trying to unravel this mystery, to figure out whatever we need to.

"Why was he trying to contact me?" I ask, my brain running in a million and seven directions, trying to understand the situation and the consequences and what my future could look like.

"What?" I'm still in Andre's lap in his office, still wrapped in him, but I need to pace.

I do my best thinking when I'm pacing.

Moving off him, I start doing just that in the small room, trying to work this out like it's not a potential felony, but a PR nightmare that needs to be worked on and refined.

That I can handle.

"Why is Bradley reaching out? Did he leave messages? Did he text me?"

Andre slowly understands.

"No messages, but I interrupted a few text messages." He looks guilty, but I shake my head.

"No time for that. What did they say?"

"Mostly just asking you to call him."

"Anything else? Why would he need to talk to me when he couldn't even bother to put my things in a box?"

"He mentioned a frame? A photo?"

I smile.

There it is.

There's the in.

FIFTY-SIX

Is going undercover hard?

TUESDAY, NOVEMBER 14

Two weeks ago, I was cleaning out my townhouse and decorating for fall, as a basic bitch does, and I tipped over the cardboard box with all of my stuff I hadn't found a home for yet from Bradley's. The gilded frame I gifted him that was hiding in the closet was in there, and it tipped over as well. While the glass was just fine, the back had popped off, and a slip of paper was between the backing and the photo.

In one column was a list of one or two digits, and in the middle column was a list of four, five, or six digits and letters. A third had a wide range of long strings of numbers, anywhere from just five to seventeen of them.

I sat for an hour googling the different combinations until I went cross-eyed and eventually figured out it was country and city postal codes.

The final column remained a mystery and I got bored, so I popped it back and basically forgot about it.

Until now, when it's all making sense.

"I have the account numbers and country and city info." Andre stares at me, watching me pace as I put the pieces together. "I saw a gift I gave him hidden in a corner and I was mad he just threw it there. Took it with me when I got my things. But a few weeks ago, the frame fell, and inside, there was a slip of paper."

"That's why you asked if I was watching your search history.

"I was looking up the numbers, trying to figure it out. That's why he's calling me, Andre. He needs those numbers."

"But it still doesn't help—"

"I'll talk to him."

"Absolutely not." His words are firm, and I know he wants them to be final. Too bad.

"Why not!?"

"Because I don't like it."

"What's he going to do, say mean stuff to me? I have what he needs, Andre. And if he set up the accounts in my name, I have the power. I can call all those banks and transfer the money wherever I want. I could turn it all into your boss, try and get a plea deal or something—"

"It doesn't work that way, Olivia." I reveal what my mind has really been thinking.

"I could get a confession, Andre."

Silence rings in the small room, and I stop pacing, turning to face him.

"Absolutely not," he says.

"Andre—"

"No. No, Olivia. No. You're not doing that. You're not getting yourself deeper into this."

"What's the other option? I hope you can find something before your boss gets too antsy? Something that isn't in my name? We do this, I could be clear. You could get your promotion—"

"No fucking way." He's getting angry now, flustered. "There's no way I'm sending my woman off to some potential criminal so I can get a fucking promotion, Olivia."

I ignore the *so I can get a promotion* since he's clearly missing the point.

But I don't skip the other part.

"Is that what I am?" I ask.

"What?"

"Your woman. Is that what I am?"

"I'm on edge right now, Olivia. Now is not the right time to fuck with me."

"I'm just asking," I say with a smile.

"We cleared this up a while ago, Olivia. Of course you're mine." Warmth takes over, the confirmation feeling so good every single time.

"Well, then, you should know me. And you should know that I will absolutely be doing this."

"No, you won't."

"You can't stop me, Andre," I say, then he raises an incredulous eyebrow. I sigh.

"I don't want you any further involved."

"Do you have a better plan?" I ask, and his brows come together.

"What?"

"Do you have a better plan? To get me out of this?"

"I-I-I," he stutters, unsure of how to answer but still wanting to, needing my safety.

"You come up with a better plan, I'm happy to follow your lead."

He glares at me.

Somehow, I know I'm going to win this one.

FIFTY-SEVEN

How to get your ex arrested	🔍

FRIDAY, NOVEMBER 17

I do, in fact, get my way a few days later when I sit in Andre's kitchen with him and send off a text to Bradley, asking what he needs.

He replies almost instantly, asking about the frame, and I tell him I want to have dinner and I'll bring it with me.

Andre *hates* this part of my plan, but I was right.

We're at a dead end, and there's *nowhere else to go.*

This leads to today, me wearing a wire underneath an extremely tight dress Bradley'll hate. He'll think it's too flashy and cheap even though I feel hot in it. In contrast, Andre can't take his eyes off me as I get dressed for my dinner with my ex.

"Why are you wearing that again?" he asks with a glare. I smile as I brush eyeshadow onto my lid meticulously.

"Because Bradley will hate it."

"Isn't the point to get him on your side?" he grumbles.

"Yes, but I'm also not going back to pushover Liv, who lived and died for his approval." A gleam comes to Andre's eyes, and the battle there is so clear. He wants to protect me but also wants to give me this moment.

It makes me smile.

"I hate this, you know?" He leans in the doorway and watches me.

"I know. It's why I love you. You hate this, but you know I want to do it, so you make it as safe as possible." I turn to him, leaning in to press my lips to his before turning back to the mirror.

"Anything you want, menace, it's yours."

And I know he means that.

●●●

Two hours later, I'm in the tight red dress at a fancy restaurant Bradley picked out, sitting across from him and wondering what in the fuck ever made me think I could be legally bound to this man. He's insulted at least three people, two right to their faces, and terrorized the server, and we've been here for five minutes.

And now, his eyes won't leave my cleavage.

"If his eyes don't leave your tits, I'm coming over and punching him in the face," Andre says in the earpiece I'm wearing, hidden by my hair. I'm in his line of sight as he sits at a table about fifteen feet behind me and can picture his brows furrowed in total frustration.

"Valenti, get it together," another man Andre introduced to me as a coworker named Nico Mancini says.

"Do you fucking see him?"

"Kind of the point, man. If her tits are out, he can't concentrate on his lies."

I take a sip of my wine to try and hide my laugh.

"You look good, Olivia," Bradley says, leaning forward. His face is what I once would have thought was sincere and caring, but I see it for what it is now.

A mask.

A mask concealing neutrality, concealing he literally does not give a fuck about me or how I look; complimenting me just fits into his end goal.

"Thank you," I say, placing my wine glass down and staring at him. I let him guide the conversation, his perfect little doll like he always wanted.

But a doll designed for his downfall. It's almost poetic when you think of it.

"I miss you, Olivia," he says, and I forgot how much I hated that, how no matter how many times I asked, he always called me Olivia. My full name on his lips feels like disrespect.

Your name is Olivia; that's what I'll call you. That's what my mom always says when I ask her to call me Liv or Livi.

God. How did it take me so long to realize I was headed toward marrying my *mother?*

"It's really good to see you, Bradley," I say, not acknowledging or affirming the *I miss you.*

I don't.

Not even a bit.

"I'm sorry for how things . . . ended." He says it like it was just a little blip, like we got into a tiff and ended on bad terms instead of him cancelling an entire marriage minutes before it was to happen.

I stare at him for a moment and decide I'm already tired of being here. We might as well get this over with. The sooner I do, the sooner I can go back home with Andre.

"Oh, I understand why you did it," I say, twirling my hair around my fingers and leaning in so my tits pop out a bit more. His eyes move directly there, focusing on them and not moving even as he answers.

But before he does, I don't miss the growl of anger in my ear, Andre clearly pissed at a man staring at what he deems to be *his.*

Should going undercover turn me on? Is that normal?

"You do?" Bradley asks.

"Oh, you don't have to play the game with me, Bradley." I flip my wrist at him then use the hand to brush my hair on one side behind my back, making it easier to stare at my breasts.

"I swear to fuck, woman—" Andre says in my ear, but I ignore him.

He'll be more fun tonight if he gets mad now anyway. So instead of stopping, I roll my shoulders back and move one hand behind my back to twirl my hair there.

"The . . . game?"

"Well, yeah. I get it now. I get why you left me that day, why you couldn't reach out or be seen with me."

"Olivia, I—"

It's clear from the way panic flashes on his face, he thinks I'm going to reveal his true plan, that he did it because he essentially needed an alibi, needed to be able to lie and say he found out what *I* was doing and ended things in order to pin it all on me. That's the truth, after all, but I don't. I need him to believe I *trust* him. I need a confession, and accusing him won't get me that.

"You wanted to keep me safe, of course." I add a bit of Laceigh to my voice, just dumb enough to make men comfortable, just delusional enough to make them think they can drop their guard. A silly little woman like that, she won't remember anything, right?

In fact, over the years, I've wondered if Laceigh really *is* as dumb as she makes herself out to be or if it's her way of protecting herself. Too dumb to be competition for her sister, too dumb to be a threat.

"I wanted to keep you . . . safe." His words are skeptical, urging me to continue, waiting for me to fill in the blanks and so he can decide his next steps.

"Well, if we got married, we were tied legally, you know?" I twirl my hair on my finger, really amping it up, partly because it's interesting to see him *not* questioning the alarmingly new behaviors. I can't decide if he always saw me as dumb and naive or if he just never took notice of me at all.

"That's how marriage works, Olivia."

"Yes, but if we were tied legally, all of those accounts in my name . . . Well, I couldn't play dumb."

His face goes white, devoid of life and color.

"The accounts."

My hand reaches out, and I lean forward, basically letting my breasts that his eyes, despite his panic, have not left sit on the table-top. Then, I grab his hand reassuringly and smile.

"Yes, silly. The accounts. With all of the . . ." I lower my voice and lean farther forward. "*Money.*" He swallows, eyes moving from my boobs to my face for a millisecond then, of course, back to my boobs.

It's like they're a security blanket.

They do look spectacular in this dress, so I can't say I blame him.

"You know about the accounts?" he asks.

"Well, a bit. I don't know about them all, I'm sure. You're so good at what you do. I don't quite get exactly how it all got there, but I do know you made those accounts and put them in my name to keep me safe." Now he looks at me, trying to understand.

"To keep you safe . . ."

"Well, not safe, but . . ." I flutter my eyelashes like I'm truly honored instead of disgusted, as if stealing from people who trust you with their financial security in order to pad your own pockets is a romantic gesture. "Cared for." He doesn't speak, and my god, was he always this dumb? You'd think if he was trying to frame me for a crime and he had a reason for me to *play along with it,* he'd jump at the chance.

"You're doing so fucking well, baby," Andre murmurs in my ear, and those words, his small praise, drop into my belly, making me warm.

"I know you set those accounts up for me just in case someone found out what you were doing and you had to go away from *me.* At least then, I wouldn't have to worry about money while I waited for you to . . . come back to me."

I try not to gag on the words, try to keep my face serene as I speak of some kind of fictional universe where I would be stoically waiting for Bradley Reed to leave prison and come back to me after going to jail for stealing millions of dollars.

There's no way anyone is going to buy this, much less a man I dated for—

But again, I'm proven wrong.

I'm proven *so* wrong when understanding washes over his face.

"I'm relieved," he says then leans forward to caress my cheek.

My skin crawls when he touches me.

"I thought you wouldn't understand, would never forgive me for doing that. But you're right. If we were married, those accounts would be *our* accounts. Both of our assets would have been frozen instantly, so anything in your name would be stuck. I wanted to keep you comfortable. I was waiting for the right time to reach out, to tell you everything . . ." Then, he makes a face like he's hurt, a lie to make me feel guilty. "But when I tried to call you, you never picked up."

I fight an eye roll.

"I was so hurt, Bradley. I didn't understand, not at first. I only took that frame because I thought you didn't care. I didn't even find the numbers until a few weeks ago." The kindness melts from his face.

"I need that frame back." He says the words, and behind them is a hint of venom he probably thinks I can't hear.

But I can.

It churns my stomach. I once would have done anything to help this man, to keep him happy. And all along, I was just a pawn in a messy game for him. A game he still thinks I'm blind to.

"Because of the numbers?"

"Yes. Those are your account numbers. I need to access them so . . ." He pauses, trying to think of a lie on the fly. "So we can go."

"Go?"

"We can take everything and run."

"Won't that be dangerous?" He gives me his frat-boy smile and I fight the nausea.

"Come on, Olivia. You were always my lucky charm. It would be fine. We could run away," he says, his voice low. "We could run away somewhere where they'll never find us."

"But how?" I ask, and somehow, intuitively, I know this is it.

This is the moment that two things are going to happen.

One, I'm finally going to get my closure.

I thought I had it, thought that what the girls and I did had eased that, thought finding Andre did, thought coming to an understanding I was being used for my connections and my name did, but I know now, I didn't have that.

Not yet.

But right now, I'm about to get it.

Whether it's by him fully admitting everything to me or by knowing that in him doing that, in him trusting me the way I trusted him, he's locking the door and throwing away the key, I don't know.

But I am getting the closure I didn't know I needed.

And two, he's about to give Andre all the evidence he needs to make his case airtight.

"All of the accounts . . . they're in your name. They won't even know to look for you," he lies. I watch gears move in his head like he's putting together a new story, trying to piece together truths and lies, what I know and what he thinks will win me over in order to make a new story, a new plan. "Like you said, I had a plan to get those funds to you if something happened, to take care of you."

Bullshit, I think, and Andre echoes the word in my ear, always so in tune with me even when he's nowhere near me.

"I can't access them without you giving me the numbers, but we could . . . go now. Take all the money out, run from all of this."

"Right now?" He nods vigorously, a new, crazed look in his eyes.

"Come on, Olivia. We could go now, get married." He pauses, thinking before he nods. "Yes, we'd have to get married, I think. Then you couldn't testify against me."

"But all of that money, Bradley . . . it was . . . stolen."

Finally, for the first time, he pauses.

"What?"

And this is where it could all fall apart.

Because he admitted to the accounts, to setting them up and putting them in my name, but it's not a slam dunk without this confession. "It isn't . . . I would feel so guilty. That money . . . you took it from people." I twirl my hair again and pray to fucking God this isn't the downfall.

I need this to work.

We need this to work.

All of those people who lost money *need this to work.*

And then it happens.

I watch in real time what I used to think was charming, when he'd turn to someone at one of his work parties and smile and say something that was either a straight-up lie or should offend them, and how he always knew he'd get away with it.

"They don't even know it's gone, Olivia. I just took the extra interest. Barely anything. And they are all so rich, they won't miss it. You know how it is." He thinks that will work. He thinks because I know what that lie is like, because I get so easily frustrated with my mother, that I'll let this go, no big deal.

But I know the lie.

I know while some of his accounts were that, even more were people he manipulated who will lose their entire life savings, their retirements if this money goes missing.

He is a crook.

He is a criminal with no heart.

And we have his confession.

My job is done here.

"Okay," I whisper, the lump in my throat heavy, guilt seeping into my veins by even *pretending* to go with this. "Okay. I need to go back to my place to pack." His eyes lose the softness of trying to convince me.

"Give me the frame first."

"What?" I say with confusion.

"Give me the frame. Is it in your car? We can pay and get it right now."

"I don't . . ."

"Get it for me and I can start the process of moving things now. By the time you pack, I'll be done and we can go." His hand reaches out, and he gives me a look that, a few years ago, I would think was kind. Genuine, even.

But it's condescending and manipulative. Calculated.

It clicks.

He wants the numbers because he's going to run.

"I don't have it. I left it at home."

"What do you mean you don't have it?" That mean look crosses his face, one I've seen before but ignored. "God, Olivia, the whole point of meeting here was that fucking frame."

I furrow my brows, like I'm genuinely confused and hurt, and in a heartbeat, he catches himself, his face changing back to sweet and kind.

"I'm sorry. I'm just excited to run with you." He sighs.

"Look, I'll go get it and bring it back, okay? You can stay here. I won't be longer than"—I shrug—"fifteen minutes."

Gears turn in his mind for a few moments before he nods.

"Okay. Yes, that works. Fifteen minutes. No longer, though, okay?"

My stomach hurts, not from lying to him but from how little I mattered to him. I purse my lips and nod before grabbing my bag and standing.

"I'll be right back."

And then I leave him behind me forever.

FIFTY-EIGHT

MONDAY, NOVEMBER 20

From *Starlight* magazine:

Sources tell us here at Starlight *that Bradley Reed has been charged with embezzling funds from his finance group. According to the white-collar division of the FBI, they've been working closely with the SEC for over a year to get all of the intel needed for the case.*

He was officially charged on multiple accounts.

Inside sources tell us his former fiancée, Olivia Anderson, daughter of reality star Melanie St. George, was seen having dinner with him just minutes before he was arrested and was a lynchpin in the case.

And to that, we say hell hath no fury like a woman scorned.

FIFTY-NINE

how to deal with a narcissistic mother 🔍

THURSDAY, NOVEMBER 23

"So, we'll go to your mother's for . . . ?" Andre starts, leaning with his back on the wall next to the vanity I use to put on my makeup in my townhouse.

He's like this, I've realized.

When I'm in a room with him, he's close.

He likes to be near me—if he can, he's touching me, his hand always on my body, not in a suffocating way, not in a controlling way, just in a way that always tells me he wants to be with me. He needs to be with me.

He needs that connection almost as much as I do, and I think it's beautiful.

"Ideally, nothing," I say under my breath.

"Olivia . . ." I roll my eyes and groan, tipping my head back and looking to the ceiling with a huff. He pushes off the wall, walking close to me and kneeling beside me, putting a hand on my knee, squeezing gently before he looks at me. "If you want to bail, we're good. We don't go. We go straight to my mom's place, eat amazing food and laugh, and you let your guard down."

That sounds good.

It sounds so good, especially when I think about the uptight Thanksgiving my mother always puts on. Since I had my formal *meet the mother* last weekend, I know Gloria's dinner will be welcoming and kind and low-key, come as you are.

My mom will say *come as you are . . . so long as it passes my standards.*

And I just never do. I've come to understand—to accept that—but it doesn't make it suck any less.

But I also can't bail.

I don't know if the reason is my mother would be hurt, or I want to be with my family on this *family* holiday, or if I just *don't want to hear it* at the end of the day, but regardless, I can't do it.

I can't *not* go.

"But I know you, Livi, baby. I know if we don't go, that shit will eat at you until you're sick, and I know it will just be another thing your mother can hold over your head." His hand moves to tip my head—I was still looking at the ceiling with its stupid popcorn texture I hate— so I see him.

His eyes are so warm.

"So we're going to go, say our hellos, do the bare minimum, and as soon as you're ready to go, I'll tell everyone we have to go to my mom's place."

"She's going to give you shit."

"So let her give *me* shit. So long as she leaves you alone, I don't care, Olivia."

"But then she might not like you," I say under my breath, and even as I do, I know it wasn't the right thing to say.

Because Andre only cares about me.

His hands move, tugging me until I'm standing in front of him, his thumb going under my chin to tip it up.

"I do not give two fucks about your mother. If you want my honest opinion of her, I'll give it to you—it's not good. But you *are* good. And for you, I'll do whatever you want me to do. If that means she ends up mad at me, what do I care? I'm there for you. And I'm telling you right now, Olivia, she tries shit, I'm your shield. You decide if that's to absorb a hit or send it right back at her, but nothing hits you." I stare at him, wondering how I got him, how I got so lucky to win this man who is so amazing and gracious and kind.

"How did I get you?" I whisper, my filter rarely in place when he's touching me.

"I ask myself the same thing every day, Liv," he whispers, then he kisses me.

The first ten minutes go as well as one could expect. We arrive at my mother's home in New York she rarely even visits anymore, spending all of her time in California with her husband and for the show. Andre makes wide, amused eyes when a butler comes and takes our coats as we walk in, and when a server brings us glasses of Champagne in flutes, I fight the giggle that bubbles in my throat.

I think then this might be a tolerable couple of hours. We'll stay for appetizers and small talk and leave before my mom has one too many glasses of wine and forgets nitpicking in front of her friends isn't the best look on her. And, of course, I'll have Andre in my corner.

Until someone, one of her friends who is only a friend for the gossip, brings up Bradley Reed.

My back goes straight as the conversation moves across multiple people, each giving their own insight and opinions on the topic as if I'm not sitting in the room with them, as if they have any basis to *have* opinions. It's then I realize it's a room full of people who all have families of their own but have been intentionally excluded from them.

A room full of people who love to talk about others, but those closest to them don't even want to spend time with them.

Sunday is my Thanksgiving with my dad and Cami, a tradition

my parents started when I was a kid and my mom would have him fly me out to wherever she was as soon as I was off school, sending me home on Saturday once I'd played the role of sweet, dutiful daughter. On Sunday, my dad would make us a small Thanksgiving of our own with all of the fixings I liked, and we'd eat way too much pie and watch the Thanksgiving Day Parade he taped for me.

As I look around, I wonder why I kept that tradition and why I let my guilt and loyalty dictate how I spend this family holiday even now as an adult.

"I just wish you would have stayed out of it, Olivia," my mother says, breaking into my thoughts and bringing me into the conversation. My fingers play with the edge of my sweaterdress, but I keep my head up and my shoulders back.

I so desperately want out.

I want this conversation to end.

"And really, was what he did *so bad*?" she asks honestly. "From what the papers say, the people wouldn't have even noticed." I roll my lips into my mouth, taking a deep breath.

Normally, I would nod and apologize and hope it would be over quickly.

But I'm tired of that. That's not me anymore.

"It was still illegal. And I was being *framed* for it. I didn't exactly have a choice," I say.

"Yes, but now your name is being dragged through the mud." *In what circles?!* "And is that really fair? I bet if you had been more amendable, it wouldn't have even been an issue. He wouldn't have broken things off with you. You know how *stubborn* you can be. Then you could have lived comfortably for the rest of your life."

I blink at her, unsure of what to say, as Andre's hand reaches out to grab mine.

An anchor in the impending storm that is my mother.

"I don't need to worry about a man helping me live comfortably, Mother. I have my own incredibly successful business."

And then it happens.

The ship hits a fucking iceberg.

"Well, I also don't know why you're doing *that* either, Olivia. It just doesn't make any sense whatsoever." She says it with a chuckle, looking at the room of misfits who start laughing along as if on cue. The acid in my stomach churns, the canapé I had a few minutes prior suddenly not sitting well.

"I'm really proud of what I've done so far." My voice is as small as I feel. As much as I want to be this new version of myself, it just feels impossible.

"You're wasting your time on this silly little venture. I don't know why you encourage it, Daddy. You know as well as I do, she should be focusing on other things."

My grandfather, who has been silently watching, looks like he might speak, but then it happens.

My worst fucking nightmare.

Andre speaks instead.

"You'd think as her mother, you'd be the one championing her the most." My mother looks at him in confusion, like she both forgot he was here and is confused as to why he's speaking.

"What?"

"You're her mother. You'd think a mother would see what an amazing job her daughter is doing with her business—both in revenue and in community impact—and would be proud as hell. Fuck, *I* am proud of her. It just seems weird that you aren't."

The face she makes when Andre says *fuck* is almost humorous.

But her reaction to what he says is . . . less so.

"As her mother, I know what is best for her. You're . . . Well, I doubt you'll be around for long."

The nausea builds. The mean look in her eye says so much without a single word and all of it is terrible. It's classic Melanie, but something about it being directed at someone I care for . . . Fuck.

I open my mouth to argue, but Andre beats me there.

"If she were my daughter, I'd stand on the top of every fucking mountain and scream about her greatness. If I'm ever lucky enough to have a daughter, I'll be sure she spends every single moment of her life knowing she's loved and cherished and successful no matter *what* she does. She'll know she is doing amazing things even if they don't align exactly with what I would choose for her."

"You've only known Olivia for a few months. I have known her her whole life. She has a very long history of making poor choices. I'm just trying to help before she throws everything away." A beat passes, and again, I try to cut in, to tell my mom she has overstepped, to let Andre know I'm okay, that he doesn't have to fight my battles, but I don't get the chance.

"I don't get it," he says low. My mother rolls her eyes like he's an idiot.

"You wouldn't, but just trust me on this."

"I won't." Her annoyance turns to confusion.

"Andre—" I whisper.

I want this to end.

I want to leave, and I want him to *stop talking* so we can change the subject.

But I know there's no option for that. If nothing else, Andre is violently loyal, and hearing anyone, even my mother, talk about me in a way he would not approve of will never go over well.

"No. I'm tired of you making yourself smaller for everyone." He doesn't say it, but I can hear it. *Especially for her.* He's confessed he listened to conversations with my mother over the year, to our weekly calls, and didn't like the way she spoke to or about me.

This is the pot bubbling over. "I can't understand how a mother can't wholeheartedly support her daughter in following her own dreams. How a mother can look at her *successful* daughter, who has spent her entire life *catering to her mother,* and think she isn't enough. That she isn't living up to some expectation."

My mother tries to cut in, anger burning behind her eyes, but he doesn't let her.

"I've heard how you speak to her, how you constantly pick at her, try and tear her down, and I don't get it." He's officially snapped, and my mom is the obvious target. "How could you look at her, how gorgeous she is, how kind, how successful and hardworking—all despite being raised by *you*, I might add—and not think she's the most amazing thing on this earth? How can you look at this woman, look at *your daughter*, and not think God looked so fucking favorably on you the day he chose you to be her mother? Because I'm telling you right now, Olivia Anderson is the absolute *best thing* I've ever had the joy of being able to call mine. My only regret is it took so long to get here." My mom huffs and rolls her eyes like this is an inconvenience for her.

"You clearly don't—"

"No. *You* clearly don't. When I met her, every moment of her life, of her personality, was centered on making sure those around her felt good. That they were happy, even if it went against what was set for her or what she wanted, what she needed."

"Well—" my mother tries, but he keeps speaking. As he does, my grandfather continues to stare at Andre, his face stoic.

"I've watched her slowly find her own, slowly stop living for everyone else, dig herself out from under the guilt of not living up to the expectations of *you* and how her own desires for *her life* clash with yours. I've watched her stand up to a man who was *using* her for years, and today, I've watched you try and tell her she should have stood by him. The man who is a *criminal*." Andre shakes his head in disgust. "And she might not have had this, not with you around, but I won't let this fly anymore. When I'm around Olivia, there will be no more of this bullshit, of you casting your expectations on her, of you insisting she follows the path you outline for her. No more talking shit about her, not about her choices, not about her looks, not about her relationships. When I'm around her, you will speak with love and kindness or not at all."

"This is ridic—"

"And I'll tell you now, I'll always be around. If you're within ten feet of her, I'll be there as her fucking shield. So you can make your choice right now. Play nice and change the subject and never talk to her like that again or we're leaving."

She stares at him for a long moment, and for a heartbeat, I think the best will come.

For a split second, I think there might be hope, might be change. For a moment, I think this explicit callout is exactly what she needs to see the error of her ways.

And then her gaze, cold as ice, turns to me.

"You're going to let him talk to me like this, Olivia?" she asks.

And I think of the times she's talked to *me* with malice.

The times she's let her friends make small digs at me in her presence and didn't bother to defend me.

The times she's witnessed the twins talk to me are much worse than this.

And the bandage falls off.

The bandage I used to hide the damaged part of my heart, to pretend it didn't exist or was healing, falls off, revealing the deep, ugly bruise she has left after years and years of poking it. A permanent disfigurement that, even if it does heal at some point, with space and time and growth, will always be a sore reminder of what my mother will never be.

The rose-colored glasses have fallen to the ground, crunched under her shiny red sole, and I see it for what it is: a relationship that will never be what I need it to be.

So I stand.

I grab Andre's hand.

He squeezes so tight, it might have hurt if I didn't already hurt all over.

And I nod.

"Yeah. I think I am," I say.

And then we head to the door to leave.

SIXTY

how to choose your family 🔍

THURSDAY, NOVEMBER 23

We leave my mother's house and drive to Andre's mom's, where I'm welcomed with open arms. No one questions when I tear up throughout the day; no one asks anything when I keep staring at my phone, waiting for my mother to reach out.

Instead, the day is filled with kind words.

And hugs.

And homemade food is eaten without the worry of calorie count and on paper plates instead of fine china that will be bragged about and not used again until next year.

The day is filled with joking insults with no pointy barbs, not meant to maim but to bond.

And when I leave, I feel an aching clash of joy and pain. Joy that I got to spend the day with these people who welcomed me, joy that Andre has this, has *had* this his whole life, and a pain that cuts so deeply knowing I don't.

I won't ever.

I will never have a joyful gathering with no strings. Will never have hugs and cheek kisses that are given even though they might mess up clothes or makeup. I will never have an aunt putting another slice of pie on my plate with a wink. Instead, I have a mother who is carefully tracking every bit of food that enters her mouth and counteracting it with Pilates the next morning.

I have my dad, who would give me anything I want, but since it's just him—and now Cami—I'll never have the big gatherings, the loud, crazy family, the need to make seventeen sides just to feed everyone.

Andre lets me stew for thirty minutes after we get back to my place before he speaks, just enough time to get ready for bed and snuggle into his side.

"You don't see her without me anymore," he says.

"What?"

"And it's on our terms. Our location, always somewhere we can leave if things get to be too much."

"I don't—"

"I'm telling you now, Liv, she says anything that even *smells* like a fuckin' hint of disrespect to you, we leave."

There it is.

There's Andre, forever sticking up for me.

"Andre, it's not—"

"I know you won't cut her off, not completely, so this is the best we'll do. If you ever disagree, I'm willing to talk about things, but after today, I'm not going to budge. After a year of listening to that woman tear you down, it's going to take a while for me."

"Honey, there's no—"

"And again, this isn't something we have to worry about right now, but when we have kids, they are never alone with her for her to spit that venom at."

My heart stops.

My breathing stops.

I try to move, but his arm holds me in place.

"Andre—"

"I will never allow her to talk to someone I love like that. Not in my presence. Not ever."

Silence fills the room. and I determine he's done with his soliloquy.

"Kids?"

"Don't play dumb, Liv. You know where this is going." My hands shake as adrenaline and emotion and *everything* starts to take over my body.

Kids.

Love.

He wants to protect me from my mother—from everyone, really.

A part of me wants to argue with him. A part of me wants to tell him she was overwhelmed, that it wasn't her fault, that it was because her friends were watching.

But I'm done making excuses for her.

He stares at me expectantly, probably anticipating my argument, calculating what I'll say and how to counteract it, how to convince me to follow his lead. I surprise him.

Surprising Andre is my favorite thing to do.

Instead, I move and press my lips to his. Hard.

He freezes for a moment before his hand moves to my waist, pulling me closer as he deepens the kiss. It's filled with love and admiration and confidence and gratitude all rolled up into this feverish moment that instantly has me needing him, needing some kind of connection to him.

I direct my hands to his pajama pants, ready to put my mouth on him, to thank him for giving me this, for protecting me, but he swats me away.

"No, no, no," he says. "No way."

"What? Andre, come on, I want to—"

"After that, I serve you, Liv. After that, you lie here and take all the fucking pleasure I can give you." He puts a hand on my chest, pushing me until I'm on my back.

"Andre." I try and argue, but his fingers are hooking into my sleep shorts, taking them and my undies down as he crawls down my body. Once they're past my feet, he uses both hands to spread me wide before running his tongue flat against me from entrance to clit, and I lose any remaining will to argue.

His lips move to the inside of my knee and slowly, such a tortuously slow ascension, he begins pressing open-mouthed kisses along my skin. "Do you know," he starts, pausing to kiss another spot slightly higher. "How fucking beautiful you are?" Another kiss. "Do you know how badly I wanted to skip Thanksgiving and drag you and that tight sweaterdress home and spend all day in this bed?" Another kiss and a nip of his teeth pulls a moan from me. "Do you know how it is to watch you question yourself and not be able to set you straight?" A kiss. "Not be able to claim what's *mine*?" I moan again and not from his touch.

He smiles.

It's a feral smile, a wolf spotting a bunny rabbit.

"Do you like that? Me being wildly protective of you?" He licks up an inch. "Possessive?"

"Yes," I moan, my hips arching as his mouth gets closer to where I need him. "I love it. I want to make you crazy."

His lips hit the juncture of my thigh and my pussy before he starts over on the other side. "You fucking do. So crazy, Olivia." He kisses up my thigh once more, and each inch he moves feels like a mile as he nears where I need him most.

"I need you to know every moment of every single day how fucking beautiful and smart and kind you are." He hits the crease at the other side before smiling wide at me. "I'm determined to spend however long it takes and then every day after that proving to you just how fucking magnificent you are. How worthy you are." His breath is brushing across my clit with each word.

"Andre, please." I moan.

"Yes, tell me exactly what you need, Liv. Take it from me." Without thinking, I move my hips up a fraction, his bottom lip brushing against where I need him most.

"Oh god."

"There she is." He puts a hand on either thigh. "What do you need, Olivia? Take it."

"I need . . ." Desire burns me, turning any hesitance to ash. "I need you to lick my clit."

"Good girl," he murmurs but doesn't move. I groan, both at his words and his lack of movement. "Now take it."

I don't understand.

I'm lost in a haze of lust, pushing my thin cami up so I can play with my nipples in an attempt at getting *some kind* of relief. But I don't understand what he's asking, what he wants.

He must see the confusion playing on my face because one of his hands moves up, grabs mine, and puts it in his hair. "Take it, menace," he says.

I *get it now.*

And I do as he demands,

"Oh, fuck." I moan, my hips moving to get his mouth where I need him. With a mind of its own, my hand presses his face down farther into my pussy and I start to move, start to ride his face, to guide the movement.

To take what I need.

"A finger," I demand, giving into the need for more, and he obliges instantly, sliding a thick finger inside of me as he sucks on my clit. "Shit!" Another finger joins the first and now, as I rock my hips, I'm fucking myself, but his lips and tongue work to take me higher and higher, and my fingers twine in his thick hair, holding him where I need him most. "Fuck, fuck, right there, I'm so close."

And then he stops.

"Andre!" He shakes his head as he sits up, his chest bare and his hard-on tenting his pajama pants as he smiles at me before pushing them down. Then, he lies next to me.

"What are you—" His hands move to my waist, pulling me up before sitting me on his upper thighs, his cock standing proud right in front of me.

"You on top," he says. His hands slide down my sides and my widened thighs before moving back up.

"I don't—"

"You on top, Liv." He grabs my hips, lifting me, and I help, moving to my knees and hovering over him. One hand leaves my hip, going to his cock as he notches the head before letting go again, letting me take full control of this.

"I don't know—"

"Do what feels right," he says. And with his cock barely in me, my body already so on edge, I have no choice but to nod. Slowly—a torture for both of us—I lower myself onto him, my breath going faint as he slowly stretches me, as I take every inch until he's as deep as he can be.

"Oh god." I moan, loud and low. His other hand on my hip leaves, both resting behind his head like he's just here for the show.

"Take what you need, Olivia. Take what you've earned," he says, and I smile a lust-filled smile before doing just that. I don't even question it, don't even feel those old questions and worries creep in because I'm with *him*.

I was never an on-top girl. It puts me on display which I don't love, but it also puts too much responsibility on me.

On top, I'm in control of my *and* his pleasure, and the old me could never focus on myself.

But with Andre's praise and the way he's staring at me, it's the only choice I have.

And it feels *natural*.

"Oh," I murmur as I lift my hips, trying it out, using my shins in the bed and lifting then falling. "*Oh*."

"Find what you like, Liv. No rush. What feels good." I grind down, my clit on his pelvis, and that feels fucking phenomenal so I do it again. I grind up and down, and his hands move to my hips, helping me find pleasure for myself. I'm full of him and grinding, and it feels so fucking good, I know I can come like this and it won't take long at all.

"Try leaning back," he suggests, his voice tight. I do as he says, leaning back, using my hands on his legs to steady myself, and the moan I let out is low and needy. "There it is." A strained smile hits his lips like he knows the unreliable jolt of pleasure that cracks through me.

"Andre, oh fuck, it's . . ." My voice trails off as I lift and fall, feeling the head of his cock swipe my G-spot with each movement at this angle. "So good."

"That's it. That's it, Liv. God, you're beautiful." His hands roam like he can't help himself, like he needs to feel me all over. They graze up my arms, down my back, grabbing my ass. Each inch of skin his hands move over erupts in a trail of goose bumps in their wake. "Ride me."

I do what he demands, speeding up then slowing down, trying circles, playing to see what I like best.

Taking my time.

Focusing only on myself.

"You should see yourself, Olivia. Riding me. A fucking queen." My hand roams my body, over my belly and up until I'm pinching my nipples as the pleasure builds low in my back.

"Fuck, it's gonna be huge," I say, panting now. My hand moves back down, ready to circle my clit and make me fall.

His hand slaps mine out of the way.

"No. Just like this. You're gonna come just like this." I smile at him through hooded eyes.

"I thought you said this was all about me, all about getting me whatever—" My breath hitches as he lifts his hips a bit, meeting me so he goes a bit deeper. "Whatever I want."

"I lied. Now be a good girl for your man and ride my cock until you find it."

I should be annoyed but . . .

I do as he says.

And in a few moments, I'm close, teetering on the edge.

"Oh god, fuck, Andre, please." I moan.

"What do you need?" he asks.

"My clit, please, god, fuck. Rub my clit so I can come."

"Anything but that," he says with a laugh. It's a bit forced, and I know he's waiting on me to fall.

"What do you need, Liv?" What I *need* is for him to rub my clit and make me come, but I know that won't get me anywhere. His hands move up my thighs, massaging as they do, like he's both trying to encourage me and use my skin as his hold to stop himself from coming.

He grips tight enough I'll probably bruise, the pain shooting to my throbbing clit.

It's then I remember our first time together.

"Slap my thigh," I murmur, riding him, leaning back farther and spreading wide to give him room. He doesn't hesitate, giving me everything and anything when he *knows* it's what I need. The slap reverberates in the room and I moan loudly. It throbs in my pussy, ratcheting up my pleasure a notch, like a dam slowly crumbling apart, waiting to burst.

"Again," I moan, the word a plea.

He obliges on the opposite thigh, and I shout this time, the pleasure so close. I keep riding him, the head of his cock grinding on my swollen G-spot.

"Fuck, fuck, fuck, Andre. More." This time, it's Andre who groans as he starts to fuck me as well, his hips lifting to meet mine, and he slaps me on the first thigh again, slightly higher than the other.

"Such a pretty little thing, aren't you?" he says through gritted teeth. "You like this, me turning your thighs pink?"

"Yes, god, please, I'm so close, Andre. I need to come."

It's then he smiles at me like the devil himself. "Alright, baby. I'll take care of you."

I moan in relief as his hand, three fingers lined up, starts to rub my aching clit hard.

"Fuck, yea—AH!" He pulls his hand back and slaps my clit. My hips buck, and I moan louder before he's back, rubbing where he hit.

Then he repeats the move.

Slapping my clit then rubbing the sting away roughly.

It only takes three before I scream.

My entire body convulses as I come harder than I even thought possible, my voice cutting out halfway through as he holds my hips in place and fucks me hard before slamming in deep and coming in me, groaning his relief into my neck as I fall forward, another small orgasm rocketing through me, or maybe just the tail end of the last one, I don't know.

But I do know I can't breathe.

I can't see.

I can't function.

My entire being just transcended to another plane.

Andre works on recovering his breathing for a minute before he lets out a small chuckle.

"So, I guess we can add slapping your pussy to the list of shit you like."

I mumble, "Fuck off," against his skin but don't move.

Another full minute passes.

"I'm really fucking proud of you, Olivia," he says low. "You've come along way. I don't think the Liv I met a few months ago would have let me take her out of there."

I wait another minute, my breathing regulating as I do, but that's not why I pause.

It's because of the tears I'm fighting back.

"I'm proud of me, too," I say.

Because I am. I never saw myself as this person, and I love her so fucking much.

And I have this man to thank for helping me find her.

◆◆◆

The next day, I call Cami.

"Hey, babe, how was your mo—" she says when she answers, but I cut her off.

"I'm ready, Cam." Silence fills the line before she speaks.

"I don't understand."

"I'm ready to . . ." The lump in my throat I've been fighting since yesterday throbs.

Yesterday, we went to Andre's family Thanksgiving after the disaster of my mother's, and we were surrounded by love. And joy. And hugs and *kindness*.

And then we came home and Andre reminded me what it felt like to be loved. And I went to bed feeling that love.

But this morning, I woke up, the bed cold because Andre had work too early, and I knew.

I knew I was ready.

"I'm ready to cry over wine."

I leave it at that, and to anyone else, they might think it meant something along the lines of crying over spilled wine.

But I know Cami remembers the words she said to me months ago.

Your mom fucked you up. One day, you'll talk about it more and we'll cry over wine about it.

"I'll be there in an hour," she says.

And hours later, when I'm spent from tears and more than a little drunk, but still full of love and adoration and a fucked-up sense of *family,* when Cami pulls a blanket over my shoulders and presses a kiss to my forehead, I wonder if whatever god or higher power exists knew.

If that being knew I needed someone to fill the gap my mother will always leave and sent Cami into our lives to fit the exact way my dad and I need her to.

I fall asleep with her words swirling around me.

You are not a burden, Olivia.

And when I wake up, Andre is at my place, making me breakfast like nothing strange happened the night before. But when he hugs me good morning, pressing a kiss into my hair, his whisper of, "I love you, Olivia," feels like the same sentiment.

You are not a burden.

You are loved.

You are worthy.

And every day from that point on, I thank whatever force brought on the fall of Bradley Reed.

how to get your happily ever after

EPILOGUE

Two years later

"When are you going to marry me, Olivia?" Andre asks me in the dark of night, pushing my hair back.

I smile the way I always do when he asks, giving him the same answer I always give him.

"When all this shit is behind us." The ceiling fan of the bedroom circles above us slowly. With May hitting New Jersey, it's finally starting to warm up.

Next week, it should be warm enough to plant some rose bushes out front, and I could scream from the excitement. Once the case was finished on Andre's end, once we recovered the funds that were stolen and I gave about a million and seven testimonies (all of which Andre insisted he watched from the observation room at the very least, always my protective agent) I was informed I had the opportunity to purchase the house from them.

The price was a bit discounted from market value, and it would forever have the mark of a *crime scene* on it, but the offer was on the table.

At first, I was absolutely against it. Why the fuck would I want to live in the house my ex used to live in, the house that helped hide stolen funds, the house that almost ruined me?

But then I remembered Edna lived next door.

And I remembered, for better or worse, this place was where I met Andre.

And at the end of the day, it was a really nice house.

With all of the memories we made here, with all of the growth *I* made here, the way this place changed my life for the better despite the initial pain it put me through . . . I decided to take it.

So I added it to my list of unhinged revenge—*buy the house he never let me live in right out from under him.*

I wrote it right under *testify and put him in prison for life.* I haven't been able to cross that one completely out yet.

"It is. It's done. It's over," Andre says, but I shake my head.

"Your part might be, the investigation, but mine isn't." He sighs.

This is not the first time we've had this conversation.

His investigation into Bradley is long over, all of the evidence and research handed off to the prosecutors, but technically, I'm a witness.

I'm a *victim.*

And I'm already scheduled to testify against him at the trial, which still doesn't have a concrete date as Bradley's lawyers continue to grasp at straws and get the case thrown out on several grounds.

Thankfully, none of which being *my ex is fucking a federal agent.* But that doesn't mean it isn't a concern keeping me up at night.

"What does it matter if we're married?" he asks, voice low.

God.

There's such a deep level of want and need and longing in his words. He wants that so freaking badly.

"I won't give them anything at all to screw with this case. It's bad enough that we're together, that I have your ring on my finger, that we live together—"

"Technically, we don't live together," he says with a pout.

"Andre, just because we kept your place *because I don't want to fuck with the case* does not mean all of our worldly possessions aren't in this home and I spend every damn night sleeping next to you."

"Exactly. What would being married change?"

"Everything," I say in a whisper.

He smiles, knowing I mean that in the best way possible.

"Yeah, it will, won't it?" he asks.

"The minute this case is done, Andre, I'm yours. I'll run to city hall with you, get married by a justice of the peace. I don't care," I whisper in the dark.

"You promise?"

"Promise."

He smiles wide, white teeth gleaming in the minimal light, before rolling me over onto my back underneath him and showing me exactly how much he likes that answer.

✱✱✱

Four months later

"You ready?" he asks, coming up from behind me. I turn to face him, anxiety bubbling in my gut but easing just a bit when I see his stern face. We're in a hallway, waiting for the judge to call us in.

For me to tell my story.

"As ready as I'll ever be," I say in a whisper. My fingers play with my engagement ring, twisting it round and round on my finger. He slid it on months ago in the quiet of my bed late at night, not even bothering to ask, simply slipping it on and pressing his lips there.

It was *perfect*.

His hand comes to my neck, trailing up until his thumb rests in the spot right under my chin, tipping it up.

"Keep this up, Liv. Keep your chin up. You don't cower; you don't hide from anyone. Ever." Suddenly, it clicks then, all those years of him doing this exact move, of placing his thumb there and tipping my chin up until I was looking at him.

Always when I was most unsure.

When I was second-guessing or nervous.

A silent reminder I think I've always internalized.

"You've been doing that for so long."

"I never want you looking at people who are beneath you ever again, Olivia. Only up."

"God, I love you," I whisper through the lump in my throat.

"Good, because I plan to love you forever, little menace." The bailiff opens the door then, the sound of the old wood unsticking from the doorframe jolting me, and calls us into the courtroom. My heart skips a beat. "Now, let's go get that forever started," Andre says in my ear.

* * *

My testimony is the last before final statements, before the jury goes off to deliberate.

It takes them less than an hour to come back with a verdict.

Guilty.

Guilty on *all charges*.

And when we walk out of the courtroom, my hands shake in Andre's. They shake as we walk past the reporters and as I keep my chin up without responding to any questions.

They shake as we stand in front of my house, which will be *our* house very soon if Andre has his way.

And they shake when he stops me before we walk in, pulling me into him.

"Let's go," he says, his hand on the back of my neck, his forehead on mine as we stand on the front step. I painted the front door red because it made me happy, and Andre helped me dig up multiple flower beds in the front and back, so we're surrounded by color and beauty and everything I didn't think I'd have two, three years ago.

"Go? Go where?" I ask in a whisper.

"To get married."

The world stops spinning. "What?"

"You said once this was over, we'd make it official."

"Andre, I . . ." I pause, my chest swelling with both excitement and nerves. "There's no time. Everyone isn't here, and we'd need—"

"Do you want a big wedding?" he asks, cutting me off, his eyes warm on mine. He knows the answer, of course, knowing me like the back of his hand and remembering what I told him. I shake my head.

"No."

"Good. Let's go then." He steps back then starts to lead me up the steps.

"Andre, I don't understand." His smile goes wide, the good one he doesn't share often but when he does, it's directed at me. The one that makes me melt, that makes me feel so damn loved since the very first time I saw it.

"You said we would get married as soon as this case was over. It was the last obstacle." I've told him this *numerous* times since he proposed.

"But . . ."

"You said in your perfect world, you'd hand it all off to Cami and just show up." He reaches into his pocket and pulls out the keys for the house like this is a normal, run-of-the-mill conversation and not like he's talking about *marrying me* right now. I watch him, my eyes wide and my mouth open.

"But she can't do it in a few *hours,* Andre. I—" He means well, but he doesn't understand how much *work* goes into an event like this.

"She's been planning this for months, Liv."

Months. "Months?"

"Everything is set. Let's go into the house." He pushes the door open and inside, my best friends, the people who held me up over the past years, are standing there.

"What is going on?" I ask in a whisper that hurts my throat as it leaves my lips. Andre tugs me into the house, closing the door behind me, but I barely process all of that.

"You're getting married, Liv," Cami says. I blink at her.

"I can't." It's all I can say. Nothing is making sense right now.

"Why not?" Andre asks.

"We . . . I-I don't have a dress," I say because that makes sense. Abbie reaches for the couch, grabs a dress bag by the hanger, and lifts it.

"I got you."

I have a dress.

My heart begins to race.

This isn't some kind of spur-of-the-moment thing. Not really at least.

"We don't have a venue."

"Cami has it covered," Andre says, and Cami smiles. My eyes start to water.

"Invites?"

"I handled it all," Cici says. "Full disclosure, your mom is coming, but she doesn't know what she's coming *to* so she couldn't spoil it. I'm sitting her in the way back, and no photos or press are allowed. Phones are going in a basket on the way in." A lump forms in my throat from knowing everyone in my life has worked together without me knowing to make this happen for me. After Thanksgiving, the few visits with my mother have been short and cordial, Andre always at my side and my mother always on her best behavior. It's not perfect, but I don't dread her visits anymore.

I turn to him fully. "Flowers. I need flowers," I whisper, excitement bubbling in my belly. "Lots of them."

"I know," he says with a smile.

"We can go to a florist, or—" I start because if there's one thing this man has taught me, it's I won't settle on *anything* I want.

If I'm getting married today, I want flowers.

"I have that covered," Andre says with a smile, and I should have known. He knows me better than I know myself. He would know that would be the most important factor in a wedding for me.

"You ordered flowers?" I ask, confused. "How did you know today would be the day?"

"Not quite," he says then grabs my hand. "Come on."

"I thought we were—"

"We are. Come on, Liv."

"Andre, what is going on? We're getting married, and I have to get ready, and there's—"

His hand goes to the back of my neck, fisting my hair and tugging just enough so the panic quiets and all I can see is him. All I can focus on is the man in front of me.

"Do you trust me?" he whispers against my lips.

"With my life," I reply instantly.

"God, I love you." I smile and press my lips to his, a short, sweet kiss. "Come with me, menace." The words flow through my bones, pooling in my fingertips and my toes and my heart until I'm nothing but warmth and happiness.

"Okay."

And then he steps back, dropping my hand.

"Turn around."

"What?"

"Turn away from me," he says then dangles a tie from his hand.

"What is that for?" Cami lets out a snorted laugh and I glare at her. For a moment, I forgot they were all there, but now Abbie, Cami, Cici, and Kat are all staring at me with small smiles.

"A blindfold. Turn away from me."

"Uh, no," I say with a shake.

"Olivia, play along please."

"Why are you putting a blindfold on me?"

"Because it's a surprise."

"What kind of surprise?" I ask, and he tips his head to the ceiling and shakes his head. "Haven't there been enough surprises today?"

"Can you just let me have this, Olivia?" When his head tips back down to me, his eyes are genuine and soft, with a hint of pleading there. "Please?"

I sigh. He must know by now when he looks at me like that, when he asks me to trust him, I can't say no—the last human in my life I'm allowed to give into my people-pleaser tendencies for. Not because I'm afraid he'll leave me or I'll hurt him or he'll reject me if I don't, but because I know he would *never* do any of that. He'll never take advantage of me, of the kindness I'm offering him.

"Okay," I say, and he ties me up then grabs my waist, helping me back outside and down the steps before holding me by my hand and guiding me . . . somewhere. My feet step over grass and cement before I hear the sound of metal on metal, like the latch of a gate, and we keep walking before he stops me. Finally, he unties the blindfold and holds my hand. I blink a few times, trying to understand what I'm seeing.

"What is—"

"It's a garden." I stare at the six boxes filled with flowers of various colors and sizes and textures in neat little rows before answering.

"I see that," I say.

"It's *your* garden, Liv."

"My . . . garden?"

"I mean, to be fair, there's not much more for you to do with it, and it's technically at Edna's house, but it's yours."

"It's . . . mine."

"I know you have gardens next door, but they're in the ground, and you put a bunch of those rose bushes and stuff there, so nothing like . . . this. You can use these as cut gardens. The internet said this style was best for that, so you can make bouquets and stuff. I mean, I guess we could move them, but . . ." He shrugs. "This also gives you a reason to be over here, check in on Edna. I know this year was too crazy to put in gardens at our place, and I kept putting off building them, but . . . that was kind of because I knew you'd want flowers for our wedding and I wanted to give you this surprise."

"You knew . . ." It seems I'm unable to let out more than two words at a time right now.

"So, your flowers. I, uh—" His hand moves up, cupping the back of his neck as he moves away from me, taking a step toward the boxes. "There's some zinnias, and ah, those are black-eyed Susans. Weird name, but whatever. Over there, there are some dahlias—did you know those aren't a seed? They're a tuber, like a sweet potato or something. And there are a few sunflowers, but they're kind of huge. I didn't expect those to get so big when I planted them."

"Wait, what?" I ask, his final words snapping me out of some kind of trance.

"Sunflowers? Those big yellow ones over there."

"No, no, after that."

"They're big?"

"No, the planting them part."

"Oh. I didn't pay attention to the package. I should have, but this isn't exactly my forte, you know?" I stare at him, a mix of confusion and all-consuming love taking over me.

"You planted them." His brow furrows like he can't understand what I'm asking, like the question is silly.

"Yeah?"

"From seeds."

"Yeah. I actually got kind of lucky since the trial dragged on. I didn't know they'd take so long to bloom if I planted them outside as seeds. Next year, we can get you a little greenhouse if you want, and you can start them early. Have flowers all season." My mind can't get over this, this act of love and kindness with zero expectation behind it.

"You started this entire garden from seeds?" I ask for clarification.

"Yes."

"You don't like flowers. Or gardens. Or the outdoors really." He stares at me, confused, like *I'm* the crazy one.

"But you do."

The words swirl around me, warmth suffusing every part of me. *But you do.* It's like it's the obvious answer, like there's no other conclusion.

"But I do."

A long moment passes, and I can't tell if he finally understands my confusion, but he steps farther from me again, closer to the gardens, before turning to me, his arm out.

"This is your wedding gift."

My entire body tingles with the words.

"You, uh, can pick what you want. Abbie said she'll make a bouquet and anything else you need. Vases and boutonnieres or whatever. It's small, though. Only a handful of guests. Your family, mine. The girls. A couple of guys from work."

"Where?"

"What?"

"Where is it? Our wedding?" His lips tip up in a smile, and he takes the three steps back to me, thumb swiping against where I know my smile is making an indent in my cheek.

"Here. In Edna's backyard. Where I realized I was so completely fucked and going to fall for you."

My hand moves to his eyebrow, a permanent cut memorializing the moment I met him. "You mean back when you were a stalker?" He blushes, his tan skin going a bit darker with the embarrassment.

"So, you're telling me Edna knows about this wedding and her big mouth hasn't slipped yet?" He smiles wide.

"She's surprisingly good at keeping secrets," my fiancé says, his thumb lifting to wipe a tear I hadn't realized fell.

"And you grew my wedding flowers." That puts a lump in my throat all over again.

"Yeah."

"From seeds."

He nods. "Yeah."

"God, you really love me, don't you?" I look at him, my brows furrowed, my hand on his jaw that is shaved close, trying to decode him the way he has *always* been able to dissect me.

To find the truth in his words and actions and try and figure out why.

How.

What I did in this life to deserve this, to deserve him.

He shakes his head, his eyes shutting gently as he does before both of his warm, rough hands grab my face, forcing me to look into his eyes, to see the truth of what he's about to say.

"I'm shocked you still believe anyone could ever not risk the world to make you happy, Olivia." He whispers the words with reverence, with such love and adoration, it shakes me to my core. "Ready to make it official?"

How could I say no to that?

How could I say no to a man who planned my dream wedding months in advance with no real date in mind, a man who heard what I wanted *years ago* and did whatever it took to make it happen?

A man who heard I wanted a flower garden and grew one so my wedding bouquet would be filled with as much love and beauty as humanly possible.

Who got all of our friends to help.

A man who is giving me a day that is all me—no pleasing anyone, no other opinions in the mix.

Just me and him.

I nod because what other answer could there be?

He smiles and I mimic it, joy and elation and love bubbling in my chest with no end in sight. His thumb moves to the spot under my chin, tipping it up.

"Only one thing you should know," he says, that smile widening despite sounding like whatever he's going to say is a huge disappointment, a bit of rain on my perfect day.

"What?" I ask. I'm smiling still, knowing nothing—*nothing*—could hinder this day, especially if Andre is in charge.

He simply won't let it happen.

"I had to let Edna be a flower girl." I stare at him, the words not quite computing. "She threatened to tell you if I said no."

A single moment passes.

A single moment before the late summer air is *filled* with the sound of my uncontrolled laughter and joy.

* * *

Cici pins up half of my hair using an antique comb Ms. Valenti brought me, an heirloom from Andre's grandmother that we've deemed my *something old,* and my eyes catch hers.

"You look gorgeous, Liv," she says, her voice soft.

I do.

My hair is half down in loose waves, my makeup simple. The silk sheath dress Abbie picked out fits perfectly, the neckline a loose cowl and the end barely grazing the floor, no train to be found. My bouquet is sitting in a vase next to Cici's, an explosion of whites and pinks and oranges and fresh greenery.

And I'm about to walk down a pathway at the place I first met my soon-to-be-husband, surrounded by flowers my fiancé planted just for me, only our closest friends and family witnessing this moment.

This is what I wanted all those years ago.

This is me.

It's the me Andre dug out, carefully using brushes and gentle touches like a paleontologist discovering a fossil that was never meant to see the light of day, buried under the desires of everyone else.

Working tirelessly until I was free.

"I'm not scared," I say in a whisper, and when her brow furrows, when her eyes meet mine, I know I need to expand.

She doesn't get it.

Of course, she doesn't.

"I don't feel it. That panic. The feeling in my belly something is going to go wrong."

Slowly, a smile spreads on her lips.

"Like last time."

She remembers that day in the fancy bridal suite, the day I asked if someone died because it felt like someone did, my intuition telling me what I wouldn't admit.

"Like last time."

"I didn't want to say it then, mostly because your mom is a cunt and I knew it was a lost cause, but that feeling? It's not normal. Nerves and excitement? Yeah. Feeling like someone just died before you're about to walk down the aisle to the supposed love of your life? Not normal." I nod.

"If I was scared, if I thought something was wrong, I'd run *to* Andre. Not away from him." I whisper the truth, the contrast to what I once felt so starkly.

"He takes care of you," she says, her fingers running through the loose curls.

"He saved me from myself," I whisper. And it's the truth. Andre thinks he saved me from doing something stupid and landing myself in jail and from Bradley's scheme. And he did, but it isn't what matters. He saved me from myself, from a life of putting everyone else first, from being *happy enough* but never overjoyed. A lifetime of accepting and internalizing criticism I didn't earn, of not knowing my own worth.

And there it is.

The ultimate revenge.

Fuck glitter and brake lines and beehives. Andre was right all along, though I'll never admit it—the best revenge is thriving without him. Thriving *in spite* of him.

And as I walk down the aisle on my dad's arm, holding a bouquet of flowers grown with love and adoration, Andre tearing up as he sees me, nothing has ever been sweeter than revenge.

ACKNOWLEDGMENTS

I don't know when it happened, but at some point over the past two years, writing these acknowledgments has become one of my favorite things to do. (I even figured out how to spell the word on the first try. I hope.)

I am a words of affirmation girl—giving them, not receiving them, to be clear. So having a spot where you, dear reader, are held captive to listen to me brag about the amazing people in life is kind of my version of heaven.

First and foremost, forever and always, thank you Alex. You're my best friend, my biggest protector. Thank you for being my Andre, for teaching me my worth and pushing me when I'm too scared to ask for it. Thank you for being overly protective of me, even when it drives me crazy. Thank you for taking the kids to the park for hours on end so I can sit in my delusions with no interruptions, for bringing me my icy Cokes and lunches since you know I won't eat real food if you don't. Thank you for believing in me more than I ever believe in myself and for putting your own dreams on hold to help me chase mine. I love you more.

Thank you to Ryan, Owen, and Ella for letting me be your mom. Thank you for enduring my Taylor Swift dance parties and pointing out every pink thing in the universe because *it's your favorite*. I'm so incredibly lucky to get to watch you grow up. Now shut this book and never talk about it again, thanks.

Thank you to Madi, the most amazing cover designer on the planet. Thank you for talking me through the mid-book slump, reminding me to ignore the haters, for remembering the things I never will, and for enduring my million and seven voice memos and endless texts. I'm so grateful to have found you, even if I didn't even know you when *Midnights* came out. Watching you grow and stick up for yourself and put yourself first over the past year has been absolutely incredible. I love you to the moon and to Saturn and truly believe you are the little sister I never got.

Thank you to Rae for being the sanity to my psychosis. Thank you for patience and kindness and grace and unending reminders to do the most basic shit. Thank you for taking on things you know will stress me TF out before I even have to look at them and for making me laugh my ass off when we trauma-dump our mommy issues. I'm so lucky to have you working and spilling tea and sharing Noah Kahan news and memes with me. I love you, please never get tired of me.

Thank you, Lindsey, the OG Morgan Elizabeth Team member. Thank you for not hating me when my deadlines come and go and I never meet them. Thank you for your unending patience and kindness and support. Thank you for talking me off ledges and pushing me to try new, scary things. I love you so much and I'm unbearably proud of you and the things you've accomplished in the last year.

Thank you to Shaye, the one who keeps our business calls on track so we do more than talk and whine and complain. Thank you for always ensuring we have time to talk and whine and complain. Thank you for handling all of my crises with grace and professionalism and getting stabby if anyone makes me cry. Thank you for teaching me to fuck the haters and to aim for the sky even when I think I'm stuck to the ground. I love you and I'm so grateful for you every day.

Thank you to Norma for taking my disaster and fixing it. Thank you for getting insane emails where I tell you I'm not done with my book, but I'm sending you half because I'm always behind my deadlines and basically just nodding and saying okay.

Thank you to Tavi for letting me send you all of my insane Taylor theories and staying up late every night so you can live-text me the LA dates while I sleep. Thank you for trusting me with your dreams and letting me bounce ideas off of you. I love you so much, and I can't wait to read the heart book and cry everywhere and watch the universe fall in love with you.

Thank you to Emily for letting me vent and whine and send you the most chaotic texts and for laughing about our trauma because if we don't laugh, then we actually have to process it, and no, thank you. I can't wait to see what the next year brings you!!

Thank you to Booktok, all of you who trusted me and gave me a chance and shared my stories the sole reason I'm here today. You've changed my life and I'm forever thankful.

Thank you, of course, to my readers. Anytime I start to question myself, you all are there, sending me messages and comments to remind me why I do this. You've all accepted me so kindly and with such grace I don't always feel like I deserve, and I am forever grateful for the ways you have changed my life for the better.

WANT MORE LIV AND ANDRE?

Read a bonus scene of Andre and Liv going to Finch Farms to cut down their Christmas tree!

WHAT'S NEXT?

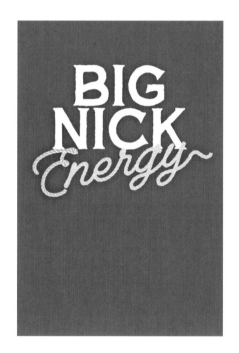

Meet Shae and Nick in my holiday release coming October 25!

When Connor Finch insists his one-time Tinder match, Shae, comes to his dad's house for Thanksgiving with her two daughters, it's because he refuses to let them be alone on her first holiday post-divorce.

But when she arrives at the Christmas tree farm and ranch he grew up on, she meets his father—the crazy tall, built, golden retriever cowboy who tells her girls all about the magic of the *stupid* elf on a shelf.

Of course, when she later corners him and tells him *thanks a lot for nothing* and that she's way too overwhelmed to have to deal with *yet another* responsibility, he feels terrible.

So terrible, he finds himself driving two hours every night just to deliver an elf, move him about, and create some Christmas magic for her girls.

But what happens when he decides meeting her the way he did was some kind of Christmas miracle and he needs to convince Shae to give him a shot?

Preorder Big Nick Energy here!

WANT THE CHANCE TO WIN KINDLE STICKERS AND SIGNED COPIES?

Leave an honest review on Amazon or Goodreads and send the link to reviewteam@authormorganelizabeth.com and you'll be entered to win a signed copy of one of Morgan Elizabeth's books and a pack of bookish stickers!

Each email is an entry (you can send one email with your Goodreads review and another with your Kindle review for two entries per book) and two winners will be chosen at the beginning of each month!

ALSO BY MORGAN ELIZABETH

The Springbrook Hills Series

The Distraction

The Protector

The Substitution

The Connection

The Playlist

Season of Revenge Series:

Tis the Season for Revenge

Cruel Summer

The Fall of Bradley Reed

Ick Factor, Coming March '24

Interconnected Holiday Standalone

Big Nick Energy, Coming Oct 25, 2023

The Ocean View Series

The Ex Files

Walking Red Flag

Bittersweet

The Mastermind Duet

Ivory Tower

Diamond Fortress

ABOUT THE AUTHOR

Morgan is a born and raised Jersey girl, living there with her two boys, toddler daughter, and mechanic husband. She's addicted to iced espresso, barbecue chips, and Starburst jellybeans. She usually has headphones on, listening to some spicy audiobook or Taylor Swift. There is rarely an in between.

Writing has been her calling for as long as she can remember. There's a framed 'page one' of a book she wrote at seven hanging in her childhood home to prove the point. Her entire life she's crafted stories in her mind, begging to be released but it wasn't until recently she finally gave them the reigns.

I'm so grateful you've agreed to take this journey with me.

Stay up to date via TikTok and Instagram

Stay up to date with future stories, get sneak peeks and bonus chapters by joining the Reader Group on Facebook!

Made in the USA
Thornton, CO
10/23/23 12:46:11

10b882c7-a527-4377-87ff-fa430af24004R01